PHOENIX FILE

PHOENIX FILE

Pete Scales

SBR Press
Halifax, Nova Scotia, Canada

SBR Press
20 Keefe Road, Halifax, Nova Scotia, Canada B3P 2J1

PHOENIX FILE
SBR Press Book
Published by Arrangement With The Author

Printed and Bound in Canada

Canadian Cataloguing in Publication Data

Scales, Pete, 1954-
Phoenix File

ISBN 0-9686449-1-0

I. Sandoz AG--Fire, 1986--Fiction. I. Title.

PS8587.C3913P48 2000 C813'.54 C99-901643-1
PR9199.3.S254P48 2000

...to Tricia, Sam and Alex.

For more titles from SBR Press
contact us at our web site or email us at...
Web Site: www.sbrpress.ns.ca
Email: pbscale@attglobal.net

Acknowledgements

Schweizerhalle is a real place and an environmental catastrophe actually happened there. The question of why and the subsequent events presented here are the results of my imagination.

The idea for the story would not have progressed much past barroom chit chat if not for the interest of three Swiss who, because of the continued sensitivity of the topic, will have to remain nameless.Thank you.

To Ian MacSween, Dr. Don Eddy, Jim Clarke and Staff Sergeant Mike Clark, the Wednesday Nighters, a bunch of guys who sat around my kitchen table discussing the nuances of spycraft and environmental terrorism, thanks guys.

Many staffers at the Township of Langley offered up their time and efforts to edit the book. My hat is off to Kory Down, Arne Badke, Linda Floyd, Fred Peters, Edie Mowat, David Wright, Judi Donald, Sharla Mauger, now Councillor Mauger and, Vicki Robinson and Cheryl Dickson.

To my hired gun (Editor that is) Richard Sherbaniuk, master of pacing, flow and the art of describing some really tasty snacks, thanks man and good luck with your upcoming novel, *The Fifth Horseman.*

The work and encouragement of three Haligonians, Tom Donovan, Odette Murphy and Kirk (don't call me Captain) MacDonald who helped put the finishing touches to the manuscript, is much appreciated.

Karen Rempel of Vivid Page Productions Inc in Vancouver, as usual, has done a wonderful job with the cover and typesetting.

And when it come to encouragement and book craft, there is none better than Peter Hawkins.

I couldn't say my thanks properly if I didn't mention my family, Tricia ("where's my book?") for reading my manuscripts for the umpteenth time and still managing a smile. And to Sam and Alex who are not yet old enough to appreciate *Phoenix File*, but do however, like the cover and want to take it to show and tell.

If I have neglected to mention some names of all you others who have read the book and made your comments, trust me, its a matter of space, not memory. To all of you, thank you for your encouragement and great ideas.

PHOENIX FILE

PROLOGUE

November 1, 1986, Muttenz, Switzerland

The black BMW shot through the night like a stealth missile headed unerringly toward an unsuspecting target. A funeral pall of inky darkness cloaked the almost deserted Basel-Zurich autobahn.

As he steered the big car along the familiar route, he could feel his guts churn and the palms of his hands burn. Don't panic, he thought, don't panic. You can handle this - it's your business to handle this kind of thing. He glanced at the speedometer - two hundred and twenty kilometres an hour - and eased off slightly on the accelerator. You're going way too fast. No point making this journey tonight if you roll the car - at this speed they'll find parts strewn on the highway for a full kilometre.

And it wasn't just him who would be killed. Anxiously, protectively, he glanced over at the young boy sleeping in the seat next to him. He cursed himself under his breath, remembering the first threatening call. I should've done something then, he thought. But even now, he couldn't think of anything he could have done, given the circumstances.

He rolled his head on his shoulders without for an instant taking his eyes from the ribbon of darkness unspooling in front of him. He licked his lips and swallowed, then breathed deeply, hoping the extra oxygen would clear the alcohol induced fog from his brain. The taste in his mouth, sour, like fruit gone bad, made him wonder for the hundredth time why he'd drunk so much cherry kirsch earlier in the evening. Good thing he held his liquor well. His eyes flicked to the luminous face of the clock on the dashboard. Just before 1:00 a.m. What the hell was going on?

The vehicle drove soundlessly, like a car in a dream, and the opulence of the interior, combined with the seamless perfection of German engineering, gave an oddly comforting feeling of solidity to what was rapidly becoming his increasingly disjointed life. He waggled his tense fingers to keep them limber on the steering wheel and settled back into the leather seat with a sigh. Not too far now. Keep your mind clear, he thought, and don't relax too much; otherwise you'll make mistakes. He tried not to think of whatever it was that might be awaiting him.

Just as he crested the hill adjacent to St. Jacob's Stadium he saw it for the first time. An ominous purple-red haze that lit up the Rhine valley, just ahead. He could see pillars of tangerine orange-and electric blue flame erupting amidst roiling clouds of yellow smoke, as if the entire sky was on fire. With each new eruption of flame, shooting hundreds of meters into the air, the smoky layer that hung over the inferno shifted and undulated in a sickening, poisonous dance.

"My God," he said aloud. He knew his business, and he knew that the combined fire departments of the entire canton couldn't extinguish a devouring conflagration like that for hours. It seemed to him that a gigantic lump of white-hot phosphorus was hidden just over the horizon, glowing and hissing and spitting deadly vapors. Thank God it's the middle of the night, he thought. Imagine how many employees might have died if this had erupted during the daytime work shift.

The sound of his voice had awakened his son. Hands clutching the edge of the dashboard, the boy was staring wide-eyed through the windshield at the raging inferno in the distance. "Papa," he whispered, "what is it?"

"A fire," he replied. "A big fire. At a factory where a fire means catastrophe."

Suddenly there was a series of powerful explosions and moments later the car was buffeted by the aftershocks. He struggled with the wheel to keep the screaming tires on the road. In the distance, the hellish glow suddenly roared higher, as if it had been doused with jet fuel. There were more explosions, louder now and closer together. Again the car was rocked and he fought to keep control.

"Papa ..."

"Please don't talk now, son, I have to concentrate. I'll tell you later." Obediently the boy clutched the dashboard again and watched the night sky, hypnotised, as if it were some sort of satanic fireworks display. Out of the corner of his eye the man watched his son for a moment. Christ, I love you, boy, maybe even more than your mama. And I've never really taken the time to tell you, always too absorbed in myself.

There was another blinding white-orange flare on the horizon and even in the cool sealed interior of the vehicle he thought he could smell the rotten egg stink of molten sulphur and the uniquely foul stench of burning mercaptans. He felt a slow spike of rage building inside him. Bastards, he thought savagely, whoever it was who had done this to him. His eyes narrowed. When this is over, I'll find you - I know how to do it. And I know how to make you pay. Bastards!

Beside him there was a soft beep. Startled out of his thoughts of revenge, it took him a moment to realise what it was. Of course – the cell phone in the car. Still watching the road, he picked up the receiver with his right hand. "Yes?"

He never heard an answer. Suddenly the steering on the huge rocketing car went spongy. He dropped the phone to grab the wheel with both hands. No response. Veering sharply to the right, out of control, he felt a jolt as the car's right front tire vaporised and the bare rim dug deep into the gravel verge at more than two hundred kilometres an hour. He had just an instant to reach for his beloved son to shield him from the inevitable, but before his fingers touched the boy the right front bumper shattered against the concrete retaining wall, pivoting the entire vehicle up and over in a sideways arc. The howling scrape of the vehicle's skin against ribbed concrete sheared the body panels from their anchors and ripped off the gas cap. The friction of steel against concrete sparked enough heat to ignite the fuel and in an instant the vehicle was a pirouetting furnace. Finishing its macabre dance after thirty meters, it fell onto its roof and continued down the highway, a spinning, screeching metal banshee, engulfed in flames and sparks like a small mobile version of the sinister inferno on the horizon.

****

Environmental Disaster at Schweizerhalle
International Herald Tribune, front page headline,
November 2, 1986

One of the worst environmental disasters in European history occurred last night at the Sandoz chemical works at Schweizerhalle near Basel, Switzerland.

Sandoz Warehouse 956 burned to the ground, releasing toxic fumes into the atmosphere. The warehouse contained an estimated 1350 metric tonnes of hazardous pesticides and agrochemicals, as well as an estimated 100 kilograms of mercury. The cause of the fire is unknown.

One hundred and sixty fire fighters from eight separate fire services battled the blaze all night. Although it was extinguished by 5 a.m., firemen continued to pour water onto the smoking rubble for hours afterwards. Once Sandoz officials revealed the contents of the warehouse, firemen were rushed to hospital for toxicology tests, as were several hundred people from the on-site police and emergency command staff.

Another cause for concern, according to sources, is that the enormous volumes of water used to battle the inferno, estimated at 10-15,000 cubic meters, are heavily contaminated with toxic chemicals and have flowed directly into the Rhine river.

"This is the worst environmental disaster in European history, second only to Chernobyl just seven months ago," stated environmental scientist Dr. Werner Dagmetz of the University of Zurich. "The entire river is bright red as far as the eye can see. The chemical cocktail that has been released into the Rhine will kill all living things for at least 300 kilometres and poison the drinking water of thousands of cities, towns and villages." According to Dr. Dagmetz, combustion of several of the chemicals stored in the warehouse would release large amounts of dioxins, the most toxic substances known.

Sandoz Fire Kommandant Theo Marti says the blaze was first spotted at 12:19 a.m. by a Basel cantonal police officer on a routine patrol. "I was on the scene with my men within five minutes," claims Marti, "but it was impossible to control the fire." Marti refused to speculate as to the cause of the blaze, the reason for its white-hot intensity, or why it spread so rapidly, stating it would be "irresponsible" to comment until a full investigation has been completed.

A visibly shaken Sandoz spokesman, Hubert Kasselman, refused to answer questions from reporters. He said in a formal statement, "We are frankly baffled by this incident. Our environmental protection measures and emergency response plans are second to none. I am confident there was no negligence on the part of Sandoz. I wish to assure the people of Switzerland and our neighbours downstream that we will extend every effort to find the cause of this unprecedented event and ensure that such an occurrence will never happen again."

The Canton of Basel-Land states it has notified the West German and French governments of the disaster and its possible environmental and human health implications. A full briefing will be provided as soon as possible. A government spokesman also said that a special commission would be established to investigate the disaster.

An immediate fishing ban has been imposed along the entire length of the Rhine. Residents of municipalities along the Rhine are warned that under no circumstances should they drink water from the tap or venture near the river. Health authorities recommend that only bottled water be consumed until further notice (for details on human health and safety measures, see separate story, page A2).

In a related incident, Christian Von Bessel, senior vice president of research and development for Sandoz, and his seven year old son, Daniel, died in an automobile crash at 1:05 a.m. on the Basel-Zurich autobahn, approximately four kilometres from the Sandoz site.

According to a witness, the vehicle driven by Von Bessel was travelling toward the burning facility at over two hundred kilometres an hour when it veered sharply, struck a concrete abutment and burst into flames. A Sandoz spokesman expressed the company's deep regrets, saying that Von Bessel must have been notified of the fire and was driving toward it when he was killed. Police are investigating the accident.

Death of Sandoz Executive Deemed Mishap
International Herald Tribune,
bottom of page 10, November 7, 1986

Zurich police have finished their investigation into the deaths of Christian Von Bessel, 40, senior vice president of research and development for Sandoz Chemical Corporation, and his seven-year-old son, Daniel. Both were killed November 1 in a fiery automobile crash. Von Bessel was travelling at high speed to the scene of last week's Sandoz fire at Schweizerhalle when his vehicle struck a concrete wall.

Police say the two died instantly. Both bodies were burned beyond recognition. Identification of Von Bessel was made through dental records and serial numbers found on car parts recovered at the scene. Sandoz officials state the cause of the accident was most probably due to Von Bessel, described as a brilliant employee, being distracted by the blaze that lit up the valley. However, police state autopsy results clearly indicate alcohol was a factor in the crash.

Von Bessel is survived by his wife, Marie Françoise.

ONE

August 12, 1988, Fao Marshes, Iraq

The pre-dawn desert air was chilly and indistinct, like fog, the earth deciding whether it wanted to be reborn this day. Low dun-coloured hills, interspersed with rocky outcroppings, sat in squat sullenness as if they knew what was coming.

Soldiers not assigned to sentry duty tried to catch any opportunity for sleep, arms wrapped around themselves for warmth as they crouched uncomfortably in the rough, hastily constructed sandbag berm that functioned as the forward observation post. Most of them didn't even know where they were, but they'd had enough sense not to ask questions.

A faint purple-orange line on the horizon silently heralded the sun's imminent arrival. With the approach of dawn, slumbering soldiers were urgently shoved awake by their comrades but as previously ordered no one made a sound. At the far end of the berm, a match flared as a cigarette was lit, only to be immediately extinguished as the sleepy soldier was cuffed across the head and his cigarette crushed.

Within seconds of being awakened, the twenty-five military personnel at the berm were uneasily attentive at their posts. Binoculars, telescopes and cameras were trained downhill toward the shabby hamlet half a mile to the north. Nestled between the base of the low brown hill and the fetid swamps of the mighty Euphrates River, the place looked peaceful and inviting despite its obvious poverty, as blue smoke from morning cooking fires began to rise. The sounds of barking mongrel dogs and clanging goat bells carried easily up the hill.

Signals for 'get ready' filtered down the line of crouching soldiers. Drill or the real thing? It was impossible to tell, but there was no hesitation as swift fingers fumbled for the gas masks hanging from every man's belt. Even if today was just another drill, the men knew enough about what might happen to quickly don the masks of their NCB's - nuclear, biological and chemical warfare gear. They had done this many times before, always the same men, always the same secrecy. And always the same captain, a big brutal man with a close-cropped head, shoulders like a bull, and a temper to match. But today, for the first time, there were two unfamiliar faces, and the soldier's questing eyes kept flicking furtively toward them. They had arrived at the camp at sunset the previous day.

One of the new arrivals was a full colonel of the elite Republican Guard. He was six feet tall, about thirty-five, with a square head, a bristling black moustache, and prematurely salt and pepper hair as immaculately styled as his combat greens. Every gesture bespoke imperious command, and their feared captain was as deferential as if he were the colonel's valet. Those closest heard the captain refer to the Republican Guard officer, in a tone of grovelling respect, as 'Colonel Hamani'. Despite his meticulous appearance, there was something about the man that said he had once been a line soldier, carrying his own gear and coming under fire, a warrior like themselves.

The other stranger was a civilian, six foot two, perhaps forty, with brown hair and eyes the colour of a rich woman's emeralds. He was dressed in a khaki bush photographer's vest with a dozen pockets, baggy khaki pants and expensive looking desert issue combat boots. He showed no sign of fear at being amongst battle hardened commandos, and indeed seemed not to acknowledge their presence at all. Like them, he had spent the long, cold night up against the sandbags but, as they would later discuss among themselves, those emerald eyes had never closed. And they also whispered that he had not had a proper name, that the colonel had referred to him as 'Sword'.

Now, with the rising sun, both colonel and civilian were staring expectantly downhill, although neither had bothered to don the masks they held in their hands. As the next fifteen minutes crept by, every soldier reached up to make sure his mask was secure. Something big must be happening today or why else would the two newcomers be present? As the sun rose, so did the temperature and the tension among the men. Beads of itchy sweat began to trickle down the brown faces inside the masks, but they dared not remove them. It was almost a relief when the radioman's back tightened at the receipt of a message over his earphones. He signalled to the captain, who tentatively reached out to touch the colonel's shoulder and whisper something. In turn, the colonel said something to the civilian, who remained aloof and impassive, staring straight ahead.

The colonel expertly slipped on his mask. Again he whispered to the civilian, who turned and looked over his shoulder at the grotesque, insect-like faces of the crouching soldiers. With no sign of emotion, he donned his mask with a swiftness and sureness that took the watching troops by surprise, adjusting the tension straps with a single fluid tug.

The colonel looked at his watch, then pointed down the hill. All of the men tensed as they peered over the edge of the berm. From the Southeast, on a bluff overlooking the hamlet, came a series of hollow, metallic pops that broke the tranquillity of the hamlet's domestic routine. Soldiers' heads snapped around to where faint puffs of white smoke smeared the bluff. Attention was immediately directed back downhill, in anticipation of the mortar shells striking their target.

As each projectile hit, the resulting explosions sent pillars of fire and brown dust skyward. In the terrible expectant lull between thudding explosions, as new mortar shells rained down, they could faintly hear the screams and shouts of people, and the panicked barks and whinnies of animals. Through binoculars they could see the hamlet's inhabitants dashing pell mell out of doorways and down narrow alleys, desperately trying to escape the shells.

One mortar shell did not send up dirty smoke and a spray of dirt. Instead, it released a yellow-orange cloud that billowed languidly skyward until it was caught by the faint prevailing wind and dragged over the shanties. Within seconds other shells landed around it, releasing, with a strange fizzing sound, puffs of soupy, grey fog that crept along the alleys, engulfing building after building.

There were more screams now, agonised shrieks. Villagers ran clutching their faces, slamming into crumbling walls they could no longer see. Once on the ground, they thrashed convulsively, fingers rigid as claws raking their throats and chests, until with a final tortured thrash they were still. Others stopped screaming and began choking, as a mingled stream of green bile and bright red arterial blood shot from their mouths. Slowly they fell to their knees, then onto their sides, limp and unmoving.

As quickly as the shelling began, it ceased. The smoke from the bombed, burning village climbed slowly into the now soot smudged sky. Soon, the only remaining sound reaching the men behind the berm was the snapping crackle of flames. Masked heads dipped and shoulders slumped as the faint, muted sounds of gagging came from behind the black sheathing of the NBC masks that the sickened soldiers dared not remove.

But through teary eyes they saw that the civilian had no such fears. They saw him remove his mask, and saw with a chill that his face was completely unemotional. He turned to the colonel and made an impatient gesture. After an interrogatory movement of his shoulders, the officer seemed to be reassured and in turn removed his own mask. The two men began to speak. The soldiers were too far away to hear the words, which the prevailing breeze carried like a different sort of doom towards the now dead hamlet.

"They're just Kurds," said Colonel Hamani. "Human vermin who want their own homeland, carved out of Iraqi soil. The Rais is sending them a message." As he looked again at his watch, he thought: But even Kurds don't deserve to die like this. It was not a sentiment he could safely voice aloud. Instead he said, "From beginning to end, less than four minutes. Most impressive."

"As I told you," replied the man known as Mohammed's Sword. "XP29, a derivative of the Nazi nerve gas Sarin, is the most effective chemical warfare agent in history. The Rais will be pleased, I trust."

Hamani frowned and nodded as he turned away, lifting his binoculars to gaze once more over the murdered village. He made a mental note of the arrogant tone in Sword's voice. It was just one of a thousand silent notes he had filed away in his mind over the years, years he had spent handling this unstable genius as if he were a badly designed weapon that might explode with no warning. A genius, he reminded himself, that he had personally recruited. That he had done so was a thought on which he tried not to dwell.

Other totalitarian states had called their leaders Duce and Fuhrer. Iraq called theirs Rais. As a heavily decorated, battle hardened field commander, thanks to eight years of war with Iran, Colonel Aziz Hamani often reported directly to his Rais, Saddam Hussein. This distinction was due to the discovery that he had a special talent, far removed from his skills on the battlefield. This talent lay in finding intellects for hire, scientific talent with a mercenary bent, and then persuading them to work for Iraq, to help sate its leader's hunger for weapons of mass destruction that would make the fatherland a superpower. Iraq was unable to purchase such weapons on the open or even the black market, given the suspicions of the U.S. in particular. As a result, it was vital to find renegade scientists - mental mercenaries - who could build them while using out-dated technology, so as not to attract the attention of international regulatory agencies or intelligence services.

But finding such scientists, and persuading them to work for Iraq, was the easiest part of Hamani's job as officer in charge of the Science Intelligence and Procurement Unit of Iraq's Ministry of Industry and Military Industrialisation (MIMI). Managing them once they were recruited was a different story. It was a supremely delicate matter – once they were working for Iraq, they were privy to all sorts of secrets and under no circumstances could they be allowed to change their minds or defect back to their own countries. They had to be kept happy, and that was the most difficult part of Hamani's job. He was very good at it.

The mental mercenaries generally came in three types: those who wanted money; those who wanted revenge against their own country; and those who were obsessed with their work and wanted to pursue it at any cost. Often all three were mixed together in one man. At the moment, one of the most promising renegade scientists was the Canadian engineer, Dr. Gerald Bull, an expert in artillery. He was obsessed with his dream of building a cannon - a supergun - over one hundred meters long that could fire telephone booth sized shells hundreds of kilometres. Bull's work was coming along well, at secret factories in Germany and the Netherlands. Soon the components of the massive gun would be smuggled into Iraq, disguised as lengths of oil pipeline. Once the gun was assembled, Israel would start to receive its own very special version of long distance calls. Bull had been enraged when the Canadian then American governments had cancelled his research program, so he had been easy to recruit. But, like so many of the scientists Hamani had to manage, Bull was a difficult and eccentric personality. He insisted on living in Brussels, under his own name, and refused all overt protection. Hamani knew this arrangement would be fine as long as U.S. or Israeli Intelligence remained ignorant of the supergun project. But if they ever found out...

Colonel Hamani lowered his binoculars and sighed. At least Bull was merely angry and obsessive. At least he was more or less normal.

The Colonel's watchful brown eyes slid sideways, to where his companion was intently scribbling formulae in a notebook. And then there was the fourth type of renegade scientist, the rarest of them all, whose motives were like black spiders, buried deep in the gloomy, dank basement of the human soul. Those motives were very hard for normal people to understand. They tended, just like spiders, to skitter off in unexpected directions, spinning ugly webs in dark corners where you least wanted to find them.

In evaluating the very few such men he had had to deal with over his career, Hamani relied on his own vast knowledge of psychology, as well as the efforts of the Iraqi intelligence agency, Mukhabarat, and the State Secret Police, Amn-al-Amm. Based on what he had learned of Sword, he had recommended against his recruitment. The man was too unstable, and there was too much of his personality that Hamani had been unable to either explore or explain, something to do with his mother, and his father, who had also been famous in his field. A wife as well. And then there was the unreasoning devotion Sword had for his son, the only remotely normal human emotion Hamani ever saw the man demonstrate. And without knowledge of such things, Hamani knew he would not be in control, would not be able to anticipate which way the black spiders would scuttle. And he dreaded not having that kind of control over any of his wards, especially this particular man.

But he had been overruled, instructed to recruit him on the direct orders of Hussein Kamil, head of MIMI and son-in-law to Saddam Hussein. Unlike Dr. Bull, he had at least agreed to security measures, such as the use of a code name, a code name suggested by the Rais himself. And in the course of his efforts to keep Mohammed's Sword happy, Hamani had learned the contents of the man's mind, had counted the number of black spiders that lived there, and he was revolted. He tried not to think of the countless messes he had cleaned up over the years. Keep the Sword happy, the Rais had said, no matter how many suffer. And the irony of it all was that, in a very real way, it was his fault.

A fervent patriot, Hamani had for the first time in his life started to wonder just how many innocent lives must be sacrificed in the name of national security. Like virtually all professional soldiers he was not a particularly religious man, nor was he a philosopher. But he had taken to dipping into the Koran, finding an unexpected comfort in the teachings of the Prophet Mohammed. He wondered what the Prophet would make of his most dangerous namesake. I have to stop thinking about this, he thought wearily. Just do your duty. But what was duty when it involved dealing with a man like this? I can't stop thinking about it. That's the reason, he thought bitterly, why I'm thirty-five and my hair is already going grey.

The Sword stopped writing for a moment and spoke, pointing with his pen toward the hamlet. "Note also the effectiveness of the new delivery system. Not one shell failed."

Hamani nodded, forcing himself to concentrate on the task at hand. A technical man himself, though the first to admit that Organo-phosphate chemistry was not his strong suit, he knew that the commonly used chemical nerve agents were binary weapons. They consisted of a canister containing two non-toxic compounds, separated by an impervious membrane. Only when the membrane was ruptured and the two compounds mixed did they form deadly nerve toxin. The canisters were pre-loaded into shells. With careful handling, these could be stored and transported with reasonable safely. Prior to the Sword's recruitment, Iraq's delivery method involved initiating pre-load on the ground before the shell was fired from the artillery piece. This was a risky business, with significant potential for error in the heat of battle - in fact, there had been a couple of disastrous accidents during training exercises.

"Tell me again how your new system works," said Hamani to the Sword, who was once again scribbling furiously. The scientist waved his hand impatiently without lifting his eyes from his notebook. "You wouldn't understand the details. As I said, XP29 is a derivative of Sarin, but five hundred times more lethal. Adding a third agent to the binary cocktail, in this case a DMSO-like chemical, one that facilitates absorption through the skin, greatly increases the kill speed. Another feature of the product is that doesn't linger in the environment so ground forces have to wait much less time before occupying the affected area. Upon firing the shell, the now tertiary canister's membrane is mechanically ruptured, allowing the chemical components to mix. Utilising the pressures of trajectory and the spinning of the shell, determined by the rifling of the artillery piece, complete mixing can be effected before the shell explodes, even over very short distances."

Hamani was about to ask another question when the captain hesitantly saluted. "Colonel Hamani, may I order my men to stand down?"

The Republican Guard officer turned to Sword. "Do you want bodies collected for autopsy?"

"No," said the Sword, slipping the notebook into one of the pockets of his khaki bush vest. "That wouldn't tell me anything I don't already know. Let them rot."

"Give the order to stand down and retire," said Hamani to the captain.

Moments later, anxious to be away from a place of so much death, soldiers grabbed their personal kit, weapons and observation gear, scrambled along the trench, and headed for the trucks that would take them back to base.

Mohammed's Sword turned and followed, with Aziz Hamani behind him. The colonel was well aware of Western culture, particularly enjoying the American movies forbidden to ordinary Iraqis. Now he suddenly recalled seeing the old film Frankenstein. As he stared at the Sword's back and thought of the bodies back in the hamlet, he thought, we've created a chemical monster, and this is the mad scientist who did it.

With a chill he understood that this man with the emerald eyes really was mad, really was as unstable as a badly designed warhead. Hamani knew with absolute certainty that one of these days something would set off that unbalanced personality, that he would explode, and the spiders would scuttle everywhere, out in the open. It was impossible to foretell what would set him off, or where the spiders would go. All I know, thought Hamani, is that when it happens it will be a dark moment. Very dark indeed.

TWO

The darkness was absolute. Out of nothingness, the face of a man, formless, imperceptible, leered down hungrily. His mouth moved and although she heard nothing, the expression on his vicious features told all.

It was going to happen again.

She tried to cry out. What have I done? If I've done something wrong, I promise I won't do it again! Please, no! But she couldn't speak.

She felt the burning, tearing thrusts as he crammed himself inside her, the heat between her legs, the searing pain, the smell of stale sweat and fresh lust. She lay unmoving, disconnected, unable to fight him, trapped in a body that could not react.

When he was gone there was nothing but the darkness. It was a dirty darkness and she herself was filthy. She must be a very bad little girl to be punished like this. She sobbed convulsively, wanting desperately to curl up like a baby in the womb, to try to crush the pain between her legs but could not. . .

She tried to remember long ago, when this place had meant refuge and comfort instead of terror. Dimly she remembered girlish fantasies, of princesses and castles, dragons and gallant knights in armour. It was her place to be alone. Going down there was her little ritual, the first thing she did when the family returned home for the summer, to descend into her sanctuary, to check to see if everything was as it should be in her secret world.

The cellar was not a big room, the central area of it taken up by the old fashioned furnace. The walls, constructed of the same granite stones as the stairwell, their soft contours truncated by abrasive mortar, were bare. She loved the cool feel of them and how they made her conjure up images of what it must have been like to live in the castles of old.

The only source of natural daylight was a small, ground level window located high up on the south wall. Invariably in spring and early summer, a single rose bush planted in the soil in front of the glass would produce beautiful flowers which when touched by the sun's rays, would bathe the room in a marvellous amber/pink glow. To a little girl, it was a place where everything seemed possible, where hope was effortless. To her, the place was the most beautiful thing on earth. In the summer of her eighth year, something happened in that room that would change that magical impression, forever.

The north side of the room housed a steel door that her father always kept locked. It must have been very bad for her to ever have come down here. Papa had said she mustn't, because the door was very important, that it was a place to hide from bombs. She hadn't been sure what bombs were, but the word didn't sound very important.

That day, a gardener/farmhand conducting annual maintenance inadvertently left the steel door wedged ajar while he went for lunch. Working on the electrical system, he had turned off the panel, choosing to run an extension cord into the bomb shelter - a common feature of Swiss homes of the period. Young Marie Françoise, always an adventuresome soul, saw the opened door and had to see inside, just once. Managing to pry the heavy door open, enough to slip past, the wedge loosened and shifted. The sound of it scraping across the slate floor grabbed her attention, but before she could react, the heavy, spring loaded door slammed shut, pinching the electrical cord, severing it. The shelter was thrown into darkness.

For the first time in her short life, she panicked. Pushing and banging frantically against its cold hardness, she couldn't budge it. Screaming for help, which didn't come for over half an hour, she lost all control.

When the man finally returned she was in such an agitated state that when he opened the door, she sprang at him and held on so tightly he had to fight her off, violently so. Totally out of control his animal urges took over.

Later, alone, terrified, she sought the peace of her bedroom. And of course she couldn't tell Papa because she wasn't supposed to have been down here at all and he might fly into one of his furious rages.

The nuns in school had said that there was a hell, but she hadn't really believed them. Now she knew there was a hell, and that it existed in impenetrable darkness, pain and grief, seventeen steps down from the kitchen of her own home.

. . . .She thrashed, even in her tortured sleep knowing it was just an old, old memory. She tried to cry out but couldn't. Where is my gallant knight? The knight who rescued me from this horror and then disappeared? Oh Christian, my Christian, how could you leave me all alone? I miss you so much. I need you.

THREE

January 20, 1991, South-eastern Iraq

In an otherwise featureless expanse of brown desert, only the raised edges of a recent excavation the size of a soccer field offered any resistance to the frigid north-westerly wind that scraped across the ground. Swirls of grit, clawed loose from piles of dirt, coalesced into dusty tendrils and slithered south towards the Saudi Arabian frontier, less than thirty kilometres away.

At the extreme south corner of the excavation, right at the edge, a man knelt, his arms raised beseechingly toward a cold and uncaring heaven, palms straining skyward. He was covered with streaks of mud. He rocked back and forth on his haunches like an animal driven insane by confinement or abuse, an eerie keening moan issuing from mud-caked lips. A desiccated ribbon of thick, blood-flecked saliva stretched from the left corner of his half-open mouth to the front of his shirt, and the frigid breeze flicked it back and forth. The corpse of a young adolescent sprawled beside him like a broken mannequin, the skin grey-green even though he had been dead only a few hours.

It had taken a long time to find the body amongst all the others in the pit, his feet slipping on the hundreds of inert forms, all the same grey-green colour. He had exhausted himself pulling and pushing and dragging them out of the way until he had found what he sought, found what he did not want to find, found what he somehow believed, despite all the evidence, he would never find. The terrible scream that had been torn from his throat when he finally discovered the body of his son had echoed amongst emptiness. The few survivors of the village of Al Asad had fled in horror hours ago, just before the NBC-suited Iraqi soldiers had arrived with their bulldozers to dig this pit and hide any evidence of what had happened. And then it had taken almost an hour, and the last remnants of his strength, to drag the body across all the others, to the edge of the pit, and somehow pull it out. Now, at dusk, all he felt was grief, so all-encompassing it numbed him to the ravages of the frigid wind and the stinging grit that peppered his face.

Only the queasy quaking of the ground broke through his agony. In his dirty tear-streaked face, the emerald green eyes slowly opened and searched the sky. A formation of five F18s, flying very low, their tails alight, roared overhead on a flight path towards the Northwest. The sight reminded him of what had happened here, just hours earlier.

Three US Air Force F16s had bombed this area, somehow knowing what to target. Their bombs had completely avoided Al Asad and its population of impoverished civilians, striking instead a piece of desolate landscape almost two kilometres outside the village. The explosions had torn open the earth and exposed a facility buried deep underground, a facility that was now just a crater filled with a tangled wreckage of concrete and reinforced steel. But it wasn't the bombs that had killed all the people who now lay in the pit. It had been the soupy, noxious grey fog released by the explosions. It had hissed from the crater like a foul exhalation from the grave and rolled Southeast, towards the village, smothering it. And his son.

How had they known? he wondered, watching the five jet fighters scream triumphantly toward the horizon as hate, black and thick as tar, slowly filled his heart. How had they known that buried near this village was an underground laboratory manufacturing XP29? How had they known enough to be aware that the percussion bombs they had dropped so precisely were the most effective means of rupturing the super reinforced concrete of the top secret fortress and in the process, destroying canisters of the three constituents of XP29 mixing their contents to make the toxic nerve agent?

Black spiders scuttled in his mind, weaving dense webs of conspiracy. Had he been betrayed? The spiders suddenly stopped, freeze-framed, as he remembered. All the work he had put into developing XP29 and its ingenious delivery system. Colonel Aziz Hamani, his recruiter, controller and procurer, telling him that, no, the system was not yet ready and likely wouldn't see action against the Allied forces, even though Iraq would lose the Gulf War as a result of the decision, a decision he was certain came right from Saddam himself. Hamani had said the Rais had decided not to use it, or his other weapons, botulism and anthrax, because he feared a terrible retribution from his enemies if he broke the international convention against the use of biochemical weapons, a convention even Adolf Hitler had respected.

But what was the point of having such weapons if you weren't prepared to use them? Had it been the Rais's decision to hold back? Or had Hamani talked him into it?

It was a good thing he had planned for this eventuality, this possibility of being betrayed.

Betrayed. The word rang in his mind like some terrible tolling bell. The black spiders started scuttling again, faster and faster, and the webs they wove grew denser and denser. His son was dead because someone must have betrayed the location of the underground facility. Betrayed, because Hamani had persuaded Saddam Hussein not to use XP29 when its use would have annihilated those who had murdered his son.

His son. His face spasmed in grief as he gazed once more at the lifeless body, a body to which he had given life, a life he had loved more than his own. Suddenly his mask of grief was transformed into a feral snarl as he remembered the body that had incubated that life. All the flimsy cobwebs in his mind linked up, crystallised, suddenly as solid and transparent as glass and he knew what he had to do.

Behind him he heard shouts and the tramp of boots. He turned and saw Iraqi soldiers advancing toward him. At the sight of the staring, crazed emerald green eyes a couple of them faltered before resuming their advance, more slowly this time, their weapons now at the ready. Suddenly he was aware of how tired he was, could feel the painful grit on which he was kneeling dig into his numb flesh. As he slowly rose to face the troops he shook his head to clear it, already making plans. An old phrase he had once heard suddenly sprang into his mind, a Spanish proverb - 'revenge is a dish best eaten cold'. For the first time in his life he disagreed with this idea. He threw back his head and laughed soundlessly, sending it pulsing toward the dim stars winking to life in the evening sky.

It would be nice to taste it hot. Hot and smoky, spicy.

FOUR

January 23, 1991, Baghdad

It was just an hour before midnight in the upscale Mansour area of northern Baghdad. The city lay in darkness, a blackout imposed because of nightly attacks by the allied forces Saddam Hussein had engaged in the Mother of All Battles.

At the huge mansion, the bell to the exterior portico rang repeatedly. The maid, Fatima, bustled across the marble floor to answer it. Who could be calling at this hour? Peering through the security grate, she saw a soldier standing outside, a Republican Guard officer. His uniform was ripped and soiled and stained with blood. Still, he was a fine looking man. And those eyes. . .

"Who are you? What do you want?"

In obvious pain, the soldier pulled himself erect and stood at attention, every inch the officer. Despite her suspicious nature, Fatima's heart swelled with pride. This was the kind of man who would throw that infidel President Bush from the top of the White House.

"Major Hakim Guramda. I have been ordered here to give grave news to the mistress of the house, Lady Soraya Hamani. It concerns her husband, Colonel Aziz Hamani. Please let me in. I must speak with her urgently."

Fatima knew her job - to carefully screen anyone before allowing them inside. She hesitated, uncertain what to do. There was no question the accent was a little odd. Perhaps this man was an ethnic Persian, or a Marsh Arab from the Shatt al Arab. Or perhaps he was a northerner, born near the Turkish border. That must be it. Certainly that would account for the eyes. Everyone knew that certain kinds of Turks had eyes like gemstones. But the man was clearly injured and he did wear the uniform of the colonel's regiment. And, if it concerned the master of the house.

"What is the message?" asked Fatima, trying to buy time so she could think a little longer before admitting the stranger.

"I must inform the Lady Soraya that her husband has been gravely injured in his defence of the fatherland. He urgently requests that she join him at his sick bed. Hurry, woman, there isn't much time!"

Trained to instantly obey direct commands, the impatient tone made Fatima throw off her indecision and unlock the door. "Come in. I will fetch my mistress. She has retired for the night."

They walked across the courtyard. "Your injuries, sir, are they severe?"

"Inconsequential. It is those of Colonel Hamani that worry me."

At these words Fatima moved faster than she ever had in her life. She motioned the officer to a chair in the foyer, into which he gratefully collapsed, while she bustled down the long hallway.

When she returned a few minutes later, she walked respectfully behind Soraya Hamani, who was tugging at the tie of her red silk robe. The sleepy pink flush of the newly awakened made her flawless coffee-and-cream complexion even more beautiful under her tousled, jet-black hair. Even without makeup she was stunning, and her huge hazel eyes shone with concern and fear. She had the build and fluid motion of a model, and her rapid pace made heavy, melon-shaped breasts swing under the taut silk. At the sight of her the major was immediately on his feet, straining to bow low, even though it was obvious it pained him. "Lady Soraya, I bring terrible news of your husband."

Lilting and musical though it was, her voice showed the strain of trying to maintain her composure. "What has happened to him? Where is he?"

"We were defending an air base near the Saudi border when we came under artillery fire. The Colonel was injured in the chest by shrapnel and moved to a field hospital. It did not look serious at first, but now . . . well, there is a problem."

Soraya Hamani stiffened visibly as his voice trailed off. "He asked for me?"

"Yes, my lady. He personally dispatched me to find you and bring you to him. You are very lucky in the love of your husband."

Fatima thought this a bold thing to say, but her mistress seemed not to notice. "We will leave immediately."

Major Guramda nodded wearily. "I have a vehicle but it is heavily damaged. I do not think it will make the journey back."

"Then we will take mine," said Soraya imperiously. "Of course I do not drive, and the chauffeur has gone home for the day. Major, are you strong enough to drive?"

"Of course, my lady."

Ten minutes later they were in the black 1990 Mercedes sedan, the two women in the back, the major driving. Soraya had insisted on taking Fatima in case there were errands to be run at the hospital as she stayed by her husband's bedside. With the streetlights out, the darkness was complete. Neither woman could make out any landmarks as they made their tortuous way to the outskirts of the city. It was only after about half an hour that they realised they were heading north.

"Major?" inquired Soraya. "We are going north, away from the Saudi border. Why?"

"The roads through the city are largely impassable," Guramda replied. "I was forced to come to you taking a circuitous route. We must continue in this direction for a few more kilometres until we reach the road to Basra and then move south from there."

"Very well," Soraya nodded, suddenly craning her elegant neck to see what was ahead.

It was a military checkpoint, with a long line of vehicles waiting to pass through, and they were at the very end of it. After two minutes of waiting and no movement, Major Guramda suddenly swung the Mercedes out of line and veered along the shoulder towards the barricade. As he approached a squad of tense looking soldiers bolted toward the vehicle and surrounded it, weapons pointed. A sergeant rapped with his pistol butt on the driver's window.

The major hit the button to roll down the window, then flashed an ID badge in the man's face. Because of the blackout even this checkpoint was largely in darkness. Before the sergeant could peer at the badge and get a good look at the photograph, the major was already putting it back in his pocket. "Just a moment," said the NCO. "I didn't get a good look at that. And who do you think you are, breaking the line?"

An expression of controlled rage on his face, Guramda leaned closer to the window and reached theatrically for his sidearm. The officer blanched as he saw the Republican Guard uniform. "Major. A thousand apologies, sir. I am just doing my duty, sir. I-

Soraya leaned forward. "Sergeant, thank you for your diligence at your post but we are on a grave mission. We must reach the major's commander, who has been injured. No doubt you have heard of him. Colonel Aziz Hamani. I am his wife. Here are my papers." She rummaged in her bag. "These should convince you."

But the sergeant was already backing away, a look of near panic on his face, spreading his arms wide to tell his men to do the same. "Advance! Private, raise the barricade for this vehicle." Looking at Guramda, he gave the crispest salute of his life. "My most humble apologies, major."

Major Guramda nodded curtly and they shot through the barricade onto the black and deserted highway. Five kilometres further on, the sign for the Basra turnoff glinted in the headlights. The major pulled to the side of the road. "It's a long drive from here. We'll stop for a moment so you can stretch your legs."

Gratefully, both women got out of the car. As they walked back and forth along the verge, the major disappeared for a few moments - both thought, probably to relieve himself. When he returned he was carrying a leather satchel that Fatima was sure he hadn't had when he left. Her mistress, preoccupied, gazing at the night sky, didn't notice. Striding purposefully to the vehicle's trunk, he opened it with the key. He called to Fatima, asking for help with something, she wasn't sure what and she bustled to assist him. As she leaned to peer into the trunk, a pistol butt sliced out of the darkness and smashed into her temple.

When she awoke, hours later it seemed, dawn was throwing a dull grey light. At first she didn't understand how she could have fallen asleep standing up. Slowly she saw that she was being held upright by strips of plastic binding her wrists to the wire of a chain link fence. Her ankles seemed to be tied too, but she couldn't tell for sure because when she tried to move her head, she discovered it was also bound to the wire, forcing her to gaze to the left. When her blinking eyes finally cleared she saw with horror that her mistress was tied as well, in a spread-eagled position against the fence. She was naked and Fatima felt acid bile rise in her throat and closed her eyes.

"Look!" a man's voice screamed, high-pitched and hysterical. She felt a tremendous blow to her kidney and opened her eyes again as she struggled to find her breath. Major Guramda seized her by the hair and shook her head viciously. "Look and remember!"

Soraya had been beaten so badly about the face that her magnificent eyes were hidden behind bruises the size and colour of plums. Dried blood caked her chin. Her mouth was half-open and Fatima could see black gaps where teeth were missing. Her breasts were swollen to twice their normal size and ugly purple welts covered her back and buttocks. Streaks of blood ran down her legs. At first Fatima couldn't tell if she was conscious, but then a slight movement of her head told her that she was, just barely. With sickening surety, Fatima knew her mistress would never be beautiful again.

The major walked over to Soraya. Fatima saw his fly was open and that his stroking hand was encouraging a huge purple erection, with bulging green veins. "Do not shut your eyes or you will get the same!" he commanded. "Look and remember. Tell Hamani the Sword did this. And tell him how much he enjoyed it."

He pressed his body against Soraya's, from behind. Grabbing at her swollen breasts with both hands, he kneaded them with such brutality Fatima thought he was going to tear them from her chest. Then, with a show of delicacy, he parted Soraya's buttocks with both hands. "Watch and remember. Or you will get the same." Not for a moment did he take his emerald green eyes from Fatima's. Soraya made an animal grunt and her head twisted from side to side in near extinguished defiance.

"Remember. Tell Colonel Hamani the Sword did this. And how much he enjoyed it."

FIVE

February 3, 1991, Baghdad

Colonel Aziz Hamani sat on the edge of his chair, perfectly still, his back ramrod straight. He did not rest his hands on his thighs because he knew his damp palms would soften the knife-edged crease of his immaculately pressed white, red and gold Republican Guard dress uniform. His palms were damp even though he was in the air-conditioned underground bunker his Rais had called home since the beginning of the war.

Only once before in his career had he had a formal audience with Saddam Hussein, and that had taken place at the presidential palace. It had been several months before the August 2, 1990 invasion of Kuwait that precipitated the Gulf War, a war now coming to an inglorious end. March 18, 1990, the day after Dr. Gerald Bull had been assassinated at the door of his Brussels apartment by agents of Mossad. The Rais had been furious, wanting to know how Bull could be murdered so close to the completion of the supergun project. Why hadn't he been living safely in Iraq? If he had to be in Brussels, why hadn't he been living under an assumed name? Under protection? Who was responsible for this carelessness? Hamani had known at the time that Saddam needed someone to blame, and as Bull's minder he, Hamani, was the obvious target.

Now, his eyes staring unseeingly forward, the colonel remembered that day. How he had kissed his beloved Soraya good-bye, smelling, as she always did, of the frankincense and myrrh perfume whose recipe she had somehow retrieved from an ancient source. He had kissed her that way because he knew his Rais and his moods, and was not sure of coming back alive. In the course of the interview with Saddam, he had explained what Bull was like, how improbable it was that Mossad would find out about the supergun project, and more he couldn't remember in detail. All he remembered was his slow, careful, logical marshalling of the facts, and how he was convinced that it wouldn't matter that he was a dead man.

To his surprise, Saddam had accepted his explanation. To this day, he could remember the sense of relief and exultation he had felt as he was driven home by his chauffeur, to kiss Soraya again and drink champagne and make love to her all night in an ecstasy of relief.

Reflecting later upon the incident, using his knowledge of psychology, he had guessed what the Rais had probably been thinking: I am surrounded by sycophants, idiots and killers; this man is not only intelligent but has never failed me; he is a genius at what he does and probably cannot be replaced; my sources tell me he is incorruptible and a patriot. I may need such a man again.

The door to the cavernous room opened and an officer's booted steps banged on the floor. He nodded to Hamani, who rose and followed. Inside, Saddam Hussein stood with his back to the door, gazing at a wall map of the Gulf War battlefield. Like a man, Hamani thought, who has been told checkmate a dozen times but refuses to believe the match is lost.

After a calculated twenty seconds, Saddam turned from the map and walked towards Hamani. The colonel saw that he looked very tired, that his face was congested and little red veins seemed to be growing in the whites of his dark brown eyes. With a sagging sense of unease, he saw that the eyes had that odd look, a look that flicked in and out, from opaque inwardness to predatory searching brightness. A bad sign. Saddam stopped some ten feet away, his eyes bright. The colonel expected this usual wary distance - he knew the Rais wouldn't shake hands with anyone, not even foreign diplomats, for fear that they might have a poisoned spike on their signet ring. Practical man and paranoid man faced each other, although practical man knew enough to stare at his leader's chest, a direct facial gaze perhaps being the cause of murderous hostility.

"So," said Saddam Hussein. "Mohammed's Sword is gone?"

"Yes Excellency, it is true."

"How and why, Colonel Hamani?"

Hamani knew that every syllable counted, that the smallest mistake in tone or detail could be a death sentence. With some surprise, he realised he didn't much care anymore. He had thought of bringing his reports and files, his recommendation that the Sword not be recruited in the first place. But he hadn't brought such documents, and the Iraqi president was a slow and tentative reader anyway. So he reverted by force of habit to his usual careful, logical style. It had worked before, and it might again.

"If your Excellency will recall, I advised most strongly against recruiting this person," knowing full well that it was Hussein Kamil, Saddam's son-in-law, who insisted that the Sword be approached with every possible incentive. He knew too that Kamil was just a mouthpiece for the Rais, that the actual recruitment decision had been made by Saddam himself. As his gaze flicked briefly upwards he saw Saddam's pupils enlarge; he could read the intimate body signals that could only be interpreted by those from an Islamic culture. There, thought Hamani, I've passed the buck. If he doesn't remember, he can look it up. And maybe, just maybe, Kamil will be the scapegoat instead of me. At least I've given him a choice. He knows it and he will respect my intelligence and consideration at allowing him to save face. An animal trapped in a burrow is always grateful for a way out.

"With regards to how, Excellency, the Sword had been travelling with a Major Guramda, a colleague of mine in the Republican Guard, looking at various testing sites. Then word was radioed that the Allies had bombed the village he had been living in, the village of Al Asad and that everyone was dead. The Sword's son was living in the village as well and was a regular authorised visitor to the underground manufacturing facility. Sword flew into a rage and insisted on being driven immediately at high speed back to the village."

Saddam's heavy face was guarded but intent. "Go on."

"The highway was strafed by Allied fighters and the armoured car spun out of control. The driver was killed. Major Guramda was thrown from the vehicle and injured. When he awoke, he found that he had been stripped of his uniform and his identification. The armoured car was gone. The vehicle was found later at the village site, near the mass grave. The Sword was there, grieving over the body of his son, although Guramda's uniform was nowhere in evidence. The Sword was detained by troops and was awaiting interrogation when two British pilots from a downed Tornado fighter were brought to the Al Asad air base. Survivors from the village saw them and rioted in fury. The base commander called for all available hands to regain control. Of the four men guarding the Sword, three were called away. When they returned, they found the lone guard strangled and the Sword gone."

Saddam's eyes were still predator bright in his otherwise weary, congested face. "Why would he do this?"

Hamani knew he was pushing his luck by being repetitive, but he couldn't think of any other way. "As I advised in my original evaluation, Excellency, the Sword's personality is unstable. For a long time, despite his brilliance, he has been teetering on the cliffs of insanity. I have thought long and hard about his. I believe the death of his son has driven him over the edge."

"And ... the unfortunate incident with your wife?"

For the first time ever during a formal interview, Colonel Aziz Hamani looked his Rais right in the eye and locked his gaze. It was provocative, perhaps even suicidal, but he didn't care any more. "Sword was very upset when I told him the fatherland would not be using his invention against the Allies. Given the way his mind works, he probably thought I advised you in this course of action. Unable to revenge himself upon you, or me, he chose to exact his revenge himself upon my wife."

The Rais flicked his eyes away. He stared at the ceiling for a moment, as if remembering something he had once read in childhood in a book of etiquette. Then he gestured at a sofa and chair facing each other in the corner. They strode stiffly toward them and sat down, Saddam on the sofa and Hamani in the chair.

Once seated, Saddam still stared at the ceiling. "And how is your wife now?"

"She's dead," said Hamani. "She was still alive when she was taken to hospital, but once there she died from her injuries." And shame, he wanted to add. He had been told her last words were, I love you, my colonel, and I cannot bear to have you see me like this, or hear of my humiliation. But he knew he couldn't say those words without weeping, and he suspected the Rais already knew, which was why he was being so uncharacteristically sympathetic.

Saddam's gaze was once again level. "And what did the maid say?"

With unprecedented insolence, Hamani not only stared the Iraqi president in the eye, but did not reply directly. "She answered every question put to her. It took some time however. She was most distraught."

Again the Rais looked at the ceiling. "Major Guramda. What had he to do with this?"

"Nothing, Excellency. He had the misfortune to be involved in an accident, have his identity stolen and used for criminal purposes. His . . . interrogation was conducted under a perfectly understandable misapprehension. When I discovered they had him I ordered it halted. I am told he is in stable condition, although still heavily sedated. Six hours of electric shocks to the genitals would have killed a weaker man."

The Rais was now staring at the floor, his heavy face unreadable. Slowly he raised his bloodshot eyes and Hamani knew that his leader's show of sympathy was at an end. Saddam was intent on asserting dominance, and if Hamani wanted to live he must now be the one to look away. "You know of course that he cannot be allowed to escape. You have taken measures?"

Hamani looked away and nodded. "Of course, Excellency. We immediately froze his bank accounts in Switzerland and the Bahamas. But despite our swiftness, we found they had already been emptied. The same with his weapons materials acquisition account. I assume he has also fled with copies of the blueprints for his devices, as well as the formulae." The colonel shrugged, to indicate he was stating the obvious. "The Sword had plans already in place to flee." To forestall an explosion of rage, he said quietly, "We will find him." Now was the dangerous part. "But it might take time."

"Find him," said Saddam Hussein. "Soon. And kill him. Whatever the cost. With what he knows . . ."

"I will need money and backup," said Hamani.

"Whatever you need," said the Rais. "Anything."

"I want Major Guramda."

Saddam's heavy caterpillar eyebrows contracted in a spasm of paranoia. "Why?"

"Both he and I have suffered personal injury as a result of the Sword. I want an assistant who is motivated to work day and night."

Hamani knew this appeal to personal revenge would make perfect psychological sense to a man like the Rais. Iraq's president nodded curtly, then rose and strode across the room to the map on the wall, as if gazing at it long enough would give him the answer to ultimate victory.

Colonel Hamani knew the interview was over. He was still alive. Once more, against all the odds, he had survived. In a newly cold part of his soul, he realised he didn't care either way. Perhaps it was that coldness that had saved him, the sort of coldness a soulless man like the Rais respected. He rose from his chair and spun smartly on his heel, marching for the door. Just as he reached it, his Rais said, "Colonel. My condolences on the death of your wife, the lady Soraya. May Allah watch over her. Her death was one of martyrs."

Tears springing to his eyes, Hamani seized the door handle and left the room, not trusting himself to reply. He had underestimated Saddam's capacity for manipulation. He told himself, I must always remember that this man is smarter than I think he is - that is why he is the Rais, and I am not. But then, he thought again. Who cares if he is the Rais? All he knew was that it had nothing to do with recruiting and minding renegade scientists, national security, the Rais's ambitions, or anything else on earth. Except vengeance. He was not a vindictive man by nature, but his search for the Sword would be nothing but pure, unadulterated vendetta.

SIX
The Present

Over the following months, Hamani brooded and planned, sitting in his office, chain smoking pungent Turkish cigarettes, his intent and serious face wreathed in clouds of blue smoke. With Major fully recovered and out of hospital, the tall, stocky thirty-year-old with the grey eyes proved to be a tireless, intelligent and ruthless assistant. The mansion in Mansour had been sold, and Fatima given a handsome pension, the colonel unable to bear living there without Soraya. So he lived in his office, sleeping on a cot, eating little, seemingly able to exist on tea, coffee and cigarettes. The secretaries wondered why this handsome man was so obsessed, so willing to live without comfort, so intense and angry.

Time and again the colonel leafed through the stacks of files that teetered on every flat surface of his office, and were piled on the floor. Every day he phoned his contacts at the Iraqi intelligence agency, Mukhabarat, and the State Secret Police, Amm-al-Amm. Every day he slowly replaced the receiver in its cradle.

Nothing. The Sword had vanished.

He wrote meticulously detailed notes on sheets of paper that invariably were balled up and thrown into the overflowing wastebasket. Then one day he reviewed a particular red file. After writing slowly for almost an hour, he rubbed his face and drummed his fingers on the desktop.

Idiot. Of course, that was it. Why hadn't he seen it sooner? Then, with a sprinting, fluid pen he rewrote those notes until they occupied just one sheet of paper. Then he opened the drawer of his desk and deposited the single sheet. Others slowly joined this, over a period of weeks, until finally one day he took them all out in a moment of decisiveness. He made a single photocopy, and gave the ten-page document to Guramda.

After reading the first page the major's black eyebrows shot toward his hairline and he threw the colonel a questioning look. Hamani waved an impatient hand to tell him to read to the end. When he had finished, the colonel waved again, to tell him to be seated.

For a long time Guramda was silent, lost in thought, alternately nodding and shaking his head, his legs crossed, the crossed left leg bouncing up and down in an excess of nervous energy. Finally he said, "Sir, with respect. Are you sure this is a wise course of action? If you want to make Iraq a pariah forever, this is the best way to do it. I cannot believe the Rais would approve."

Hamani rubbed his eyes wearily. "Look at the facts. It's been months now. He's disappeared. Our agents cannot find him. He has a great deal of money and the blueprints and formulae for his devices. He also has all the time in the world, and we do not. The Rais is getting impatient. He told me to do anything to find and kill the Sword, and that is what I intend to do. We must flush him out. I know his mind and how it works. The combination of a challenge, a threat and his obsession will prove irresistible."

Weeks earlier, his grey eyes widened in disbelief, Major Guramda had read the files about Mohammed's Sword and the compulsions that drove him. As he remembered those files now, he rubbed his face as if trying to scrub away something unclean.

Hamani leaned forward, his eyes intent. "It is risky, of course. And if we fail. . ." He could tell Guramda was under no illusions about what that would mean. "The key with this plan is that we will no longer be working alone. Every Western intelligence service will be searching for Mohammed's Sword. Even I never imagined that we might be able to recruit the Americans, the British and the French to find the Sword for us. And they won't even know they're doing it."

Guramda had to smile. "That is true. This could be the most ingenious intelligence feint in history." His smile vanished. "But, Allah, the risk."

Hamani lit another cigarette and waved his hand. "Risk is relative. If it works, we gain everything. If it doesn't, we lose our lives. Do nothing; we will also lose our lives when the Rais's patience runs out. Do you trust me?"

Guramda nodded. "Of course. When Mukhabarat was frying my balls, you rescued me. I respected you before, sir, and the past weeks have simply increased my opinion of your abilities."

"Do you have any questions or suggestions about the plan?" asked Hamani, oblivious to the compliment.

The major stood and began pacing the room, once again leafing through the document. Finally he stopped. "Which part of the plan do you initiate first? It is not clear."

"It's not clear because until now I wasn't sure," replied Hamani. "Now, I know."

He made a little temple with his fingers and tucked it under his chin. "First, the tease, to make Sword curious. Get him a little off balance, get him excited and intrigued. Then the leak and the first piece of bait. The Accountant. That will open the jaws of the trap."

"Where is this Accountant?"

"I have him," said Colonel Hamani. "I've been saving him for years, just in case."

Guramda probed for holes. "But how can you leak information about the Accountant without implicating the fatherland? Not to mention yourself."

"That is the riskiest part of the operation," admitted Hamani. "One false step and the Rais will know. If the facts are revealed, even our few remaining allies will shun us. Our nation will be an international pariah for the foreseeable future. And both of us, my friend, will be dead."

He stood and walked over to a stack of files, removing a red one, third from the top. "But it must be done. Leaked information about the Accountant will, by itself, make the Sword very worried. He will become even more alarmed when Western intelligence agencies start hunting him. He will have to move, have to come out of hiding."

The colonel opened the file, but his eyes were unseeing as he thought aloud. "It is absolutely vital that the leak be channelled through the woman at the Phoenix Foundation. If Western intelligence gets even the slightest whiff of the fact that the information comes from us, they will not search for the Sword. In Sword's twisted mind, his fixation with the woman will fuse with the fact that she possesses information that will destroy him. He will desire, hate and fear her, all at once."

Guramda shook his head. "I am used to dealing with animal minds but this one, he is like nothing I have seen before. I do not understand his motivations."

"Likely because you're normal," said Hamani. "The Sword definitely is not. The point is, given his psychology, that desire, hate and fear will make her absolutely irresistible. He will be compulsively drawn to her. And of course, we will know where both pieces of bait are, and we will be waiting when he shows up. Then we spring the trap and crush his foul life forever."

"How will you tease the Sword? I mean, you can't tease him if you don't know where he is."

Hamani's face was inscrutable. "It can be done. We have a shared history and mutual contacts. I am sure the Sword is maintaining a one-way blind approach, and the information will pass through many hands. There is no point in trying to track him through such a trail - Mukhabarat has tried already without success, and if we do it while the plan is in progress we may jeopardise it. But he will get what we feed him."

The colonel handed the red file to his assistant. "Read this. It will tell you about the woman and her value to us."

As Guramda took the file, he asked, "Are you willing to risk losing both pieces of bait?"

"Yes," said Hamani curtly. He opened the door and walked out.

The major began reading. As he remembered once again what he had learned about the Sword, his lip curled. He wouldn't want to be in her shoes, being stalked by a man like that. He felt a stab of pity for the poor woman. No, he thought. Not for anything in this world would I want to be Marie Françoise Von Bessel.

Neither he nor Colonel Hamani could possibly know that years would pass before the perfect circumstances to spring the trap would present themselves.

SEVEN

Basel, Switzerland, February 1
The Present

Rolf Muller accepted the room key from the desk agent of the Basel Hilton. Tall, blond, and athletically built, his confident easy manner extracted a smile from the young clerk as she gazed into his friendly blue eyes.

He was deeply sun-tanned, as if he had spent months in a hot sunny climate; the Aga Khan's fabulous resort on Sardinia's Costa Smeralda, perhaps, or somewhere in Tunisia. His expensive navy Armani jacket, pale green slacks, snow white shirt and red tie made him look like a cover model for Gentleman's Quarterly. It certainly seemed as if the flaxen haired woman in the short tight black leather skirt and the floor length mink coat, hanging adoringly onto his arm, would agree. The clerk recognised her - Gabriella Kuhn, at twenty-one already an internationally famous model, based in Zurich. This handsome man must be a model as well. She felt a pang of envy. It must be wonderful to be so beautiful.

"Are you enjoying your stay, sir?" she asked.

"Very much," he replied, looking hungrily at Gabriella. We have had a splendid day together, haven't we, my dear?"

"Yes," giggled Gabriella. "A gorgeous evening. I must say I'm a little tipsy. That wonderful meal, and all those brandies at the Cafe Chic. It certainly helps to take off the winter chill."

Rolf Muller bowed. "Nothing is too good for a woman as beautiful as you." Gabriella giggled again as they headed for the elevators, arm in arm. Enviously, the desk clerk watched them go. She sighed and started leafing through a pile of room service receipts. Some women have all the luck.

Gabriella entered the suite and gasped as she tossed her mink onto the chair nearest the door. "My God, it's huge!"

Muller smiled. "I like to live well."

She pouted. "It must be nice to have so much money. Ooooh, a round bed! I love round beds!"

She bounced on the embroidered silk coverlet. As she did so, her short leather skirt rode up her thighs and Muller could see the white triangle of her panties. He felt a stabbing spike of almost uncontrollable lust. Keeping his voice calm, he said, "I'll get you another drink. Make yourself comfortable." With an effort he adopted a light, teasing tone. "Has anyone ever told you that your eyes are like topazes? There was that lovely topaz necklace we saw this afternoon at Bergman's. When is your birthday, by the way?" He smiled thinly as Gabriella clapped her hands together and squealed.

Less than three minutes later they were on the bed, Rolf Muller's hands tearing at her clothes. "Rolf," she gasped. "Not so rough!"

He didn't seem to hear. His eyes were closed; his face, transformed, no longer handsome, was a mask of tension. She was suddenly aware of the rank smell coming from his body, a smell like a goat, that not even his expensive cologne could hide.

Suddenly she heard the electronic warble. The hands scrabbling at her slowed and stopped. The phone rang and rang. As if awakening from a trance, Rolf Muller lifted his head and slowly reached for the receiver.

"Yes. This is Muller. Where? Winterplatz, Brussels, two days from now, at 14:30 hours. I understand. No, no, I'm fine. My chest is congested with this winter air. Leaves me a little breathless."

He replaced the receiver in the cradle as Gabriella whimpered. His staring eyes seemed to bore into her soul. "Get out."

She scrabbled from the bed. She seized her coat and managed to put it on. Rolf Muller was still watching her with those staring blue eyes. Fumbling, Gabriella Kuhn managed to get the door open. It was just after two a.m. and the hallway was deserted. She stumbled down the corridor, forever ignorant of just how lucky she really was.

The man on the bed picked a few of Gabriella's blond hairs from the pillow and looked at them with distaste. He walked to the bathroom and flushed them down the toilet. He undressed and stepped into the shower, scrubbing himself clean and towelling off. Standing in front of the mirror, he stared into his own blue eyes. He suddenly decided they bothered him. Leaning over the sink, he popped out first one, then the other, contact lens and rinsed them, finally putting them into the case. Now blinking emerald green eyes stared back.

He wondered briefly if the model would go to the police. He smiled. No. He could always tell. And it was just as well that the phone had rung when it did. He licked his index finger and slowly ran it along his right eyebrow, to smooth it. It had been stupid of him to take a risk like this - he knew he was having more and more trouble controlling his urges.

He felt a prickle of excitement, remembering the last time he had had to control his urges. It had been years ago. It had been very difficult. He had never been able to do to her what he wanted to do. What he still wanted to do. He shrugged. Well, one of these days. One of these days, soon.

He threw on a heavy terrycloth robe and padded back into the main room. Dialing the combination, he threw open the lid of the smallest of his three Louis Vuitton suitcases. Hands on his hips, he contemplated his collection of videotapes.

He had acquired this collection at odd places and odd times over the previous few weeks. A package at a café in Amsterdam, an envelope at a train station locker in Rheims, a plastic bag concealed in the branches of a tree way out in the Black Forest. He had always been very careful not to collect these items himself, but as far as he could tell from his couriers, there had been no attempts at tracking or ambush. At first he had been surprised and a little amused, especially since he suspected where the tapes came from. Then he had started to wonder. What was going on? It irritated him that he couldn't figure it out. The tapes consisted of film taken at various places and various times, often at a convention or an international symposium. But the person on the tapes was always the same. And in spite of himself, he found he was increasingly intrigued, then finally obsessed.

He removed the latest tape and inserted it into the VCR above the TV. As he fiddled with the remote control, he remembered his initial reaction upon seeing this particular tape. He had not been amused; in fact, he had been very unpleasantly surprised.

He opened the minibar in the room and removed a small bottle of Glenfiddich. He sat down in front of the TV screen and drained the bottle in two convulsive swallows, remembering the length of time he had not been able to drink, all those excuses and explanations. But it had been necessary - if you already have trouble controlling your urges, alcohol made it that much more difficult.

He aimed the remote and settled back in his chair. He'd watched this two dozen times. It was a tape of an American CNN broadcast, consisting of a special report and an interview, televised just days before. He had been in a safe house and hadn't read the European papers or watched the news, so this was the first time he had become aware of the story. He leaned forward as he stared hungrily at the screen, unaware that his mouth was open. As the woman on the screen spoke in her correct but heavily accented English, he was also unaware that he had begun to mouth silent curses in several languages.

"...Correct, Mr. Kingsley. We have just learned that the disastrous fire at the Sandoz chemical facility five and a half years ago that poisoned the Rhine River was a terrorist attack."

"Mrs. Von Bessel, could you tell us why the facility would have been a terrorist target?"

"Apparently the warehouse housed large quantities of two precursor chemicals used in the manufacture of a deadly nerve toxin. It was deliberately destroyed because a bogus ship's manifest had been discovered at Hamburg. Apparently those involved in the plot feared the operation would be discovered so the facility was burned as a precaution."

"When you say large quantities, what are we talking about?"

"Over fifty thousand litres."

"I take it that's a lot of nerve gas component?"

"Yes, indeed. Evidence indicates these materials were prepared at a secret laboratory in Germany, then smuggled under bogus manifest documentation to Sandoz's Schweizerhalle facility. Once the materials were inside the warehouse, small shipments were distributed, mixed in with legitimate agro-chemical products. This apparently went on for several years, right under the nose of Sandoz."

"Who manufactured these deadly materials, and what was their ultimate destination?"

"At the moment, we do not know. I find our present ignorance deeply disturbing. The fact that it has taken so long for this information to come to light, and that those responsible have never been caught, means it is highly likely that such terrible weapons are still being manufactured. Possibly even using the same technique, at some unsuspecting chemical facility."

"So, we don't know who concocted this deadly brew, or who they concocted it for?

"That is correct."

"So that is why you have given this information to the CIA and other Western intelligence services?"

"Yes. They are most interested in discovering more, especially about who was responsible. Given the fact that use of such a chemical weapon could kill millions of innocent people, I am sure a world-wide hunt is being launched."

"That brings us to the only really important clue you have at the moment. Now, I understand the Sandoz Corporation itself was not involved in this plot?"

"It is unlikely. They are a perfectly legitimate company."

"But I understand there was a Sandoz employee who was the mastermind behind all of this?"

"Yes. He was apparently known as the Accountant. According to our information, he was responsible for preparing the false papers and manifests and concealing the true nature of the shipments that were exported containing the illegal chemicals."

"Was he the only Sandoz employee involved?"

"At this time, we simply do not know. It is possible. We intend to find out."

"Mrs. Von Bessel, can you give us some idea of how the intelligence services involved are going to conduct their investigation? I mean, the trail is pretty cold by now."

"I'm sorry. I do have other information, but I have been asked to keep it confidential."

"I understand. Thank you."

The Sword ejected the tape and pulled it from the machine. Holding it in both powerful hands, he twisted the plastic casing until it shattered. He pulled out several meters of videotape and wrapped it around one of the pillars in the room. His face a mask of rage, he pulled it tight, around two imaginary necks.

Hamani had said the Accountant was dead. And what other information did the bitch have?

EIGHT

Brussels, February 3

The voice had a haunting, sensual quality, a strange amalgam of honey, smoke and music. Perhaps it was the intense conviction behind her words, words she uttered with the experience of long practice, but in which she obviously believed with every fibre of her being. The huge crowd jammed into the main convention hall of the Brussels Winterplatz hung on every syllable.

Having spoken in her native French for five minutes, she now switched to moderately accented English. "The Phoenix Foundation was established after the second worst environmental catastrophe in European history, the Sandoz chemical works fire at Schweizerhalle near Basel on November 1, 1986. In this day and age, there is no excuse for such disasters. We at the Foundation have met with the heads of virtually every large company in Europe, to urge the adoption of stringent environmental protection measures. Our hazardous materials management philosophy is based on the principle of industry product stewardship. Those who manufacture and sell hazardous chemicals must be responsible for such products, from cradle to grave. . ."

Impassively, Colonel Aziz Hamani watched the chairman of the board and CEO of the Phoenix Foundation as she spoke. Standing at the front of the crowd on the mezzanine of the convention hall, right against the railing, he was dressed in a dark civilian suit. The tag in his lapel said his name was Nizar Naboulsi of Saudi Arabia. With a pang he realised that Marie Françoise Von Bessel was a classic beauty, not unlike his beloved Soraya - the same oval face, brown eyes and finely sculptured features. Just over five feet tall, her trademark - familiar to anyone in Western Europe who picked up a newspaper or watched TV - was a cap of glistening, chestnut hair cut in a medium length page boy that she tended to flip haughtily at the first sign of displeasure or challenge. Her Channel suit fit her perfectly and Hamani knew that her petite figure hid a dynamo of energy and determination, which was why the Foundation was the most feared organisation of its type in the world.

Taking his eyes away from her momentarily, he glanced down and caught sight of Major Guramda, also in a dark civilian suit. Their eyes locked and Guramda nodded slightly. His men were scattered throughout the crowd, and had discretely watched every delegate enter the hall, trying to spot the Sword. Hamani scanned the crowd anxiously, then turned his attention back to Von Bessel as he heard a familiar word.

"Believe it or not, the recent revelations about terrorism that night at Schweizerhalle prompted Sandoz officials to ask the Phoenix Foundation for a formal apology for our accusations about their environmental protection measures. I have refused to apologise. Their measures were inadequate, since runoff from the smoking rubble was allowed to drain directly into the Rhine. Even though this defect has now been corrected, along with many others, it should never have been allowed in the first place. The revelations about the terrorist attack have simply driven home the necessity of taking ever greater precautions, of safeguarding. . ."

Again Hamani scanned the crowd from his vantagepoint. Because of the aggressiveness with which Von Bessel pursued companies she felt were environmentally irresponsible, there had been threats against her life. As a result, she only rarely appeared in large crowds. That was why he was so confident the Sword would make his move here - he had to kill her soon, because the colonel knew the man couldn't stand the idea that Von Bessel might have damaging information of which he was unaware. And he also knew with absolute certainty that the Sword, given his crazed obsession with this woman, would attempt the assassination himself. For the thousandth time, he wondered how he would do it. For the thousandth time, he tried to reassure himself that he wouldn't use poison gas, a bomb or a missile. Then again, with the Sword you never really knew.

It sounded as if Von Bessel was winding up her speech. She faltered momentarily and Hamani peered, concerned. He became fully aware of something that had been bothering her for some time. Someone in the audience near the podium was constantly coughing, a hacking, phlegmy cough. Bird-like, she rotated her head, searching for the source of the distraction. Hamani followed her gaze and saw a stooped and dishevelled old man in a threadbare naval pea coat and a wool cap. He was standing in the third row back, over towards the curtained fringe at the edge of the display area. Hamani shook his head. Some of these Western environmentalists should be ashamed of themselves, dressing like bums. Wanted to clean up the environment but couldn't be bothered to clean up themselves.

Von Bessel took a deep breath and continued. "But again I remind you that it is not just large corporations who carry a heavy burden of responsibility. As individual citizens, we are all responsible for ensuring the protection, enhancement and wise use of our environment. On a personal note, I wish to end today by talking about individuals. My husband, Christian Von Bessel, and my young son, Daniel, were both tragically killed in a road accident the very night of the Schweizerhalle fire. They would not have died if not for that fire. It was their loss that drove me to establish the Phoenix Foundation. It is their loss that drives me to this day. . ."

Hamani saw a sudden movement out of the corner of his eye, saw the man in the threadbare coat aim the pistol. He shouted at the same time Major Guramda did, as everything began to move in slow motion. Allah, no. In a situation like this, women always freeze like a deer caught in headlights. Then to his astonishment, he realised that Von Bessel had dropped behind the lectern just as a shot rang out. And an other. He thought to himself, either she's had special training from an expert or her life has been such that she has often had to hide very quickly. He didn't have time to pursue the thought.

Two more blasts, as huge splinters of wood exploded from the lectern and spun across the stage. Realising he had missed, the shooter suddenly dropped, cat-like, into a crouch and Hamani lost sight of him. He saw the crowd sway and part like a field of grain through which a lion was running. The curtained barrier twitched aside and he was gone.

The assassin was not alone. There was a blur of activity as several other people, obviously accomplices, darted through the curtains, pistols in the air to dissuade any heroic bystanders. The entire episode had lasted less than ten seconds; executed with such military precision that even Hamani was impressed. And sickened, that the Sword had entered the trap, only to escape. He could see Guramda trying to fight his way to the exit, unable to make way against the panicked crowd fleeing from the sight of the guns.

Half an hour later, Hamani and his team regrouped at a nearby hotel. His men expected one of the colonel's infamous dressing downs, but instead found him remarkably controlled, even calm. Recruited just for this action, and unaware of the scope of the full operation, they could not know what their leader knew: that he still had the Accountant and Von Bessel, and that the Sword would have to try again.

They also did not know another reason for his icy calm. Knowledge was power, and Hamani now knew that the Sword had an expert team assisting him. He also knew that the Sword had a completely new face. It must have cost tens of thousands of dollars, thought the colonel. But there was no way he could have changed his eye colour. He must be using contact lenses.

But he had been forced to come out of hiding. This particular trap had failed, but he was confident the next one wouldn't.

The plan was working.

****

Four days later, Major Guramda strode briskly down the hallway to Colonel Hamani's office. He glanced at his watch. Three in the morning.

He threw open the door to be greeted by a cloud of pungent blue smoke. Through it he could see his boss sitting at his desk in his shirtsleeves, elbows on the table, his head in his hands. An overflowing ashtray sat in front of him, as well as a slim manila folder.

"Colonel, I came as soon as I was informed. I apologise that it was not easy to reach me."

Hamani waved a weary arm. "Come in and shut the door."

The major had never seen his boss look so tired. "What is it? What on earth has happened?"

The colonel reached for a cigarette, put it to his lips and made a face. He threw it onto the table and reached for the folder. He began to read.

"At 10 p.m. this evening - or rather yesterday evening - a team of north Baghdad firemen responded to an anonymous tip. They initiated a search of homes on a particular street. On the roof of the fourth home, which was vacant, they discovered a large mechanical assembly. This assembly featured three cylindrical stainless steel canisters; each equipped with pneumatic pistons and affixed radically to a central shiny metallic sphere. Attached below the sphere was an assortment of electronics and timers. Along its lower edge, a cup of grey plastic-like putty."

Hamani looked up from the folder. "Allah be praised that one of the firemen had been in the army and had worked with explosives. They all backed away from the device and called in the army bomb disposal unit. The bomb unit commander also called me, and I listened in as they were on the rooftop. They described the device to me and I was able to tell them what it was. I recognised it immediately from a set of preliminary blueprints I once saw by accident."

He continued reading. "The bomb disposal unit confirmed that the device was remote controlled through a connection to the home's telephone line. A simple telephone call would trigger the putty, the plastic explosive Semtex. The Semtex would then fire off the rest of the device. The device is something new, a three-part canister filled with the two chemical precursors of XP29 and a new, as yet unidentified reagent which appears to intensify the efficacy of the nerve gas by an order of magnitude."

Guramda was staring in horror. Hamani closed the file and tossed it on the table. "Had it gone off, with the wind blowing the way it was tonight, a sizeable portion of the population of north

Baghdad would now be dead."

"Mohammed's Sword?"

Hamani shrugged. "Who else?"

"What possibly could be the purpose of-" The colonel's phone rang. They both stared at it and Guramda looked reflexively at his watch. Hamani reached for the phone and picked up the receiver. "Hamani here." He listened in silence, scribbling notes on the cover of the manila folder. He hung up but continued writing. When he had finished, he picked up the phone again and dialed a number. "I want a trace on that call. No? Well try anyway."

"What?" asked Major Guramda, dreading the answer.

"That was the Sword," said Hamani. "He's figured out our game. His message, 'two can play'."

"What does he mean?"

Wearily Hamani rubbed his face. "He wants us to kill Marie Françoise Von Bessel. Or he will annihilate the entire population of an unspecified large city somewhere in the world, and provide incontrovertible evidence that it was the Rais who did it."

NINE

San Pedro, Belize, March 15

Douglas Baker was awake but knew enough not to open his eyes. He checked himself out. Apart from the pounding in his head, and the fact that his tongue felt like it was coated with something that grew on the east side of Mars, everything else seemed to be functional. Experimentally he moved his legs. Bad idea. When the sound of sheets against your body got on your nerves, you had a bad one. Not for the first time in his life he wondered how you could feel so good at two in the morning and so bad just a few hours later.

A rhythmic metallic sound came from the other side of the room. It set his teeth on edge, as well as triggering a reflex action in his foggy brain. His right hand swept instinctively under the pillow to locate his weapon. It wasn't there. Fight or flight hormones surging, he was about to dive for cover when the sound came again and he finally recognised it - creaking bedsprings.

But he wasn't married anymore. Slowly he turned his head and squinted. A wonderfully tanned, finely sculpted female back shifted and restlessly turned on the single bed across the room.

What the hell was her name? He knew from past experience that they always reacted really badly if you didn't remember their name the morning after. He commanded himself to relax. Bertha? No, Betty. That was it. Betty from Dallas. Female cop. Good looking, could hold her tequila like nobody's business.

Painfully he raised himself on one elbow and contemplated the red-blond curls on the pillow, now glowing with hot, early morning sunlight. He smiled as clearer images of the previous night's adventures seeped into his brain. How many times? Four? Not bad. Not bad at all. He felt an anticipatory tingle in his groin.

Rise and shine ... what else was there to do in a lazy tropical paradise?

The past four years running Douglas Baker had retreated for his annual holiday to the easy, laid back village of San Pedro, Belize. Each time he stayed at Señor Paz's. The eight room hotel, totally lacking in pretension, had everything he needed. The attractions of the place, other than Señor Paz himself, included a wide balcony big enough for him to stretch out his six foot, four inch frame on a deck chair and sip Belekian beer from his well-stocked cooler while enjoying a splendid view of the longest barrier reef in the northern hemisphere. Without a doubt, San Pedro was his personal paradise and each time it became more difficult to leave.

Baker lay back on his bed, wondering whether to finish off the four inches left in the tequila bottle on the beside table. He decided the hair of the dog could wait. And so could sex. An arm crooked over his eyes, he tried to block out the now excruciating light streaming through the ill-fitting window louvers. He was just starting to doze off again when the familiar pad of barefoot steps sounded on the stairs, stopping in front of his door. He knew what this meant. He winced as he visualised the bony, well-tanned arm. A sharp rap on the door was echoed in his aching head.

"Señor Baker?"

"Si, Señor Paz. Que pasa?"

In strongly accented English Paz answered, "There is a man here to see you. From the consulate, in Mexico City."

"The consulate? Who?"

"Señor Carter. You want me to say you no here?"

"The consulate?" Baker heaved himself off the creaking bed. He winced at the sudden squeal. They must creak so much because they're rusted from the salt air. He called, "Senor, give me a minute to get on some clothes."

"Si. Momentito." The bare feet padded away.

Baker had just thrown on a well-used T-shirt when a new set of footfalls, shod this time, sounded on the stairs. There was a smart rap at the door. Taking his time, he drained a couple of ounces from the tequila bottle. He was on holidays, after all. No law against a morning eye opener. He flipped a Camel out of the packet, took the filter between his thumb and forefinger, and crushed it. He flicked his old Ronson lighter and inhaled deeply, enjoying the burning sensation of both tobacco and liquor. Unlatching the rickety door, he strolled lazily out to face a tall spindly young man with a thin moustache, obviously grown in the hopes that it made him look older. Baker noted he was fashionably dressed in the sort of white short-sleeved dress shirt and comfortable tropic weight trousers that you buy at Abercrombie and Fitch for too much money. As soon as he saw Baker's square unshaven face squinting down at him the young man blinked and took a step backwards. "Baker? Staff Sergeant Douglas Baker, RCMP?" he asked sceptically.

"No, I'm the other Staff Sergeant Douglas Baker. What do you want?"

"Name's Carter." He flipped open a leather wallet and flashed a laminated picture ID. "Adrian Carter, External Affairs."

Baker reached for the card and scrutinised it before handing it back. "So you are. What do you want? I'm a busy man."

Baker could tell Carter didn't know what to make of him. He saw the kid's doubtful eyes say, this is the legendary Doug Baker? At forty-three his hair was already slate grey and it needed a trim. He had the beginnings of a small hard gut on his otherwise trim, muscular frame. He knew his cold grey eyes were bloodshot and that he probably reeked of booze, stale tobacco smoke and sex. So what - I'm on holiday. What'd he expect, a tuxedo?

"I don't quite know how to say this."

"With words, preferably. C'mon, Carter, spit it out."

"If you insist. Congratulations, your vacation just ended." He withdrew a manila folder from under his arm and held it out. "Here are your orders. You're to report back to E Division tonight. If you'll kindly get your things, we can just make the 9:30 a.m. plane out of here."

"Just like that? No explanation, nothing?" came Baker's incredulous reply. "Where the hell do you intelligence fairies get off ordering real cops around?"

"I got my orders." He pushed the envelope into the crook of Baker's bent arm. "Just like you got yours." He looked at his watch. "We don't have much time." He squinted suddenly. "And who said I was with intelligence?"

"How did you find me? I didn't tell anyone where I was."

"It's no secret you've been coming here for, what is it, three years ever since that Washington fiasco? Besides, Paz is very helpful in keeping you people safe, if you know what I mean."

Baker nodded glumly. Paz, in his youth, had very useful to the British in their struggles against the Guatemalans, who to this day contended that Belize is theirs. As safe havens went, Paz's place was well known in British aligned intelligence circles. "I'll have to talk to the little guy about his big mouth," he growled, although he didn't really mean it.

"Sorry to do this to you, but you know how it is. Everything you need is in the envelope - money, ticket and info on your new assignment. By the way, you're back in VIP for this one. I'm going to see if I can scrounge up some breakfast downstairs. I'll be back in half an hour. We got a plane to catch."

Baker nodded irritably. "So you keep saying." He turned and walked back through the open door into the room. Slumping down on the bed, he took a huge drag on the cigarette, as if it could smother his frustration. Instead, he just felt dizzy and coughed. Betty was now sitting on the edge of her bed, the sheet pulled around her, red-gold hair tumbling around her shoulders. She was fuming.

"A cop? Why didn't you tell me?"

Baker opened his mouth to answer but she cut him off. "I came down here to forget about cops, especially the prick I just divorced. Oh man," she moaned, turning away from him. "How could you be a cop? And now you're gonna just pack up and leave!" She gathered the sheet around her and charged for the bathroom, slamming the door.

Douglas Baker reached for the bottle. Hell of a way to start the day, he thought. He tipped the remaining two ounces of tequila down his throat and coughed again.

Morning, sunshine.

TEN

It was dark when the JAL flight from Mexico City landed at Vancouver International Airport, eight hours late, thanks to an earthquake in the Mexican capital. Baker exited the sliding doors at the Arrivals Level and was immediately jolted by a blast of March air. It was enough to make him turn around and get right back on the next plane south. "God damn, I hate the cold!" he groused to nothing but the frigid air.

Fifteen minutes later, after a taxi ride from the airport, he was deposited at the front entrance of E Division, the RCMP headquarters for British Columbia and the Yukon Territory. He slipped his ID card into the slot, only to be informed by a fidgeting LED that the card was no longer valid. Fucking high technology. His irritation rose another notch as he shivered in disgust. He hadn't taken a jacket south and still wore stained tropical togs. He scratched his unshaven face, stuck a battered straw hat on his head and again picked up his only luggage, a loaded daypack and a trusty cooler. He humped them around the back of the expansive complex, to a parking lot filled with a number of portables. After fumbling around in the dark he finally found the one marked VIP.

Very important prick, he thought savagely. He disliked politicians and professional activists of any stripe, and from what he'd read in the file about his current assignment, coming home on the plane, he was particularly unhappy. To top it all off, they were sending him back to work for a man he had once commanded in Special Operations, the intelligence section of the RCMP. It had been disbanded after a well-organised dirty tricks campaign had discredited it. It was then that his career had gone off the rails onto a siding, where it had remained ever since.

Once inside the portable, he stood at a desk for a couple of minutes before shouting, "Hello?" It was a full two minutes before a plain-clothes member of the Force ambled around the partition to stare at him suspiciously. It was a young Asian, Japanese from the look of him. He was about twenty-five, five foot nine, maybe a hundred and sixty pounds, with piercing black eyes. Middleweight, thought Baker. He saw the look on the young man's face as he took in the cut-off T shirt, faded blue jeans with a red wine stain down one leg, sandals, non-regulation hair and two day's worth of beard.

"Help you?"

He doffed his battered straw hat. "Baker. Staff Sergeant Douglas Baker. Skipper's expecting me." Recognising he was already half an hour late, he added hopefully, "Unless of course he's not here?" Seeing that the young officer still didn't believe him he said, "Close your mouth, son, makes you look like the village idiot. I'm here to see Inspector Wattington. Some time this century would be great."

"Sorry. Yeah, come on in." He shot Baker an embarrassed glance. "Can I get you a coffee or something?"

"No thanks. Any place I can put my gear?"

"I'll take it." With his free hand he pointed over his shoulder. "Down the hall, first door on your left."

Baker strode purposefully down the hall, his battered sandals slapping on the worn linoleum, and knocked on the door.

"Come in."

Sitting at a desk, with his back to Baker, on the phone, was Inspector Jim Wattington, thirty-nine, a slender, slightly stooped officer in a rumpled brown suit. Baker had both trained and commanded him, and now this guy was his superior officer. Who ever said life was fair? Then again, the man was adept at political games and administrative intrigue and Baker wasn't. Wattington hung up, turned and stared. Languidly he rose, straightening his lanky form until his slightly goggley eyes were almost level with Baker's. He looked him up and down. "Well, if it isn't Robinson Crusoe. Where's your man Friday?"

"Hello, Skipper," said Baker, ignoring the jibe by trying to think of the inspector as Gilligan, to whom he bore a slight resemblance. The nautical term had stuck after Wattington had purchased a thirty-eight foot Bayliner cruiser. Brand new, at that.

"Been a while."

"Good to see you again, Doug. Have a seat."

"Thanks." Baker threw himself into a chair and placed his straw hat on one knee. "What's up, and why me?"

Wattington hitched his hip onto the edge of the desk. "Sorry about your vacation, but it was unavoidable. A couple of days ago we lost four senior NCOs to a case of food poisoning. They went out for dinner together, ate bad seafood, you get the picture. They're all pretty sick and won't be much use for at least a week. That's why you're here. You read the file?"

"Yes. Once again, why me? I've been out of the VIP game for over two years now. Why not one of your young hotshots?"

"Two reasons. First, all four of my young hotshots will be doing nothing but sitting on toilets for the next week. And this one has me worried. I want you because you are experienced and I have absolute faith in your abilities."

Baker's eyebrow arched as he thought of his last performance appraisal. Wattington caught the look and sighed. "You know as well as I do that a performance appraisal is like an IQ test - it measures some things really well but fails to account for other things that might be just as important. If you just weren't so damn insubordinate-

"And the second reason?"

"You trained me and I owe you. This is a very important assignment and I want to see you pull it off, get your career back on track."

Baker kept his face impassive. He wasn't much good at office politics, but he could read this situation perfectly well. If Wattington was willing to admit that he was worried, it meant he was really worried. That meant he thought there was a strong chance that something bad could happen, something that would derail his own career. If you're a guy like Wattington, what do you do? Find a fall guy. 'Honestly, Commissioner, with my four best men out of action, Baker looked like the best possibility, despite his age and recent inactivity. I'm as disappointed as you are, sir, that he wasn't up to it. I feel for the guy, but I'm afraid I must agree that a desk job would be the best thing for him.'

Baker tried to keep a sneer from his lips as he said, "Gee, thanks Skipper." He saw Wattington's eyes narrow at his tone. He pulled a pack of Camels out of his shirt pocket and flicked his Ronson.

"I don't remember you ever being a smoker," said Wattington.

"Started up again, couple months back," replied Baker nonchalantly. "Stress and all that." Before the inspector could reply, he continued, "Let's get down to business. Describe this scenario from your point of view."

"Okay," said Wattington, beginning to pace the room. "There's going to be a huge international environmental conference in town, called GLOBE. Lots of bigwigs floating around. One of the biggest of the wigs is Marie Françoise Von Bessel, chairman and CEO of the Phoenix Foundation. She also occupies the environmental seat with the European Commission - nominated two years ago by the German Christian Democratic Party and won in a landslide. As you know, there was an assassination attempt on her about six weeks ago, in Brussels. A very professional assassination attempt. That it failed was a miracle."

Baker interrupted. "And you're afraid the same people might try again at GLOBE."

"That's right."

"Here in Vancouver, the assassination capital of Canada."

"Doug, this isn't something to be taken lightly."

"C'mon, Skipper, when was the last time a politician was assassinated in this part of the country? Here, politicians do their own assassinations, character that is?"

"I'm not concerned about the last time," snapped the inspector. "I'm worried about the next time. And I don't want it to be this Von Bessel woman. Not on my watch. Besides, the very fact that this country is not a hotbed of political terrorism might lead potential assassins to believe that our security will be complacent or inept, and that she'll be a much easier target here than she is in Europe."

Baker had to admit the man had a point. Thoughtfully he blew a plume of smoke into the air as Wattington continued. "As you know, we are party, along with a lot of other countries, to the international protected-persons agreement. A country like Switzerland or Germany asks us to provide security for someone like Von Bessel and we do it. They do the same when our VIPs go over there. Very simple."

Baker nodded - he knew this already. "You're forgetting something."

Wattington's eyes widened in irritation. He hated being told that he had overlooked some detail. "What?"

"I haven't had a refresher course in French in years. How can I guard someone if I can't communicate with her?"

The inspector looked relieved. "Not a problem. She speaks English fluently and so does her assistant."

Baker shrugged. "So, what's the plan?"

"You'll be commanding a five man team assigned to the Von Bessel woman. You have the day shift, along with your partner, Barry Nakamura, the young Japanese constable you met out front. Your night team is O'Neal and Slodnick. You know them." Baker nodded. They were good, solid professionals. "Right now they're down at the Waterfront Centre Hotel, just across the road from Canada Place where the business part of GLOBE will be happening. Given the size of the conference, the trade show and opening ceremonies will be occurring thirteen blocks away at BC Place stadium. Right now they're completing the security check on the set of hotel rooms assigned to Von Bessel and her executive assistant, Marta Rudd. The boys will stay there tonight and be replaced by an uniformed member of the force in the morning. I don't know yet who that will be. He'll secure the rooms during the day. All of you are on duty for the next six days, until this conference is over and Von Bessel is on the plane. Everything clear so far?"

"Yeah. Do I report to you?"

"No. The ranking NCO in charge of the whole operation is Staff Sergeant Steve Owen."

Baker suppressed the urge to whistle. Wattington must be really worried if he was inserting yet another layer of responsibility between himself and possible disaster.

Wattington continued, "Owen's been heading up the section for about a year now. Know him?"

"Heard of him. Wonder boy, right? Rises like a rocket into the career stratosphere."

The inspector frowned disapprovingly. "Owen is very impressive. He's done some good work keeping tabs on the radical environmentalists in this country and their contacts abroad. Apparently he knows a lot about Von Bessel. In fact, he volunteered for this assignment."

Baker knew Steve Owen was one career intelligence officer who had done everything right, taking on a variety of assignments, most of them in isolated postings, but inevitably ones that put him on a career command track. He also knew Owen was a friend of a friend, Sergeant Joan Chan. If Joanie said Owen was okay, then Owen was okay.

"You got your gun?"

"Yup."

"What is it? The issue Walther .38."

"Not that piece of shit. Small profile Smith and Wesson." The Force purchased the Walthers for all undercover operatives but few if any used them due to a bad history of jamming at just the wrong time.

Wattington nodded as he opened a side drawer of his desk and pulled out a communications unit about twice the bulk of a cell phone, with a lapel microphone and earplug. He also extracted an ID badge and a manila envelope. He handed them all to Baker. "The envelope contains more biographical information on Marie Françoise Von Bessel and her assistant Marta Rudd, as well as a detailed map of the GLOBE site. Nakamura will fill you in on protocol, frequencies, activation codes and the like. He'll also tell you any new info we've picked up on the two women since we prepared the dossiers. He's been instructed to get you to the hotel tonight so you can meet your crew. Tomorrow morning at 7:30, here in the Superintendent's auditorium, there's going to be a final security briefing. All eleven VIP team heads will be attending."

"Okay. When does Von Bessel arrive?"

"Tomorrow afternoon at 1:15. Lufthansa flight 656 from Frankfurt. I want you to be there to meet her. There's a car for you at the motor pool. Why don't you pick it up first thing in the morning?" As an afterthought he added, "You might want to have the bomb squad go over it."

Baker suppressed a smile. Skipper was worried as hell.

"Questions?"

"Just one. What about the rest of my damn vacation?"

Wattington regarded Baker with disbelief. "You just don't get it, do you? This is a chance to get back on track, and you're worried about missing some rays. Get outta here. And for Christ's sake, get cleaned up. I can smell you from here."

"Aye aye, Skipper," Baker grinned, his sandals slapping the floor as he left.

ELEVEN

Forty-five minutes later, Baker and Nakamura arrived at the Waterfront Centre Hotel on Vancouver's Coal Harbour area. Once in the suite, Baker greeted corporals Paul O'Neal and Steve Slodnick, seated on the sofa.

"Look, Paul," said Slodnick. "It's Jimmy Buffet. Cool hat. Hey, Jimbo, how about a chorus of Wasting Away Again in Margaritaville?" Short and stocky, Slodnick had a dark brown crew-cut, a craggy face, and a voice that could blister paint. He looked and sounded like a Marine drill instructor after a hard night on the town.

As Baker grinned at his old friend, O'Neal said, "So how're they hangin', big fella?" Baker remembered Betty. "They were hanging a lot better on the beach, I'll tell you." O'Neal was slender and wiry, with an unruly thatch of dirty blond hair, bushy eyebrows and fierce eyes that hid his essential good nature.

They joshed around for a few more minutes until Baker threw himself into a chair and yawned. "Let's get this over with," he said. "I'm tired. And hungry. Guys, let's get something to eat."

"Sure," rasped Slodnick. "Pizza, Chinese or Mexican?"

Baker grunted. "I've been eating Mexican for days now. How about pizza?"

After the others agreed on four twelve inch pies, loaded, O'Neal phoned in the order, then left to pick them up. "A case of beer, too!" called Baker. "Moosehead or Kokanee, whatever they've got!"

They sifted through piles of paper until O'Neal returned twenty minutes later and they all dug in. Baker cracked open a Kokanee and said, around a mouthful of pizza, "Housekeeping first. Equipment and locale. Barry?"

Nakamura took five minutes to explain protocol, frequencies and activation codes. None of it was news to the others. Then they spent a few minutes reviewing the map of the GLOBE convention site and Von Bessel's itinerary. They all agreed that, from a logistical point of view, the site was a security nightmare.

Finally Baker leaned back and lit a smoke. "Now for the human element. Why are bad people trying to turn nice Mrs. Von Bessel into a colander? I read the file on the plane, but I understand from Skipper that there's more information. I don't like reading these files because they're written in bureaucratese. Who'd like to give me a nice crisp briefing that doesn't leave out anything important?"

"I can," volunteered Barry Nakamura. "I've gone through all this stuff and made notes."

"Fire away," said Baker. Kid was a keener. Nothing wrong with that. He'd been a keener too, long ago.

"First of all," said Nakamura, "she's not very nice at all."

Baker raised his eyebrows. "Really?"

Barry slid a couple of photos across the table. Baker scrutinised the first one closely. "Good looking woman. Audrey Hepburn." He peered a little closer. "Audrey Hepburn with an attitude."

Nakamura grinned. "You got that nailed. You just came back from Belize, right?"

"Yeah."

"Well, here's a stab at describing her in Spanish - 'el bitcho supremo'. It looks like that goes as well for her executive assistant, Marta Rudd. At least Von Bessel doesn't have a record. Rudd does. Heroin addiction and prostitution. And apparently the two ladies are very close."

The three other men contemplated this information for a moment, each fully aware of their collective experience with a wide range of personalities and personality types, both criminal and otherwise. It was Slodnick who broke the silence with his raspy foghorn voice. "Bunch of do-gooders running around Europe hugging trees and the rich bitch in charge has a former pincushion and whore as an EA? You trying to say they're a couple of dykes?"

"It's possible," said Barry. "That's how I read it."

Baker was now studying the photo of Marta Rudd. "This woman looks hard enough to scratch diamond. This is getting interesting. Why don't we start at the beginning?" He opened another Kokanee, leaned back in his chair and closed his eyes as Nakamura began to speak.

"Marie Françoise Von Bessel, born Bertrand, December 17, 1956. Her father was French-born Jean-Claude Bertrand and her mother, French-Swiss Rebecca Marie. She's a vegetarian and a dyed-in-the-wool pacifist. Wealthy family upbringing - Paris apartment, Swiss country chateau, that kind of thing. Sounds pretty idyllic. Father was founder of a chemical manufacturing company. Reputation as a ruthless hard-ass. In her teens and early twenties Marie apparently underwent extensive psychotherapy, reason unknown. Something of a coconut from day one, I guess."

"Fucking swell," growled Baker, eyes still closed.

"Marie graduated from the Sorbonne with the equivalent of a master's degree in languages. Went to work for her father's company, in public relations. There, she met a young chemical engineer, German-born Christian Von Bessel. He pursued her ardently, wouldn't take no for an answer. Romance blossomed, blah-de-blah, they got married in August, 1978. One child, Daniel, born September, 1979. During this time Christian Von Bessel advanced quickly through the ranks of Bertrand's firm. Then Mr. Bertrand sold out his major interest to the Swiss chemical giant Sandoz and retired. Christian went over to the larger company as veep in charge of R&D. Moved with his family to Basel, Switzerland to live happily ever after."

Nakamura took a swig of his beer. "Only they didn't. Late evening and early morning of October 31 and November 1, 1986. Marie Françoise is out on the town being a party girl at a local fundraising charity while hubby stays home working. Those sound pretty typical, guys? There's a big fire at the Sandoz plant, which according to the news over the past few weeks was a terrorist attack. Anyway, Christian hears about the fire, the maid's gone home, Marie's being a party animal, he can't leave their seven year old kid alone in the house, so he takes Daniel with him as he drives to the fire. There's a terrible single vehicle accident and both husband and son are killed. According to the autopsy, Christian had three times the Swiss legal limit in his blood and was doing over two hundreds klicks an hour when he hit a wall."

"Jesus," said O'Neal. "Strawberry jam."

"Nah," said Nakamura. "Crispy critters. The car burned. Anyway, the missus arrives home to a ringing telephone. She's told both hubby and pup are toast. Next morning the maid comes in and finds the lady of the house curled up in a corner in the foetal position, sobbing and incoherent. Back to the psyche ward. Following four months of hospitalisation she'd recovered enough to be released into her parents' care. Two weeks later, daddy has a heart attack while driving to Paris with his wife, Marie's mother, crosses two lanes of traffic at high speed and hits a loaded transport truck. End of the rainbow for the folks, back to the psyche ward for Marie. Released after eight months. Sorry guys, gotta take a leak."

When he returned, Barry Nakamura picked up where he had left off.

"Where was I? Oh yeah. According to friends, Marie Françoise had changed dramatically. She was obsessed with the death of her husband and child and blamed the Sandoz Corporation for allowing the warehouse fire to happen in the first place." He read quickly and turned a couple of pages. "This is one driven woman. Hounds the company unmercifully, gets them to open up to the public the results of the largely secret fire investigation. Fights skilfully for billions in corporate funding to clean up the entire Rhine watershed. Makes business enemies by the score, but lots of friends among the Greens. Makes such a nuisance of herself that corporate interests secretly lobby to have her kicked out of the country. There are also death threats. On some sort of legal technicality the Swiss civil authorities are able to politely ask her to leave. As a naturalised German citizen, the result of her marriage to Christian, she moves to Darmstadt on the outskirts of Frankfurt, but retains possession of the family chateau near Neuchatel in Switzerland. Blah-de-blah."

Barry flipped more pages. Baker looked as if he'd fallen asleep.

"Almost at the end. Runs the Phoenix Foundation ruthlessly, just as her daddy ran his business. Demanding, emotionally frigid, unforgiving. Never takes no for an answer. Control freak, hates being told what to do. Fast with her mouth, brilliant at public relations, fundraising and media manipulation. Feared but respected, and even her enemies don't doubt her commitment. Elected in a landslide to a seat on the European Commission."

Nakamura grabbed another wedge of pizza and leaned back in his chair. "Now we get into our territory. Six weeks ago, at a convention centre in Brussels, there was an assassination attempt. Lots of people with guns present, but only one shooter. He missed, even though he was close, she was the only person on stage and she was standing still. Everybody got away. Brussels police discovered some of the delegates had bogus credentials but the trail went cold. No leads, no arrests, nothing."

Douglas Baker's eyes finally opened. "I remember reading about that. Struck me as odd at the time. Whole thing was obviously superbly organised, yet they're incompetent enough that they miss an unmissable target, yet good enough that everyone gets away scot-free."

O'Neal frowned. "Yeah, it does sound strange. What do you think of the idea that-"

Baker held up his hand. "Let's hear the pincushion's story first."

Nakamura nodded. "Marta Rudd. Never married. Born in West Berlin, August 24, 1963. Mother was the editor of a left-leaning entertainment weekly, her father a musician and heroin addict. Left the family when Marta was four. Mama takes up with a variety of abusive male companions. One of them rapes Marta when she's thirteen and when she threatens to tell mama the creep beats her up so bad she's in hospital for a month. She returns home, only to leave a few days later. Disappears. Nothing for four years. Her mother dies during this time, apparently found beaten to death in an alley. One week before her seventeenth birthday police pick her up in a raid on a non-complying brothel. Put into a halfway house run by a Catholic rehab organisation. Female social worker takes a shine to her, she blossoms, finishes high school and enters university while living with said social worker. Dykesville. As an undergraduate, Marta becomes heavily involved in women's rights. Graduates 1984. Is a known member of a number of left-wing fringe organisations. Proves to be skilled at media relations, organising demonstrations, and so on. Rumoured connection, never substantiated, with the Red Brigade baddies."

"That's playing with fire," observed Slodnick.

Nakamura nodded in agreement as he continued. "Met Marie Françoise Von Bessel in mid-1988. With the Phoenix Foundation from day one, when it was just Von Bessel and a couple of others. Started as a volunteer, soon became executive assistant. It was Marta who masterminded Von Bessel's campaign to win the seat. Regarded by her boss as indispensable. Tough and shrewd. The two women are inseparable and appear devoted to each other. That's it."

"Thanks," said Baker. "Who put all that together so fast?"

"A Sergeant Joan Chan." At Baker's big grin he said, "You know her?"

"Yeah. I'll have to stop by and thank her in person. She's been over at the Canadian Security and Intelligence Service for a few years now, in Ottawa. I'm glad to hear she's in town." For the second time that evening, he warmly remembered his old friend. They'd been through a lot together. Chan was a superb intelligence officer and a computer whiz to boot. They had first met when assigned to a combined Scotland Yard/Strategic Air Services (SAS) anti-terrorist training program in England. As the only Canadians in the group, they naturally gravitated together and struck up an enduring friendship - one of the closest relationships the taciturn Baker had ever had. Back in Canada, Joan was there to prop him up when his wife Renate locked him out of the house. And he'd propped Joan up when she left her deputy minister husband after she caught him bedding one of his female aides.

O'Neal broke his reverie. "So you think any potential assassins have arrived here in Vancouver, based on what happened in Brussels?"

Baker started ticking off his fingers. "Any one of a thousand corporations in the Rhine watershed who'd love to get this harridan off their backs for good. Any one of half a dozen governments, ditto. Political enemies from other parties." He frowned, pausing. "She's had death threats before but there have never been any attempts. The one attempt happens after she breaks the story about the Sandoz fire being arson. Could be a connection there." He frowned again. "This Marta Rudd. Disappears for four years. The Red Brigade - I forget how many people they killed before they got caught."

He fell into a brooding contemplation of his empty beer bottle. O'Neal looked at Slodnick - they'd seen this before. "What is it, Doug?" asked O'Neal.

Baker raised his eyes. "I don't like it when things don't make sense. This friendship between Von Bessel and Rudd doesn't make sense at all. The pampered woman of privilege, grieving for her husband and son, and the dyke former junkie and whore. What the hell do they have in common?"

"But don't forget that Von Bessel's head wiring is all screwed up," said Slodnick.

Nakamura yawned uncontrollably and looked at his watch. "Jesus. It's midnight."

Baker heaved from his chair and stretched his full six foot four, bones cracking. "All right. I'm going home." He looked at the devastation of pizza boxes and empty bottles. "And clean this place up, will you? Looks like a bunch of cops had a meeting here or something. See you tomorrow morning at 6:30 for shift change. Barry, can you give me a lift?"

On the way home to his apartment, Douglas Baker stared out of the car window at the Vancouver skyline and discouraged the young constable's attempts at conversation. He was not looking forward to the next six days.

He knew he wasn't going to get a lot of sleep tonight. He'd sit up, smoke cigarettes, have a stiff whiskey and think. Despite appearances, he hadn't been asleep during Nakamura's briefing. Wattington might be a five-sided snake in the grass, but he wasn't stupid - if he was worried, it was for a damn good reason. He wondered if maybe the inspector was holding back on something. And based on what he'd learned tonight, Von Bessel was going to be a problem.

What was it Barry had said? 'Never takes no for an answer. Control freak, hates being told what to do.' Well, sweetheart, thought Baker grimly, I don't care how much money you have or how wilful and headstrong you are. You're going to hear 'no' a lot while you're in Vancouver, maybe more than you've ever heard it before in your entire pampered life, and I'll be telling you what you can and cannot do every minute of the six days you're here.

He rubbed his eyes. 'El bitcho supremo'. But she was a guest of the country, a VIP, which meant she would have to be handled very carefully. And he would have to figure out how to do that. Tonight.

As they approached the Four Seasons Hotel he glanced at his watch. Almost one a.m. He wondered what Betty was doing tonight on the beach back in Belize. He was sure that whatever it might be, it was a hell of a lot more fun than this.

He noticed a few lights on in the hotel as they drove by. He knew it was a favourite haven for foreign businessmen. Maybe someone else has to work late tonight, he thought, preparing for a big day tomorrow. Poor bastard, you have my sympathies, whoever you are.

TWELVE

Cigarette in hand, Colonel Aziz Hamani gazed out of the window of his room at the Four Seasons Hotel. He'd never been to Vancouver before, although he had agents here, as he had agents in every major city in the world. From the tourist brochures he'd seen he had concluded that Canada was a land of ice and snow and grim dark coniferous forests filled with carnivores. He'd assumed the population consisted mainly of immigrants from the British Isles, and was thus astonished to discover how many Chinese, East Indians and other Asians people were living in this city.

He looked at his watch. One a.m. He turned and walked back to the desk where his briefcase was open. Lots of work to do. Next to the briefcase was his passport, in the name of Hatem Faruzi, identified as a businessman from the Republic of Turkey. The briefcase contained the appropriate documentation and invoices proving that he specialised in the sale and purchase of oil field equipment.

Ever since the discovery of the sinister device on the rooftop and the call from Sword, Hamani had struggled to find some way to deal with his dilemma. If he did as Sword requested, and killed Marie Françoise Von Bessel, he would have one less piece of bait. He would be left with only the Accountant. And he knew that by doing what the Sword demanded, he was giving in to blackmail. There was no telling what demands Sword might make in the future, what terrible threats there might be to millions of innocent people, and to Iraq and the Rais. Sword must be found and killed, whatever else might happen.

And in a deep part of his soul, Hamani did not believe Sword. He had thought again and again about the phone call that night at three in the morning, and he didn't believe it. He wants her for himself, he thought. If I kill her, he won't have that gratification, and it is that kind of gratification that gives meaning to his twisted life. He must still be after her. He might even be here now, in Vancouver.

He pressed his hands to his aching temples. He hadn't told the Rais about the discovery by the firemen, or Sword's phone call. He had simply said that he knew Sword was pursuing Von Bessel and that he might now be in Vancouver. Only he and Guramda knew the truth. Only he and Guramda could find a way out of this terrible trap.

There must be a way.

With the sureness of a professional gambler dealing cards, he reached into the briefcase and swiftly laid three files on the desktop. The way out must be in here. He knew these files by heart, was almost sick to death of reading them over and over, but he believed they were like Tarot cards - they might always look the same, but if you dealt them over and over again, in different combinations, destiny might suddenly reveal itself.

He opened the first file and began to read.

The Sword had come from a privileged home. His mother was a famously vain and empty-headed beauty, prone to alcoholism, a habit regarded by her upright family as a disgraceful vice. His father was a gentleman, a brilliant research chemist educated at several prestigious institutions in five countries. The marriage had been arranged, the way they often were in those days, between wealthy families.

The father had a laboratory in his home and demonstrated his work to his only child. A specialist in pesticides, he communicated to his son his fascination with the interaction of organic compounds and their effect on animal nervous systems. With the patience of the dedicated scientist, he explained that the biochemical mechanism he was interested in was the inhibition of the enzyme acetylcholinesterase and its action in nerve impulse transmission. The young Sword learned that the chemical acetylcholine, produced at nerve endings upon stimulation by an electrical impulse, flows across the space between the nerve and muscle, causing a change in electrical potential, stimulating the muscle to contract. Then acetylcholine is hydrolysed by an enzyme, acteo-cholinesterase, which allows the muscle to relax. The presence of Organo-phosphates in nerve agents effectively shuts down production of the enzyme, leading to continuous firing at the muscle-nerve interface, leading to convulsion and death. The Sword quickly absorbed everything his father had to teach.

But his father never managed to make much money and had no head for business. He'd been fired from the only well-paying job he had ever held, as a research chemist at a French research and manufacturing facility. His parents' marriage had seemed to go rapidly downhill after that, as his mother increasingly found his father's lack of practicality intolerable. As the tentacles of her addiction tightened their grip, his mother's constant nagging became much worse and she also became increasingly prone to violent rages, during which she would physically attack her husband, who took refuge behind the locked doors of his library, or her son, who had no such refuge. Finally she had packed up her belongings one day, secure in the knowledge that her family would support her no matter what, and left her husband forever, taking her tearful son with her.

During the two years that followed, living in a large and luxurious mansion, the young Sword yearned for his father, but never heard a word - not a phone call, not a letter. His mother told him constantly that it had been her husband's fault that she had had to leave, that he had not loved her, nor had he loved his son. In the trusting, naïve way of children, the Sword reluctantly came to believe his mother. The proof of his uncaring, she declared, was the absence of calls or letters, and the boy had to admit that the evidence of that silence was irrefutable.

But he had insisted on having her buy him his own small laboratory, so he could conduct experiments based on what he remembered of his father's teachings. She had screamed no, he had screamed yes, and they had screamed at each other until he ran upstairs to his mother's bathroom, locked himself in and swallowed a container of pills chosen at random from the overflowing shelves of amphetamines and barbiturates. After the doctors and the month in hospital, his mother had reluctantly relented, but she always found reasons why he couldn't work in his little lab, and he resented it bitterly. Eventually, hearing nothing from his father and absorbed in his own experiments with insects, he had not even much cared when his mother changed his name, from his father's to her family's.

Hamani closed the first file - there was much more in here, concerning the boy's friends, his hobbies and such, but instinctively he knew it wasn't relevant.

He reached over to the phone and dialed room service. It was now two in the morning. In excellent English, with just the trace of an accent and more than a trace of charm and courtesy, he asked for a plain four egg omelette, a rack of buttered whole wheat toast, a large glass of orange juice and a pot of fresh strong coffee. He stood at the window and gazed at the ocean until he heard the knock on the door. Giving the boy a handsome tip, he sat down at the desk and ate his meal. Draining his coffee cup, he lit another cigarette and opened the second file.

Just before his thirteenth birthday, the Sword made a discovery that profoundly changed his life. His tutor was ill, the weather unseasonably rainy. His mother was out at a ladies' lunch of the sort held by women who couldn't be seen drinking in public without arousing the stern disapproval of their families, and she had locked his lab. Frustrated and bored, he was kicking his soccer ball up and down the corridors of the upper floor. A wild kick sent the ball through the door of his mother's boudoir, striking a carved wooden box on a shelf full of expensive glass carvings and other knickknacks. The carvings shattered on the parquet, and the locked box fell on its edge in such a way that the flimsy lock failed and the contents spilled all over the floor.

Fearfully collecting the mess, the young Sword found a single piece of paper with a code from the phone company, informing his mother that the code would block all calls from a certain set of phone numbers. He'd then noticed that the rest of the box's contents consisted entirely of stacks and stacks of letters, bound with elastic bands. With a chill he recognised his father's handwriting, and with a spiky sense of psychic dislocation realised that they were all addressed to him.

He opened them and started to read. They were passionate, imploring letters of love and longing. Where are you, my beloved son? Why don't you write to me? The last one was dated just three days previous. He read it with mounting horror. The adolescent Sword didn't know what liver cancer was, but whatever it was it could, according to his father, be caused by decades of exposure to laboratory solvents. His father had the disease, and just days to live.

The boy was waiting when his drunken mother came home. He accused her, first in tears, then in a rage. She sneered at the weakness of his beloved father and at his own stupidity. Shrieking at each other, they ended up fighting and snarling like beasts. But she, drunk as she was, knew how to fight and he did not. She'd ripped a length of electrical cord from a lamp and bound his thrashing limbs. She'd whipped him within an inch of his life, seized his testicles in a crushing grip and jeered with hot stinking breath in his ear, mocking him for his weakness. Once again he found himself in the hospital, and it was there that he learned how his father had died an agonising death, all alone.

Upon his release from hospital, the young Sword had changed. His got down on her knees to beg his forgiveness. He'd smiled, his emerald eyes glowing, and forgiven her, on condition that she quit drinking. She had done so, and resolutely stayed off the bottle.

Eighteen months later, when he was fifteen, she died. Her death, with its bizarre range of symptoms, baffled the attending physicians. The failure of her thyroid gland made her eyes bulge from her head like Ping-Pong balls. The sudden disintegration of her pancreas rapidly led to severe diabetes, and resultant gangrene forced the amputation of both legs just below the knee. A deadly mixture of white lead and arsenic trioxide was then discovered in the pipes that fed the old mansion's drinking water supply. Doctors concluded that the lead had leached from the decaying pipes, while the arsenic could have either come from the lead itself or somehow been an infiltration from pesticides used in the area. These two substances explained the woman's loss of all her hair, along with her sudden blindness, grossly swollen abdomen, and partial paralysis. That her son did not suffer the same symptoms was attributed to the fact that his mother indulged him: she permitted him to follow the new fashion for drinking nothing but bottled mineral water, and allowed him to cook his own meals in his own suite of rooms, where he had his lab. The Sword explained how distilled water from his lab was the best way of cooking tasty vegetables, and no one was in a position to disagree.

Finally, ulcers the size of silver coins were discovered in the woman's stomach and small bowel. When these finally perforated one night, at two in the morning, and she began to fill with blood from rectum to throat, the attending nurse urgently awakened the son so he could attend his mother as the doctors were summoned.

The nurse returned to the room to find the young Sword bent over his dying mother, tenderly stroking her bald head, kissing her blind popping eyes and whispering in her ear, as the woman's hands twitched convulsively.

After the funeral, no one saw the young Sword carefully place several containers of used pipettes and half-empty ampoules of chemical reagents into a furnace at the municipal dump.

Colonel Aziz Hamani stared at the last page of the file. He knew where all of this information had come from - himself. Sword had told him all of this, in bits and pieces over time, usually when he'd had too much to drink. Hamani remembered hearing these stories, especially the one about how Sword had slowly poisoned his own mother. He remembered what a struggle it had been to keep the alarm from showing on his face, to keep making sympathetic noises. Afterwards, he'd written it all down, even though he desperately wanted to believe it was some sort of sick fantasy. Finally he had had Mukhabarat check it out, and everything had rung true.

With an effort, he read the last page. With his inheritance, the Sword had applied to go to school in a foreign country. At just sixteen he had easily passed the notoriously difficult entrance exams. Once in an academic environment, he excelled. His work ethic and intelligence did not go unnoticed, although some of the more thoughtful professors noticed a tendency toward arrogance, bordering on hysteria when contradicted.

The colonel slowly closed the second file. He laid the palm of his hand on the third folder and felt his heart start to pound.

The first two files contained a life, and events in that life, that he hadn't known and hadn't influenced. The third file was different, a future that needn't be imagined. The fact that it had was his fault. In this file was XP29, thousands of Kurdish deaths, the torture-murder of his wife Soraya, the torture of Major Guramda, and his present dilemma.

He lit another cigarette and inhaled the bitter smoke, felt it rasp in his lungs, as his heart filled with bitterness beyond measure. Today would not exist if it weren't for him. Was he as guilty as the Sword? At least he wasn't insane, driven by compulsion, his brain stuffed with black spiders. Which meant he should have known better. He thought he'd known, known what he was doing, every step of the way, in the name of patriotism and national security.

A muscle twitched in his cheek. I must be honest with myself, he thought. They weren't the only reasons. He'd been showing off, eager to demonstrate his intelligence and insight, bask in the praise of those who benefited from his eager diligence. Such eager young men were the bane of the world; too much energy to pause and contemplate the consequences of what they were doing, too little experience with error and failure to be cautious. Caution and contemplation always came when you were older. Often, when it was too late.

Slowly he opened the file.

The Sword completed his chemical engineering degree one year early, then went into a masters program at the Hamburg Technical Institute, then into their Ph.D. program. His thesis topic was innovative nerve toxins and their use as pesticides. He had also, as part of his research, studied the use of poison gas in World War I and the use of chemical weapons by the Japanese in Manchuria during the 1930s.

In the final year of his studies at the institute, in the library one day, Sword met a first year student named Aziz Hamani, from an old and politically influential Iraqi family, training to be a civil engineer. The young Hamani had been very impressed by the energy and charm of the Sword, and hero-worshipped the older graduate student.

Unbeknownst to anyone, Hamani had another purpose besides getting a degree. At the behest of his country, he fed intelligence reports back to the government, first to General Abd al-Rahman Aref; then, upon his overthrow, he had continued his work for the new president, Major-General Ahmad Hasan al-Bakr. It was during the heyday of the left-wing student movement in European universities, and many students and instructors professed to despise the capitalist governments who afforded them such a handsome living and the freedom to study. Hamani made many suggestions to his minders back in Iraq about whom to approach, and his talent for spotting such people was duly noted. It was then that he had first highly recommended the Sword as a possible recruit, although no action was taken at the time.

He and the Sword caroused together. The older student had a knack for making the younger feel important and special. The Sword seemed to find the basically shy and sexually repressed Arab youth a challenge. They visited bars and brothels together, Hamani finding the sophisticated life of the West a thrilling departure from his stern Islamic upbringing. Those were giddy days for young Iraqis - billions of dollars in oil revenues were flooding the country and it seemed as if everything was possible.

But as he saw more of the Sword in his uninhibited moments, Hamani began to have tiny nagging doubts. First there were the horrible stories Sword told about his childhood and what he had done to his mother. Then the two of them were banned from several of the classier brothels in Hamburg because of the way Sword treated the women there. Apart from that, the maturing Arab student saw aspects of the Sword's personality, his rages and arrogance, that suddenly did not seem so worthy of hero-worship. He had slowly begun to distance himself from the Sword, as the graduate student became more demanding on their friendship. They'd finally parted, although Sword phoned constantly. It had come as a relief when, upon his own graduation, Hamani was summoned back to Iraq. And it was just a year later, on July 16, 1979, that President Bakr resigned and Saddam Hussein occupied the office of president.

It was then that Hamani's career took off. In 1980 the Iraq-Iran war had broken out, during which Hamani distinguished himself on the battlefield. Shortly thereafter, the Rais decided to put to full use his talent for finding and managing renegade scientists. It was then, to Hamani's horror, that his recommendation to recruit the Sword had been revived. Hamani further researched the Sword's career in the years since they had last seen each other, and was very disturbed by what he discovered. He had recommended against recruitment and been overruled.

And now he was sitting in a hotel room in Canada, contemplating a blackmail demand, the possible assassination of an innocent woman, and a plan for finally getting rid of the Sword before he murdered millions of innocent people.

He closed the third file and placed all three back in the briefcase. He went into the bathroom and slapped his face with cold water, then lay down on the bed. I must sleep, he thought. The phrase, 'my fault, my fault', ran incessantly through his head.

I have sinned. But now I will atone.

THIRTEEN

Vancouver, March 16

In less than twelve hours, Staff Sergeant Douglas Baker had thrown off any sign of Belize except his tan.

Instead of tequila and beer, his mouth now tasted of mint toothpaste. When he had gone to the Waterfront Centre Hotel at 6:30 a.m. for the changeover so Slodnick and O'Neal could go home, the barbershop had just been opening, so he got a hair cut. He wore an immaculately pressed white shirt, a conservative blue and gold tie, a Harris Tweed sports coat in blue herringbone and navy slacks. And his gun, in a shoulder holster under his left armpit. He had to admit he even felt crisp and precise, despite the fact that he'd had only three hours sleep. The 7:30 meeting in the Superintendent's auditorium had gone well. He had inquired at the personnel office about Joan Chan and left a message for her. Then he and Nakamura had talked strategy for a couple of hours before grabbing an early lunch, getting the car from the motor pool and heading for the Vancouver International Airport.

Now, they stood side by side and watched Lufthansa flight 656 dock at Gate 23. They were the first on board when the door of the Boeing 747 opened. Baker and Nakamura both flashed their ID at the female chief steward. "RCMP," said Baker. "We're here to escort the Von Bessel party."

She scrutized the ID, looking several times at both the photos and the faces. Finally she beamed.

"Ja. Officers, you will be so kind as to take good care of Frau Von Bessel for us? She is a hero in our country, you know." Baker smiled noncommittally. "Please come this way." She led them forward to the first class compartment.

Half way along the cabin, on the left-hand side, she stopped where another flight attendant was helping a petite woman with a chestnut bob, dressed in a navy skirt and jacket with a white blouse, into a stylish blue wool overcoat. Baker noted the discreet label on the inside - Channel. Beside Von Bessel, a tall, red haired woman in a dark green pantsuit was plucking a portable computer off her seat with one hand while pulling a bulging briefcase from between the seats with the other.

"Frau Von Bessel?" The brunette turned, an agitated and irritated expression on her perfectly made-up face. Keeping his tone neutral, he said, "My name is Staff Sergeant Baker, Royal Canadian Mounted Police. This is Constable Nakamura. Welcome to Canada."

She looked him up and down with a perfunctory glance, as if immediately deciding she didn't like what she saw. "Bonjour," she said. "Parlez vous français, s'il vous plaît?" She could have made it sound like a request, but instead she made it sound like an order.

Baker felt his jaw muscles bunch. God damn you, Wattington. "I'm sorry, Madame, but I was given to understand that you are fluent in English."

She gave a little snort, whether of astonishment or disgust, he couldn't tell. All he knew was that she was intent on being rude. Her eyes flickered over Nakamura and she said something out of the corner of her mouth to the redhead. It sounded like some sort of witticism but all he caught was the word japonais. He glanced over at Nakamura and saw that he was looking intently and unsmilingly at the brunette.

This was going to be worse than he had imagined. It was not Baker's nature to be smiley-faced at the best of times, and definitely not when confronted with something like this. His blood pressure climbing, he stood silently and watched the two women gather their possessions. Just be calm and neutral, he told himself. Despite what she thinks, I'm the boss here.

Finally they were ready. Von Bessel tossed her head and turned to face him. She was politer this time. "Oui, sergeant, we were told to expect you." Then, in an obvious and gratuitous snub to Baker, she turned to Nakamura and continued with, "Constable Nakamura, may I present my assistant, Frauline Marta Rudd."

Nakamura inclined his head courteously.

"Sergeant, Frauline Rudd." Baker didn't incline his head. He stared at the woman, deciding in an instant he didn't like her at all.

She was obviously a natural redhead. Her complexion was the kind of very pale, peaches and cream. Even so he observed, with the practice that comes only from long years of experience in reading people, that despite the fine skin there were no laugh lines at the corners of her eyes. Was the woman completely devoid of a sense of humour? The eyes themselves were as blue and opaque as marbles under sandy lashes. Her mouth was a straight unsmiling line, so thin it looked as if she didn't have an upper lip.

When Baker didn't respond she extended her arm straight out, as if about to touch a large and potentially dangerous animal. It was a challenge. He extended his own arm. She had unusually long , delicate looking hands but her grip was firm and dry and she squeezed hard in a handshake designed to be remembered. He squeezed back as they appraised each other, looking right in each other's eyes, for two seconds longer than was polite. Rudd appeared to come to some sort of decision and flicked her eyes away first. Baker then released her hand. He'd come to a decision as well. This woman has missed her calling in life, he thought, born two generations too late. She should have been dressed in a black uniform, whip in hand, directing a line of shuffling inmates toward the Dachau ovens.

Baker stepped aside. The other first class passengers were getting restless at the delay, wanting to disembark and stretch their legs. "Ladies, shall we leave?"

Baker gave Nakamura a near imperceptible hand signal, telling him to move into the aisle and take the point. In the close confines of the crowded aisle way, Marta Rudd effortlessly handled her bags, but her smaller boss struggled with her briefcase and a large purse with a Gucci label on it. Exasperated, she snagged the purse and looked expectantly at Baker. He gazed at her impassively, knowing he had to keep his hands free. I'm a bodyguard, not a fucking bellboy, he thought. As she finally freed the purse she tossed her head and pushed furiously past him, muttering under her breath, "Gauche rustre."

The two officers guided the women out of the aircraft and up the first section of the jet-way. Rounding the corner, they had a clear view of the main hallway and an exuberant welcoming party for the many European dignitaries arriving on the flight. An honour guard of three RCMP members, two males and one female, in full ceremonial dress - traditional Stetson, scarlet serge tunics, blue riding breeches with a yellow stripe running down the outer seam, mirror-buffed riding boots - stood at the head of a line of local dignitaries. Baker empathised with his fellow members of the Force, having to stand at attention, ramrod straight. The sight of them brought back vivid and painful memories of squeezing himself into his own ceremonial uniform, the one that always made him feel like the granite jawed cartoon character Sergeant Preston of the Yukon.

Welcoming committee members were already starting to pump the hands of arriving dignitaries who had passed the four of them - they were moving less rapidly than Baker would have liked because of Von Bessel's slow progress. The media were there, cameras and microphones at the ready. Baker could tell Marta Rudd was gearing herself up to face the horde and obviously relished the idea.

Nakamura strode ahead of the two women and Baker brought up the rear in a 'by the book' wedge formation. Just as the young officer was about to enter the main hall he passed a female Canadian Airlines International passenger agent sporting an innocuous lapel pin - five tiny white doves in a circle around a small green earth - identical to those worn by Baker and Nakamura. The pins served as an event identification device for security personnel at GLOBE. A simple flip of Nakamura's ID was enough to have the woman key in a four digit code on the security panel to open the door beside her.

Nakamura turned and halted at the side door to block Rudd's passage and get her to move down the stairs. She attempted to side-step him but he was too quick for her. He touched her upper arm to guide her down the stairs and she snatched it away, a look of fury pinking her pale face. Baker took Von Bessel by the shoulders and physically turned her through the door and toward the stairs. Seeing her boss being hustled down the flight of steps, Rudd followed. As the four of them headed down, Rudd said loudly, in clear, good English, "What is going on here? You have no right to prevent us from meeting the media. I demand an explanation!"

"Ma'am," said Nakamura, "this is for your safety. We are following our orders." Baker thought, good way of putting it. Just the sort of phrasing that would appeal to a born-again Nazi.

"This is ridiculous!" snapped Von Bessel. "Take your hands off me! Our lives are not in danger and I do not believe you two toy soldiers could do anything about it if they were!"

I love you too, thought Baker. "Ladies, if you'll follow us, there's a car waiting to take you to your hotel. As for meeting the media, there will be a scheduled conference this evening. There will be ample opportunity for coverage then. We know security arrangements can sometimes be bothersome but they're designed to keep you as safe as possible. Please let us do our jobs."

Rudd was still intent on protesting. To Baker's surprise, Von Bessel said sharply, "That is enough, Marta." Rudd didn't look happy, but she did shut up.

The stairway ended at another security door. They exited, to see a black Ford Crown Victoria on the concrete outside, attended by two uniformed RCMP officers. The trunk, rear and front passenger doors were open. Baker gestured for the two men to be on alert, and relieved Von Bessel of her two pieces of luggage. She snatched her purse back. "I do not like American cars. I want a Mercedes."

Baker suppressed a smile at her petulant tone, remembering how the word 'pampered' had occurred to him in the small hours of the morning. "We have no Mercedes in the fleet, Madame. But this vehicle is guaranteed to be free of bombs. Frankly, I'd prefer to have you return to your home in one piece, as opposed to by the cupful, a distinct possibility with the quality of today's explosives."

Von Bessel made an irritated sound and flounced into the car. Nakamura relieved Marta Rudd of her bags and she did the same. Nakamura, in turn gave the two uniforms a twitch of the head, instructing them to take up positions by the doors. Baker and Nakamura moved to the rear of the car.

As the two men placed the luggage in the trunk, Baker said to Nakamura, "How's your French?"

"Pas mal," he replied. "Although I'm really only an expert in profanity. Why?"

"When I didn't help Her Highness with her bags on the plane, she called me a gauche rustre. I know gauche means clumsy, but what's the other word?"

Barry was grinning. "The woman's sure got your number. Damn. Should've noticed it myself, the first time I met you."

"Give," growled Baker.

"Rustre' means 'oaf' or 'lout'. You're a clumsy oaf."

Douglas Baker slammed the trunk shut and gave his partner a crooked smile. "Thought it might mean something like that. Jeez, Barry, my feelings are hurt."

"You'll get over it. Look on the bright side there's probably worse to come."

****

From his vantagepoint up in the airport's observation area, Colonel Aziz Hamani watched the two men enter the car and prepare to drive off. One of his agents had just whispered in his ear a description of how the two Mounties had escorted the women, and of the expertly executed dash down the stairwell. Hamani scratched his cheek meditatively, his brown eyes focused on the big Mountie with the slate grey hair. He had been thoroughly briefed on this man by another of his agents here in Vancouver, an agent who occupied a position of great sensitivity. Paying special attention to the big Mountie and how he handled the situation, he was impressed. So far, Staff Sergeant Douglas Baker was acting just as the agent said he would.

But it wouldn't do him any good in the long run. I will know everything you do and every place you go, the colonel thought. It gave him comfort to have such knowledge.

He wanted to turn and scrutinise the observation area, but he resisted the urge. Over the past two days he had been unable to shake the sensation that the Sword was watching him. He took a deep breath and looked at the 'No Smoking' sign on the wall. No point thinking about it now. He had to concentrate on the task ahead. And the first order of business was Marta Rudd.

FOURTEEN

As they drove along Granville Street, northward toward Vancouver City centre, the atmosphere in the car was thick with tension. Nakamura was driving, with Baker next to him. The two women were fuming in the back seat. For a long time no one spoke.

Absently, Baker flipped a cigarette out of the pack, squeezing the filter before lighting the Camel with his Ronson. He inhaled deeply, luxuriously, holding it in before letting the smoke escape in a billowing cloud.

Marie Françoise Von Bessel coughed, a barking, pointed cough. Lost in thought, Baker looked over his shoulder inquiringly. "Sergeant, I must insist that you refrain from smoking in our presence. It is a filthy habit. I expect to be shown respect and consideration, or I shall report you to your superiors."

Baker reached over to the ashtray and stubbed out the cigarette. "Of course, Madame, how thoughtless of me."

He considered briefly, then thought, what the hell. He chose his words more carefully than he ordinarily would have, formal words, speaking more slowly than he ordinarily would have to lend the formal words extra weight. "But as I am sure you are aware, respect and consideration, like politeness, are habits that require cultivation. Civilised behaviour is not possible without their mutual exchange. I trust you will agree. As for reporting me to my superiors, Madame, I am pleased to inform you that I have none."

He waited just long enough to see Von Bessel's mouth form an "O" and Rudd's eyes throw sparks like a couple of blue flints. As he turned to once again face the windshield, he could see from the corner of his eye that in an effort to keep from laughing out loud Nakamura was biting his lip so hard he was about to draw blood.

Baker tried to remember more of his French. What was the word? Ah, yes. Salope. Bitch.

In the small hours earlier that morning, in his apartment after the meeting with O'Neal, Slodnick and Nakamura, he had pondered what he had heard about Von Bessel during the briefing. He had concluded that, difficult and neurotic though she might be, the woman had been through a fair amount of tragedy. As a result, he had decided that he was willing to cut her some slack. After the experience of the past hour, no more. You push me, Salope, and I'll push back.

It was in dead silence that the two Mounties escorted the icy-eyed women into the Harbourside Centre Hotel, leaving the two waiting Vancouver Police officers, one to watch the car and one to move the luggage. Once registered, Baker and Nakamura accompanied the women up to their door. Introducing them to Slodnik and O'Neal, Baker added, "We'll be back here at 7:30, to escort you to the opening ceremonies thirteen blocks from here, at the BC Place stadium."

Von Bessel completely ignored him. Remembering what Nakamura had said the previous evening, about the woman being a control freak who didn't like being told what to do, Baker couldn't resist. "You are forbidden to leave this hotel without the permission of one member of my team and then, not without an escort." There was a sound from Marta Rudd like steam escaping from a kettle. They spun on their heels and left. Nakamura collapsed in laughter once they got into the elevator and even Baker allowed himself a sardonic smile.

At 7:30 on the dot they picked up the two women and drove in frigid silence to BC Place, arriving at 7:45. Single file, Nakamura, Rudd, Von Bessel and Baker passed through the airlock of the domed sports complex. Once through, Baker signalled Nakamura to re-group and take up the wedge formation. As they walked, he once again assessed the cavernous building.

Glancing around the echoing interior, with its balconies and maintenance shafts, thick criss-crossed girders, and GLOBE banners hung from the dome, he tried to count all the optimal locations for a shooter to hole up. He stopped counting after he hit fifty. You could hide an army of assassins in this place. He thought again of Wattington's nervousness about this assignment, and started feeling a little edgy himself.

The sports floor of the facility was more than three-quarters covered with carpeted aisles and display booths. The remaining open space was lined with chairs and a large raised stage. Up on the pedestrian apron that circled the entire building, where the seats of the red section met the blue, he spotted uniformed members of the City of Vancouver Police Department. Higher up, in the nosebleed section, directly across from the giant Sanyo viewing screen, he spied two more uniforms that he pegged as sharpshooters. The obviously tight security not withstanding, he saw ample opportunities for a seasoned professional to make an easy hit, no matter where he looked. If someone was intent on killing Marie Françoise Von Bessel and getting away with it, he thought, this is the place to do it.

Mentally he shrugged - don't waste your time worrying about something you can't do anything about. He concentrated on the task at hand, which was to get Von Bessel to the podium, wait for ninety minutes until she'd done her dog and pony show, then get her safely out.

The earpiece of his communications unit crackled. "GLOBE twelve. GLOBE one. Glad you could join us." It was Wattington's voice. Following protocol, with the purpose of not giving away a surveillance position, Baker didn't look up in the direction of the pre-arranged command location beside the big screen, where he knew the inspector was.

"You're the first team to arrive," continued Wattington. "Take up your positions. GLOBE two is directly ahead of you." Baker knew that was Staff Sergeant Steve Owen, the event commander. "He's got two people to help you get your lady onto the stage. Once there, he will be directing the action. Have fun and keep your eyes open."

"Roger that, Skipper. Any sign of unfriendlies?"

"Nothing yet."

Baker removed his hand from the lapel microphone and glanced over at Von Bessel. She looked very pale and uneasy, but when she realised he was looking at her she threw her head back, tossed her glossy chestnut hair and aggressively shot him a poisonous glance. He wondered briefly at the theatricality of the gesture until Marta Rudd reached out with her hand and tenderly touched the smaller woman's wrist. Von Bessel gave her a teary grateful smile.

Slowly the light of understanding dawned in Baker's mind.

This kind of public appearance doesn't come naturally to her, he thought. She's a shy, retiring private person who has forced herself to become a controversial public figure. And she hates every minute of it. That's why she needs Rudd - to run interference and provide support and comfort.

He filed this away in his mind under 'interesting insights' as he caught sight of two plain clothed VIP officers, a male and a female, striding up. To his right he saw Steve Owen chatting to a female usher. As their eyes met Owen squeezed off the slightest of nods to Baker and then to Nakamura. Owen was six feet tall and blond, the image of a California surfer. Baker couldn't remember how old he was, but he knew for sure he was at least ten years younger. Good luck to you, fast tracker. May your wheels always stay on the rails.

Baker looked around again at the sea of bodies washing back and forth. He never tired of this. The intricate ballet he always called in his mind 'Security Lake' had always fascinated him. If you did it right, nobody tripped, stumbled, fell off the stage, or crashed into the wings. Or got shot. If you didn't do it right, people got hurt.

Proceeding up the aisle to the front row, Baker signalled for Nakamura to break off with Rudd. As they turned away, Baker, accompanied by the two guide officers, walked Von Bessel the remaining twenty feet to the stage. At the bottom of the stairs he stopped, motioning the two officers to ascend with the VIP. He moved in front of the stage to a display booth where he stopped, turned and appeared to be looking over the display, while unobtrusively scanning the audience.

Over the next twenty minutes he looked on as the show's director-general introduced dignitary after dignitary. Political notables from Canada, the U.S., England, Indonesia and a host of other nations gave presentations that were supposed to be brief but weren't. Throughout, Baker continued to scan the floor and the surrounding area, turning occasionally toward the stage.

The image on the giant Sanyo screen suddenly changed, from a pan of the audience to a thirty-foot high head-and-shoulders of Dr. Gro Harlem Brundtland, revered environmental leader and Prime Minister of Norway, speaking via satellite from Brazil. This was the signal for Von Bessel to rise and move to the podium to welcome her friend through the miracle of modern technology.

Baker didn't even hear the exchange of pleasantries between the two women, concentrating instead on trying to spot sudden movements or the sinuous weaving of someone trying to slip through the crowd to a better shooting position. Von Bessel started speaking. Fidgety and nervous, it was not until two minutes into her presentation that she began to relax. Three minutes later, swept up in a Gaulish torrent of emotion, her voice was as thick and rich as ripe Camembert, and the hall was absolutely silent.

As Von Bessel cast her spell over the audience, Baker's earpiece clicked. "GLOBE twelve, this is E Control." Depressing the lapel-mounted microphone switch he whispered, "GLOBE twelve. Go ahead Control."

"Switch to channel two for a message from Division."

He frowned. What the hell was this? "Roger, Control. Nakamura?" He saw the young man look up, nod. "Hold the fort for a sec. You know what to do." Two clicks sounded. Baker reached into his jacket and switched channels. "E, GLOBE twelve. Go ahead."

A female voice said, "Regarding your inquiry this morning concerning 70341, staffing and personnel have located the party. Party requests, correction, demands, dinner this evening. Twelve to arrive communications room E when able. Acknowledge, twelve."

Baker smiled. "Roger that. Twelve clear." Switching back to

the floor channel he announced, again in a whisper, "Nakamura, I'm clear." He saw the young officer nod. He continued his scan of the audience. Trust Joan Chan to contact him like this. It would be great to see her again.

He turned to the stage. He saw Von Bessel look down at him and falter ever so slightly and do something he had never before seen. To his surprise she was smiling at him, obviously because she thought he was appreciating her speech. It was a hesitant girlish smile, really quite lovely, he thought. Still filled with the warmth at the thought of seeing Joanie, he figured oh what the hell. He nodded his head in acknowledgement. If she thinks I'm enjoying it, what's the harm? He turned once again to do his job, to scan the audience, but as he did so he was aware that for the first time, he was actually paying attention to what she was saying and though he would never admit it to anyone, he was duly impressed.

He watched on as this pale, nervous bird-like woman was now transformed into the very image of confidence. She used the podium expertly, grasping it firmly with both hands, bowing her head to emphasise a statement, or forming sensual arabesques with her hands to eloquently express a point. Baker couldn't remember the number of times he'd seen dignitaries who suffered from the Teddy Kennedy syndrome: get excited, start shouting and have your face turn brick red. Von Bessel was far removed from that kind of shrill emptiness. She is good, thought Baker. If I listen to this much longer, I'll end up hugging trees or cuddling spotted owls.

At the conclusion of her speech, Von Bessel was greeted with thunderous applause. It was everything Baker, Nakamura, Owen and the two other RCMP officers could do to plow their way through the adoring crowds and get the VIP and Marta Rudd out of the crush of bodies and into the airlock.

Once outside, the Crown Victoria was waiting and the four of them piled in. Von Bessel and Rudd chattered excitedly at each other in French on the way back to the hotel. Baker could feel the Phoenix Foundation founder's gaze resting on him periodically, but he didn't turn around. He meditated on what had happened in the course of the evening.

At the hotel, he and Nakamura escorted the ladies into the hotel and up the elevator to their respective suites, handing them over to a grim and apprehensive looking Slodnick and O'Neal in the hallway. It was obvious Nakamura had briefed them on what had happened that afternoon and they were braced for the worst.

As they said goodnight, Von Bessel extended her hand and looked him right in the eye, with a shadowed glance he had trouble reading. On the way down the elevator, Nakamura said, "She actually engaged you in human contact without an insult. What the hell was that friendly handshake about, all of a sudden?

Baker just shrugged, not feeling like talking. He looked at his watch. Not even 9:30. Still time for a late dinner with Joan Chan. As Nakamura drove the two of them back to E Division, he stared out of the window, thinking hard about a lot of things.

Marie Françoise Von Bessel's obvious loathing of her role as public speaker and activist, as high profile head of the Phoenix Foundation. The fact that she felt driven to do it, presumably because of love for her dead husband and child. The fact that she had trained herself to do it effectively, to use an actor's art to communicate the concern and conviction she had in her heart. The fact that she used coldness and rudeness to keep people at bay, to hide the vulnerability that lurked within.

Doesn't want to do it. Has to do it. Doesn't want to do it. Has to do it.

Compulsion.

Her reliance on Marta Rudd. Baker frowned. That now made more sense, but there was still something odd about it. Marie didn't strike him as a dyke. As he remembered the girlish smile she had given him while she was speaking, in response to his own inadvertent smile, he knew he had discovered a key to the woman's personality. The key had a name - needy. Von Bessel was an emotionally needy woman.

What was it Nakamura had said? That her father had been a ruthless hard-ass? That the young Marie had spent years in psychotherapy? Maybe life in the chateau hadn't been all that idyllic after all. And she'd fallen completely apart after her husband's death. Baker wondered what Christian Von Bessel had been like. How had he fed that greedy neediness?

He'd never thought of himself as being a particularly sensitive individual, but a thought suddenly occurred to him. To swim so strongly against the tide of one's own personality was a remarkable thing. A terrible thing. Terrible, as in, filled with terror.

What terror drove Marie Françoise Von Bessel?

FIFTEEN

Nakamura dropped Baker off at E Division and headed for home. The big Mountie crossed over to the main building, used his newly issued facility access card and caught the elevator down to the basement. Exiting, he turned to the right and made his way down the long, low corridor to the security desk at the end. Showing his ID to the watchman, he signed in and entered the expansive, brightly lit and windowless communications centre.

The large rectangular room was monopolised by a raised, circular equipment pedestal with seven enclosed workstation cubicles radiating from it. Each cubicle contained two computer monitors, banks of radio equipment and numerous telephone receivers. Civilian communications dispatchers occupied five of the seven positions.

Across from the central pedestal, halfway down the room, was a glassed-in cubicle. The sign over it read, 'Communications Watch Commander.' Baker nodded at the corporal on duty and once again offered his ID. "Joan Chan?"

The corporal handed back the piece of laminated plastic. "Sergeant Chan's expecting you. Down that way. Can't miss it. It's the one with the biggest, badest sign."

He wasn't kidding about the sign. Big and ominous, the black and white warning over the middle door stated: 'No Unauthorised Entry. Restricted Zone'. Underneath it someone had written in black felt pen, 'Trespassers will be shot'.

He knocked. No answer. About to knock again, a familiar, smoky female voice sounded from a nearby cubicle, with just the faintest trace of Hong Kong in it. "Over here, you big lug." He turned to find her sitting in a swivel chair in a cubicle, her feet up on the desk and a well eaten pencil protruding from the side of her mouth. Grinning broadly, she sprang out of the chair and into his arms, planting an affectionate sisterly kiss on his cheek. She came up to his shoulder.

They appraised each other at arms' length. Compact and muscular, Joan Chan was the image of fitness. Her shoulder-length ebony hair was pulled back in a pert ponytail, which accentuated the exotic features of her round face. She was forty, but like a lot of Asian women appeared practically ageless.

"Hi Joan," said Baker. "You still don't look like a spook."

"Well, you still look like a cop." She patted his abdomen just above his belt. "Didn't know men could get pregnant." She leaned forward and sniffed suspiciously. "You smoking again? After all that effort to quit? Shame on you." Joan was one of the few people who could make remarks like this without finding themselves in immediate need of orthodontic work.

"So," said Baker, "you breeze into town and don't even let me know you're here?"

"When I got here I checked in on you. I was told you were on vacation. The usual place?"

"Yeah," said Baker. "Only it was cut short. I'm playing babysitter to you know who. What are you doing here? You back on the Force?"

"God no, although I sometimes think it might not be such a bad idea. I'm the new divisional intelligence liaison officer."

"Congratulations," he said, pumping her right hand until she bounced. "So, what's the hot gossip in the spook business? The CIA or MI5 doing anything that might keep me awake at night?"

"Doug," she answered with a wry smile, "you know as well as I do that if I did tell you anything, I'd then have to kill you."

He grinned. "At least fill me in on the reorg."

Chan sighed and shrugged. Baker knew why. The rumour mill suggested that the newly minted intelligence service was going through yet another of its organisational upheavals. Formed just three years before, the Canadian Security and Intelligence Service was the result of a parliamentary study to investigate wrongdoings by the RCMP's Special Operations Branch, particularly allegations of dirty tricks. They both knew that the allegations had been planted by Soviet operatives attempting to get Special Ops off their backs, and the disinformation had worked. As a result, a Supreme Court judge had recommended that Special Ops be disbanded and replaced with CSIS. The organisation's birth had not been an easy one. All Special Ops personnel were given the option of transferring to CSIS or take on regular duties within the police Force. Baker had elected to stay with the Force, but Joan Chan had gone to the new organisation.

"No point in talking about it," she said. "The same old same old." She brightened. "So, let's go for dinner! Just let me sign off." She went back into the cubicle, sat down before the terminal and started keying information.

Baker contemplated the black and white warning sign. "I thought this locked concrete bunker with the scary sign was your office. What are you doing out here?"

"It is my office, but it's being repainted. I can't stand the fumes so I moved out here." She signed off and stood. "Where to?"

They went to the Granville Island Keg steakhouse. Once again Baker marvelled at how someone as small as Joan could eat so much. She had a twelve-ounce sirloin and a loaded baked potato, while Baker ordered a sixteen-ounce filet, home fries and a full-sized Caesar salad with double garlic. They split a bottle of excellent Chilean red. As the remains of the meal were cleared away Joan ordered a cognac, while Baker asked for a double single - the staff knew he meant a double, single malt Dalwhinnie on the rocks. Baker lit a cigarette as Joan frowned.

"What's up, big dude? Your body isn't a temple anymore or what?"

"Nope."

Chan's eyes were appraising. "You don't give a shit, or what? Is it Washington again? You've got to let that go."

Baker shrugged at the reference to the incident that had derailed his career three years previously. He'd stumbled onto a Soviet mole, a man planted during the darkest days of Stalinism.

Code-named 'Reggie,' this British medical researcher had specialised in brain function, particularly bizarre experiments to use the human brain as a weapon. Reggie had been underground for so long he was practically invisible, but hard-liners in the Kremlin had finally activated him for the biggest job of his career - assassinating the new Russian President on his first visit to Washington, D.C. It had been Baker who'd provided the bait to snap the trap on the old spy, and with the assistance of the CIA he had foiled the plot to kill the Russian leader. But at the last moment, when the spy knew the game was lost, he and his team escaped into the subway and used commuters as hostages. In the pitched gun battle that followed, Reggie and a little girl had been killed. The CIA never formally accused Baker of any wrongdoing, but they needed someone to blame and the Canadian, who had gone outside regular channels, was the perfect scapegoat. Blamed for a fiasco that was not his fault, targeted by unseen bureaucrats as the fall guy, and not able to talk about it because of national security obligations, Baker had eaten his fill of rage and humiliation. The only people he could talk to about it were Joan Chan and Colin Stewart, who had been their instructor at the Scotland Yard anti-terrorist program, where Baker had first met Joan. The three had become fast friends, and eventually Colin had immigrated to Canada after he had been crippled in an IRA attack and forced to retire.

"Seen Colin and Claire lately?" Baker asked.

"Yes. Saw them a few weeks back."

"How is he?"

"Not so good. He's in that damn wheelchair most of the time and doesn't have much energy."

In an effort to change the subject, Baker said, "Joanie, how'd you come to work on the Von Bessel bio? It was a great piece of research, but isn't it a little odd that you'd be doing it for the RCMP?"

Chan sipped her cognac. "Steve Owen asked me to do it. We've known each other for a while and he was aware that I'm now in the analysis field with CSIS. When it became apparent that Von Bessel would be coming to GLOBE, and with that attack in

Brussels, he needed some deep background thrown together right quick and my bosses said okay. And, if I may blow my own horn, there's nobody better at that kind of thing than I am."

Baker nodded. It was true. "But there are some gaps."

Chan's eyes narrowed as she sensed a challenge. "I know. Couldn't be helped, given the time frame. If I'd had more time I could tell you right now what her cholesterol level is."

As Baker drained his scotch, she said, "Any gaps in particular that you're interested in?"

Meditatively he contemplated his glass. "Why did she undergo psychotherapy when she was a kid?"

"Don't know. Patient privilege and all that. It was decades ago. The consulting physician is dead and the medical records have been archived. None of it's on-line so I can't hack the files. I could find out, but it'd be one hell of an effort."

"Are she and Marta Rudd lovers?"

"I don't think so. Just because Rudd is a lesbian doesn't mean her boss is too."

Baker's eyes were gazing off into the middle distance as he thought about his own impressions of Marie Françoise Von Bessel. "Fair enough. Not that it's important. What really interests me is that assassination attempt in Brussels. That is one mighty bizarre incident, don't you think?"

"Yes I do," said Chan. "Struck me the same way. Public place, half a dozen people with guns, very professional set-up. But only one guy is a shooter and he misses, like he's the only person in the whole op who isn't a pro. Why select as a shootist a guy who can't shoot? A dozen delegates with fake credentials but nobody can find out how they got accredited or who they really are. Everybody gets away and there are no leads, nothing. Stuff like that happens in spy novels but not in real life."

Baker was frowning, remembering his meeting with Nakamura, Slodnick and O'Neal. "I agree. And the timing is suggestive. She's had dozens of death threats, but the only time an attempt is made is just after the story breaks about that Schweizerhalle fire being arson. If her theory is right about unknown persons being involved, and with the CIA and everybody hunting them down, there might be some very edgy perps out there who want to shut her up at all costs."

Chan nodded. "There's something else as well. Something that really got me wondering."

Baker's cold grey eyes were hard. He knew Joan Chan and she didn't say such things lightly. "Such as?"

"Such as making a routine information request about the night of the fire and the death of Von Bessel's husband and son in the car accident, and hitting a wall the size of Stonehenge."

Without taking his eyes from Chan's, Douglas Baker motioned to the waiter to bring more drinks. "About the fire or the accident?"

"Both. The fire I can sort of see why there'd be a stonewall, what with the new information about it being a terrorist attack, but the accident? Unless of course it wasn't an accident."

"Anything that leads you to believe it wasn't?"

"One or two of those odd little bits of information you pick up that seem to be completely meaningless, until you find another little piece of information that doesn't fit with the first ones."

Baker crushed the filter of a Camel and fired the smoke with his Ronson. "I'm listening."

"The autopsy results on Christian Von Bessel. He was wearing a signet ring on the third finger of his left hand. It half-melted in the heat so it couldn't be identified, but it burned right into the flesh."

"So?"

"Family and friends told the coroner they couldn't remember Christian ever wearing a signet ring. The one person who would've known for sure was the wife, and she was babbling at the walls in a mental institution."

Baker's eyes were hooded. "I'm listening."

"The autopsy also showed that he had a high blood alcohol level. Swiss police attribute the crash to the fact that he was drunk."

Baker nodded. "I remember. Three times the Swiss legal

limit."

The waiter placed a snifter in front of Chan and a glass in front of Baker. The big man downed it in one gulp and rattled the ice cubes. "And the significance of this is?"

Joan tossed back her brandy. "Christian Von Bessel didn't drink. Like, never."

"Never?"

"I'm listening."

"They identified him from dental records. But they can't explain why a man who had apparently never been to Eastern Europe, or for that matter Africa, had dental work typical of what you'd find in the third world."

Baker had taken a fistful of ice cubes and was squeezing them, watching the melting waterfall back into his glass. "I'm still listening."

"And they never did a dental search on the boy's body. They just presumed it was Daniel's. According to the coroner, he was small for a seven year old."

Baker motioned once again to the waiter. "And of course, by the time Marie Von Bessel was out of the booby hatch, some four months had gone by and the bodies had been buried. Or were they cremated?"

Chan smiled sardonically. "They were cremated once already, remember?"

Baker popped an ice cube in his mouth and clicked it against his teeth. "You mention all of this to Steve Owen?"

"Yeah. He said, so what? He said, we have no jurisdiction and none of this supposition is going to help us guard Marie Von Bessel when she's here. Let it go, he said."

Baker nodded slowly. "I can see his point. Then again, he's young. Hasn't been around the block a few times, like you and me."

The waiter placed fresh glasses in front of them. For several moments Douglas Baker was lost in thought, gazing sombrely at the amber liquid. "You think it stinks?"

"Like ten week old fish," said Joan Chan, gazing at her own.

Baker poured the scotch down his throat. "You feel like doing a little freelance grave digging?"

Chan tossed back her cognac and smiled, her teeth very white in her porcelain doll face. "Try and stop me, big fella."

Baker grinned. "I love ya, babe."

"I love you too, you big lug." She waggled her empty snifter. "Deduction is thirsty work. I want another drink."

SIXTEEN

Vancouver, March 17

The shrill shriek of the phone jarred Douglas Baker from a wonderful dream involving Betty from Dallas, the balcony of his room at Senor Paz's, and a cooler filled with bottles of Belikian Beer.

"Hello?" he croaked.

"Doug, its Joan."

Baker licked his dry lips. "What the hell time is it?"

"Five thirty-seven, big guy. You should be up and at 'em pretty soon anyway. What's the matter, can't hold your liquor any more?"

Baker rubbed his face, remembering that he'd been drinking doubles to Chan's singles. And chain-smoking. The multiplier effect. "Joan, what's up?"

"I hate it when I miss things. After we left the restaurant I couldn't get our conversation out of my head. Came back to the office and started digging. I think I've hit a mother-lode."

Baker shook his rapidly clearing head. "Fire away."

"First, there's all that funny business with the autopsy results - the alcohol, the signet ring, the dental work, the kid. I think Christian Von Bessel and his son Daniel were murdered, but I don't think they died in that car. Second, Frau Von Bessel's information about how the fire was arson. Where did she get that stuff from, all of a sudden? It looks as if it was deliberately fed to her. By whom, and why? Apparently, just days before the Brussels attack, one of her key people at the Phoenix Foundation disappeared. Still hasn't been found. I think the lady knows a lot more than she's letting on. As for who actually died in the car, you won't believe. . ."

Baker was now on his feet, his queasy stomach forgotten, every instinct alert. About to fire off a series of questions, he heard the bitten-off beep sound that indicated Joan Chan was getting a call on another line.

"Damn!" she swore. "Sorry Doug. This is the fourth time this hour. Somebody's slinging a trace on me, from overseas. I must've ruffled some feathers back in Belgium or Switzerland. This is really getting interesting. Gotta go!" Before Baker could speak, the line went dead.

He tried calling back and got a busy signal. Finally, he padded into the bathroom in search of Tylenol. Swallowing two of the white pills, he stared at himself in the bathroom mirror, thinking hard. He went back into the bedroom, picked up the phone and dialed Joan's direct line. Still busy.

Quickly he showered, shaved and dressed. He looked at his watch. Just 6:05. He knew he'd have to be at the hotel at 6:30, but there was just enough time to fit this in.

He drove to E Division headquarters and parked illegally by the front entrance. To punish himself for drinking too much scotch the previous evening, he didn't take the elevator. Instead, he bounded down the stairway, two steps at a time, threw open the basement fire door and walked rapidly down the long, deserted hallway to the communications room door. There was no guard at the desk. One of the three operators on duty looked up at him and offered a wan smile before turning back to her console. The duty officer, the corporal from the night before, waved him through after he'd scribbled his signature in the logbook.

He made his way to Joan's cubicle, only to find it deserted. Sucking in a ragged, apprehensive breath, he stepped into the meagre seclusion the partitioned area offered. Not knowing what he was looking for, or what he expected to find, he quickly scanned the enclosure for anything that might be amiss. Nothing seemed out of place. He was about to leave when he realised that Joan's computer monitor was black. He frowned. Nobody ever turned off their computer in this place. Why wasn't there at least a screen saver on the monitor?

He crossed over to the restricted access office and tried the door. Maybe the paint fumes had cleared and she was in here.

Locked and no response. Even from the opposite side of the door he could smell paint fumes. He returned to the duty officer, who looked up helpfully. "Staff?"

"I need to know when Sergeant Joan Chan signed out."

The officer consulted the ledger. "Says here 5:43."

"When she left, did it look like she was in a hurry, or upset maybe?"

"Now that you mention it, she looked kind of alert for this time of the morning. And she did forget to give me one of those great smiles she always has for everyone. Must've had something on her mind."

"Did she say where she was going"

"Nope. She was carrying a package, though."

"What kind of package?"

"I didn't really notice. Think it was her lunch though. You know, one of them plastic Tupperware things."

Baker nodded. "You didn't check it?" as per protocol.

"It was her lunch Staff. And, it was Sergeant Chan. She's good people."

"You're right on that one. Where's the civilian guard who's supposed to be at the check-in? He wasn't around when I came in."

The duty officer pointed to a monitor that showed the guard now sitting at his desk. "Him? Must've gone for a piss. Pretty much standard for the old guy this time of morning. Too much coffee."

Baker nodded, filled with an intense disquiet he couldn't explain.

"Say, is there anything wrong?"

"I don't know," said Baker. "I'll give her a call later. If she comes in, tell her to phone Doug. She'll know. I'll be at the GLOBE conference all day."

"Shall do," said the duty officer. "She'll probably be back right away."

Baker was starting to feel a little foolish. "Okay. See you around." He turned and walked away, still filled with a sense of foreboding.

SEVENTEEN

Baker arrived at the hotel some five minutes late. He picked up four French dark roast coffees from the Starbucks outlet in the mall and liberally laced his with cream.

Once upstairs, he found O'Neal sitting outside the women's suite, while Nakamura was talking to Slodnick near the stairwell. The coffee was gratefully received by the three men. "Anything?" asked Baker.

"Nada," replied O'Neal. "If it was any quieter I'd think I was in church."

As O'Neal and Slodnick headed home, Baker and Nakamura escorted the two women downstairs to the hotel's restaurant. As usual, both chose to eat from the buffet's vegetarian offerings. Baker grabbed four hard-boiled eggs, four packets of salt and pepper, a smoked salmon bagel with dill cream cheese, a club soda and coffee. Nakamura watched, keeping a close eye on the restaurant. Then, it was off to the conference; a whirlwind of backroom meetings, speeches, presentations and the sort of insincere political glad-handing Baker detested. He tried to get Joan Chan a couple of times, but she still hadn't returned. He left a message on her machine at home. Finally, when there was no word by 10:30, he initiated a locator order on her pager. Where the hell was she?

At 12:45, Marta Rudd shooed her boss into one of the key events of the conference, a speech to five hundred delegates. Once again, Baker noted Von Bessel's extreme nervousness and the soothing touch on the wrist from Rudd. He had finally decided it was genuine, that these two very different women had a real bond of affection and understanding, even though he still hadn't figured out what it was. He had purposefully avoided eye contact with Von

Bessel and tried to conduct himself as neutrally as possible, still reminding himself of how needy she was and not certain how to forestall any kind of response from her. The luncheon was almost over by the time they arrived, the meal already cleared away and the coffee being served. The moderator was a dour Indonesian with a heavy accent and an ornate, flowery style of speaking. Reflexively, Baker scanned the area. Apart from the swinging doors to the kitchen area, there was only one way in or out. You'd have to be suicidal to try a hit in here, he thought. He looked over at Barry Nakamura, with his conference carryall that concealed a 9-mm Heckler and Koch-MP5. He sat at a table with Marta, four tables back from the floor level lectern. With his hair untidy and a scruffy Simon Fraser University sweat shirt, he looked like a student.

His eyes sweeping the crowd like a beacon, Baker barely heard the introductory remarks. Through his earpiece he heard a stream of information coming from other officers around the building. Occasionally, he heard Steve Owen providing terse comments and orders. Finally, the Indonesian introduced Marie Françoise Von Bessel. With nervous bird-like movements she approached the microphone and began to speak.

"Why is it that the most developed nations in the world are the worst polluters, while at the same time the ones who insist that Third World nations enforce standards that we ourselves do not adhere to? Well. . ."

Baker tuned out. Christ, this is boring. Once again, he noticed how Von Bessel's nervousness soon turned into confidence, how the eyes of every delegate were fastened on her, how they hung on every word. As he fought to ignore his still queasy stomach and concentrate, he heard a voice in his earpiece. It was Nakamura. "Hey, Baker. Try to keep your eyes open, will you? You look bored rigid."

Baker was about to reply when he heard Owen's voice. "Can the chatter! Do your job, Nakamura. GLOBE twelve, pay attention." Baker tilted his head at Barry, who rolled his eyes.

At the end of her speech, Von Bessel was greeted with a tumultuous ovation, which she acknowledged with the practised grace of a film star winning her third Oscar. Before fans could swarm her,

Baker signalled to Nakamura to close in and escort her from the hall. She had to be at another venue in less than ten minutes. They expertly wove through the crush of the crowd with Von Bessel and Rudd. Baker radioed that he wanted the car waiting in the subterranean parking garage.

Once on the elevator, they descended to parking level one. When the doors opened, Baker stepped out first, eyes searching. There were two men waiting to enter the second elevator. They leaned against a trolley carrying an ice sculpture of a humpback whale and a large covered dish. Both wore the uniforms of hotel food service staff. Baker reflexively noted the nametags - Philipe and Jesus.

Then it hit him.

They looked dark enough to be Filipino, but there was something very wrong with the bone structure and the set of the eyes. He'd never seen Filipinos with hooked noses. And they were too big to be Filipino. One was at least five ten, with a burly build, the other five eight and squat as a fireplug.

And the eyes were not the eyes of bored hotel employees. Clear and glistening, with irises so brown they appeared black, they were far too alert, the eyes of professional watchers.

Baker noted all of this in less time than it took to blink.

His mouth suddenly dry, he flashed a quick hand signal to Nakamura to stay in the elevator car. As he reached into his jacket he saw, from the corner of his eye, Nakamura's hand move to the zipper of the carryall and the Heckler and Koch concealed there. He suddenly knew that the covered tray on the trolley was big enough to hold a machine pistol.

The two men blinked as they realised he had a gun halfway out of his jacket. A faint 'ping' announced the arrival of the second elevator. The waiters stared at Baker as they pushed their cart though the open door. As the doors closed, he saw the two glance at each other. He confirmed that the elevator was in fact ascending and signalled Nakamura that everything was okay. Then he pressed the transmit button.

"Cameras. This is GLOBE twelve. What is the nearest position to the parking level elevators?"

"Camera three, directly across from door on the convention level."

"Camera one, top of escalators, restaurant level."

"Did either of you see two hotel employees with an ice sculpture on a cart?"

"This is camera one. I got them."

"Make them famous, camera one."

"Roger that, GLOBE twelve. Photographing now. Pictures ASAP."

"GLOBE twelve, this is GLOBE one," came Steve Owen's anxious voice. "What's up?"

"Don't know. Just a hunch. I want reference checks on the photos of those two. My antennae are twanging."

"Done, GLOBE twelve."

"Signing off," Baker said as he caught sight of the black Ford moving into the loading zone adjacent to the elevators. The car's tires squealed on the pavement as the driver made a turn, bringing the vehicle to a smooth stop. An uniformed constable got out and held the driver's door open while unlatching the rear door. Nakamura stepped forward, guiding Marta into the back seat. Baker helped Von Bessel into the car, suddenly anxious to be away from the garage. Nakamura slid behind the wheel and they were off.

"What was that all about?" asked the young constable.

"Instinct," said Baker, still trying to figure out what had happened back in the garage.

"What twigged?" asked Nakamura, as Baker realised Barry hadn't even seen the two men.

"Couple of guys with Filipino names who didn't look Filipino."

Nakamura's eyes slid sideways. "What did they look like?"

Baker thought for a moment. "Arabs."

The young constable's eyebrows shot toward his hairline as Marie Françoise Von Bessel said irritably, "What are you two talking about?" It was then that Baker realised the two women didn't have a clue what was going on. And they hadn't seen the two men either. As he turned to say something to Von Bessel, he saw the look on Marta Rudd's face. She was very pale and the pupils of her opaque blue eyes were like pinpricks.

"Did you say, Arabs?" she asked quietly.

"Yeah," said Baker. "Why?" Rudd shrugged and looked out of the window, pensively nibbling a fingernail. Von Bessel was watching her, concerned. What the hell was going on? Turning around again, Baker absently popped a Camel out of the pack and fished in his jacket for his Ronson.

"I demand, repeat demand, that you extinguish that foul cigarette!"

Baker looked over his shoulder. "It's not even lit yet, but I take your point." He stuffed it back into the pack and pocketed his lighter. He leaned over, made a choice and rammed the cassette into the tape deck. The sound of Dr. Hook and the Medicine Show playing Freakin' at the Freaker's Ball boomed through the car. Baker tapped his fingers on the dashboard in time to the music. "Far out, huh?" he said to Nakamura.

Deadpan, his partner replied, "Groovy, man."

"Vous! Vous, maudit! I will report you to your superiors! I insist that you turn off that dreadful music! Damn you-" She lunged at Baker, but couldn't get to him because of her seatbelt. "Give me that microphone!" she screamed. "I want to speak to your commanding officer!"

Baker turned around again. "Madame, I am astonished. This is most undignified. I suggest you relax and compose yourself." He pressed the fast forward button on the tape machine, cutting out the gravely singing voice of Dr. Hook's lead singer, Dennis Del Montier. When the music came back on, it was Van Morrison singing Avalon Sunset, a piece of music identified in Von Bessel's biographical profile. "One of your favourites, Madame?"

"Batard!" she seethed.

Baker smiled.

Two hours later, after another speech, they were back at the main conference venue. Baker saw a grave Sergeant Steve Owen walking towards him. He motioned, and the big Mountie moved to join him in the far corner of the room. Under his breath Owen said, "Signal Nakamura that you're taking a break." Baker nodded all his instincts in overdrive. "Got some bad news."

"What?"

"Joan Chan."

"I'm listening."

"Hit and run. She was on the Granville Street Bridge, just exiting onto Seymour, when she was apparently side-swiped by a car."

Baker felt his heart turn to ice. "And?"

"Intensive care at St. Paul's Hospital. She's smashed up pretty bad."

"What about the driver?"

"That's what's got everybody worried. Police found the vehicle that struck her abandoned and cleaned out, a few blocks away. It was stolen sometime early this morning."

Furiously Baker absorbed the information that it was a deliberate hit. "What time did this happen?"

"Just after six this morning."

Baker looked at his watch. "It's three in the afternoon. Why didn't we know sooner?"

"As soon as word got back to CSIS they shut everything down. The only reason I know is because of you. They want to talk to you real bad."

"What about?"

"You were listed in the communications log as being the last person to visit her, both late last night and early this morning. Her computer terminal has been cannibalised - the entire hard drive is missing. Not only that, but someone who knew exactly what they were doing has totally screwed up the local area network that connects Joan's machine with all the others. Whatever data she had on her machine is gone - now it's just a digital black hole. The spooks are right pissed. They want to know what the hell is going on and what you talked to her about. Come to think of it, I wouldn't mind knowing myself."

"It was about Von Bessel," replied Baker. "Joan found some strange stuff when she was preparing the briefing on her and

Rudd."

"Christ," said Steve Owen. "I told her to can that shit. It's not important."

"I disagree," said Baker. "I think it might have something to do with whoever tried to kill her Brussels, and whether the same people might try it here."

The two men stared at each other, until finally Owen looked away. "Doesn't matter now, I guess. I'll have to pull you off detail for an hour or two so the spooks can talk to you. We'll have Nakamura in charge until you get back."

"Okay," said Baker reluctantly. "We got any ID on the photos of those two guys in the parking garage?"

"Not yet. I'll let you know when I hear something."

Baker briefed Nakamura. "In the meantime, you're in charge here. I want you to watch for anything, anything at all. Take Gold and Collins as backup while I'm gone. Brief them thoroughly. Come up with your own strategy to make it to shift change. Anything that looks bogus to you, treat as hostile. Also, don't let Von Bessel, or Rudd for that matter, get to you. You're the boss. Hang on a sec."

He pushed the transmit button. "GLOBE two, GLOBE twelve. Request ten minute strategy session for Nakamura, Gold and Collins. Two to remain with twelve." Baker could see Owen ponder the request, then nod. "Okay Barry, it's all yours. Fill them in and then get back in here. Got it?"

"Sure. Just one question. Gold and Collins are corporals. They outrank me."

"I know. But by now you know Von Bessel and Rudd and their little idiosyncrasies better than anybody else except me. You're in charge. You'll be fine."

"Okay. Good luck with the third degree. I understand those rubber truncheons hurt like hell."

Baker grinned in spite of himself as he left.

Back at the 64th Avenue headquarters Baker made his way up to the Superintendent's office. As he entered the outer reception area, he could feel the tension in the room. Inspector Wattington was there and Baker had never seen him look so agitated. "I'm really sorry about your friend."

Baker nodded curtly - he knew this was just a courtesy and Wattington didn't give a shit about Joan Chan.

"This thing is about to blow up in our faces. These spooks are out for blood and they want some answers. You ready?" Baker shrugged. "Let's go. Make it good, and for Christ's take no lip."

EIGHTEEN

The interrogation went on for over an hour. Three senior level CSIS operatives grilled Baker about every detail of his relationship with Joan Chan, what he knew about Von Bessel and Rudd, and what it was they had discussed. It wasn't until a full forty minutes into the interview that they asked about Joan's hard drive. Then they asked the same questions over and over.

"For the tenth time, I don't know what happened to it, nor do I know what was on the damn thing," snarled Baker. "I am not a computer technician and the only way I know of to remove a hard drive is with a crowbar. So that means I didn't take it. Don't you guys back up your systems? I've told you everything I know. The duty man said she was carrying a lunch container. You've already told me it wasn't at the scene of the accident and she's been unconscious since the H and R. That's all I know, apart from the fact that Joanie would never have done anything like this unless it was vitally important. Now give. You must have some theories about what's going on. Let's hear them."

That shut them up. Baker's temper started to flare as he came to understand that the intel guys knew even less than he did. The only thing that really surprised him was that Wattington stuck up for him all the way through, instead of remaining silent or throwing him to the wolves.

At the end, Baker was no closer to finding a tangible connection between Joan's accident and Von Bessel. He finally snapped when he asked the obsequious senior officer for an update on Joan's condition and was told the information was classified. It took the two other CSIS operatives and Wattington to get him off the man, but not before he'd hit him with a couple of solid shots and scared the crap out of the little bastard. The interview ended quickly after that.

As they took the elevator down, Jim Wattington smoothed his hair and straightened his tie. "That was real smart, Doug." He examined a rip in the seam of his jacket. "Christ, have you been lifting weights or something? The only reason they aren't going to throw the book at you is because I already told them how close you and Joan are. But these guys don't forget anything. They already think you're a cowboy because of that Washington fiasco, and now you pull a stunt like this."

"Classified information my ass," growled Baker. "Bet it's classified that he can't get it up."

The elevator door opened and as they walked toward the entrance, Wattington sighed. "I know. Bunch of assholes who think they're fucking James Bond."

Baker stopped at the front door. "Aren't you coming?" asked Wattington.

"In a second. I have to use the can. Go ahead - I'll get hold of Nakamura and the others."

The inspector looked at him suspiciously. "You go to the can, then you go to the hotel. Right?"

Baker's cold grey eyes were level. "I'll be straight with you. Given that those spooks upstairs couldn't find their own asses with both hands and a flashlight, they might've missed something."

Wattington held up a hand. "I didn't hear that last remark. I stuck up for you, and don't forget that. I've done my good deed for the day. You start poking around and get caught, you're on your own." He turned and marched out.

Baker took the stairs to the basement and the communications centre. They knew him by now but they did log in his visit. Chan's cubicle was criss-crossed shut with yellow crime scene tape, a crime right in the heart of police operations. A young uniformed constable stood guard next to the office and was about to deny Baker access until the big man showed his ID. He peered down the hallway. "I heard about you. Any friend of Joan's is a friend of mine. Just don't be too long, okay? And if someone comes down here, I'll have to say you pulled rank."

"Thanks, kid." Ducking under the tape barrier, Baker moved over to the lone chair in the cubicle. Taking care not to touch anything, he sat down, swivelling slowly in the chair, looking at the minutest details.

His eyes finally came to rest on the computer tower. It was on its side and he could now see what he hadn't seen this morning - a gaping hole on the right side of the box, where the hard drive should be. He leaned and peered. The quick release memory module was missing.

Pulling a clean handkerchief from his jacket pocket, he started opening drawers, flipping through file folders, looking for anything that might give him a hint. After ten minutes of detailed examination, there was still no hint of why Joan had bolted.

It was almost 6:20 when he finally signed out of the communications room. Knowing he would miss shift change at the hotel, he had the duty officer get a message to Nakamura at the GLOBE site, ordering the constable to stay with Slodnick and O'Neal until he arrived back at the hotel. Nothing short of a bullet in the heart was going to prevent him from going to his next destination.

The intensive care unit of St. Paul's Hospital was hushed and subdued, filled with murmurs, the swish of nurses' polyester uniforms, the squeak of their shoes on the gleaming linoleum. Baker hated hospitals at the best of times, and ICUs in particular. Death in a holding pattern, he thought.

There were four square rooms on each side of the floor, all bounded by sliding glass doors. Joan was in the ninth suite, at the far end. A cordon of three uniformed officers from the Vancouver Police Department restricted access to the end of the corridor to everyone but a tiny group of cleared medical staff.

Standing just beyond the human cordon, only making it that far after having his ID evaluated by a plainclothes operative at the nurses' station, he could just see all the electronic gadgetry keeping Joan alive, the snaking transparent IVs that hooked her to the two clear plastic bags, one with saline drip and the other with glucose. He noticed the green LED of an antibiotic pump. Damn, he thought, wounds infected already? An infection for someone in Joan's condition could be the little nudge over the edge, into eternity.

He stood there for more than ten minutes, unaccustomed to being in a situation where he was completely useless. To take his mind off his own helplessness, he cast his mind back over the details of the accident. Joan had been on the Granville Street Bridge, just exiting onto Seymour. Where had she been going? Why had she been walking? Sideswiped by a car that had catapulted her over the bridge railing. Then the twenty-foot drop to the road underneath. Baker knew if it had been rush hour she would've been instantly run over. Given the lacerations on her left hand, investigators figured she'd grabbed at the railing, maybe swung there for several seconds before she lost consciousness or couldn't hold on any longer. That was his Joanie - tough and strong. Where was the package she'd been carrying? The car that hit her, stolen that morning, found abandoned a few streets away. Completely cleaned out, not even a partial print anywhere in the car, no hairs, no cloth fibres, nothing.

A professional hit.

What was it she'd said to him on the phone? 'Somebody's slinging a trace on me, from overseas. I must've ruffled some feathers' and that business she'd mentioned, about who had actually perished in the fiery crash that Christian Von Bessel and his son were supposed to have died in.

He was lost in thought until one of the young officers tapped him lightly on the elbow to break him out of his trance. Baker nodded at the man and pointed toward the unconscious Chan. "It was a professional hit. You see anything, I don't care if it's a God damn budgie bird trying to get into that room, you start blasting." The officer nodded. Without another word Baker turned and walked out.

He stopped off at home, intending to clean himself up and put on a new shirt, to free his nostrils of the smell of adrenaline and rage. Approaching the door of his condominium, on the top floor of the complex, still lost in thought, he took out his key.

Then he stopped dead and stared at the floor. He looked at the front door, then reached into his jacket for his gun. He quickly knelt and peered, so no one could see him through the peephole. He had a mat in front of his door, almost the same wine purple colour as the hallway carpet. It had a distinctive nap to it. Baker always made sure that as he left every day he shuffled his shoes on it so the nap lay a certain way, catching the light in such a manner that the mat had a velvety, deep purple sheen. But now the mat was flattened, and some pinkish-purple footprints could be seen on it.

Leading into the apartment.

He examined the keyhole. No scratches. Very quietly he opened the door, gun at the ready. Moving fast, he searched all the rooms, but there was no one there and no other trace of entry. He noticed that the light was flashing on his answering machine, but there was something more important he had to do first. Holstering his gun, he threw off his sports coat and rummaged in an old athletic bag in the back of his bedroom closet. Two minutes of electronic sleuthing with the very effective sniffer unit he'd picked up at a recent surveillance trade show in Los Angeles told him there was a bug attached to his phone. He left it in place, put the sniffer unit away, sat down on the sofa and lit a Camel. He had a pretty good idea who had done it, especially after the grilling they'd given him earlier.

Walking into the bedroom, he stripped off his clothes and took a long hot shower. Then he shaved and changed. He was just doing up his tie when the doorbell sounded. At the peephole he saw the friendly face of Karen Stedman, his neighbour from the unit directly across the hall. Nice girl. Forcing himself to smile, he opened the door. Remembering the bug, and having no idea how sensitive it was, he stepped into the hallway and closed the door behind him. "Hello, Karen. What can I do for you?"

"Hi, Doug. Just delivering this FedEx package. Came this afternoon. Instructions were, if you're not home, it was to be left with me."

Baker took the package, resisting the urge to look at the label. "Thanks. Hey, you see anybody else around here today? Repairmen perhaps?"

"Nope. I was in the sack most of the day - on graveyard shift until the end of the week. I only heard the doorbell going off when they brought the package. You okay? You look kind of pale."

"I'm fine. Thanks for playing messenger."

"Any time. Gotta fly. See you around."

Baker nodded as she headed down the hall. He went back into his apartment and closed the door. Once seated on the sofa, he opened the package and extracted the thick envelope inside as he read the packing slip: Marika, 657 Laurel St., Vancouver, BC. He frowned. He didn't know any Marika. He scanned the slip again. No phone number, no last name. But the address was one block north of E Division headquarters. He ripped open the package. Inside was a large rectangular Tupperware container. He pulled off the plastic lid. A dirty container that had recently contained lasagne. Something had obviously been hastily wrapped in blank computer paper, now red and transparent, stained with tomato sauce and grease. He tore the paper apart and stared.

A modularised hard drive unit.

He noticed that something was scribbled in heavy black felt pen across one corner of the lasagne-stained computer paper: 'See Julia!' What was all this cryptic stuff with the strange names?

Slowly it came to him.

The three of them had finished their anti-terrorism training in Britain and Colin Stewart had taken them over to Amsterdam for a wild weekend. Joan Chan had insisted on being treated like one of the boys, so they'd gone to the notorious red light district to see a strip show. They'd all had too much to drink, but one of the strippers had taken a shine to him. Her name had been Marika. Colin received a lot of attention from a girl named Julia.

Joanie was telling him to take the hard drive to Colin Stewart. A man who, even though crippled and semi-retired, was still one of the world's leading experts on terrorism.

Baker's grey eyes were cold. Terrorism. So his hunch had been right - it was about the Schweizerhalle fire in 1986. Joanie must've locked onto someone's tail and they were scared as hell.

Suddenly he remembered, cursing himself for his carelessness. He heaved from the sofa and reached for the answering machine. His hand froze in mid-air. He thought for a moment, remembering the bug attached to the phone. He unplugged the machine and carried it to the balcony. He opened the sliding glass door, then plugged the machine into the phone jack right next to the window. Stepping outside, he closed the glass panel and hit the play button.

Beep. "Hi, Doug. It's Karen. Got a FedEx package for you. Hope you get home before I go to work." There were no more messages following Karen's. Frowning, he rewound the tape. There were other messages - and presumably whoever had broken into his condo had listened to them.

Beep. "Hey Doug!" It was Joan's voice. "Sorry about that. Took me a bit to ditch that asshole. I assume you've left. This whole thing's got somebody big time ticked off. For sure, Doug, it's all about Schweizerhalle. And there's this guy, Tousignant. I think he-" An electronic warble momentarily clouded her voice. "Christ! Who are these guys? Another trace."

There was a pause of almost ten seconds. Baker could hear Joan's excited breathing. "Holy fuck. It's coming from inside this building. Doug, they're in the building! Fuck, I'm out of here. I'll be in touch pronto."

Beep. "Doug! Me again!" This time the voice was strained, panting as if she was rushing, barely audible over traffic noise. She was calling from a cell phone. "It's this guy Tousignant. He's got to be the key. I-

Baker started violently as there was a tremendous thump and a deafening screeching sound, accompanied by the sound of breaking glass. The last thing he heard was an electronic shriek, then silence. That last sound he'd heard was the cell phone shattering on the roadway. He stared at the machine, only turning it off when Karen's message came on again.

He re-entered the apartment, thinking furiously, and plugged the machine back in. Whoever had broken into his place had probably listened to the messages. He started pacing.

But they hadn't heard the last one. They didn't know he had a package.

The phone rang. As he walked toward it he threw on his holster and jacket. "Yeah?"

It was Barry Nakamura. "Man, I'm glad you're home. We got your message and I figured you'd probably gone to the hospital to visit your friend. We got trouble."

"What?"

"I'm at the hotel. Von Bessel threw a fit and decided she wanted to go out for dinner. Even Rudd tried to tell her it was a bad idea, but I guess she's going a little stir-crazy. Quite the tantrum, I gather. Gold and Collins obviously didn't listen carefully to my briefing about how the two women are under lock and key for the duration. They're corporals, I'm a constable, I don't know. They let them leave before I even got back to the hotel."

Baker swore.

"It gets worse. Remember you asked for photos of those two Arabic-looking Filipinos?"

"Of course."

"Just had a call from CSIS. There are two Filipino employees named Philipe and Jesus at the convention centre. Or should I say, were. They're dead, bodies found stuffed in the trunk of a car in the parkade. Because they're a lot smaller than the guys you described we figure they were killed just for their ID badges. And CSIS has a make on the one with the Jesus nametag. Took them hours but it looks like they've got a positive. A couple of Ay-rabs, like you said."

"Barry, I haven't got all day. Spit it out!"

"An Iraqi spook named Guramda. A major in the army, only - get this - he's attached to the Iraqi spook org, Mukhab-something. I can't pronounce this shit. Anyway, word is this Mukhab-something works for him. Anyway, apparently the guy is big time bad news. CSIS figures they were going to hit Rudd and Von Bessel in the parkade, but hadn't been expecting you to be so sharp. And this Guramda works for another guy, who believe it or not has a Canadian connection. Name's Hamani, connection's a corpse named Dr. Gerald Bull."

Baker tried to recall. "Rocketry, right? Was working on something to blow Israel to powder?"

"Something like that. Anyway, that's why CSIS has so much stuff on these two otherwise shadowy guys. Why do you think?"

"Barry, you can brief me later. Where are Von Bessel and Rudd?"

"Waterfront Cafe in Gastown. We're on our way now. I've called for backup but it's shift change."

"I'm on my way too." As he headed for the door, Baker knew that whoever had tried to kill Joan Chan might also have another crack at Von Bessel and Rudd.

He grabbed the lasagne container, threw it into the old athletic bag in his closet with the electronic sniffer unit, and ran to the door.

NINETEEN

"Dammit!" yelled Baker, viciously punching the steering wheel of the marked cruiser as the vehicle ahead of him failed to pull over. "Are you deaf as well as blind? Get out of the fucking way!"

More than once on the sirens-and-lights dash into town he'd fought to hold back his seething rage at Von Bessel in favour of keeping the Chevy Caprice police special under control. He swung sharply into the left lane, around the gaping idiot in the Toyota Tercel, and entered a sliding turn onto the Seymour Street ramp.

Expertly he wove the screaming cruiser at top speed through the tangled streets of Gastown. Three blocks away from his destination on Cambie and Water Street, he cut the siren and lights and slowed down. In an alley, one street up the hill from the restaurant, he squeezed the big cruiser between two overfilled dumpsters. Out of the vehicle and running, he struggled to set the earphone to the com unit. Depressing the transmitter button he called out, "GLOBE twenty-two, twelve."

"Hey boss. Glad you're here. Where are you?"

"Block away. Anything happening?"

"No. Nice quiet place. We're trying to blend in, but this is a pretty ritzy joint and we don't look like we belong. Which I guess means we stick out. Too bad we didn't have time to plan."

Baker approached the door to the restaurant and swung it open. He stopped by the desk, beside the sign that said, 'please wait to be seated' and sized the place up. He decided he didn't like what he saw.

Located on the south side of Water Street and Cambie, the Waterfront Cafe was well lit. The streetside of the place, save for a bare brick wall that went from the floor to about waist height, was paned glass. Someone sitting at a streetside table could have their head blown off by a shooter a hundred yards away. The place was big and rectangular, with easy lines of fire from virtually anywhere in the room. There were twenty or so tables, all but three occupied. He had entered through the main door off Cambie Street. To the left were the bar and the door to the kitchen. Straight ahead, a wide, ornate wooden stairway led up to the banquet floor. To the right, half the tables and windows looked out onto Water Street and Gastown's world famous steam clock.

Von Bessel and three others sat at a large table in the far right hand corner of the restaurant, one position away from the Water Street window. The environmentalist was wearing a dark red dress and sitting next to an elegant African woman in traditional head-dress and a caftan of orange and green, whom he recognised as a senior government representative from Nigeria. The two were engaged in animated discussion, Von Bessel oblivious to her surroundings. To Von Bessel's left, facing the kitchen, sat Marta Rudd. She was very pale and kept moving her head in a funny, surveying, bird-like motion she must have picked up from her boss. Baker didn't have time to wonder what it was she expected to see. The fourth member of the party was the Nigerian woman's male executive assistant, who kept trying to engage the distracted Rudd in conversation without much success. Baker's assessment of the situation was that it stunk.

Nakamura sat alone at a window table just inside and to the right of the door, two tables away from the Von Bessel party. Good positioning, thought Baker. Slodnick stood at the bar, on the left-hand side of the restaurant, just paces away from the kitchen door. He was chatting up the bartender and had good visual coverage of the place, although there were a couple of bar tables between him and the main room. O'Neal was nowhere in sight. Guessing that the lanky man with the fierce eyes was stationed in the kitchen, Baker called in for a position check.

"O'Neal? Tell me you're in the kitchen."

"I'll tell you anything you want. Including when supper's ready. Looks mighty good. I love saltimbocca."

"Screw the food. Staff look okay?"

"Yeah. All knew each other for years. No shifty-eyed temps who just arrived today. Waiting for the bread delivery. According to the staff, customers demand fresh-baked and all that."

"So you got an eye on the back door that leads into the alley?"

"Roger."

Baker breathed a bit easier. At least they had a good view of any unfriendlies who might come into the place. He looked again at the open lines of fire. Once they were actually in the place it would be a different story. It'd be like shooting a squirrel trapped in a box. He clicked the transmit button. "When's the cavalry arrive?"

"Another ten to fifteen minutes. GLOBE two says he has his own problems, says Her Highness isn't the only VIP who needs protection around here."

"Roger twenty-two." He knew GLOBE two was Steve Owen. Baker tried to smile at the hostess as she walked up and leafed together a menu and wine list. "Table for one, miss."

"Certainly sir. But the only free table we have left is in smoking. The others are reserved."

"That would be just fine."

She led him to a table four places in from the window. It wasn't ideal, but it would have to do. He positioned himself so he faced Von Bessel's table while still having a decent view of the front door and the kitchen. The woman noticed him for the first time and tossed her arrogant head. I know where I'd like to toss you, thought Baker sourly.

He ordered a club soda but didn't touch it as he waited. He wanted to light a cigarette but didn't do that either. He looked at his watch. Just after seven. About to contact GLOBE two again and urge their imminent arrival, he suddenly saw Slodnick twist his head toward the front door. Following his gaze, he saw a dark skinned man. He was wearing an expensive but baggy cream trenchcoat, a brown fedora and wrap-around sunglasses. His hands were in his pockets. Baker couldn't get a good look at him but he could hear what he was saying.

Smiling easily, with very white teeth, he asked the hostess in some sort of mild foreign accent, "Miss, a table for Mercado?"

She checked. "I'm sorry sir, I have no record of that name."

"Ah. It is a business meeting, arranged by a friend, so perhaps the reservation is under a different name. Would you be so kind as to guide me while I look to see if there is anyone here I recognise?"

"Certainly sir. Please follow me."

Take off the fucking hat and glasses, thought Baker as he unbuttoned his jacket and reached inside. You could hide a howitzer under that coat. Take them off now.

As the man turned there was something about the shape of the head.

Jesus, a.k.a. Major Guramda.

The man's head turned to Baker and froze. Then suddenly everything started to happen at once.

From the corner of his eye Baker saw two men in white cook's uniforms come through the swinging doors with trays of French bread. Each was grasping a loaf with his right hand. O'Neal must be down. Baker pulled his gun and aimed. He saw Nakamura lunge from his chair and heard Slodnick vault a table by the bar. He saw the bulge in the right hand pocket of Guramda's trenchcoat, saw the man remove his sunglasses with his left. . .

Baker fired three times at his easiest targets. The two cooks. He hit the first square in the chest, but the other twisted away so he had to drill him twice. They collapsed to the floor just as he saw the look of absolute terror on Marta Rudd's face as she stared at Guramda.

With his heart in his throat it was clear to him, she knows this guy.

He saw her mouth start to form a word that started with an 'n', but the word she screamed wasn't 'No!', it was 'Nein!'.

Out of the corner of his eye he realised a shadowy figure had stopped on the street, directly opposite Von Bessel's table. Nakamura was spinning, spotted him through the glass.

"Down!" he yelled. "Everyone get down!"

The constable fired through the windowpane as glass exploded all around.

As Baker lowered the arm he had raised to shield his eyes from the chunks of shattered glass that sprayed through the room, he saw the Nigerian woman and her assistant surge to their feet. She was a big woman, partially blocking Guramda's aim. He darted around her. Marta Rudd was also on her feet, arms outstretched, throwing herself in front of Von Bessel. She slipped on something, perhaps a shard of glass, and slammed heavily onto the table, leaving Von Bessel completely exposed. Guramda aimed deliberately and fired three shots.

At Marta Rudd.

The German caught a slug in her lily-pale throat as it instantly grew an ugly crimson blossom, like some sinister liquid corsage. The second drilled her right through the forehead, a smoking little grey hole. The third took out her right eye and blew off the back of her head, spattering Von Bessel with coin-sized drops of bright red arterial blood. The Nigerian and her assistant hit the floor.

Baker fired twice at Guramda and thought he hit him right between the shoulder blades. He saw the Iraqi duck and spin. But instead of falling he grabbed the hostess and pulled her to him, his gun at her temple. Her body shielded the assassin from Baker's fire. He saw Nakamura throw a terrified patron to the floor and aim at the major's profile. Spinning, Guramda snapped off two shots that caught Nakamura in the thigh. He crashed onto a table and slid to the floor in an explosion of porcelain and crystal.

Desperately Baker thought, guy's a sharpshooter. I've fired five shots and so has he. Four left apiece. He shouted at Slodnick but the patrons writhing on the floor were screaming and he couldn't make himself heard.

There was still a man on the sidewalk outside, rising from his crouch below the brick section of the wall. Nakamura had missed. The lone figure threw open a long duster coat and levelled a sawed-off shotgun directly at Baker. He dived, snapping off two shots as a booming blast shredded the wooden table he had rolled under. Desperately trying to steady himself before the next hail of shot, he heard three crisp explosions. It was Slodnick. He saw the bullets pluck like fingers at the major's voluminous trenchcoat but it looked like all he'd hit was fabric. The Iraqi was wearing body armour. Von Bessel was nowhere in sight.

From his crouch Baker could see Guramda snap off a shot at Slodnick to make him back off, still jerking the whimpering hostess back and forth to cover himself from the two Mounties.

Two bullets left. He prayed the major wasn't counting. He fumbled in his jacket for another clip, knowing instinctively there wouldn't be time. Have to go for a headshot. He thought, I've got to get myself a bigger gun.

"Respect for human life is a wonderful thing, Sergeant Baker. Wouldn't you agree?"

Startled that the man would know his name, Baker hesitated for one vital second. Seeing movement out of the corner of his eye, he swivelled. It was a patron scrambling for the kitchen door. He swung back.

Too late.

Guramda, dragging the girl like she was stuffed with straw, was in a full run toward the gaping window. Just as he reached it he gave the girl a savage shove, sending her staggering into Baker. Then he vaulted the brick wainscoting and the splintered shards of glass. The man on the sidewalk loosed another blast as Baker fired his last two bullets. One hit the man in the chest and he staggered, but didn't fall. Body armour too.

Then they were gone. Baker held the sobbing hostess, mechanically muttering words of comfort. "It's okay, it's over."

I think. Had they got what they'd come for? Marta Rudd? Not Marie Françoise Von Bessel? Or had Rudd been the primary target and Von Bessel some sort of extra? It just didn't make sense.

Leaving the hostess, he crawled over to Nakamura, reaching him just as Slodnick did. "Steve," panted Baker, "check on O'Neal." Slodnick darted off to the kitchen.

"Stay down!" roared Baker, to keep the civilians on the floor.

Barry's eyes were open, his pupils widening in what Baker knew was shock. Quickly he checked the wound. Just missed the femoral artery. He ran his hands over his partner's body. Some nasty cuts from the flying glass, but otherwise he seemed to be okay. But his breathing was shallow, panting. He tore off his tie, wrapped it around the top of Nakamura's thigh and pulled it tight to stanch the bleeding.

"Hey Barry."

The young constable's eyes slid over to him. "Yeah?"

"You're a lousy shot."

The cop gave a forced grin. "That's what my mama always said. Barry, you're a lousy shot."

It was a feeble joke, but at least the kid's brain was still functioning. "You're going to be okay," said Baker. He knew that if he were too comforting Nakamura would think he was in real bad shape. "Flesh wound. I've seen worse mosquito bites."

Nakamura nodded and his mouth twitched in another attempt to smile. Baker thought, where the hell is Slodnick? Just then the bullfrog-voiced man slid across the floor. "O'Neal's going to have an Olympic record concussion, far as I can tell, but they didn't kill him. Rest of the staff is unconscious. Must've used gas or something."

Slodnick looked down at Barry, then up at Baker, who half-closed his eyes and nodded. The gruff guy got the message. Again he looked down at Nakamura. "You still alive, samurai? Shit, I thought the whole point to kamikaze is, you don't survive."

Baker motioned for Slodnick to take over, then slid across the floor to Von Bessel's table, dreading what he would find there. From the remains of Marta Rudd's destroyed face, a single opaque blue eye stared at him like a searchlight someone had forgotten to turn off. The force of the three gunshots had thrown Rudd's body on top of Von Bessel's. He hadn't seen the environmentalist get hit, but then bullets were funny things. Then he realised she was alive, but curled up in a foetal position and moaning. He shook her shoulder.

Still no sirens. Where were they? He remembered his briefing. Any kind of trauma, back to the psyche ward. He gritted his teeth. Not on my watch. He shook her violently, finally standing and heaving her to her feet. He felt her as she tried to bat his hands away. Not wounded. She was drenched in Rudd's blood, but it was hard to tell unless you were real close, because of the dark red dress. She was trembling violently.

Baker looked over at Slodnick, holding Nakamura. He could read the man's eyes, could see the urgent message there.

No sound of squealing tires. No getaway.

They were still outside, probably reloading. When they heard the sirens, they'd have to either run or attack the restaurant again to finish the job. Baker could tell Slodnick read the situation the same way he did. The gruff cop started reloading his weapon, tilting his chin at Baker in an unmistakable signal. Baker nodded.

"C'mon," he said to Von Bessel. "We have to get out of here."

"Quoi?" She sounded confused.

"The men who killed Marta knew you were here. How could they know? Did you tell anyone you were coming to this restaurant? Did Marta tell anyone?"

The woman shook her head. "Just the police," she said vaguely. Then her legs buckled.

Baker dragged her toward the kitchen, his mind racing. Must get out of here before they regroup. His car was in the alley, but a block away - a block away, uphill. And they'll have to regroup before the GLOBE two team arrives. If they knew Von Bessel would be at this restaurant tonight, after a spur of the moment decision, they might know a lot more, too. If they were waiting, where would they be waiting?

He halted at the swinging doors, his arm around the limp Von Bessel. They'd think he'd take her out the alley exit. He hauled her toward the Cambie street front entrance. There, he ejected the used clip and rammed another home, tossing the empty container on the floor.

Just before he threw open the door, he slapped her face hard, until she started to struggle. "That's right!" he hissed. "Salope! You hear that? Vouz êtes une Salope!" She was thrashing now, enraged. He was surprised, afraid that he'd been going to have to carry her.

"Allez!" he directed, throwing open the door. The next moment they were running down the sidewalk.

TWENTY

In an instant Baker knew he'd been right.

Behind him he heard the rapid patter of running steps coming from the alley, then a blast and the twang of lead on concrete, inches from his ear. He dodged, pulling the woman around the corner just as the glass panel beside them turned milky and exploded.

As he heard pursuing footsteps also round the corner, he turned suddenly around and fired two shots at the men behind him. He aimed at their feet because of the body armour, knowing that a ricochet from the pavement doubled his chances of hitting something. They dodged behind a parked car.

Baker had never seen such a small woman run so fast, except for Joan Chan. He thanked the gods that Von Bessel, with her busy schedule and hours of speeches, favoured sensible flats instead of ankle-shattering stiletto heels. He grabbed her by the hand and dodged into traffic as tires screamed and voices yelled.

They ran across the well-lit common square of the Granville Place office tower. Baker knew where he wanted to go and pushed Von Bessel toward Howe Street. They dashed past the gawking outdoor patrons of Forrester's restaurant. Baker heard one man shout, "Hey honey, look, they're making a movie!"

At the far end of the terrace they reached the head of a steep flight of stairs that led down to the sidewalk level of the Howe Street causeway. Von Bessel stumbled and almost pitched headlong over the side of the concrete railing until Baker caught her. They stumbled down the stairs, Baker half-carrying the small woman, dreading the thought of being shot in the back. He could hear the patter of running feet and knew the two attackers were gaining quickly. At the bottom of the steps, Baker slung Von Bessel over his shoulder like a sack of cement and ran heavily across the wide expanse of concrete separating them from the Waterfront Centre Hotel. Only one way out. The escalator down to the Sky Train station. He plunged down the escalator, two steps at a time. Just as he reached the passageway he heard the whine of a ricochet near his ear as a slug hit the stainless steel framework of the escalator well. He felt something like a hard punch in his lower back. Turning with difficulty, he twisted his gun arm back and snapped off a shot at the two figures descending pell mell down the moving staircase. The shotgun-toting attacker grabbed his leg and fell headlong. Guramda had to leap over the falling body to avoid tripping, but twisted his ankle and fell, crashing down the stairs, his gun flying.

There was a train at the platform about to depart, its doors open, caution alarms ringing. Baker threw Von Bessel into a near empty car and spun. At the sight of the gun the other four passengers in the car hit the floor. The doors swished shut.

Baker crouched, one hand holding his gun, the other on top of the woman's head to keep her down. Guramda was running heavily beside the accelerating train. He fired at the compartment and a hail of shattered Plexiglas imploded into the car. Baker aimed carefully through the hole. Head shot. Just as he pulled the trigger the train jerked and the shot went over the major's head. Baker staggered, trying to keep his feet. Guramda now had his hand through the gaping hole in the door, his hand clamping around the frame, trying to steady his gun as he ran faster and faster to keep up with the train.

From his crouch, rocking from the motion of the train, Baker fired blindly. The bullet slammed into the door, loosening the stainless steel post of the frame the Iraqi was holding on to. Suddenly it gave way, and the major disappeared. Baker looked back and saw him tumbling along the concrete.

Baker sat down on the seat and looked at Von Bessel. She was staring blankly at the shattered window, her chestnut hair swirling from the wind that whipped through the gaping hole. He looked over at the four wide-eyed commuters lying on the floor as he holstered his gun. "I'd stay down, if I were you." They stayed down.

Baker waited three stops, then hauled the trembling environmentalist out of the car. They took the escalator up to street level. At the Dunsmuir street crosswalk, while they waited for a break in the traffic, Baker thought hard. He had to get help, and soon. He had to hand Von Bessel over to Steve Owen.

Upon reaching the other side they moved west toward the main entrance of Vancouver Community College. "GLOBE two, GLOBE twelve come in." Nothing. He tried again, receiving only static. He twisted the communications unit forward in its sling. The aluminium face and its underlying circuitry had been obliterated, replaced by a shiny, mushroom-shaped bullet indent. He shoved the unit back into place and felt just above his right kidney. There was a hole in his jacket. He felt cold sweat break out on his face.

They entered the foyer for the college and walked toward the bank of telephones. He shoved a quarter into the slot and dialed the number of the communications room at E Division.

"RCMP Communications. Corporal Chalmers speaking." Baker recognised the voice of the man who had been on duty the previous evening.

"Chalmers, this is Staff Sergeant Baker, assigned to VIP."

"Jesus Christ," said Chalmers. "Half the Force is out looking for you."

"Look, I need to talk to somebody. Wattington around?"

"No. He's on his way to the restaurant. What the hell happened out there?"

"Tell you later. Where's Steve Owen?"

"He's at the restaurant. I'll patch through a feed. Hang on."

While he waited, Baker scanned the area. Von Bessel still looked dazed. At least she wasn't talking.

"Baker, where the hell are you?"

"I'm at VCC on Dunsmuir. I need a pickup and I need it now."

"What was with the gunfight at the OK 0Corral?"

"Shut the fuck up and listen," snarled Baker. "Get a cruiser and officers over here now!"

"How's Von Bessel?"

"Drenched with Marta Rudd's blood and blank-eyed, but otherwise unharmed. How are Nakamura and O'Neal?"

"They'll be all right. Go out into the parking lot and I'll have men there pronto."

Baker hung up. He took Von Bessel by the shoulder and directed her outside. The two of them sat down on a bench and it was only then that he felt the strain his legs, they were like lead. After three minutes he heard the distant sound of a police siren. Sweetest sound I've heard in a long time, he thought. He heaved himself and Marie Françoise upright and waited. Approaching from the east, along the Dunsmuir viaduct, he saw the flashing blue and red lights of a cruiser. Suddenly he heard the sound of squealing tires behind him. He turned to see a dark blue Chevy four door skidding into the parking lot some twenty yards away.

With slow disbelief he saw Guramda get out of the car.

"What the hell!" Baker drew his gun, trying to remember how many bullets he had left. He fired twice and the major ducked behind the open door of his car. Then suddenly the cruiser was there, screaming to a halt between him and the Iraqi. Baker fired again to get the officers' attention, pointing toward Guramda's car. In an instant the two uniformed officers were out of the vehicle and aiming their Smith and Wesson 9mil automatics. He saw the assassin reach into the vehicle and bring out a machine pistol.

Baker pulled Von Bessel away from the bench and ran to the line of Yellow Top taxis parked in front of the College. Protecting the VIP was his job, and he had to get her out of here. He reached the last car in the line, pulled open the back door and threw her in. As he closed the door he yelled at the wide-eyed Sikh cabby, "Go!"

The driver, seeing the gun in Baker's hand and the impending gun battle outside, needed no further encouragement. The vehicle shot out of its space and smoked down the driveway.

TWENTY ONE

An hour later, after three changes of cabs, a dash across a park and down several alleys, they reached Baker's Granville Island condominium. Von Bessel had started to weep from fatigue and fear.

Baker stopped at a pay phone and dropped a coin into the slot. Refusing to say where he was and intent on keeping the conversation as brief as possible so they couldn't do a trace, he asked about the outcome of the gun battle at the Dunsmuir bus terminal. Both officers dead, Guramda fled. He slammed down the receiver and grabbed the woman by the arm.

As soon as they got onto the elevator Von Bessel fainted. He had to slap her to bring her around. Gun drawn, he eased the door open as quietly as he could and they crept into the apartment. It was just as he had left it. Putting his finger to his lips, he left her on the sofa and tiptoed to the bedroom. He checked the athletic bag in his closet. The Tupperware container and the hard drive were still there. He took out the electronic sniffer and looked at the settings, selecting the one he wanted. He walked back into the living room and stared at the phone and answering machine. No messages. He placed the sniffer next to the phone and initialised the masking sequence. The white noise it generated would render the bug inoperative. He knew the sniffer's batteries were fresh and it could mask the bug for hours. If CSIS or anyone else were listening in, they wouldn't hear a thing and they'd presume the apartment was empty.

He contemplated Marie Françoise Von Bessel, her makeup smeared and tears streaking her face. He walked into the kitchen and poured some milk into a saucepan, thinking hard. How the hell had Major Guramda known that the two women would be at the Waterfront Café? He'd obviously had time to outfit two of his men with cook's uniforms and find out the delivery schedule from the Bread Company. How could he have done it so fast? He remembered what Von Bessel had said about the attack, that the only people who had been told they were going to be there were the police. And how had Guramda found them at the college? If the cruiser had arrived thirty seconds later, he had no doubts that both he and the VIP would now be piles of shredded flesh. He remembered what Joan Chan had said in the second phone message: 'It's coming from inside this building. Doug, they're in the building!'

Someone on the inside, someone at E Division, was working for Guramda.

The milk was beginning to simmer. No way he could take her back there, and no way he could let E Division staff know where he was. He tested the milk with his finger. Scalding hot. He went to the fridge and took the carton, poured more milk in to cool it down. They wouldn't think he'd go back to his own condo. And not knowing that the bug was masked, any listeners would assume he wasn't there. He thought hard. Couldn't put on any lights.

He poured the milk into a mug and walked back into the living room. "Drink this. It'll calm you down. I'll run a bath so you can get cleaned up."

She wiped her eyes with the back of her hand, smearing mascara. She took the mug with both hands and gazed up at him. She looks like a pathetic, abused little girl, he thought.

"Why did you call me that ugly name?"

"What?"

"Salope." In her blank, pitiful eyes tears were welling.

"I had to make you angry," he said gruffly. "No one runs faster or fights harder than someone who's angry. I had to do it. I apologise."

She nodded and sipped her milk as salt tears fell into it.

He ran the bath for her and laid out some fresh towels. He hunted around in one of the drawers to find some of the stuff he knew his wife had left behind - ladies' shampoo, a bar of the honey-almond soap she'd always liked so much, a half-empty container of aloe vera skin moisturiser. There was even a dish with some jewel-like gelatine capsules of bubble bath. He laid the items out and looked at them thoughtfully. What else did women like when they cleaned themselves up? He shrugged, unable to remember.

He walked into the second bedroom and opened his wife's closet to find some clothes. She'd left behind a few items. He found some older jeans and a flannel shirt. They'd still be too big for Von Bessel but that couldn't be helped.

When he went back into the living room she had finished her milk. He guided her to the bathroom and paused at the door, watching her eyes carefully. They were no longer blank, but rather looked at him with a searching, questing gaze he couldn't read. It was a little like the look she'd given him the first night, when she thought he was smiling with approval at her speech.

"Ça va?" he asked.

She nodded that she was okay.

"Toss that dress out the door and I'll get rid of it. I'm afraid it's garbage. Blood is hard to get out of fabric at the best of times and I'm sure it isn't exactly going to bring fond memories anyway." She nodded again as her eyes filled with tears. She closed the door.

He walked back into the living room, wondering if she was going to fall apart like she'd done after the deaths of her husband and son and her parents. He took off his jacket, holster and the dead communications unit and threw them on a chair. Staying away from the front window, in the deepening gloom of evening, he poured himself two ounces of Glenfiddich. He shrugged, then splashed in two more. His lungs still ached from all the running and so, increasingly, did the area over his kidney where the bullet had smashed into the radio. Wearily he sat down on the couch and took a long swallow of his drink. Nothing took the starch out of you faster than almost being shot to death. He tried briefly to formulate some sort of plan but couldn't concentrate. He drained the rest of the scotch, tucked the empty glass between his legs, leaned back and closed his eyes.

Twenty minutes later he started awake. It took him a moment to remember where he was. He looked at his watch. Heaving to his feet, he walked to the bathroom. The door was still closed and he couldn't hear anything.

"Madame? We have to get out of here. Madame?"

There was no response. He hesitated. Christ, had she drowned? Praying that she hadn't locked the door, he twisted the knob. It opened and he stuck his head in, prepared to beat a hasty retreat.

The mirror was steamed up but the bathtub, still filled with bubbles, appeared to be empty. It took a moment before he saw her, curled up in the space between the tub and the toilet bowl, a towel wrapped clumsily around her shivering body. Her chestnut hair was still wet and looked black. She was staring blankly into space, rocking aimlessly back and forth as huge silent sobs wracked her slim frame.

Back to the psyche ward. He had to snap her out of this fast before she descended too deeply into despair. Swiftly he entered the room and took her by the arms to lift her to her feet. He realised she was naked under the towel, but there wasn't anything he could do about that at the moment. She was limp in his arms. Supporting her with one hand at the base of her spine, he tipped her head back and gazed intently into her eyes. They were haunted pools of overwhelming sadness.

Slowly her eyes cleared as she looked at him. She raised her hand and stroked his cheek. "Vaillant," she whispered. Baker struggled to remember what the word meant. Brave?

She cupped his face with both hands. "Protecteur." Her mouth closed over his. As he felt her tongue against his teeth he felt the slow surge of desire. She pulled his head down and kissed his eyes. Suddenly her arms were around him, clutching with surprising strength as her lips again found his. Her skin smelled sweetly of honey-almond soap, and he remembered how much he had always liked the scent. He cupped her buttocks with his big hands and drew her towards him. The towel fell to the floor and he felt her hand inside his shirt. He could feel her hard nipples against his chest as her hips surged at the hard muscles of his thigh. Effortlessly he picked her up and carried her into the bedroom.

He was startled by the clawing violence of her lovemaking, had to restrain her, make her slow down. When she finally adjusted to his rhythm, their bodies made sensual arabesque after sensual arabesque.

Later, she lay in his arms, her ragged breathing slowly deepening. Baker rose on one elbow to gaze into her face. She was flushed but frowning, looking thoughtful. Christ, she's a small woman, he thought. He stroked her face gently with a big hand. "I wasn't too rough, was I?"

"Non," she whispered. "It was wonderful." She turned her head to look at him as if she was puzzled. "I had no idea it could be gentle like that."

What on earth was she talking about? He remembered how violent she had been at the beginning. Was she used to rough sex? She didn't seem the type at all. Once again, he wondered if this woman and Marta Rudd had been lovers. And what sort of lover had her husband been? Before he could formulate any kind of answer to this riddle, she pulled his head down and kissed him gently. "Thank you."

"You're welcome," he said, feeling both proud and a little foolish. She lay back and closed her eyes.

He waited until she was asleep before quietly easing out of bed, throwing on a robe and padding into the living room. The moonlight was coming through the big picture window so he could see what he was doing. He poured himself a scotch and sat on the sofa, deep in thought.

Suddenly his head snapped up. What was that noise? He looked over at the clock. Just after two a.m.

Then he heard it again. A creaking sound just above his head. He looked over at the kitchen skylight and saw a shadow fall across it. He tiptoed over to his holster and pulled out his gun. Moving to the wall, pressed tightly against it, he watched the skylight but saw nothing. He slid to the side window and looked down at the courtyard, three floors below. A quick scan showed a man standing in the shadows by the service entrance.

Baker darted to the big picture window. It overlooked the man-made marina harbour. Beyond it, to the west, lay False Creek and English Bay. Between his building and the marina was a string of businesses, a pub and a trendy restaurant, Monk McQueens. Scanning the alley below, he spotted another shadowy form for sure. Squinting, but unable to tell for certain, he thought there might be at least one more man outside, watching the building. And the man on the roof. Three or four. Too many.

He thought furiously and made up his mind. He crept over to the sniffer unit, still sitting next to the phone, still masking the bug. He turned it off and lifted the receiver, rapidly dialing a number he knew by heart from too many lonely nights in this place.

"Panagopolis Pizza," answered the sleepy voice on the other end. "Can I help you?"

He spoke as softly as he could. "Yeah. I want to order a couple of large number sixes, thin crust, double cheese." He gave his name, phone number and address and waited until the man hung up.

Into the supposedly dead receiver he hissed, "You guys get that? I've been here for hours, you stupid bastards. And I've got your fucking hard drive. Now company's coming and they prefer crashing through windows to coming in by the front door, if you get my drift. Time to play cavalry, assholes." He hung up and turned the masking device on again. He hoped they weren't napping and assumed they must have a unit nearby, probably a van.

He darted into the bedroom and cupped his hand over Marie Françoise's mouth as she started awake and began to struggle. "It's me!" he hissed. "There are men with guns outside. We have to leave. Get dressed!"

She scrambled out of bed and fumbled for the clothes Baker had laid out on the chair hours earlier. He threw on a pair of jeans, a white cotton shirt, a heavy hiking jacket and a pair of Nikes. He fetched his holster and put it on. He rummaged for the Tupperware container, wrinkling his nose at the increasingly pungent smell it emitted. From the kitchen he took a big ziplock freezer bag. Stuffed the container into it and sealing it tight, he tucked the bag into the voluminous inside pocket of his bulky jacket, the one with the Velcro fastener. He grabbed his daypack and shoved in a heavy sweater, a spare shirt, some socks and underwear. After a moment's thought he tossed in several packs of cigarettes from the carton in the closet. Then he moved around the wall to the dresser. He took his car keys, as well as those for his boat and the ones for Karen's apartment across the hall. She'd given them to him several weeks earlier when she'd gone skiing and asked him to water her plants. He'd forgotten to give them back before going to Belize, and was now grateful for his absentmindedness. He stuffed five spare clips of ammo into his jacket and then took his old .38 long nose service revolver and a box of shells.

Moments later they were crouched by the front door. He peered through the peephole. Nothing now, but it wouldn't be long. He slipped the bolt and opened the door. He pushed Marie toward Karen's door as he closed and locked his own. They darted across the hall and in an instant they were in Karen's apartment. The place was pitch black, but Baker knew the layout. Still gripping her hand, he pulled her down the hall to the first door on the right and felt for the light switch.

It was a small spare bedroom. Baker went directly to the closet, hoping it was still there. It was. Karen liked climbing and she'd asked his opinion of this when she bought it. He tore open the blue bag and pulled out a bundle of yellow polypropylene rope and blue plastic doweling. Spreading the rope ladder out on the floor, he tied the loose ends to the bed frame, then pushed it so it was braced against the wall, directly below the window.

Marie Françoise crossed her arms. "Non!"

Baker looked at her. "Oui!" Despite the situation, he had to smile. In the baggy denim pants and flannel shirt, with the short hair and petulant expression, she looked like a sixteen-year-old being told she couldn't go to the mall. The bright red dress shoes from her bloodied crimson outfit peeped incongruously from the legs of the jeans.

"We are going out through the window, on a side of the building that I'm pretty sure is not covered. Just to be safe, we're going to wait until they attack my empty apartment, CSIS arrives to attack them, or the pizza guy arrives, which will at least confuse the hell out of whoever is creeping around on the roof. Either way, when they go in, we go out."

She tossed her head. "I have had my fill of running for today."

"We won't have to run far," said Baker. "If we can make it to my boat, we can cruise the rest of the way. And I have yet to hear a better plan from you." He opened the window as silently as he could and popped the screen loose, laying it on the floor. He handed her the daypack. "Put this on and get ready. We'll have to move fast."

Reluctantly she moved to the window as he gathered the ladder and arranged it on the sill so a simple push would send it unravelling down the side of the building. He knew it would make a rattling sound but hoped it wouldn't be loud enough to attract attention.

"Once you hit the bottom, make a run for the space between those two buildings, over there." She nodded. He reached inside his jacket and drew out a set of keys held together by a foam anchor fob with the name Valerie written on it with felt pen. "This one is for the first gate. This one here is for the second security fence. The last is for my boat. Remember, it's called the Valerie. You'll find her half way along G wharf." A thought occurred to him. "You familiar with boats?"

"A little. We used to sail on Lac Neuchatel."

"Sail boats? No, this is motor launch. A cruiser." He thought fast. "When you get to the boat, find a pair of pliers in the tool box under the seat in the cockpit. Then go up on deck and cut down the radar detector on the mast." He noted her look of confusion. "It's a square, metal thing with a cable. Cut the cable. Shit, never mind. Just get on board and stay out of sight. Start the motor. Wait for five minutes. If I'm not there by then, untie the boat and go, out that way!" He pointed to the Burrard Street Bridge to the west.

"Where are you going to be?" she asked, an edge of panic to her voice.

"Creating a diversion. I'll have to stay here until I know you've made it. No matter what happens or what you hear, keep going."

She shook her head.

"You've got to do it. We don't have any choice. You understand me?" He cocked his ear. "Wait."

Looking through the peep hole he saw the distorted fish eye image of a man's back as he reached up to ring the doorbell of his own apartment. He carried two pizza boxes balanced on top of his left arm. Baker grinned. It was too bad he couldn't answer his own door and ask the guy how he'd secured entry when Baker hadn't pressed his security button for admittance. Then he saw that in his right hand the man carried a gun, held low so it couldn't be seen from Baker's peephole. Briefly he wondered where they'd obtained the pizza boxes. He crept back to the bedroom and shoved the ladder out. He winced as it rattled against the side of the building. Christ, it sounded as loud as an avalanche. He lifted Marie Françoise into the air and onto the sill. He gripped her hands until she had her feet firmly on the rungs. "Go!"

She scurried down the ladder without the slightest hesitation, and with considerable alacrity. She hit the ground and started running. Baker darted back into the living room and slid open the door to Karen's balcony. Hidden in shadow, he aimed at his own window and fired. In the still of the night the noise was deafening and a cascade of glass shattered onto the concrete.

Baker headed back to the ladder. He could hear shouts and the scurrying of feet on the roof. He heard the splintering crash of his front door being kicked in and heaved himself onto the sill. There were a couple of gunshots from inside the apartment. So much for my home insurance premiums, he thought. Von Bessel was nowhere in sight. Hefting himself through the window, he made his way down the shaky, undulating ladder, still holding his gun.

Halfway down, he heard another volley of muffled shots. Lights came on in a suite above him. "Hey! Hey you! What the hell's going on?" Briefly Baker wondered what it is that some people use for brains. He moved faster, hitting the ground harder than he had planned. He grunted and rolled to get into the cover of the shrubbery. He looked up and saw a head peering down from the roof, staring at the ladder.

Shit. He waited until the head vanished, then started running as fast as he could.

It seemed like only moments before he heard the sound of pursuing footsteps. Man, he thought, I'm getting very tired of being prey instead of predator. Hugging the side of the building, he ducked and sprinted to the last bend.

Around the corner all that was between him and the water was one hundred and fifty feet of open Public Square. He swung around and for the first time got a look at his pursuer. The man was running well and very fast, despite having a radio in one hand and a gun in the other. Baker had seen this sprinting style before. Major Guramda. He aimed and fired. The Iraqi ducked and started to weave from side to side just as another man appeared, joining in the pursuit.

Running with everything he had left, Baker closed the distance towards the water, trying to achieve an optimum combination of speed and broken field running. Sparks erupted as lead made contact with the granite by his feet. Another bullet whined past him.

Ten feet more to go. He could see the water beyond the forty five-degree slope of the granite sea wall. He deftly slipped his gun in his belt, just as his right foot struck the lip of the curbing. He thrust as hard as he could. Airborne, all he could see below him was the shadowy, irregular surface of jagged rock. Would he hit rock or water?

TWENTY TWO

Marie Françoise Von Bessel rushed up to the marina's chain link fence. She looked fearfully over her shoulder, listening to the echoing gunshots from the condominium complex. The single overhead light in the alcove offered only a faint pool of illumination. In an agony of desperation, she fumbled with the keys. Which one was it? The first didn't work but the second did. Entering the fenced cage onto the gangway, she jumped with fright as the gate clanged shut behind her. She dashed for the second gate and once again had to try one key before she found the right one. Slamming the gate behind her, she ran down the gangway, frantically looking at pier numbers designated by large square placards on top of the pilings.

She found G wharf and halfway down spotted an all-white fibreglass cruiser. Valerie. She clambered aboard and threw Baker's daypack into a corner. She moved to the pilot's seat, finally finding the ignition. She inserted the key and turned. Nothing happened. She tried again. Nothing.

Her head swivelled back and forth. It was hard to see. It was hard to breathe. She felt a blood-black tide rising in her heart. The sort of situation she dreaded more than any other on earth - alone, afraid, in the dark, being hunted. She felt a strangled cry beginning deep in her throat and with a convulsive effort managed to make it die on her lips.

Mustn't panic. What was it the sergeant had said? She crashed around the cockpit. It had to be here somewhere. Finally she pulled back the engine cover in the stern. With relief she saw a switch on the cover wall and flipped it. A small light in the engine compartment came on. She was now staring at a confused mess of wiring in the suffocating, oily air.

Again her eyes searched. She spotted a large black and red rotary switch, in the 'off' position. She twisted it sideways to 'on' and immediately a noisy fan whirred to life near the ceiling. Pulling her head out of the small compartment, she noticed with relief that the control panel was lit. Rushing forward, she turned the key. At first, the engine strained to turn over, then caught with a roar.

What was it he had said? Tools, and the radar detector. She searched for the toolbox and threw back the lid. Pliers. Finding it was not half as difficult as cutting the thing off - it was attached with some sort of stainless steel cable. She could feel two blisters forming on the palm of her tiny hand. She clenched her teeth and gripped the pliers as hard as she could. Just as the cable parted she heard it.

A faint voice. Baker's voice.

"Go! Marie, for Christ's sake, go!"

Her head snapped around, searching for the sound of the voice. She saw a shadowy figure stumbling along the next pier. It was the sergeant. He was gesturing wildly back the way she had come. She turned to look down the slip. Two men, racing down the decking directly toward her, guns drawn. Dropping the pliers, she jumped from the command bridge to the moorage slip. She flung the aft docking rope off the bollard, then ran to the stern line. With a running jump, she was back on board, staring at the control panel. What to do?

The two running figures were now almost halfway along the pier.

Unfamiliar with the controls, she pushed the throttle lever down hard. The boat shot forward, out of the narrow confines of the slip, straight towards the sharp prow of a ketch moored directly across. In a fevered attempt to avoid the looming mass, she spun the wheel to the left, sending the rapidly accelerating vessel into a wild, pitching turn, out into the channel between the piers, but not before tearing the end off the slip with a deafening screech.

On her right, the two running figures were now almost level with the Valerie. She saw one aim his gun and she ducked as the muzzle flashed. The vent window beside her head exploded. From below the control console, she peered out of the windshield and saw that she was nearly at the end of the pier, rapidly approaching the opening to the main channel.

The two men were now running directly parallel to her, so close she could clearly see their dark faces, greenish in the light of the mercury vapour lamps along the pier. With a spike of dread, she recognised the man who had killed Marta in the restaurant. Panicked, she tugged at the wheel, sending the large craft into a sickening right hand turn that slammed it against G wharf. Both men fell, one into the water. But Guramda was instantly on his feet, aiming directly at her.

She saw him suddenly flinch. She turned to her left and saw Baker bounding along the adjacent pier. He was firing repeatedly. She turned back and saw the Iraqi go down on one knee and aim…

TWENTY THREE

Baker's body hit the water, his feet mere inches from the rock-water interface. His heart spasmed in the cold, but something deep within his shocked brain commanded him to stay under the icy water and kick, no matter what.

Struggling against the bulk of his clothing he pulled forward and down into the black watery void. The rippling blur of a bullet's trail spiralled across his vision. He kicked and pulled with every sinew of his being. His lungs burned. Why the hell do I smoke so much? The pain was excruciating, but he knew he was heading towards the wharf, twenty feet ahead. His eardrums squeezed into his skull as he dove down further.

Bullets made foaming white trails as they snaked past him. He knew that soon he would have to surface or let the air out of his searing lungs and inhale seawater. With white bullet snakes whirling and pirouetting past him, Baker swam until his hand hit a post. He realised he was below the concrete wharf. Surging out of the water, he gasped in a huge breath. His lungs burned so intensely he thought he could never get enough air in them to make the pain go away. His temples felt as though they would explode and the cold was already numbing his limbs. He shook his head and cleared his eyes. His two pursuers were nowhere in sight. Seconds later, still short of breath, he kicked off from the wharf towards the nearest pier, less than a dozen yards away.

Exhausted and numbed, he grasped clumsily for a bumper hanging over the stern of a small sailboat. So heavy were his limbs that he had to try three times. So, he thought, this is how people drown. With trembling arms he hauled himself up.

He knew he must be close. His eyes searched. He located the Valerie, at the next pier. With relief he knew Von Bessel must be there, because the lights were on in the cabin and he could see blue exhaust from the motor.

Then it hit him. Christ, it's three in the morning. The only people around were himself, Von Bessel and their pursuers. He saw near the darkened gate a sleek figure gliding over a fence, and a second one at the gate scanning the wharf in front of him.

He leapt from the deck of the small sailboat and landed heavily on the pier, feeling the cartilage in his left knee crack. He ran, cursing his frozen limbs and heavy soaked clothing. He shouted, "Go! Marie, for Christ's sake, go!"

He pulled his gun from his sodden waistband and fired blindly at the man nearest the Valerie. He saw his boat roar from its mooring, hit the dock, the shock sending one man into the water. But the other crouched and aimed.

He was five feet from the end of the pier. The Valerie was bucking through the water after its collision with the wharf, temporarily swamped with waves.

Now or never. He dived.

TWENTY FOUR

Vancouver Island, March 18

The view of the house from the rocky beach was spectacular. Perched at the top of the steep cliff amongst arbutus trees, the dwelling was essentially two buildings, each with moderately peaked roofs and joined by a low lying, flat roofed central area, an interesting combination of a modern-day, West coast castle and Swiss chalet.

The bow of the rubber inflatable dinghy slipped up on the beach as Baker shifted the oars. Marie Françoise jumped nimbly out onto the wet rocks, pulling the craft further up on shore. Baker clambered out and hauled it the rest of the way onto the rocky beach. He stretched to loosen his aching muscles as he looked around. Underneath his still wet clothes he could feel his skin itch from the salt water.

He had made it to the Valerie just as Von Bessel had finally figured out how to work the throttle. Hanging onto the side of the craft, he had waited until Guramda's gunfire had died away before hauling himself on board. When he could finally get his breath he had noted the bullet holes in his beloved cruiser. He had stripped off his wet clothes so they could dry, changing into the sweater and shirt he'd placed in his daypack. Just in case, he had waited for more than half an hour before finally turning on the running lights. Still shivering with exhaustion, he had wrapped himself in a scratchy wool blanket and directed Von Bessel as she steered the craft toward their destination.

And now they had arrived.

Baker led Marie Françoise Von Bessel to the steep set of rustic stairs that switchbacked up the terraced concrete retaining wall to an expansive wooden deck enclosing three sides. At the top of the stairs there was a small swimming pool that nestled against the foundation of the house. Partially overhanging the pool were the supports for the living room, just underneath the picture window with a panoramic view of the ocean. The house looked as if it were bolted to the cliff.

Von Bessel gasped at the westerly view of Patricia Bay, as Baker grinned. It had had the same effect on him, the first time he'd seen it. There was a clattering sound on the big cedar deck and a huge golden retriever bounded up to greet them. Baker grabbed the scampering beast and gave it a friendly bear hug, getting his face bathed in return. "Dave, you slobbering old bugger!" He smiled at Von Bessel. "Probably the most useless guard dog in the world, but he sure is happy."

From the garden at the north side of the house he heard enthusiastic yelps. "Uncle Doug! Monica, its Uncle Doug!" yelled a boy's voice. Baker noted that his British accent was starting to fade, although it was still pretty thick.

A skinny, dark haired six-year-old tore across the deck, followed by a redheaded girl of four. They scrambled at Baker and he lifted them both into the air. "Hey guys! How are you?"

"Great! We didn't know you were coming to see us."

"I didn't know myself until last night," answered Baker. "You remember your manners?" The boy's eyes shifted shyly to Von Bessel. "Hello, my name is Peter. Are you a friend of Uncle Doug's?"

Marie Françoise smiled. "Oui. Yes. I am pleased to meet you, Peter. And this must be Monica," she said to the little girl nestled shyly under Baker's chin.

Baker asked, "Peter, why aren't you in school today?"

"Dad said mama and us are going to Victoria to see Nanna and Poppa for a few days." Baker nodded. He had used the radiotelephone on the boat to call Colin Stewart, waking him up in the middle of the night. He'd given him a terse briefing. Obviously it had alarmed the former SAS man enough that he was getting his wife and kids out of harm's way.

"Where are your mom and dad?"

"Packing the car. Come on, we'll show you!" Peter turned and sped across the deck, his sister scampering close behind. The two adults followed the children across the deck and around the side of the house. They went through the side garden and up to the ivy-infested carport that jutted from the house.

As they arrived, Peter was leading a vivacious raven-haired woman around the side of a late model Volvo station wagon. She saw Baker and a broad warm smile spread across her face. In an Oxfordshire accent she exclaimed, "Douglas Baker! Oh, it is good to see you again!"

"Hello Claire." He strode up and gave her a warm embrace. A stranger wouldn't have been able to tell, but he could - the stiffness of her body gave it away. I'm really sorry, he thought. He knew how relieved she had been when Colin had finally retired from his uniquely dangerous profession, first as a police investigator with Scotland Yard and then later, with Her Majesty's Special Air Services. And now he had dragged the old anti-terrorism master back into the muck. Silently he vowed that he would make it up to her.

He introduced the environmentalist and Claire extended her hand. "Madame Von Bessel. I'm very familiar with your work. Welcome to Vancouver Island."

"Merci, Madame Claire."

"So where's the old man?" Baker inquired.

"Skulking," came a rich, deep, English voice. Baker turned to see a wheelchair swivel around the front of the vehicle. He tried not to let the shock show in his face. Joan Chan had said that he wasn't doing well, didn't have a lot of energy, but he hadn't been prepared for the haggard man he now saw. The only thing healthy about him seemed to be his voice. His clothes hung loosely on his bony frame and there was pain behind his eyes.

At the time Colin left Scotland Yard and his secondment to #23 Brigade of SAS in Northern Ireland and the Middle East, he chose to follow the academic route, doing postgraduate work at the University of Aberdeen, the unofficial centre for anti-terrorist studies in the western world. With a young family, he'd come to Canada after he's been crippled and taken a Ph.D. program at the

University of British Columbia. To supplement his pension and his scholarship income from the Canadian government, he did contract analysis work for local police forces, the RCMP included.

Baker knew that the IRA bomb, which had deprived him of the use of his legs, had damaged his spinal cord and that he suffered from chronic pain that for some reason couldn't be treated. And because Colin said painkillers made him feel stupid, he almost never used them, preferring to live in constant discomfort.

Now those eyes were looking at him and, as always with Colin, he had the feeling the man was reading his mind. Baker stuck out his hand. "Caught any bad guys lately?"

Colin smiled as he gave a firm shake. "Alas, no. Then again, the day is young." His eyes were appraising and Baker knew he was impatient to find out the whole story. "How is Joan?"

"Same as before, far as I know. Bad shape."

Colin nodded. "I called the hospital this morning. Her condition is unchanged."

Colin spun the chair and lifted his hand to Marie Françoise Von Bessel. "Enchanté, Madame. Bienvenue au Canada, et à notre maison."

She smiled with genuine pleasure. "Mais non monsieur, le plasier c'est tout le mien. You have a beautiful home. Thank you for helping us."

"Je vous en pris, Madame."

Colin spun back to Baker and reached inside his green Harris Tweed jacket. He pulled out two black 31/2-inch floppy disks and held them up as if he had just performed a conjuring trick. "These arrived about five minutes ago, courtesy of Federal Express. From our friend. That woman is extremely clever, and when I catch—

Claire interrupted smoothly. "Dear, I'm sure the children will be bored to tears if you start discussing business now. Let's get the car packed up so we can go."

Colin nodded. Baker looked at Von Bessel. The politician in her was wide-awake - she knew a coded conversation when she heard one, and she had also picked up on the fact that Claire was upset.

Fifteen minutes later, the three of them were standing at the end of the driveway as Claire led Dave the dog to the back seat where the children sat, buckling them in. Withdrawing from the door, she gave her husband a long embrace. Straightening, she turned to Baker and hugged him tightly, her embrace turning rigid. He could tell she could feel the gun he wore under his still damp hiking jacket. She whispered, "Take good care of him. Stay safe."

Not trusting himself to speak, he nodded. She got in and drove away.

Colin spun the chair, suddenly all business. "People, we have work to do."

TWENTY FIVE

Once inside the house, in the living room, Marie Françoise Von Bessel sat down in a chair as Baker and Stewart went into the kitchen to make coffee. When they returned, they discovered the environmentalist fast asleep. Baker gently shook her awake and suggested that she go into one of the spare bedrooms and lie down to catch up on her sleep. She gratefully agreed, as the big Mountie found himself wishing he could do the same. But, tired though he was, he forced himself to give Colin a meticulously detailed briefing about everything he knew and everything Joan Chan had discovered. Von Bessel's absence made it a lot easier. It took almost two hours, and at the end of it the anti-terrorism expert's haggard face was alert and thoughtful.

"Doug, you look exhausted. Go get cleaned up, and get some sleep yourself. I'll see if I can get that hard drive up and running and find out what's in those two disks Joan sent me."

Baker fetched the plastic ziplock bag from his hiking jacket and gave it to Colin. The Englishman grinned. "I know Tupperware is versatile, but this is a new one. Thank God you put it in a waterproof bag. Nothing fries electronics like seawater. That was excellent foresight."

"No it wasn't," said Baker wryly. "Pure luck. You'll find out why I did it when you open the container. Do me a favour and let me get out of the room first before you do. You've been warned."

When Baker awoke from a deep and dreamless nap three hours later, Von Bessel was still asleep. He found Stewart working furiously in his office, in the midst of an unmistakable scent.

"Almost there," he said. "I don't think I'm ever going to get the smell of decayed lasagne out of here. While you're waiting, could you do a tour of the perimeter security system? Make sure it's up and running, just in case?"

"Okay." Half an hour later he was back. He threw himself onto the sofa and lit a Camel. "Very impressive. And obviously very expensive. I don't think a centipede could go undetected."

Stewart was still staring at the screen. "I've made a lot of enemies in my life. Being blown up once was enough." He pointed at one of the three monitors he had on his desk. "Let me fill you in with what I've got so far."

"I'm listening," said Baker.

"I started by jury-rigging her hard drive to see if I could get it running on this PC. After twenty minutes of buggering about, I got frustrated and tried an unlikely combination of floppy disk and hard drive together. Lo and behold, the junk on the screen cleared and this series of information windows appeared. Somehow she managed to get all her security codes and compatibility information onto the floppies. In other words, possessing just the two floppies or the hard drive alone is useless. The information she sent can't be read by anyone unless they have both pieces of the puzzle. Really quite ingenious.

Baker's eyes were cold behind a cloud of blue smoke. "So what do we have?"

"Thanks to Joan we now have access to the CSIS encryption protocol database, among other things."

Baker's eyes widened. "What!"

Colin Stewart nodded. "I know. It's like being given the keys to Fort Knox, as well as a fleet of trucks to haul all the loot away. But based on what we discussed, there is sure to be some vital information missing, the sort of thing a computer can't supply."

The big Mountie nodded. "The human element."

"Precisely. I strongly suspect that information can only come from Madame Von Bessel. She may not even know she has it."

"I'm listening."

Colin Stewart went on to explain that the CSIS hard drive was essentially a sophisticated Windows application that allowed simultaneous communication on up to twenty telephone lines. The screen could register any numbers called, the location and duration of the call, and what encryption algorithm program was being used at that moment. With the floppies and hard drive together, he was tied into the Central

Computer and Communications Centre for CSIS located in the Gatineau Hills, just outside Ottawa. At his fingertips he had all the downloading protocols, as well as the encryption devices required for successful communications through a telephone line or satellite link. He also had access to a line trace alarm system. The minute by minute log of Joan's work over the previous few nights showed her making a series of linkups with various data banks around the world. As one contact was established and the data required specified, she would leave the window and initiate another link up. Any incoming information was received and automatically stored by the computer in numerically indexed files she must have set up in advance. Once a contact was established or completed, an icon on the screen would inform her. Without her actually seeing the information, the software saved it until she had time to pull up the file to review the materials.

"I'll have to be very careful accessing the CSIS databases so as not to trigger any alarms. I think I know how to break in without being detected. If I'm wrong, half an army will descend on this place. So, my task is to identify individual files and decipher what each one means," concluded Stewart. "There's one hell of a lot of information in here. She seems to have been receiving data from more than five different data bases simultaneously, all of them in Europe. Plus, she was talking to real people at the same time. I've been able to isolate some of her search trends but nothing definite so far."

"What sort of trends?" asked Baker.

"Well, she appears to have started with media data bases, acquiring material for your briefing - it is of course the logical place to begin, and it's strictly routine. Then bio background on Von Bessel and Rudd. Then she called up information on the Phoenix Foundation. Once again, strictly routine. That in turn led to the reason why the foundation was established in the first place, which was because of the Schweizerhalle fire at the chemical facility. That's when it starts to get very, very interesting."

"Interesting how?"

"She hits a great big wall of silence. Encryption codes start multiplying like mutant cells. Sophisticated ones, too." He pointed at the screen.

Baker peered at lines of code. "Looks like something Einstein might've come up with when he was really cranking."

Stewart nodded. "Almost every piece of information about the fire is locked down tighter than a prison cell block. The question is, why? From what I can tell, the Sandoz Corporation was pretty forthcoming about the whole thing. Who's locked all this stuff up? What is there to hide?"

Baker lit another Camel. "Maybe it's locked up because of the new investigation into the fact that it was terrorism."

Stewart shook his head. "Some of it, yes. But a lot of it is old, locked down years ago. Probably by the people who knew from the beginning that it was arson."

"Keep going."

"You know Joan as well as I do. This kind of thing is like waving a red flag at a bull. As she tried to figure out how to hack all this code, she kept digging around the great wall of silence. That led her to the death of Christian Von Bessel the night of the fire. Because she was now fully alert, she started to notice little anomalies that someone who wasn't alert wouldn't notice."

Baker blew smoke at the ceiling, remembering. "Alcohol, signet ring, dental work and on."

"Exactly. Did she mention the phone bill?"

Baker frowned. "No. What phone bill?"

The Englishman's smile was thin. "All of the media reports, as well as information from the company, state that Christian must have been speeding toward the fire because he'd received a call from someone at the facility telling him the blaze had broken out."

"Go on."

"But according to the phone company records Joan was able to dig up, no call from Schweizerhalle was received at the Von Bessel residence that evening."

Douglas Baker rubbed his face wearily. "I'm getting a brain cramp. What about the assassination attempt in Brussels?"

Stewart sighed. "Haven't managed to get that far yet. I've got at least a week's work here. At least."

"No indication of an Iraqi connection? Or why Major

Guramda would want to kill Marta Rudd?"

"Nothing."

Baker struggled to remember. "On two of the messages I got from her, she mentioned a guy's name, said he was the key. Tousignant, something like that."

Stewart shrugged. "Nothing so far."

The big Mountie stood and started to pace. "She said she was being traced from inside E Division headquarters."

"That has me worried too," said Colin Stewart. "Really worried. Anyone who knows anything about you and Joan is sooner or later going to make the connection that you are both friends of mine. Given my background, it wouldn't take a rocket scientist to figure out where you and Madame Von Bessel might be right now. If the phone rings I suggest neither of you answer it."

Baker grunted. "I agree. Which is why you sent Claire and the kids away. A week, huh?"

"Best I can do," replied the retired SAS man. "While I'm working on this lot, I suggest you focus on the human element. You and the lady get along?"

Baker knew he looked uncomfortable and shifty-eyed but he couldn't help it. "Off and on. Hot and cold."

Colin's eyes narrowed but he decided to let it go. "She has to know something, something she either doesn't realise she knows, or the significance of which escapes her. It's up to you to find out."

"Okay. I'll crank up my world-famous charm."

The Englishman grinned. "That'll be a sight to see. Maybe I'd better give you a hand after all."

They heard footsteps on the wheelchair ramp outside Colin's office and Von Bessel appeared in the doorway, looking tousled and still half-asleep. "Allô?"

"Aha!" said Colin. "It's sleeping beauty."

She smiled. "May I make some tea?"

"My home is your home," replied Stewart. "I wouldn't mind some myself."

The Englishman went back to work as Baker watched. The woman returned carrying a tray with a teapot, cups and saucers, cream, lemon and sugar. As they all helped themselves, Baker explained what it was they were looking at. Von Bessel frowned. "Information about me? And the Phoenix Foundation?"

"Yes," said Baker. "We believe the material in the computer will explain the assassination attempts in Brussels and Vancouver. Also Marta's death." He was about to add 'as well as your husband and child' when Stewart shot him a warning glance and he shut up.

The Englishman sipped his tea. "Perhaps, Madame, you could help us with some of this material. A great deal of it is simply miscellaneous junk. I have no idea why it is in here." Baker knew this was a lie - Joan wouldn't have left junk in the machine. Everything was in there for a reason.

"Of course," she said, moving to the bank of monitors and pointing at a screen. "What are these?"

"Your husband's EuroCard bills. The highlighted entries are for flower deliveries. There are large numbers of them. Was your husband fond of flowers?

"He knew I liked them," she said. "My husband pampered me a great deal." She had a funny look on her face. Some sort of nerve had been hit.

Seeing it, Stewart smoothly changed the subject. "How did you meet your husband?"

"At my father's factory. He was so handsome that I was completely tongue-tied. I was extremely shy and withdrawn at that time. But it seemed every time I turned around he was there, being so very charming. He quite swept me off my feet."

"What kind of a man was he?"

Once again, that odd, dubious expression. Then she looked at Baker, a shadowed glance he couldn't read. "He worked very hard and was always coming up with new ideas. That was why my father approved of our getting married. He worked even harder after he moved to Sandoz. Many nights he would work very late. He also travelled a great deal. We argued a little over it, but he told me I didn't understand the business well enough, which was quite true. But he also tried to make me happy."

Her eyes again flickered to Baker. "He was my protector." He tried to keep his face impassive but knew she could read the surprise there. He wondered if she could read the puzzlement too. Protect her from what?

"I was very easy to please. I think the English word is 'crave'. I craved affection and attention and he showered me with gifts."

Baker remembered Nakamura's description of her father as a ruthless hard-ass. If the guy had been cold and neglectful enough, that might explain the psychotherapy. Then again, Marie Françoise didn't strike him as nearly that fragile. There's a steel spine in that nifty little body, he thought. There has to be something more.

"Once he gave me a miniature crystal swan when I cried after seeing a dead swan in a park. He was always doing things like that, so thoughtful. And he adored our son Daniel. He would have been a teenager now."

Baker thought of her funny looks, the hesitation, the shadowed glances. She wasn't telling everything, not by a long shot. Joan was comatose, Nakamura's wounded leg might mean the end of his career, Marta Rudd was dead along with the two police officers Guramda had slaughtered, and he'd damn near been killed himself. And they didn't have a lot of time. Colin Stewart might prefer to use a scalpel in this kind of interview, but sometimes a blunt instrument was best. He decided to go for broke. "I understand Daniel was a small child."

She stared at him, a small frown on her face. "Not at all. He took after his father. He was tall for his age. Why would you say something like that?"

Baker half-expected Stewart to interrupt, but instead the Englishman sipped his tea, his eyes never leaving Von Bessel's face. "Can you describe your husband's signet ring?"

She tossed her head, visibly getting angry. "He didn't wear a ring. He always said it was dangerous to wear jewellery around the laboratory equipment because it might catch on something. What are you talking about?"

The big Mountie smelled blood and bored in relentlessly. "Did your husband often drive when he was drunk?"

She was turning red and her tiny fists bunched. "He never drank, not even wine. I insist that you tell me the purpose of these ridiculous questions!"

"I assure you, Madame, they are not ridiculous. Had your husband ever had dental work done in the third world? Africa, perhaps?"

Her eyes flicked to Stewart. He was impassive, watching her. The Gaulish temper finally snapped. "I will not listen to my husband and son being the object of some sort of joke!" she screamed.

If she was acting, she was damn good, thought Baker. "Then how do you explain the results of the autopsies on your husband and son?"

The look on her face was a compound of anger, grief and now confusion. "What?"

Baker frowned. "The autopsy results. Surely it must have struck you as odd that-"

He stopped as the slow, brilliant light of understanding dawned in his mind. Mentally he called himself every synonym for jackass he could think of in every language he knew.

She'd collapsed, sobbing and incoherent, the moment she'd heard of the accident, and then had been in the psyche ward for four months. What was it Joan had said? She'd been in a mental institution, babbling at the walls.

She didn't know.

Tears were now forming in her eyes. "I don't know anything about the autopsy results. I was . . . ill. People came and tried to ask me questions and I screamed at them to go away. Once I had recovered, I wanted nothing to do with it. They had been dead and buried for months and I knew if I brooded about it I would kill myself or go mad."

A retching sob tore from her throat. "Why are you tormenting me?" Tears streaking down her face, she turned and ran from the room.

There was dead silence. Baker started to go after her and felt Colin's restraining hand on his sleeve. "Let her have a good cry."

Slowly the Englishman set down his cup and saucer and looked up at Baker. As he said the words, the big Mountie knew that this kind of Anglo-Saxon understatement was the highest compliment he might ever hear. "You know, my dear chap, you really are awfully good."

TWENTY SIX

He watched as she lay in the deck chair, a heavy blanket protecting her from the cool March air. Her limbs were twitching, her head jerking back and forth as tears ran down the pale cheeks. As her agonised moans became louder and louder, he decided to intervene and wake her up.

Colin wheeled forward and reached over to touch Marie Françoise Von Bessel's arm. She started violently and stared at him uncomprehendingly, her body stiff with tension, until she recognised him and suddenly relaxed. He waited until her breathing slowed and she was fully awake, then reached into his green Harris Tweed jacket and pulled out a small packet of Kleenex. Gratefully she took a couple of tissues and dabbed at her eyes.

"Bad dream?" he asked softly.

She nodded. "It's the same one, always."

"About your husband and son?"

She shook her head. "Older than that. From when I was a little girl. About the cellar in our home." Her eyes were despairing pools of pain and suffering.

"Have you ever told anyone about it? It can help a lot if you talk about such things."

Her eyes searched his. Accusingly she said, "Why do you care?"

With the palms of his hands, Colin patted the arms of his wheelchair. "I tend most of the time to be in a lot of pain myself. Sometimes it makes me unreasonable and demanding, short-tempered and impatient. Sometimes I lash out at the people who love me the most, because it hurts so much." He contemplated her as she gazed deeply into his eyes. He knew she could see the pain there. "You too?"

She nodded. "How were you hurt?"

"Bomb. And you?"

She gazed out over the ocean, her eyes were still swollen with sleep and red from weeping. Colin could tell that the events of the last few days had shaken her up badly and she was obviously troubled. She was vulnerable, and if he were to make her reveal herself it would have to be now.

"Marie Françoise?" he prompted gently. "How were you hurt?"

She took a deep breath and came to some sort of decision. "It was in a cellar, of my home in Neuchatel. I was very young. There was a gardener on the estate. He . . . attacked me, sexually. I don't know how to say it." The tears were starting to flow again. Again her eyes searched his, seeing only deep compassion. "He hurt me in my sex. Said he would do more terrible things if I told anyone."

Colin nodded. "I understand." Unlike most Englishmen who tended to be reserved and became uncomfortable at any display of emotion, he was different, generally able to provide empathy - it was a skill that had served him well in his chosen profession. But this time her plight was too much for him. He decided to change the topic. "I apologise for being hard on you earlier today. I had no idea that you were never informed of the autopsy results. Neither did Staff Sergeant Baker. I know he feels badly about it too." He tilted his chin toward the beach, where sandstone cliffs rose abruptly out of the surf.

She saw Baker, sitting on a log, staring out to sea, puffing on a cigarette.

"Why is he so hard and angry? Sometimes I get the feeling that he almost hates me. And yet he can be so gentle-" She stopped awkwardly.

Colin's impassive face gave nothing away. "To begin with, he's a well-educated man. Degree in political science. Fluent in Spanish and German. More than passable French, as you might have noticed. Had a marriage that started out happily but ended in divorce. Wife's name was Renate. Has a teenage daughter he adores, named Valerie, but doesn't get to see very often."

Von Bessel nodded. "The same name as the boat."

"Yes. Had a spectacular start to his career. Then, several years ago, things started to fall apart. For years he had been working on a case involving a Soviet spy, living in Vancouver. The details don't matter, although it involved an assassination attempt on the Russian President during his first visit to Washington. Suffice to say things went very wrong and a spy and a young girl were killed. The press had a field day. He's never been willing to talk much about it and the actual details of the case have been buried in a locked vault someplace. The Americans were very angry and needed someone to blame. He's been shuffled around from place to place on the Force, missing out on promotions. I suspect someone really has it in for him, probably a politician. Baker loathes politicians, so that might account for some of the hostility you've sensed."

She shivered in the cold as the evening dusk gathered.

"There's also the fact that your presence here has resulted in an attempt on the life of one of his closest friends, a Sergeant Joan Chan. It was she who provided the information I'm working on right now." He looked at his watch.

"You are working on it now?"

"Yes. I'm running an encryption defrag program to try to pry open some of those files. It takes an hour to run. I just hope it works. I wish Joan hadn't been quite so good at ciphers."

She stood, gathering the blanket around her and walking to the deck railing. Baker was headed back toward the steep staircase that led to the house from the beach.

"Madame, you're cold. Would you like to go in?"

She nodded. "I will make more tea."

"That would be very nice," said Stewart. He looked again at his watch. "That defrag program should be completed by now."

She turned and looked at him. "Thank you."

The Englishman nodded. "You can thank me best by helping us make sense of the information in our possession. You must be completely honest with us and perhaps face some extremely unpleasant facts." He hesitated, not sure whether to say it or not. He decided. "Perhaps facts as ugly and hurtful as what you just trusted me with. Will you help us?"

At the memory of the 'gardener' and the set of emotions concerning the cellar that were evoked she shivered convulsively, but her voice was strong and determined. "Oui." She hesitated, then came to her own decision. "The flowers."

"What?"

"All the flowers on my husband's credit card bills. I lied about them. They were not for me. I was never fond of flowers, for reasons you have just been made aware of."

Stewart stared at her, nonplussed.

"I was pregnant with Daniel when I found out. Christian had been unfaithful to me right from the beginning. At first, I hated him for it. But what could I do? I loved him and I know he loved me, in his way. He promised me there would be no more women and he really was trying to keep his promise to me. He was very generous to me otherwise." She tossed her chestnut hair, "So you see, Monsieur Stewart-"

"Colin," he said quietly.

"So you see, Colin, I have had to face unpleasant facts before."

"I understand." Stewart pointed his chin toward the door. "You're freezing. Go on in and make some tea. I have to talk to Doug." She opened the door and went inside.

As Baker trudged to the top of the steps, he saw Colin Stewart deep in thought, his haggard head sunk on his chest, his eyes closed. "Colin? You okay?"

The Englishman roused himself. "Yes. I've made my peace with Madame Von Bessel. I suggest you do the same, preferably without shagging her again."

Baker stared at him, slowly reddening. "It just sort of happened. She told you? I meant to fill you in, but there hasn't-"

"A lapse in your professionalism that I find frankly astonishing," Colin said sternly, in his plummiest voice. Then he relented and grinned. "Never mind. She didn't tell me - I guessed. I can't say I blame you. She really is quite a lovely and sensitive woman, who I am pleased to say is now an ally instead of an adversary. Incidentally, we now know why she spent years in psychotherapy."

"We do?"

"Yes, we do. We know other valuable information besides. Didn't you say that Marta Rudd had been raped as a girl?"

"Yeah," said Baker, baffled.

"Then we also know why there was the close emotional bond between Von Bessel and Rudd. It had nothing to do with lesbianism."

Slowly Baker said, "How the hell did you find. . .?"

Stewart spun the wheelchair. "Ask her about the cellar. Just don't expect to engage in a protracted conversation. You're not the only person who's good at this sort of thing. I'll fill you in on the rest later."

TWENTY SEVEN

The three of them sat in Colin's office, drinking tea. Outside the big picture window, the sun was sinking into the ocean.

Baker had just finished briefing Marie Françoise. The woman looked stunned as he asked her the question again. "So the name of the man Joan Chan mentioned, the man she identified as the key to the whole Schweizerhalle fire, a guy named Tousignant, doesn't mean anything to you at all?"

She shook her head. "I am completely sure I have never heard it before. The name means nothing to me."

Baker poured himself some more tea. "Okay. That's it for what we know or suspect. Until Colin can finish hacking Joan's files over the next several days, we don't have much else to go on. Now we must find out what you know. All the information you gave to the CIA and the other intelligence agencies. Where did you get it from?"

She ran her hands distractedly through her hair, clutching her temples as though they hurt. "Over the years since I started the Phoenix Foundation, I became convinced that the Schweizerhalle fire was not the result of negligence on the part of the Sandoz Corporation. It was a very hard conclusion to reach because I wanted them to be at fault. Someone had to take responsibility for the deaths of Christian and Daniel."

She raised her troubled eyes. Baker could see the question there and knew what was coming. It was one of the very few pieces of information he had omitted as he'd briefed her. He had left it out because he still wasn't sure how mentally and emotionally stable she was. And the last thing on earth they needed was for her to go off the deep end now, with so much at stake. He remembered what he had neglected to tell her - Joan's comment: 'I think Christian Von

Bessel and his son Daniel were murdered, but I don't think they died in that car'. He braced himself.

"But if the autopsy results are correct, then who died in the car? There was no question it was Christian's vehicle?"

"Apparently not," admitted Baker. "Serial numbers were found on parts at the scene and I can't even imagine how you'd fake something like that. Was your husband in the habit of lending his car to strangers in the middle of the night?"

She shook her head. "Of course not. Perhaps it was stolen. But if they didn't die in the car, where are they?"

"They're dead," said Baker, watching her carefully. She'd become accustomed to the fact that they were dead, so it was the simplest answer, the one least likely to send her swan diving off the cliffs of sanity. No point at all in mentioning the word 'murder'. "How or why, we as yet have no idea." He pointed at one of the monitors. "It's probably in there somewhere."

Colin had picked up on how dangerous this particular territory was. "Please continue," he said gently. "How did you find out the fire wasn't an accident?"

"It was almost two months ago now when we received positive proof that the fire was intentionally set."

"What sort of proof?" asked Stewart.

"Documents, bills of lading, forged manifests. All delivered anonymously, impossible to trace. It took some time for us to persuade Sandoz to cooperate by opening their records, given the way we had hounded them. But finally they did and we were able to authenticate it all."

"Tell me again about the precise nature of the illicit operation," said Colin Stewart.

Marie Françoise poured more tea. "It appears that the warehouse was being used as a distribution point for some of the chemical precursors used in the manufacture of nerve gas. This had been going on for years, without the knowledge of Sandoz I might add. The chemicals were mixed in with shipments of legitimate agricultural pesticides. The point of departure for the shipments was always the port of Hamburg. Customs officials there had discovered, completely by accident, that a manifest from Schweizerhalle had been forged - something to do with a change in the appearance of the official stamps, I can't remember. Before they could board the vessel and actually obtain samples of the chemicals being illegally shipped, the freighter exploded and everything was destroyed. According to our information, a very large amount of the nerve gas precursor was left at the Schweizerhalle facility with no way of getting it out once the distribution chain was shut down. To hide the evidence and to destroy the chemicals, the fire was set and the warehouse destroyed."

"Who forged the manifest?" asked Baker. "Presumably someone at the warehouse had to certify the shipment's contents and sign for them."

Marie Françoise nodded. "Klaus Staffel. He is, or was, a senior accountant in the logistics department. Had been there for at least ten years. According to Sandoz, he abruptly resigned from the company just before we received proof that the fire was arson."

Stewart's head was nodding up and down. "Resigned just before? That means he was tipped off."

"Yeah," said Baker. "And the tip off could only have come from whoever was making the nerve gas components, his real bosses. Interesting that he'd still be with the company, such a long time after the fire, if the reason he was there in the first place was to hide evidence."

"Unless," said the Englishman, "the reason he stayed was to make sure the evidence stayed hidden. They had to keep an eye on things."

"Bingo!" exclaimed Baker.

"What do you know about this man?" Stewart asked Marie Françoise.

The environmentalist was absently running her finger around the rim of the cup. "Sandoz has run a check on his background, and so have we, but all we have been able to find out so far is that all of the manifests were forged by him. That's the main reason we contacted the CIA and the other intelligence organisations. We simply do not have the capability to evaluate this kind of sophisticated espionage."

"He forged all of the manifests?" asked Stewart.

"Yes."

"So he was the key guy," said Baker.

Von Bessel shook her head. "That's what I assumed as well. But the Sandoz people don't think so. Clever though he obviously was, he was just an accountant. Someone had to take care of the rest of it, someone who actually knew and handled chemicals, had access to the laboratories, the loading docks and trucks, and so on."

Baker turned to Colin Stewart. "Is there any way of finding out whether this Tousignant character was employed by the company? Joan did say he was the key to the whole thing. Maybe he was the guy who took care of the hands-on, non-paperwork stuff."

The Englishman nodded approvingly. "Excellent idea. I'll get on it."

The big Mountie turned back to Von Bessel. "So where is this Klaus Staffel now?"

"No one knows. Completely vanished. According to what we were told, he was actually called 'the Accountant' by the unknown parties making the nerve gas precursors.

Stewart gazed thoughtfully at the ceiling. "So the person or persons unknown who provided the documentation are the same people who decided to throw this Staffel to the wolves. You say you were told this man was the Accountant for the whole operation. Told by whom?"

"Our contact."

Baker raised his eyebrow. "You mean we have a name and a face?"

She shook her head. "Information was provided to us in a very elaborate and secretive manner. There was only one contact person on our side, a man named Heinrich Wiegl. He was one of my people, had been with the Foundation from the beginning. Our director in charge of logistics. We were specifically ordered to use him as our contact."

"Why him and not someone else?"

"Heinrich was legally blind. No matter whom he met with, he

could never provide a description. It was most ingenious. I've often wondered how our unknown information providers could have known enough about our organisation to have even been aware of Heinrich's existence. He was very shy and spent most of his time in our back rooms."

"How was contact made?" asked Baker.

"There were just two formal meetings. The first was in a park in Basel. The second was at a restaurant just outside of Zurich. The instructions were for him to go in alone and unarmed and that there be no attempt to follow or watch. He was to receive instructions there - how, I do not know - which he was to follow to the letter. From what we have been able to determine, he got into a taxicab and that was the last anyone ever saw of him. A few hours later I received an anonymous call telling me that Heinrich was dead and that I was to immediately cease all efforts to investigate the information we had received. By that time, of course, it was too late. I had been interviewed on American television and I had already contacted the CIA. It was out of my hands."

"When was this?" asked Stewart.

"About a week before my speech in Brussels."

"So what we have is the restaurant," said Baker. "What kind of restaurant?"

"Italian. But Turks run it. In Dietekon, just outside of Zurich.

Baker thought of the two Arabic-looking Filipinos. "Well, it's a start."

"You know what this means," said Colin.

"What?"

"It means we are dealing with two separate individuals or groups. The first leaked the information to you to encourage an investigation into the six-year-old Schweizerhalle fire. Why on earth would they do this? I mean, they got away with it! No one as far as I know has ever suspected that the fire was arson. By leaking this information, the perpetrators are running the risk of having you find out who they are and what their ultimate motives are."

"And the second individual or group is trying to stop the first," agreed Baker. His cold grey eyes looked at the Englishman staring sightlessly at the ocean. "Colin, it's a flush."

"I'm inclined to agree."

"What?" asked Von Bessel.

Baker rubbed his face wearily. "They're trying to flush someone out of deep cover. That person is the one who killed Heinrich. They are also trying to stop you."

Colin Stewart looked thoughtful. "How many people at the Phoenix Foundation knew, or had access to, the information you were provided with?"

"Myself, Heinrich Weigel and Marta Rudd."

Baker nodded. "Heinrich and Marta are dead. And someone is trying to kill you."

Stewart's eyes were hooded. "There's something else as well. Whoever caused the Schweizerhalle fire left Klaus Staffel in place to continue hiding evidence or otherwise keep an eye on things. The main pressure to investigate the fire, to make the results public, and to force the creation of a multi-billion dollar fund to clean up the Rhine watershed, came from you and your Foundation. I can't believe they would allow you to operate without having some way of keeping an eye on you."

"What are you trying to say?" she demanded.

Baker interjected. "In Marta Rudd's life there is a gap of four years. A complete void. Once she resurfaced, she was a prostitute and apparently a heroin addict. Then she got involved in left-wing student organisations, including a rumoured connection with the Red Brigade."

"Whose terrorist activities were sponsored by Libya and Iraq, among others," added Stewart. "And whose members trained at special desert camps in the Middle East and North Africa."

Von Bessel was once again getting angry. "This is utter nonsense! I will not hear of Marta being spoken of this way. We were very close and I always felt that I had her complete loyalty. We were very fond of each other."

"I know," said Baker. "I sensed that there was a very real bond between the two of you. What I suggest is that, at the beginning, it was not genuine on her part. I think she was deliberately planted for the express purpose of becoming your executive assistant, so that our person or persons unknown could keep an eye on you. They may even have chosen her over other agents because of the experience of the rape, which they knew would make you feel intense sympathy for her, perhaps confide in her more than you would in anyone else."

"I will not listen to this slander of someone who sacrificed her life to save mine!"

Baker bored in relentlessly. "She could've spent those four years being trained at one of the terrorist camps. Perhaps her handlers knew that she was getting too fond of you, and that's why they killed her. She was the only person who could have identified them to you and to Western intelligence agencies."

"I will not listen!"

"You have to damnit! I saw the look on Marta Rudd's face when she saw Major Guramda at the restaurant. The look was unmistakable. A look of recognition. And of sheer terror. She knew him and she was scared to death of him."

Von Bessel was close to tears. "But why would he shoot Marta? I am the head of the Foundation, not her. Why didn't he kill me, too?"

"Perhaps he didn't want to. Not yet anyway." Baker thought of the chase and the gun battles. "Perhaps they wanted to scare you enough to shut you up. Maybe they wanted to kidnap you. Or maybe they know they must keep you alive for the present, for reasons known only to them."

"Non!' she shrieked. She turned and fled from the room.

Colin Stewart sighed heavily. "Let's take a break, shall we?"

TWENTY EIGHT

Just before nine that evening, in the absolute blackness of a Vancouver Island spring night, Baker went to Colin's office to tell him dinner was ready. Going in search of Marie Françoise, he located her in one of the upstairs bedrooms, sullen and withdrawn, staring out the window at the blackness. She brushed past him without a word.

In the years since his wife had left him, Baker had developed a limited repertoire of dishes he was good at making, although he usually made enough just for himself. In the fridge and kitchen cupboards he had found all the ingredients for garlic risotto, a big bed of garlic-scented saffron rice topped with chopped, sautéed tomatoes, zucchini, green peppers, and onions, with tender sweet scallops and chunks of fresh salmon. A light salad of greens in raspberry vinaigrette, big crusty rolls and an excellent Mosel from Stewart's superb wine cellar completed the meal. Because Von Bessel was a vegetarian, he skipped the seafood on her rice and instead added walnuts and asiago cheese.

Von Bessel was silent and picked at her food, as Baker and Colin chatted in a desultory manner, having unspokenly agreed to leave the woman alone to figure out the truth of what they had said earlier in the day. Each man occasionally looked over at the petite environmentalist. It now looked as if Stewart's claim of securing her as an ally instead of an adversary had been premature.

At the end of the meal Baker cleared the dishes, then threw on his hiking jacket. "I'm going for a smoke."

The Englishman nodded. "While you're out there, why don't you check the perimeter security system again? I'll track you on the video monitors."

Baker nodded and stepped out onto the deck as Stewart wheeled himself into his office. Opposite the three computer monitors were three black and white video monitors on a hinged ledge, the eyes of the Video Motion Outdoor Detection System.

Watching the screens, he was able to easily follow Baker's progress around the grounds.

On his afternoon tour of the area, Baker had been impressed by the system. The grounds in the back of the house, while not expansive, were diverse, divided into four strips. Each was bordered by sinuously curving rows of shrubs and prize rhododendrons that ran parallel to the long, narrow driveway that connected to the main road. At the main road, about a hundred feet from the front of the house, the perimeter fence was little more than a zigzag of split cedar logs, rustic and attractive. At first Baker had seen no security value at all, until he had knelt down and looked closer. On the underside of the second to last rung he discovered a single, rubber coated wire slung snugly to the wood. Unless you were really searching for it you wouldn't see it. He'd followed the wire along to the gate, where it disappeared under the road. At the opposite gatepost, he found the wire again, continuing around the remainder of the perimeter. He assumed what he was looking at was the best small-scale anti-motion detector available, an Israeli product. And even if an intruder cut the wire in one or more places, the control monitor would reference the exact location of such a break and fill the gap with an infrared beam so the entire system was still functional.

Two of the monitors in Colin's office covered the area with an automatic scan using infrared cameras. The third monitored any intrusions across the sensor line. Its screen showed a computer-generated outline of the house and a spider web-like grid around it. Each time Baker came up to the hidden line, his location was identified on the screen. Despite Baker's presence no alarms were sounding, Colin Stewart having silenced the alarm while the big Mountie did his rounds.

The Englishman continued monitoring Baker's movement at the back of the house, to a greenhouse that bordered the western loop of the driveway. He turned away for a moment to reach for the sugar. When he next looked a second source of movement showed on the screen. Fifty feet from Baker's position, on the other side of the drive, someone was slipping along the guest wing wall. Then another, and another, coming in from the grounds of the next property.

"Damn it! He's walking right into them!" He spun the chair and shot expertly down the ramp. As he descended to the main level, he called to Marie Françoise, sitting on the sofa with a magazine. "Madame! We have unwanted guests. I need your help here. When I tell you, turn off that switch at the bottom of the stairs. When it's dark, come up to the top of the stairs and draw these curtains closed. He waved at the thick thermal tapestries tucked into alcoves at either end of the thirty-foot long feature window. Reaching the front door, he flung open the wooden door and turned on the porch lights.

"Doug!" he called. "Dinner's ready. The five of us are waiting for you. Get in here before it gets too cold."

In the midst of a dense thicket of rhododendrons and shrubbery, Baker could just make out Colin's waving arm in the light of the opened door. What the hell was going on? He noted the urgent rapidity of the waving arm. He cut back directly to the house. Rustling from the blackness of a Douglas fir to his far right made him spin. He ducked behind a berm that ran alongside the westerly part of the drive, his hand flashing to the inside of his anorak for the compact Smith and Wesson 9-millimetre, and assessed the situation. Forty feet of deeply shadowed, dimly lit lawn separated him from the house. He knew he would have to cross the gravel drive and use the grove of madronas and rhododendrons as cover.

The instant he made his move, the rustling stopped. Spotted. But they couldn't see him any more than he could see them. Dodging from tree to tree, he finally reached Colin's Ford station wagon parked on one side of the carport. He visualised the fifteen feet of open space between the carport and the door. Surging from behind the vehicle, he started a blind, dodging run. As he made it through the door, Colin threw it shut just as he heard the dull thud of a bullet slamming into the doorframe.

He checked his gun, just to be sure. "How many?"

"Three at least," replied the SAS man. "Back and south. We have a bit of time - I've set up a series of trip lines that will set off recorded gun sounds. Hopefully it'll be enough to keep them busy until they figure it out. Check the assembly. Swing the monitor unit out here where we can check." He began pulling himself along the ceramic tiles of the hallway bordering the feature window.

At the monitor display, Baker said, "Six of them."

Stewart called out, "Madame Von Bessel, could you bring me the gun in the second drawer from the bottom, in the kitchen? Then, very carefully, crawl to the living room window and draw the curtains. Stay as low as you can."

She handed him the Sig Sauer automatic, then crawled to the window and reached for the curtain drawstring. Briefly rising above the level of the sill, she saw a shadowy form, covered in black assault gear, slithering across the deck.

From his daypack Baker extracted his old long nose .38 Smith and Wesson service revolver and a box of shells. He loaded the gun, then thrust it at Marie Françoise. She shook her head, repulsed by the thought.

"Look at it as a noisemaker," said Baker. "You're not going to hit anything, but they won't know that. Just start firing." Finally she took it, the mere touch of it making her cringe.

He turned to Colin Stewart. "Suggestions?"

"Diversion. Any way possible." The eyes in the haggard face were alert. "We must get Madame Von Bessel out of here. I'm afraid with my legs I'll be almost completely useless. I suggest you leave me behind."

"When hell freezes over," growled Baker.

Quickly the Englishman explained his plan, the big Mountie nodding slowly. He ran up the ramp and fetched the hard drive and the two disks. Baker put them back into the Tupperware container then into a heavy gauge ziploc plastic bag, sealed it tight, and stuck it into his hiking jacket. Then he made his way down into the basement, carrying a flashlight, a pair of pliers, and two clean white plastic jugs.

Using the flashlight Colin had given him from a kitchen drawer, he found the panel. Pulling open the thin metal door, he found himself looking at an old-fashioned furnace in a cramped, oily enclosure. He located the fuel line running in from the outside tank and followed it along to the bleeder valve. Using a pair of pliers, he gave the copper tubing leading to the valve a quick tap. Dark, viscous oil poured out. Within seconds, the stench in the confined space was overpowering. Baker held his breath and continued with his task.

He filled the two plastic jugs with the stinky ooze. Then, leaving the valve open, he pushed his way out into the laundry room, leaving a pond of oil developing near the furnace sump and deliberately splattering a trail of oil behind him. He doused the doorframe, then crossed the room to the stairs. At the top, he discarded the first jug and started draining the second. Two minutes later, the whole bottom floor was doused.

Baker contemplated the mess. "Christ, what a mess. You sure about this?"

The Englishman shrugged. "Only thing I can think of. It's just a house. Why else do you pay insurance premiums? I'd rather burn the place down than die." He gazed meditatively at the ooze that soaked the berber carpet. "Low volatility," he murmured. "Not enough." He looked at Baker. "Suggestions?"

"Yeah. Wait here. As I get it, you guys get dressed." He thundered down the stairs back into the basement and found what he was looking for. Grunting, he heaved it and carried it back upstairs.

Baker had always admired English calm. "What a shame," sighed Colin Stewart. "Practically a capital offence."

Marie Françoise stared as well, finally lifting one of the squat, dark brown bottles out of the box. "Polignac," she breathed. "Un crime."

Baker grinned. "You want bottled volatility, that's it. Sorry, Colin. And about the rest of that magnificent wine cellar."

Stewart shrugged. "It would just go up in flames anyway."

Baker peeled back the lead sheathing and popped the cork, handing the bottle to Marie Françoise. "Take a slug. Good for what ails you. It's cold out there."

She tipped it back, then returned the bottle to Baker. He took a hit himself, then handed the bottle to Stewart. He drank deeply as Baker opened another. "Oh my," said the Englishman, wiping his chin. "The drink of heroes."

Baker grunted. "I hope we don't have to do too many heroics to get out of here. Back in a sec."

He ran down to the basement and poured half a bottle of the world's best cognac onto the pool of oil. Then he poured the amber liquid on top of the trail of oil that led upstairs. Everywhere there was oil, there was now cognac mixed with it. Reverently he placed the two empty bottles on the credenza in the corner and opened a third, splashing it in a golden trail all the way to the front door. Holding the empty bottle in his hand, Baker contemplated the other two people, dressed in winter gear and waiting by the curtained front window. "As Elvis once sang, it's now or never. Ready?"

Without waiting for an answer, he took the Ronson out of his pocket and made an adjustment. He flicked it and produced a flame half the size of his hand. He held it to the oily strip by the door. The alcohol caught with a clear blue blaze as it shot along the carpet and disappeared down the basement stairs. As the oil caught, orange-blue flames slowly rose. Within seconds, the entire house was blanketed in thick billowing clouds of sooty black smoke. Nodding at Stewart, Baker threw the heavy bottle through the side door window. Moments later, in response to the shattering glass, the room was filled with thundering staccato gunfire. As Colin stuck his Sig Sauer out of the broken pane and sprayed bullets around the area to keep the intruders at bay, Baker and Marie Françoise put their backs against the big heavy display table by the picture window and pushed. Slowly it slid toward the glass, its passage eased by the thick wool throw rug beneath it.

The table struck the picture window on an oblique angle, its left corner punching through the thick glass. For a hanging second, the entire glass sheet went milky white, then collapsed in a deadly cascade, into the swimming pool below.

As the heavy table pitched through the gaping expanse, its bulk half-hidden by billowing black smoke, Baker stuck his gun out and fired in a wide fan. One clip, two clips, three. Enough to make them think he had an arsenal.

Aiming inexpertly, Marie Françoise pressed the trigger of the .38 and was thrown back by the recoil. Baker grabbed her and threw her out of the window, knowing she would land in the far end of the pool. He ran to Colin, seized the handles of the wheelchair and pushed. The Englishman disappeared through the shattered window.

The interior of the house was now a raging inferno as the wood substructure caught fire. There was a tremendous explosion from the basement and Baker felt the entire house lurch, as if an earthquake had hit it. Suddenly he remembered. The whole thing was bolted to the cliff. And the explosions were jarring it loose. Engulfed in black smoke, heat searing his back, he mounted the sill and jumped.

He hit the water of the swimming pool, dimly realising it was filled with debris. As he fought to gain the surface, he saw with horror that the pool was emptying. The entire structure of the house had been jarred loose, the pool with it. With watery eyes he saw the huge crack in the far end, saw the surge of water that gushed through with a terrible roar. He realised he was being carried with it. He tried to remember what was below. Rocky beach and ocean. The groaning howl of grinding concrete, twisting steel and ten thousand gallons of water escaping its confines was everywhere. As Baker slipped over the edge, helplessly caught in a torrent of raging water, he caught a last brief glimpse of the house. The front was now totally engulfed in whipping flames. It was canting awkwardly as it loosened. In a ghastly, slithering lurch, a whole section broke apart and skidded downward. Christ in heaven, he thought, it's coming after me.

Moments later, dazed, Baker opened his eyes to find he was lying face up as frigid wavelets lapped at his ears. The torrent from the swimming pool had carried him into the sea. Disoriented and stunned, he roused himself. A face was staring down at him. Marie Françoise. She was pulling at his sodden clothing, mouthing something. He felt the stabbing pain as she grabbed his ears and pulled up his unresponsive head. Where the hell had she learned that trick? "Get up!" she screamed. "Get up, damn you!"

Clumsily he managed to get to his knees. "Where's Colin?"

"Voilà, la bas!" she beckoned down the beach to the frothing surfline. Straining his eyes, he finally detected a lump that was his friend. Crawling, half-swimming, he lurched over to Colin. The man was holding himself out of the water like a man doing pushups, his useless legs being rocked back and forth by the surf.

As he grabbed his old friend under the arms and heaved him upright, Baker scanned the cliff above, where the house used to be. He saw a burning mess, still bolted to the rocky face. But it was just half the house, the other half lay crumpled and smoking at the base of the cliff, some seventy feet from where they stood.

He saw flashlights flickering in the billowing smoke and shadows. A search was on. He realised it wouldn't be long before they realised what had happened, before they plunged down to the beach.

They would have to swim for the Valerie, rocking gently at anchor some fifty yards away.

Colin protested feebly. "You two go. Get out of here."

"Shut up!" whispered Baker. "Stop being noble or I'll have to pop you!" With one arm around Colin, he seized Von Bessel with the other and dragged them into the surf. He put Colin on his back so he floated, then cupped his hand under the man's chin to keep his nose and mouth out of the water and to haul him along. Every three or four strokes, he looked back to the shore. Now they were down at the beach, two flashlight beams stabbing the creaming waves while another five scanned the dark towering trees behind. He looked over his shoulder at the Valerie. Not far now.

All of the flashlights were now aiming out to sea. They were less than a body length away from the anchor buoy. He pulled Colin towards the bow, on the seaward side, away from the prying beam of light, as Von Bessel followed. They moved down the length of the darkened hull to the swim grid at the stern. Baker shifted along the grid to the partially raised power unit of the inboard-outboard. Gingerly, he craned his head out to the side to gauge the position of the flashlight beams. Hidden. He hooked his leg over the power unit. It took him three tries before he lay sprawled on the grid, fumbling with frozen hands to unzip the tarp. Finally, it opened. With every last ounce of his strength, he hauled Colin out of the water as Von Bessel pushed from below. As the Englishman sagged to the deck, he pulled at Marie Françoise until she was crouched on the deck as well, heaving salt water from her lungs.

Baker staggered to the tool kit, found the razor sharp gutting knife. Five strokes and the anchor line parted. He let the boat drift for a moment before cranking the engine. As soon as the humid, metallic coughing stopped and the engine roared to life, he heard the sound of shots being fired from the shore. A slug whined into the hull mere inches away. He heaved at the throttle and the cruiser surged into the dark ocean void.

TWENTY NINE

Colonel Aziz Hamani contemplated disaster.

His mind raced. How could it have come to this? An eight man assault team, led by Major Guramda. The blueprints for the house. The municipal maintenance truck and the uniforms for the men. A full day of preparation by some of the best professionals in the business.

Disaster.

He remembered what he had said to the team: "The property is isolated. It is hard to get to but also hard to escape from. The owner is a cripple, in a wheelchair. There is our target - the woman - and that policeman. Once the building is surrounded, they have nowhere to go."

He had to admit he'd been surprised by the elaborate security system, and the fake gunfire. That had led to an unacceptable delay. But still, one had to expect that kind of thing. He had smiled when he'd heard the first burst of bullets. They couldn't see anything in the dark, and he knew the sound of panicked gunfire when he heard it. But he hadn't believed his eyes when he saw the first flickering flames, then saw the front window shatter and the black smoke billow out.

Watching, wincing as the magnificent house plunged into the abyss, he thought, how can a simple abduction turn into this kind of catastrophe?

The darkness hampered the clean up and getaway. Even as they gathered their gear and pulled away from the smouldering site in the stolen municipal van, collecting the perimeter guard detail who had kept any neighbours out of the way, Hamani half-expected the police to show up, or at least a neighbour, who would of course have to be shot.

Cruising down the winding dark road, Hamani thought hard. He had to have the woman. Without her he had no leverage against the Sword, apart from the Accountant. The Sword had told him to kill Von Bessel, as a condition of his not annihilating some large city somewhere in the world. But he didn't believe that the black spiders imprisoned in the Sword's demented head were darting in that particular direction. He had to want her for himself. Hamani smiled grimly - he knew the Sword was bluffing. Now he must be in a towering rage, his informants having told him about the Vancouver assassination attempt at the Waterfront Café. Bluff called. And now he knew of the death of Marta Rudd. That would show him this game was deadly serious.

Hamani and Sword had met the fourteen year old Marta Rudd in a Hamburg brothel that specialised in young girls. The proprietors kept their pathetic young charges in line with easily available heroin. As he did with everyone he met, the Iraqi spy had filed her away in his mind, noting the intelligence in the opaque blue eyes, an intelligence that fought to exist behind the fog of drugs. Smart and tough, he had thought. He and Sword had patronised the girl, educating her in the most sophisticated ways of providing pleasure. Even though he was now ashamed of his youthful exploits, Hamani still felt a tingle in his groin as he thought of the hours the two of them had spent with the girl. Despite everything that happened to her, she never broke; the intelligence in those Teutonic eyes had never flickered. As a result, he had suggested the girl to his contacts in Iraqi intelligence. Through a long and convoluted double blind process, they had paid off the brothel's proprietors and recruited her. She had abandoned the heroin habit with an ease Hamani felt justified his faith in the girl's strength, and at the tactical training school in Libya had proved herself to be an assiduous student. Once introduced back into Germany, in a manner that made it virtually impossible to trace the missing four years of her life, they had pondered what to do with her. The Schweizerhalle incident had provided the perfect opportunity. They had known everything Marie Françoise Von Bessel did, even knew what she thought.

He frowned. Too bad they wouldn't have that access anymore. He had suspected for a long time that Rudd was turning, that her own emotional neediness was finding a responsive echo in Marie Françoise Von Bessel, an echo she had never expected to find. The human element. It was always so hard to gauge.

When he had told Guramda to kill Marta, he had thought the whole thing would be easy. Now, thanks to that damn Mountie Douglas Baker, it wouldn't.

THIRTY

They were drinking a combination of hot tea laced with sugar and rum, courtesy of the old bottle Baker had found in the stern locker.

Finally Colin Stewart said, "You're awfully quiet, my friend, even for you."

"Jesus, I hate the cold," shivered Baker. "Second time in two nights I've had to swim for it." He sipped his drink and fingered a bullet hole on the cabin frame. "And, they've shot the shit out of my fucking boat. If this thing had any more holes in it we'd be at the bottom of the ocean."

Marie Françoise Von Bessel was off somewhere far away, from the look on her face. She was towelling her wet chestnut hair, wrapped in the same old blanket Baker had worn the previous evening, a million years ago, it seemed.

Baker turned back to face the Englishman, sitting on the bunk seat near the space heater. He was trying not to tremble, but the big Mountie could tell he was exhausted as well as cold. But his eyes were still alert and he knew the SAS man was thinking the same thing he was.

How had they known where they were?

He remembered what Stewart had said the previous day, referring to the fact that Joan Chan's call had been traced from inside E Division headquarters: 'Anyone who knows anything about you and Joan is sooner or later going to make the connection that you are both friends of mine'. And so they had. Fast. Far too fast for his liking.

Baker's cold grey eyes appraised his friend as he tried not to let his concern show. "You okay?"

"Yes and no. What now?"

He stared down at the compass, confirming their bearing. After a lengthy pause, he said, "Switzerland."

Stewart didn't look surprised. "Logical place to hunt. Check the restaurant Heinrich Weigel disappeared from, check on the Accountant. Etcertera." He knew he didn't have to elaborate.

"You got a safe place to stay?" asked Baker.

"Of course," replied the anti-terrorism expert. "I was in the Boy Scouts and I remember the motto - be prepared. I have more safe houses than most people have leaves in their backyard in the fall."

Baker grinned in spite of himself. He reached into his soaked jacket and withdrew the heavy plastic bag with the hard drive and the disks. "Here." He knew the answer before he even asked the question. "You got access to computers?"

Stewart took the package, holding it up to the cruiser's cabin lights to check for moisture. Satisfied, he placed it in his lap. "Of course. Find me someplace where I can get hold of Claire. She'll come and pick me up. She'll bring the spare wheelchair, too. From the safe house I'll keep working on Joan's files."

It was almost three in the morning when Baker piloted the boat out of the major shipping lanes, finding moorage at an empty public dock on Maine Island, one of hundreds forming the Gulf Island chain between Vancouver Island and the mainland. They spent the remainder of the night catching up on sleep and drying their clothes. Just before sun-up, Baker had the boat untied and underway. Next stop was Ganges Harbour on Saltspring Island, the main commercial and transportation centre for the islands. They paid enough docking fees to the attendant to keep the Valerie dockside for a month. Then they went to a local hotel, Baker carrying his friend. At the set of telephones, Colin called Claire.

"I'm not looking forward to this at all," he said glumly as he dialed the number. "She's always hated my work and now our home is smoking wreckage."

Baker placed a consoling hand on his old friend's shoulder. He knew what this kind of thing was like - it was the sort of incident that had ruined his own marriage. "I know what you mean. Blame it all on me. Lay it on real thick. It's my fault anyway. Good luck."

The Englishman handed him a scrap of paper. "You'll need this. It's a telephone number you can call from wherever you are, anywhere in the world. The area code is Chilean, but that doesn't matter. The whole thing is linked to a global list of phone codes, which will change automatically and randomly each time you call. Call at twelve noon or midnight, Vancouver time, so I know it's you. Two rings, hang up, two rings, hang up, three rings. I'll be there. Keep your calls to less than two minutes to blow off any traces, just in case. I am developing a very healthy respect for our adversaries."

Pulling Baker down towards him, he bear-hugged the big Mountie. "Good luck, old man. And good hunting."

Baker nodded. "Good hunting for sure. I'll be in touch." He turned and walked away, gesturing for the Swiss/French woman to follow.

THIRTY ONE

Vancouver, March 19

Douglas Baker ran his hand over his dark brown hair and wondered if the dye job looked as fake as it felt. He tried not to think of how much money was in the briefcase sitting in his lap.

He glanced at his watch. She must be almost finished by now and they had a plane to catch. He gazed at the elegant skyline of downtown Vancouver, back set by snow-capped mountains. The weather turns nice all of a sudden, he thought glumly, and I won't be here to enjoy it. He checked the cuff of his new jacket. Good thing he was a natural 44 long and didn't have to wait for alterations. He knew from the call he'd made earlier that Colin Stewart was now about as far west as he could go without finding himself in Hawaii, holed up in a picturesque cabin resort three miles south of the remote village of Tofino on the extreme west coast of Vancouver Island.

He'd learned that the owner was an ex-cop and old friend of Colin's named Ned Flanagan. Long ago he'd offered the use of the hidden loft above his office, should the SAS man ever need a safe place to hide. It came complete with bed, toilet and bath, telephone lines, and a powerful desk top computer set-up. When Baker had spoken to him to explain his plan for getting out of the country, Stewart had given his approval.

"I'll be perfectly safe here. Ned can handle any intruders and also function as my legs to run any errands. I have a gorgeous view from the window of a private sandy beach and raging waves. Just to be absolutely safe, I've jury-rigged a system that will route all of my calls through a remote phone miles from here. If anything gets traced, as it did with Joan, it won't lead them directly to me. Always handy to have an escape hatch. I intend on doing nothing but hacking Joan's hard drive until I've found everything. Don't forget to call on a regular basis so I can keep you posted."

Impatiently Baker looked again at this new watch - two dousings in seawater had ruined the old one. Jesus Christ, is she buying the entire store? Strongly suspecting that she would not be in and out of the shops in five minutes or less, he'd given her a wad of bills - credit cards could be too easily traced - and let her go off to buy new clothing so he could make his three calls. The first had been to Colin, the second to a low life piece of Ottawa scum named Henri Bergerant who, despite his almost infinite deficiencies, had one very rare talent. The third had been to an old friend at the Department of National Defence, someone who owed both Baker and Chan big time and did not have an excessive amount of respect for rules and regulations.

He drummed his fingers on the briefcase. It held the contents of his 'rainy day' box, which he moved around from place to place and which currently resided at the downtown bus terminal. It held almost twenty-five thousand dollars in Canadian and US currency and some blank official documents Baker had somehow just never got around to returning to the documents section when they accidentally fell into his hands a few months earlier. He also had a set of credit cards in different names, but all signed with his slashing handwriting despite the different identities. There were a few other odds and ends as well, all of them innocuous looking to the untrained eye.

He was about to start looking for Marie Françoise Von Bessel when he saw her hurrying down the street. He had to admit the frosted hair and the glasses were a pretty effective disguise, and he had specifically told her to buy nondescript, casual travelling clothes. He stood and hailed a cab.

They arrived at Vancouver International Airport with twenty minutes to spare before boarding a domestic flight for Ottawa.

After checking in, he said to her, "From here on, just go along with whatever happens. Got it? Just remember to keep your mouth shut." And before she could react she felt the shock of cold steel closing over her left wrist. As she stared down uncomprehendingly, she saw him snap the cuffs over his own wrist. "Mon

Dieu-" she exclaimed as he grinned at her.

"Just try to control that famous Gaulish temperament of yours, okay?" Baker said as he dragged her kicking and screaming across the floor, directly past an uniformed member of the airport RCMP detachment.

"Voyou!" she screamed. Baker tried not to smile. What did it mean? Ah yes. Hoodlum. Warily the officer moved in to assist, only to see Baker wave his badge. "Fucking transfer duty," he said to the man. "Doesn't look like a serial killer, does she?" As Von Bessel pounded his shoulder with her tiny fist, he said, "Regular little hellcat, this one!" as the other officer grinned sympathetically.

"You gonna be okay?" he asked.

"Yeah," said Baker. "She'll calm down once we get on the plane."

The uniformed Mountie eyed the furious Von Bessel. "Better you than me, my friend. I suggest you don't turn your back." He waved him through.

Baker nodded and walked down the corridor. He waited until they were well past the still chuckling officer, then around the corner and out of sight. He pulled her into an alcove and removed the cuffs.

"You sickening chien! You tricked me!"

"I didn't so much trick you as use you," grinned Baker. "We're past him, aren't we? You deflected his attention away from what we look like to his sympathy for me as a fellow cop. These damned dye jobs aren't bad but if anyone looks real hard, we're history. Just remember, in this game there's nothing more unpleasant to deal with than a hysterical woman in handcuffs, acting like you just did. Nobody wants to have anything to do with it."

He tossed the cuffs into the nearest trash bin. "Okay, now we're ready for the security X ray. I sure feel naked without my gun." They went through security and boarded the plane without incident. Baker slipped the briefcase under his seat. It wasn't until an hour into the flight that Von Bessel even deigned to look at him.

****

Despite all his years on the Force, Douglas Baker didn't think he'd ever run into anyone who looked more untrustworthy than Henri Bergerant. Short and fat, his gnomic face was a purple, scarred and swollen mess, the result of too much cheap booze and too many drunken brawls in seedy taverns. He reeked of stale sweat, rye whisky and cigarette smoke. Right now he was leering at an alarmed Marie Françoise Von Bessel, who was sticking to the big Mountie like Velcro. "Sergeant. . .?" she whispered, her hand over her nose.

"I know," grunted Baker. "But sometimes it's handy to have friends in low places. It helps if you try not to breathe."

But what Henri lacked in charm and a sense of personal hygiene he more than made up for in the quality of his limited but very special talent. He was an artist of a sort, the Picasso of forgery. Any document, from stock certificates to passports, Henri could duplicate with uncanny precision. Baker had always wondered how someone like the squat little criminal could be successful in his chosen career when he drank so much. He knew that if most people sucked back the booze like Henri they'd be in a permanent state of delirium tremors, their hands fluttering like autumn leaves.

But for some reason the forger liked Baker. He had utilised the repulsive little man's services over the years, which was why they were now standing in the fetid confines of the forger's basement apartment. Among Bergerant's less attractive habits was his fondness for exposing himself to women in parks, which he tended to do when he was really drunk and the moon was full. Baker had been able to intercede on occasion, for which Bergerant was grateful - the little pervert knew as well as the big Mountie did that other convicts loathed flashers and he ran the risk of getting a handmade shiv between his ribs if he went to jail.

Baker handed over a wad of cash. "Henri, this is fucking highway robbery."

The little man wiped his hand on his filthy undershirt and fingered the bills with obvious satisfaction. He shrugged. "To do it so fast, you pay a premium. You don't like the cost, try picking this stuff up at the drug store."

"Once again, Henri, who was here tonight?" asked Baker, flicking through the two authentically dog-eared passports and other ID.

Bergerant leered. "Madonna and the Pope. Anyone but you."

Baker nodded and they left. They had used the forger's filthy bathroom to rinse the water-based dye from their hair and change the colour once again. Marie Françoise was now a blond, with a haircut she detested, saying it looked too military. Baker hadn't commented on the very good reason he'd chopped it so short. He was now a redhead and thought he looked rather Irish. They got into the car and drove.

Twenty minutes later, at a residence in the bedroom community of Kanata, they stopped and walked up the drive to the front door. Baker rang - short, long, long and short - and the door creaked open. He said, "Hello, sport. Long time no see."

Their host was gaunt and appeared nervous. He appraised Baker's hair. "Very fetching. For the upcoming Esquire photo shoot?" The big Mountie grinned.

"Sorry I can't tell you any more. I can't tell you how much I appreciate this."

"I don't know and I don't want to know. Just don't get caught, for Christ's sake."

Baker looked around the home's gloomy interior. "Everything set?"

The man nodded. Within minutes Marie Françoise was wearing a rather seedy looking military uniform, field fatigues, showing the rank of lance corporal in the Canadian army, while Baker wore the dress greens of a senior warrant officer, Criminal Investigation Division. He nodded approvingly as he patted the standard issue Glok sidearm. "Very convincing."

The gaunt man grinned. "I must say you look rather dashing." He looked at the woman. "And you look suitably shabby, whoever you are."

"What do we do with the uniforms afterwards?" asked Baker.

"Burn them, preferably at a high heat. Local incinerator at the landfill should do it. Or acid. Throw the gun in the river or something."

Refusing to answer Marie Françoise's questions, Baker just shook his head and pointed to his watch. They sat in silence and waited. At 8:05 p.m., a knock sounded at the front door. Their shadowy host answered it. Two enlisted military police entered. At the sight of Baker standing down the hall, they offered a deferential nod - certainly not the snappy salute Baker was hoping for, until he remembered the rank he was wearing didn't require a salute. He waved off their lack lustre response with friendly bonhomie. "Gentlemen," he said, gesturing at Marie Françoise, "this is Lance Corporal Lisse." Seized her arms, roughly pulling them behind her he snapped on a set of cuffs. "Your prisoner."

"Non!" she shouted. "You cannot do this to me again! Damn you!"

"Lance Corporal Lisse, shut up!" Baker shook his head at the two military cops. "Worst disciplinary case I've ever seen. Watch out for her - she's dangerous, especially those feet." The two young soldiers flanked her, grabbed her elbows and strong-armed her out the door into the freezing night. Baker shook David Williams' hand and bounded down the front steps. Marie Françoise fought and kicked all the way down to the camouflaged lock-up van parked at the front of the house. They threw her into the back of the van and slammed the door. Baker got into the front with the two men. "See what I mean? Regular little hellcat."

Two and a half hours later, cold and miserable, they hauled her out of the van into the chain linked compound with barbed hoops running along the upper level of the fence. A well lit sign bolted to the fence announced: Stockade, Canadian Forces-Airforce Base, Trenton. An hour later, at five minutes after midnight, she was escorted aboard a Canadian Forces A320 bound for Lahr, Germany.

Baker directed her to the rear of the craft and sat her down. He unlocked the cuffs and she rubbed her wrists. Then she raised both heavy boots into the air and brought them down as hard as she could. Baker grinned lazily as he dodged to avoid having his toes crushed. "I was expecting something like that. Can't say I blame you. Look, I know I wasn't exactly candid with you about my plans. But you've got to admit we are still alive and we're on our way to Europe. And we didn't have to run a gauntlet of spooks and Mounties at passport control, which would've been the case if we'd tried to board a commercial flight."

She crossed her arms across her chest, as Baker sat down across the aisle from her. He could see in her eyes that she knew he was right. "When you cool down, try to get some sleep. I have a feeling we're going to be very busy in Europe."

THIRTY TWO

His eyes red-rimmed with fatigue and rage, Major Hakim Guramda stared at the view from apartment 703. It was a panorama of winter greys, of mists rising up from a warming earth. But there was no warmth in his heart. His back still ached between his shoulder blades where Baker's two bullets had slammed into his body armour.

Nestled on the south face of rolling hills, the apartment was one of a cluster of five high rises in the residential section of Dietekon, an industrial town eleven kilometres north west of Zurich. Two of the five towers in the complex were joined by a ground level commercial complex, a PTT (Swiss Post, Telephone & Telegraph) office, a beauty salon, a Co-op grocery store in the middle and, to the far right, a restaurant and bar. Out front, bordering the semi-circular driveway and parking lot, a magazine and tobacco kiosk served the drive-through clientele.

As he watched the busy crowds of shoppers, he thought to himself, where the hell are you? You must be out there somewhere. He knew that Colonel Hamani had finally leaked word of the Accountant's location in an attempt to bring the Sword out of hiding and provoke him into an attack.

He looked down at the floor. Room 603, right below his feet. He turned toward the dining room; the command centre of the surveillance unit, with its banks of audio, infrared video and electronic recording devices, as well as computer terminals and communication satellite set up. "You are absolutely sure that no one who does not live in the building has entered in the last two days?"

"No one," answered the head of the five person surveillance

team. "We have the entire building covered." More than two months earlier, they had taken up residence in apartment 703. The apartment complex's managers had been offered an all expenses paid, extended Greek vacation, courtesy of what they thought was a representative of their own government but in fact was an agent of Colonel Hamani's. Both the vacation offer and the fact that they were participating in a matter vital to national security and thus were sworn to absolute secrecy had thrilled the elderly couple. To the building's residents, the man and wife who the managers introduced as their temporary replacements were completely believable, a typically sober and hardworking young Swiss couple who minded their own business and kept the building running smoothly.

Again Guramda stared unseeingly at the late winter landscape as he recalled the plan. The subject of all this effort was the Accountant, Klaus Staffel, the new resident of apartment 603. When Hamani had tipped him off that he was about to be blown, the man had panicked and nearly bolted the country. Only the colonel's assurance that he was perfectly safe and would be taken care of had calmed him down. Hamani had supplied the apartment on the sixth floor, which unbeknownst to Staffel until his arrival was also the home of a very attractive young Swiss blond who had made herself very attentive, as she had been trained to do by Mukhabarat. The Iraqi military man had said it was the best arrangement, as all the bills would be in her name and she could run errands so the Accountant would almost never have to venture outdoors. Also unbeknownst to Staffel was the fact that every room in his new home was fitted with surveillance monitoring equipment. The exterior of the complex was also tightly monitored. He was the bait in the trap, to be kept happy until he had to be used.

Now it was time. Guramda knew that the Sword must be waiting and watching. He glanced back over his shoulder at the five-man team. They hadn't been told - the watchers didn't know that they had now become watched themselves. Couldn't let too many people in on the operation.

Wearily he rubbed his face. At least Marta Rudd was dead. But now Marie Françoise Von Bessel and that accursed Mountie had disappeared, as had Colin Stewart. No bait, no hard drive, nothing now but the Accountant. He knew Colonel Hamani had his people in Canada working non-stop on locating them. They'd found Baker's boat but that didn't tell them anything except that they hadn't sunk in the middle of the ocean. And they had to trap and kill the Sword before Sergeant Joan Chan woke up. If they found out about Tousignant. Chan had to die, that much was clear. Strike and be done with it, just in case. She was a tough one and Guranda could not help feeling a grudging respect for the scrappy spy.

THIRTY THREE

Lahr, Germany, March 20

Brilliant morning sun flooding through the window of the A320 brought Marie Françoise to wakefulness. The sight of the snow-laden German countryside below brought a burst of warmth that complemented the brightness. Baker didn't waken until ten minutes later, when the Captain announced their preparation for landing in Lahr.

Waiting until all the other military and support personnel passengers had deplaned and walked toward the transfer bus, Baker guided Von Bessel to the door and down the stairs, directly towards an ugly but efficient-looking GM personnel carrier guarded by two hulking MPs. Without a word, he displayed his and the woman's ID. This was examined more carefully than he would have liked, and he prayed Henri Bergerant had done his usual impeccable work. The big soldier then looked at Baker's orders and again he held his breath. The detail sergeant gazed at Marie Françoise with a faint smirk, then at Baker. "Really?"

"Yes," said Baker, winking conspiratorially.

The sergeant's smile broadened. "Don't suppose you could fill me in?"

Baker grinned back. "Wish I could, but you know how it is."

"Yeah, I know how it is." He looked Marie Françoise up and down. "Some people have all the luck." He tipped the edge of his purple airborne beret, directing them inside the personnel carrier.

Once they were underway, heading in the opposite direction from the flight processing centre and the prying eyes of German immigration officials, Baker silently gave thanks to friends in places both high and low.

Five minutes later, the carrier turned into an aircraft servicing area, coming to a halt behind a dolly supporting an F18 engine. They followed the sergeant over to a door in the nearby fence and slipped through. Outside, he handed Baker a set of ignition keys and pointed to an older model Mercedes coupe. Baker nodded and they climbed in. Moments later they easily cleared base security and were on the way south. Looking back in the mirror, Baker let out a huge sigh of relief. "Well lady, after this little caper, I'm definitely back in a deficit situation with my IOUs."

She was staring at him suspiciously. "I insist on an answer."

Baker feigned innocence. "Answer to what?"

"What charge is listed against Lance Corporal Lisse on those orders of yours? What is it that the Canadian government thinks she, or rather I, did to deserve all this attention?"

He grinned. "Pandering. Sex with an officer. A very senior officer." He coughed. "Actually, to be absolutely honest, sex with three senior officers. Simultaneously." He watched her carefully, ready to defend himself if she attacked.

She tossed her head. "I suppose you think it is just so amusing," she snorted. "Men are such children sometimes." But he noticed that as she turned to gaze out of the side window at the winter countryside, a small smile was playing on her lips.

****

"Hello, old man," came Colin's relaxed, Oxfordshire tone over the line. "I'll be brief. The people who are after you are definitely Iraqi and definitely very ugly pieces of work. Major Guramda, who killed Rudd and the two police officers, has a boss named Colonel Aziz Hamani. You know that already. What's new is that he works for MIMI, the Ministry of Industry and Military Industrialisation. Specialises in procurement of both weapons and expertise."

Baker's mind raced. "Barry Nakamura told me before about the connection between Hamani and Dr. Gerald Bull. You think he's involved with chemical weapons?"

"No doubt about it. It's obvious this whole thing is about the Schweizerhalle fire. Probably Hamani was the mastermind behind the chemicals operation, the bogus manifests, everything."

"But he didn't work at the Sandoz facility."

"No."

"Then that leaves us with the Accountant, and he's just a book keeper. There must've been someone else working with him." The big Mountie frowned. "But why is Hamani leaking information about Iraqi involvement?"

"He's not," reminded Colin Stewart. "He's trying to avoid any kind of Iraqi link as he tries to flush out whoever it is he's trying to flush out. Given the assassination of Rudd, the attack on Joan, and the full-scale military assault on my home, they're becoming desperate."

"The key has to be this Tousignant person. Maybe he's the guy Hamani is trying to flush. Have you found anything at all?"

"Nothing. According to Sandoz, no one with a name remotely like that has ever worked for the company in any capacity. Could be a pseudonym, but Joan would've checked that right off, so I assume it's his real name. It's possible Joan was getting local information over the voice phone and hadn't entered it. Personally, I doubt it. There has to be a file on the man somewhere, or some indication of where to look. I'll keep digging."

"Okay," said Baker. "And keep in mind, we don't even have a first name. For all we know, it could be a woman."

"Damn," replied Stewart. "Never even occurred to me. And speaking of women, I have what may be extremely valuable information."

"Finally," growled Baker. "I could use a little good news. What is it?"

"A contact for you in Basel. Seems to be a friend of Joan's, although I can't find out anything more yet than that Joan sent an information request to her and asked her to respond electronically. Whether it was sent or not I don't know. But the point is, the woman is a criminal inspector with Basel City Police. She must be good, or connected, or both - women don't feature prominently in the Swiss police hierarchy. Inspector Erika Haus. Here's the spelling of her name and her work number."

As Baker scribbled it down, he said, "Last question."

"Make it quick, Doug. Time is running out. I don't want this traced."

"How is Joan doing?"

"Considerable improvement but still unconscious. That's according to an old source of mine at the hospital, who's been sworn to secrecy in case anyone asks who it is that's phoning. That trace from E Division still bothers the hell out of me. I don't think we can be too careful."

Baker thought furiously. "I agree. It's just occurred to me that the only reason we know about Tousignant, whoever the hell he is, is because Joan knows about him. If I were Colonel Hamani and knew he was the key to this whole mess, I'd get Joan out of the way right quick, before she wakes up and spills what she knows."

There was dead silence on the other end. Finally the SAS man said, "You know, my dear chap, you really are awfully good. I'm on it immediately. Good hunting."

Baker rang off.

THIRTY FOUR

Basel, Switzerland, March 21

Baker shook Marie Françoise, who barely stirred against his touch. A second try had more effect. She sat bolt upright and looked at him, then at the rough brick wall beside her. He saw recognition dawn in her face as she remembered.

"Seven a.m. Gotta move. Here, I got you a coffee and a croissant that looks like it was made during the Crimean war. How'd you sleep?" The question was rhetorical, because no matter how she'd slept it had to have been a more restful slumber than he'd had. She got the bed, lumpy and rickety though it was. He had tossed and turned on a sprung old sofa that was both too short and too narrow. It hadn't been gallantry, just an old fashioned coin toss, and she'd won.

They were in a flophouse in Klein Basel, or Little Town, the most rundown section of the city. Had they not been so exhausted, the junkies partying next door might have kept them awake. But it was exactly what Baker required. It put them right in the heart of old Basel, in a milieu where it was unlikely anyone would recognise Von Bessel, especially the way she looked now. Blond, dishevelled, unwashed, no makeup and dressed in the black bikers' leathers he had insisted on buying for her: "The biggest contrast possible with your old Channel and Gucci persona." Baker was in jeans, a black leather jacket and heavy navy turtleneck. The uniforms had been burned but he'd kept the Glok.

She sipped the coffee and made a face. "So, what do we do?"

"First, we try and make contact again with Colin. We've got a couple of hours to kill before we can call him. Then, I want to look at the Sandoz facility. I find that when I look at a place, I get a better idea of what I'm up against. How far is it from here? Then, depending on what we hear, we could start trying to track down the Accountant, Herr Staffel. Or get hold of Erika Haus."

"The facility is a ten or fifteen minute car ride across the river. The traffic right now will be terrible."

"Okay, then let's find a cell phone supplier and see if we can secure a phone. Any suggestions?" Baker hated to use cell phones but it was looking like his only option. He didn't want to use hotel phones, in case people were looking for them, and he also didn't want to find himself stuck someplace, needing to make a fast call and not being able to do so. He was far away from the handy gadgets and connections of his professional world, and he felt exposed and isolated.

"I believe we should start at the Post Office. All major Swiss PTT offices have telephones for sale. Their sign-up restrictions might be severe, however. There should be private operations nearby that will be better, especially if the price is right."

"Okay, biker girl."

She frowned. "Aren't you going to shave?"

"Nope."

She sighed. "All right, let's go." She drained the rest of the coffee and heaved out of bed, putting the stale croissant on the grimy bedside table.

"Don't you want it?"

She shook her head. "Leave it for the rats."

They had changed a big wad of American cash into Swiss francs the previous day. Baker bought a phone, and by the time the purchase was completed it was time to call. The sound was full of static, but it couldn't be helped.

"Doug, are you on a cell phone?"

Baker took a drag on his cigarette and squinted in the early morning sunshine. "Yeah. That a problem?"

"Possibly. Cell calls can be monitored and pulled off the ether. Let's keep this brief."

Colin sounded worried and harassed. Baker frowned. "You okay?"

"Actually, no I'm not."

Baker felt his heart sink. "Please tell me it's not Claire and the kids."

"It's not Claire and the kids. There's nothing whatever you can do about it. I'll tell you at the end of the conversation."

"Okay. What's new?"

"Joan called Erika Haus's work number just before she detected the last trace. I strongly suggest that Inspector Haus might be a gold mine of information. And I might have a line on the Accountant. One of his credit cards was used recently, near Zurich, in a place called Dietekon. At a grocery store."

Baker furiously scribbled down the information, after asking how to spell 'Dietekon'. "Colin, I don't know anything about this Inspector Haus. For all we know, she's the one who slung the trace on her own phone call with Joan. Or maybe her office is bugged. I'm not willing to take a blind chance on a stranger."

"I thought you might say that. I've dug up a bio and a photo. Give me a fax number and I'll get it to you. In fact, I'll also give you the address of the grocery store in Dietekon. Give me twenty minutes or so. And try not to use a cell phone if you can avoid it."

"Okay."

They got into the BMW they had rented after abandoning the Mercedes coupe, using one of the fake credit cards from Baker's briefcase, because it was impossible to rent a car using cash. They headed toward the outskirts of Basel, heading east. What the hell was Colin so upset about? Baker spotted a Bier Stube, pulled over and left Von Bessel in the car as he entered. He discovered they had a fax and would accept cash for an international transmission. He got the number and used the phone, relieved that the proprietors spoke poor English.

"Hi, Colin."

"Greetings. Got a fax number?" Baker told him what it was. "I'll transmit the information now. How is Von Bessel?"

"Hard to tell. She gets real quiet sometimes, especially whenever I mention the fire and checking out Schweizerhalle. I don't think she wants to go there. I also have a suspicion that she's brooding about the conversation we had before the Iraqis incinerated your house."

"Which part of the conversation?"

"The part about, if the bodies in the car weren't those of her husband and son, who the hell were they? If she starts thinking that maybe they were murdered, that would be bad enough. But if it occurs to her that maybe they're not dead after all. . ."

Colin Stewart completed the thought. "She might go off like a bad batch of nitro. Back to the mental hospital. Just try to keep her mind off it, if possible. Don't know what else to suggest." There was a pause. "The fax should be coming through right now. It's only two pages."

Baker looked over the big jolly Swiss woman behind the counter where the fax machine was. She was smiling at him and pointing at a slowly unspooling curl of paper.

"It's here. Now tell me what's wrong."

"It's bad. They got Henri Bergerant. Savage beating, apparently. Then they slit his throat. Blood all over the place, which incidentally was completely trashed. Henri wouldn't have been dumb enough to keep copies of any documents he made for you, would he?"

Baker closed his eyes. "Yeah, he might've been dumb enough. All his talent was concentrated in his fingers, not his fucking brain."

"More bad news."

"Jesus, Colin, you are just one barrel of laughs today."

"They also got your friend at National Defence. Body was found in his garage, in the car, which was running and had a hose leading from the tail pipe to the passenger compartment. If it weren't for the fact that he was missing most of his teeth and six of his fingers had been clipped off with a pair of pruning shears you might almost say he'd committed suicide."

Baker leaned against the wall, cool against his forehead, as he bit his lip.

"Doug, you there?"

He tried to find his voice and couldn't.

"Doug, for God's sake talk to me!"

He cleared his throat. "Yeah, I'm here."

"You think they talked?"

"Henri for sure. They wouldn't have been able to shut him up, he would've been so eager to talk. The other, I don't know." But he was thinking to himself, six fucking fingers. If he hadn't talked, they would've done all ten. And then started on his toes.

"You may be completely blown."

"Shit!"

"Next falls into the category of bad news, good news. Just as you said, they made another try on Joan. Just about did it, too. Two police officers hurt bad, but she's okay. Still unconscious."

"How'd they fail?"

"Like you, I have some friends in low places. Contacted and briefed a couple of them. Thanks to my friend at the hospital they got posted as night-time floor cleaners. Had miniature metal detectors hidden in the swabs and very specific instructions from me. Assassin shoots the officers, but before he could pull the pin and toss the grenade my guys got him. Wounded him. Then the bastard committed suicide. Looks like he had a cyanide capsule in his mouth, one of the glass-encased ones that doesn't dissolve and doesn't work until you bite down on it. No ID on him, of course, but he looks like an Arab."

"Colin, they may try again."

The Englishman's voice was grim. "Then they'd better use a nuclear weapon, because that hospital is now a fortress. Doug, I have to go. Read that fax." He hung up.

Baker stared at the receiver before slowly replacing it in the cradle. He walked over, forcing himself to smile, collected the fax and paid for it. As he walked to the car, he tried to keep his face impassive so as not to alarm Von Bessel.

How the hell did they know so much, so fast? And what was so important that it elicited such murderous desperation?

When Marie Françoise asked him if there was anything new, he said no. When she asked why he looked so thoughtful, he said he was trying to figure out a way of talking to someone in the know at Schweizerhalle. “I mean, it’s an industrial facility manufacturing hazardous chemicals and it’s already been torched once. I assume security is tight and I can’t just walk in off the street and start asking questions.”

“I have an idea,” she said.

THIRTY FIVE

I know the company and the way it is run, "Von Bessel continued. Because the 1986 catastrophe caused terrible public relations problems for the firm, they are very good at dealing with the public. I just hope they don't recognise my voice."

The two of them re-entered the Bier Stube and again used the phone. Baker fired up a Camel and listened as Von Bessel called the main public relations office of Sandoz and asked to speak to one of the media relations officers. Finally she was connected with one who was fluent in English. She explained that she and her husband were on vacation in the Basel area and that her husband was a fireman, specialising in industrial accidents involving hazardous chemicals, that he'd had a long-standing interest in the Schweizerhalle incident, and could he visit the site? Grudgingly Baker had to concede that the story was not half bad. Then the woman held up the phone so he could hear as the man on the other end of the line spluttered that he was much too busy to entertain complete strangers without a previous appointment, and that he had to leave immediately for a meeting in Zurich. Then he calmed down a little and said he could see no reason why they couldn't view the site from the back public access road. He asked only that they check in with the guards at the front gate of the facility and have their identification verified. Marie Françoise thanked him and hung up.

They drove back to the hotel and Baker shaved. They checked out, stashing their clothing and suitcases in the trunk. Five minutes later, in a new set of clothing, they were on the autobahn, travelling east towards the small industrial village of Muttenz. The closer they got to their destination, Baker noticed her mood progressively darken as she stared out of the window. This, he recalled, was the road on which her husband and son had died. He wondered where. Muttenz looked inconsequential as they entered from the west. Resting on a long plateau and nestled amongst thick deciduous forest, the land to the north dropped-off gently to the Rhine. Down the hill, on a thickly forested steppe, sprawled the extensive manufacturing facilities of industrial giants Sandoz and Ciba Geigy, as well as the tank farms of international petroleum producers. Beyond the rapidly flowing, green waters of the Rhine, was the German frontier.

Baker drove down the hill, turning onto a riverside service road at the north-western fringe of the Sandoz enclosure. They got out of the car. Standing on a rail siding facing the wide expanse of the Rhine, Marie Françoise stared blankly in the direction of the thick groves of oak choking the German side.

Baker stood next to her, trying to figure out a way of lifting her from her funk. "So this is where Phoenix got started?" She nodded mutely, her eyes filling with tears. He gave up and turned to look back at the Sandoz plant.

He had to admit he was impressed. He'd already noted that Switzerland was one of the tidiest places he'd ever seen. Now he marvelled at how even large industrial facilities like these were designed to fit into the landscape. All the structures he could see were painted in a sandy beige colour, giving a soothing impression of neutrality and cleanliness, as if they were some sort of impossibly square boulders, indigenous to the landscape. Scanning the sprawling site from east to west, he took in the six story high research and administrative building, by far the tallest structure on the site, bordered on two sides by hulking refinery superstructure. In the central zone, warehousing and support buildings were separated by service lanes providing a buffer zone to the barren expanse of concrete spreading about a hundred meters south to the far fence line, where the property ended in a rail siding, and another two hundred meters or so west to the Shell oil facility.

He knew that the flat, stark expanse before him was the sole memorial to the ill-fated Warehouse 956.

To the south-west, beyond the rail siding, a thickly treed verge monopolised the slope up the plateau to Muttenz. To the north, downhill to the river, Baker could easily visualise how the fire and the release of toxic chemicals would have been so difficult to stop. Remembering television news coverage of the fire, he recalled how torrents of contaminated fire control water had flowed downhill, unhindered by any storm water retention system, directly into the Rhine. He shook his head. Staging any clean-up activities in a river flowing so fast would have been impossible. He had a sudden mental image of a poisonous plume spreading for hundreds of kilometres, killing everything it encountered.

They drove back up the street separating the two chemical behemoths and parked at the main gate guard post. As they sat and looked at Schweizerhalle, Baker said, "I have an idea. But it depends on you staying in the car and the possibility that these guys speak lousy English."

With a big friendly smile, Baker walked up to the two young guards. Using English only and playing dumb, even though he understood their Swiss-German, Baker attempted to explain why he was there, and that he had been invited to see the facility. The two guards scratched their heads as they failed to find his name on the duty sheet of scheduled visitors. Feigning agitation, Baker provided the name of the media relations officer Von Bessel had spoken to.

One of the guards phoned head office to confirm the story, only to discover that the man had gone to Zurich, as Baker already knew. But his secretary remembered overhearing a little of the earlier conversation, and confirmed that permission had been given for something. Then she suggested that Baker be allowed into the facility to speak to the only man who could really answer questions about fire safety, the very man who had commanded the fire teams the night of November 1, 1986. Baker couldn't believe his luck. As Sandoz was obviously adhering to their policy of having nothing to hide from the public, he was welcomed in to big smiles from the guards. He gathered that one of the junior firemen would arrive shortly to direct him to the Fewer Kommandant's office. He turned and waved to Marie Françoise, still in the car. She nodded.

The young fire fighter who arrived explained, in very good English, that he was one of five full time fire specialists on the site. The remainder of the force consisted of volunteers from all production departments. As they toured the fire hall, it struck him that it was as well appointed as any he had ever seen. It was obvious the company was determined to avoid a repetition of the 1986 disaster. Then, he was escorted to the Fewer Kommandant's office. On the way, the big Mountie tried to remember everything he knew about hazardous chemicals management and fire fighting. It wasn't a lot. He hoped he knew enough to at least ask intelligent questions, even if the answers were beyond him.

Fewer Kommandant Theo Marti was a short, stocky alert man in his late fifties. Baker immediately decided that he liked him. Marti stated that he spoke no English, and asked the young fire fighter to stay and act as a translator, if necessary. Baker thought that maybe by playing up the language disability thing again would enable him to hide his ignorance.

He found himself smiling as Marti described that hellish November 1 night as the "worst bitch of a fire" any of them had ever seen. The rest of the details he remembered from his previous briefings. He nodded sympathetically as the stocky man said that he'd grown up along the Rhine and had been "sick with grief" at the devastation.

Baker chose his words carefully. "Kommandant, I have never been clear on the cause of the fire, or why it spread so fast and burned so hot."

Marti's eyes were appraising. "The first question, I believe we can answer. The other two. . ." He shrugged. "The official investigation determined the fire started as a result of some labelling work that was done earlier in the day on containers. As the labels in question required shrink fitting, a propane torch was used. It is the accepted means of heating during this procedure. But in this case, there appears to have been a freak accident. The containers in question contained a paint tint, azimuth blue, a compound that burns with no visible flame."

Baker nodded sagely, not knowing what Marti was talking about but trying to hide it.

"In the final analysis, the investigation teams theorised that somehow azimuth residues, the result of sloppy filling technique, were present on the outside of one of the containers. Somehow it ignited because of contact with the propane torch and no one noticed because there was no flame. Over the afternoon and evening it must have continued to smoulder until later that evening, it caught. Then, POOF, the whole place went up. That is the official explanation." It was plain the Kommandant was thinking, in a pig's eye.

Baker nodded. This was going to be delicate. "Are you personally convinced of the merits of the official investigation?"

Marti shrugged again. "I'm not totally sure of anything, except that the price of good beer is far too high." Baker could tell that the German side of the little man was coming out. "It is official. I have to live with it, for what good it does now."

Once again, the appraising gaze. "You are perhaps referring to the current investigation about terrorism?" Baker nodded. "And why would you be interested in that aspect?"

The man deserved a straight answer and Baker felt badly that he couldn't give one. "I've done investigative work for insurance companies and police forces in cases where arson has been suspected as the cause of a fire. The fact that the blaze spread so fast and burned so hot is suggestive. That it was carefully planned and set on purpose."

Marti's eyes were hooded. "You would not be the first to think so, I assure you. I cannot of course comment in my official capacity, but the possibility occurred to me that very night. One only has to look at the lay of the land at the back of the warehouse site and see that it wouldn't have taken much to jump the fence, get in, do the job, then get the hell away with absolutely no one being the wiser. The person who did it would have to be an expert, but. . ." Again, the shrug.

"I appreciate your honesty, Kommandant." Baker liked the little guy more and more. "What about the inventory in the warehouse? Have they ever pinned down what and how much material was lost that day? Into the Rhine, I mean?"

Marti was now more definite as he moved away from conjecture and back into the realm of hard fact. "That is something we are quite sure about. Come over here." He directed Baker to his desk and an active computer screen. "Just one moment and I'll clear the screen I was working on. Ja, here it is. A complete listing of the inventory at the time of the fire." He swung the screen around for Baker to see. "Look at this. What a bloody mess. Agrochemicals, paints, solvents, pharmaceuticals, you name it. Over one hundred thousand kilograms."

Transfixed by the length of the list and struggling to remember his organic chemistry courses, he tried to pick out what components could be used in nerve toxins. He drew a blank. "Amazing," he said, just to say something.

"Ja, it was incredible. Little wonder the fire was such a bitch. Most of the stuff in there would have gone up by itself. Mixed together-" He didn't have to say it. He contemplated Baker. "This list is common knowledge now. Would you like a copy?"

Surprised, Baker said, "Please, if I could." As Marti hit the print button the Canadian said, "I must say this is quite the system you have here. Are you independent of the rest of Sandoz or tied in?"

"As I am considered a department head, I have access to almost every other department. It helps to have the communication integrated. Helps ward off any potential fire emergencies."

The two of them contemplated the list spewing from the high-speed printer. When it had finished the Fewer Kommandant handed him the sheets of paper. "And now, if you will excuse me, I have another meeting. I will have someone show you further around the site, if you wish. It was a pleasure to speak with you." Baker could tell the man had been on the verge of saying, 'with another fireman' but had changed his mind. One last appraising glance and he was gone.

The young fire fighter was enthusiastic, almost to a fault. Baker encouraged him to talk, learning far more than he had ever wanted to know about hoses and sprinklers, storm water drains and settling ponds. But, Baker couldn't stop from gawking at the storm water runoff management system, a huge underground cavern stretching the equivalent of a city block. The techno-talk was interspersed with personal information about himself, his team and even the tavern in little Muttenz, where they all went for a drink after work - including, on most occasions, Herr Kommandant himself.

Finally Baker said, "So this is the system that was put in place by the company after the fire?"

The fireman nodded. "If this had been in place in 1986, not a drop of anything would have reached the Rhine. Not a drop. Some of the older men don't have a very high opinion of the Phoenix Foundation, but I do."

The staff sergeant nodded. "So it was Phoenix that agitated to have this system built?"

"Ja. And now it is emulated by most chemical facilities across Europe." Baker found himself engaged in a substantial upward revision of his estimate of Marie Françoise Von Bessel's abilities.

Finally the tour was over and he had his hand pumped by the young fireman. Back at the main gate Marie Françoise was still in the car, fitfully snoozing in the front seat. She woke when he opened the car door.

"Did it go well?"

"Yes. Let's grab some lunch. And later on today there is a happening little Bier Stube in Muttenz we need to check out."

THIRTY SIX

A magnum of Feldsclossen beer in his hand, his head filled with pounding music and his nostrils with some of the pale blue cloud of cigarette smoke hanging over a full house, Douglas Baker surveyed his surroundings. Every wooden table was filled, the walls covered with stag's heads and shelving holding every imaginable kind of beer mug or stein. Despite some of the kitsch touches, this was obviously a real place where real people came to unwind after work, not the sort of Ye Olde English Pub that he'd seen elsewhere in Europe, that served watery beer, overpriced sandwiches and prefab fries, and catered only to tourists. Nothing could be finer and Baker was in his element.

It was 4:45 in the afternoon. He'd made a few discreet phone calls, including one to Colin Stewart. He'd also faxed Colin a copy of Theo Marti's printout and grilled Von Bessel, then called the SAS man again. He'd been given some new information - Stewart wouldn't say where he'd got his from - and he was turning it over in his mind as he contemplated his probable plan of action. Until he saw how this particular gambit was going to play out, he'd banished Marie Françoise Von Bessel to a remote booth behind the fireplace, several tables away from the one at which he had chosen to wait. At exactly 5 p.m., Fewer Kommandant Theo Marti entered with three young firemen and surveyed the room. His smile vanished as his eyes fastened unblinkingly on Baker, then narrowed slightly as the Canadian waved. He gestured at a table and his three companions sat down. Marti walked over and stood next to the table, but did not acknowledge either Baker's smile or his proffered hand. "Guten Abend. Getrank?"

"Your German has improved remarkably since this afternoon,"

replied Marti coldly. "I do not wish to be rude, but I am not in the habit of having a drink with men who first misrepresent themselves and then follow me. I am sure you understand I feel somewhat taken advantage of? I suggest you state your business and be quick about it."

"I apologise for the deceit, Kommandant. It was necessary until I had a chance to size you up. The fact that I am here at all is something you should take as a compliment. I am Staff Sergeant Douglas Baker of the Royal Canadian Mounted Police and I am working on a case. One that involves you and the Schweizerhalle fire of 1986. Please sit down and let me buy you a drink."

Marti sat down. Baker handed him his RCMP ID card. He grunted. "A nice badge, good picture on the card. My ten year old son could forge this." He handed it back. "I'm waiting. But not for much longer."

"The fire was intentionally set. In the past few weeks those who did it have attempted two assassinations and murdered half a dozen people. You know about the attempts on the head of the Phoenix Foundation? One in Brussels and one in Vancouver?"

"Of course." Marti suddenly looked very alert.

"They have also tried to kill me. We still don't know why this is happening, but we have very strong evidence that the Iraqi government is behind it."

The Kommandant's eyes widened. "Iraqis?"

"Yes."

"Why?"

Baker lit a Camel as the mug of beer was placed in front of the fireman. "Haven't you heard the details?"

The fireman sipped his beer. "I know there is an investigation underway at the highest levels. I am not a policy person nor am I an executive, which means I am not privy to such information. I understand it concerns nerve gas components that were mixed in with legitimate shipments of chemicals. Frankly, I find it almost impossible to believe."

"Impossible? How?"

"As you may know, we Swiss are a most efficient lot. The company I work for is what I think in English you call 'a tight ship'. You are not familiar with how this company is run, but I am. There are hundreds of chemical facilities across Europe where it would be much easier to do the secret storing and transportation of nerve gas. Any plant at all in Eastern Europe. There are facilities on the Italian peninsula and in Sicily where security is as leaky as an old whore's bladder. Places where they would be far more responsive to penetration by Iraqis than we are. What proof do you have?"

The Canadian contemplated his mug. "There's a man, a recent employee of Sandoz, who's disappeared. Klaus Staffel, an accountant. He forged the manifests to hide the nature of the shipments, but he was just a bookkeeper. There had to be someone else in the company, right in the facility, who actually supervised the mixing of the shipments, the actual handling and loading." Baker took another swallow of beer and frowned. "As you say, why Sandoz and not some other company, one easier to infiltrate? I think I know the answer."

The Kommandant was motionless. "I like answers. Please continue."

"The answer is, it was your facility at Schweizerhalle where the man who did the actual handling worked, probably for many years and probably with a spotless reputation. Based on what I have learned today, the inventory sheets you showed me this morning are incomplete."

"My inventory sheets are never incomplete," snapped Marti.

Baker bored in. He'd got this information from Von Bessel, who'd in turn got hers from mysterious contacts. This was the stuff she'd also given to the CIA, the information she hadn't revealed to the public. "Missing from it are two chemicals, phosphorus oxychloride and dimethylamine. Alone, they're next to harmless. But together, they are the foundation compounds for a very toxic nerve agent, based on the Nazi gas Sarin. The handling of these two chemicals in such huge quantities is not a task you would give to an amateur. The secret operation was done at your facility because the Iraqi agent or agents with the expertise to do it just happened to work there. And if security is as tight as you say it is, they must have been in a responsible position or positions. Do you understand?"

Theo Marti drained his beer. "First, we have never had Iraqis working at our facility. Second, I am a loyal company man and I do not like such insinuations. Third, I still have no proof that you even are who you claim to be. Anyone can make up such nonsense. Thank you for the drink. If you will excuse me. . ."

"I understand your hesitation. I have a way to convince you." He gave the high sign to Marie Françoise, who rose, picked up her drink and came over to the table. Obviously uncertain whether to be rude to a woman, the Kommandant watched as she approached.

She stood right in front of him and removed her sunglasses. "Hello, Theo."

There was a look of complete shock on the stocky fireman's face. Finally he found his voice. "Frau Von Bessel?" he whispered. He looked at Baker. "He is my bodyguard and protector," she said. "You may trust him implicitly." Again, a hooded glance. "As I do."

Marti sat down again. "All of this, about the Iraqis and the nerve gas, all of it - is true?" She nodded.

"How can I help?" asked Marti. The Canadian smiled. When Swiss Germans decided to be decisive, they were all business.

"Did you know Klaus Staffel?" queried Baker.

"By sight. Nothing else."

"Can you think of anyone in the facility who could have had the kind of expertise necessary to handle the nerve gas components, which are not exactly standard issue chemicals, on almost a daily basis and not be found out?"

The Kommandant's eyes flickered. Baker frowned as he saw it. He seemed about to say something and then changed his mind. "No."

"Have you ever heard the name Tousignant?"

"No." No hesitation this time.

"Will you think about all of this?" asked Baker. "Someone, somewhere, knows something that they are either hiding or that they don't know the significance of."

The little man nodded decisively. "I will think. I will ask around." He rose from the table and bowed. "Frau Von Bessel." He turned to Baker. "Staff Sergeant. You may phone me at any time." He scribbled his work and home phone numbers on a napkin and handed it to Baker. The Canadian nodded his thanks and Marti rejoined his three companions. Baker threw some francs on the table and they left.

****

Later that evening Baker used the public telephone in the very noisy nightclub at the end of the street from their new hotel.

"I can barely hear you," complained Colin. "What is that in the background, a train wreck?"

Baker turned his head away from the sounds of the cyberpunk group called Second Captain. "Any better?"

"Yes. Your taste in music seems to have gone berserk. But I don't have time for this. It appears they are on to you and hot on your trail. They have you all the way to Basel. Once again, I strongly suggest you make contact with Inspector Erika Haus. Did you read the fax?"

"Yes." He'd read it before the meeting with Theo Marti.

"Do you intend to contact her?"

"Yes. But I'll do it my way, just in case."

"Fair enough. Your discretion. I suggest you enlist her assistance in checking on missing persons, around about the time of the Schweizerhalle fire. Don't have any details, but Joan was definitely pursuing that line of inquiry. As for Colonel Aziz Hamani, it seems he's been very active here in British Columbia. Was involved with a couple of Iraqi bigwigs who settled in North Vancouver after the Gulf war. It appears he has agents here. That may be our link to the leak at E Division." There was a brief pause, a soft click, then "Damn. I'm gone." Click.

Baker stared at the receiver, his sixth sense on overdrive.

THIRTY SEVEN

Basel, Switzerland, March 22

The underground parking garage was cavernous. Despite being well lit, the fluorescent lights threw eerie pools of foreboding shadow.

Silently the elevator door opened and a tall, leggy brunette stepped out. In her mid thirties, she was attractive in a healthy, outdoorsy way, and looked athletic enough to take care of herself in most situations. She had long dark brown hair and stood just over six feet tall. She was dressed in a navy suit with a pale green blouse, carried a shoulder purse almost as large as a brief case and wore a dark grey London Fog raincoat. She was hurrying, as if she was late for work.

She bent to insert the key into the driver's door of a late model Peugeot. As she did so, she felt an arm snake around her neck and tighten mercilessly against her carotid arteries, while her left arm was twisted behind her back. Panicked, she maintained enough presence of mind to judge that the pressure applied, while not enough to make her black out, indicated that whoever had hold of her was a professional. Adrenaline surging, she was about to let go of the car key with her right hand, reach up and seize the little finger of the man's hand - no matter how big and strong someone was, their pinkie finger would snap like a twig and it would hurt like hell - then turn around and deliver a swift knee to the groin.

She felt the cold pressure of a gun barrel against her temple. In German, with a slight trace of an accent she couldn't quite place, a voice said in her ear. "Don't make any sudden moves. Do exactly as I say and you will not be harmed. I just want to ask you a few questions. Do you understand?" She nodded. The man's body pressed her against the car door and she gritted her teeth. He took the keys from her hand and opened it. "Get behind the wheel, lower the rear view mirror and stare straight ahead. Do it now please." She complied. She heard him press the button that would unlock all of the other doors, then open the rear door and enter the car. She could feel the gun on her at all times. The vehicle creaked and rocked as he got in and shut the door. Big man.

Then she heard the other rear door open. She closed her eyes, trying not to panic. Christ, there are two of them. Then she smelled the faint bouquet of expensive perfume. A woman.

"Now drive out of the lot. Go to the meat packing plant two blocks away and park in the alley near the rear entrance to the Kit Kat Club. Drive slowly and don't do anything stupid." Once at their destination, she parked the car and waited, staring straight ahead at a brick wall.

"Criminal Inspector Erika Haus, Basel Police Department? Interpol representative here in Basel?" asked the man's voice from the back seat.

"Ja." She was surprised.

"This is about Sergeant Joan Chan. The name familiar to you?"

She felt her eyes widen. "Yes. Why-"

"I will ask the questions. When were you last in contact with Sergeant Chan?"

She had finally placed the accent. "Three, four months ago, perhaps. Would you like me to speak English if that will make this easier for you?"

"Okay," he said. "You're sure it was that long ago?"

"Yes. I received a phone message several days ago but when I called back I was told she was on sick leave."

"How did you meet Sergeant Chan?"

"A few years ago at an Interpol workshop. We have been friends ever since, although of necessity, long distance."

"Do you know that she attempted to access information from both Basel City police and Interpol concerning a motor vehicle fatality that occurred several years ago just outside of Basel and that her request was denied?"

"No, I did not know that." Haus frowned. "An ordinary MVA? There is no reason for access to be denied. What is this all about? I do not believe a friend of Joan's would abduct me at gun point."

"Someone's tried to kill her. Twice. She's in a coma and may not pull out of it. The first assassination attempt occurred about twenty minutes after she submitted the information request to you as Interpol rep and she realised she was being traced."

"Mein Gott," breathed the tall brunette. It was clear the news was a genuine surprise. "Why?"

"I believe the attack was tied to a case she was working on. I'm investigating that case. I need your help. She was trying to contact you just before the first attempt was made on her life. You may know something, or have access to information, that may assist me. I need to know if I can trust you, and whether you will help me."

Inspector Haus considered her words carefully before she spoke. "I don't know who you are, or the lady either. It is usual in such cases to go through channels. Sticking a gun to my head and kidnapping me is hardly proper procedure. I must trust you as well. At least you know who I am."

"We'll get to show and tell a little later. The reason I'm not doing this through channels is because the channels all seem to be filled with shadowy figures with microphones in their ears, if you catch my drift. I suspect who some of them are, but there seem to be people within my own organisation."

"Which is?" asked Haus, with more confidence than she had felt since the beginning of this ordeal. It was funny what you could tell about a person's motives and sincerity just from the sound of their voice.

"Royal Canadian Mounted Police."

"I see."

"I can't seem to take a piss without these people knowing about it."

"And who are these listeners?"

"Some of them are Iraqi military intelligence. The others, I don't know."

Haus digested this for several moments. Before she could speak again, the man said, "Any request from Joan that was directed to you as Interpol rep you would have seen personally, right?"

"Yes. When was the request sent?"

"About four days ago."

"In that case, no." She started to raise her left arm and suddenly felt the gun again at the back of her head. "I'm not suicidal, you know," she chided.

"Slowly, then."

The woman raised her arm and pulled back the cuff of her blouse with right hand. Half of her hand and her wrist were encased in a flesh-coloured plastic wrist cast. "I was on vacation, skiing in Grindlwald. Fell on the last run of the day. Always a mistake to do one last run when you are tired. I only got back to work yesterday. There was no record of such a request on my files, I assure you."

"But there should have been, correct?"

"Correct."

"I believe it was intercepted," said the man.

He could tell she didn't believe him. "Mr. Mountie, if that is what you really are, I do not believe that Iraqi military intelligence would have the slightest interest in the Basel office of Interpol. We have been a neutral nation for five hundred years, remember?"

"I think they do have an interest. And I know why."

"Ja? Weshalb?" she asked sceptically.

"Why? Schweizerhalle, the night of November 1, 1986."

The inspector nodded slowly. "The current investigation into allegations of terrorism, with information supplied by Frau Von Bessel of the Phoenix Foundation. The attempt on her life in Brussels. And in Vancouver."

"Joan Chan was investigating the Schweizerhalle fire and Von Bessel when the first attempt was made on her own life."

Involuntarily Erika Haus's eyes flicked to the rear view mirror. It was still down and she couldn't see anything of the two people in the back seat. She decided to be bold and hazard a guess. "And you feel your life is still in danger, Frau Von Bessel?"

"Yes," replied the environmentalist, before she knew what she was doing.

The inspector tensed, then realised the rasping sound in her ear was the man behind her chuckling. "Inspector," he said, "I like your style."

Five minutes later, Erika Haus drove her Peugeot up to a busy intersection. "Remember, don't look around," said the man. "You have my cell phone number. Call me when you have something. Do not under any circumstances use the phones in your office - use a pay phone instead, preferably one outside the building. When you call back I'll tell you where we will meet. It will be a public place so I feel safe. I will initiate contact on my own terms and only if I am sure you are alone. If you are not alone, I will know you cannot be trusted. Before you give me any information, I will establish my bona fides. Auf Wiedersehen for now."

And then they were gone. She quickly turned up the mirror, then twisted around. All she could see were the crammed sidewalks of Basel during morning rush hour. The light changed and she drove off, thinking hard.

Baker met Marie Françoise five minutes later in a small cafe next to the main train station.

"So, what did you think of our friend back there?" inquired Baker.

"I trust her," replied Von Bessel. She hesitated briefly. "I am sorry for responding the way I did."

Baker grinned. "Not your fault. Oldest trick in the book. Know how you can tell for sure if someone is just pretending to be deaf or catatonic?" She shook her head. "Stare at them in sudden horror and say, 'There's a spider on top of your head!' When they move to brush it off, bingo."

She smiled.

Baker sipped his coffee. "She'll contact us when she has something. Since she knows what she's looking for, it shouldn't take long. You know this town, I don't. Where is a meeting place we can use when we see her again? I need some place that's near the main police station, with lots of people, but quiet. I want a place where we can see her clearly at all times but she can't see us until we're ready. I want to check it out thoroughly before we schedule a meeting, to make sure it meets our purposes."

Marie Françoise thought for a moment and her eyes brightened. "Oui, there is such a place."

Erika Haus telephoned at 5:45 that afternoon to say that she had information. Baker said, "Meet me in fifteen minutes at the main municipal library, the reading section off the main hall." Marie Françoise stationed herself on the mezzanine, overlooking Baker's position on the main floor in a small reading cubicle. The Mountie had insisted on this: "If she's going to betray us and bring company, then I'll be the only one to go down. With the dyed hair and the glasses and the clothes, you should be able to get away." He'd given her Colin Stewart's number. "If I'm taken, call Colin. He'll tell you what to do."

At exactly six p.m. Inspector Haus found her place at the study table, next to a copy of the Swiss Train System Baker had laid out for her. She sat down and began inspecting both covers as instructed. He studied her from his location across the hall. She was not visibly nervous. He continued to watch her and the entrances for a further ten minutes, convincing himself that she hadn't set a trap. Standing, he began pushing the loaded book cart he'd commandeered, the one that hid most of him from view as he sat in the cubicle. The Glok from the Canadian army uniform was wedged between a stack of periodicals, within inches of his right hand. He crossed the twenty-metre space, leisurely picking up discarded books as he went. Reaching her table, he placed a German language translation of John Le Carre's The Secret Pilgrim in front of her. It had somehow seemed like the right touch under the circumstances. He remembered her snort of derision when he had told her this would be the signal to initiate contact. He liked Erika Haus more and more.

He backed away from her table, pulling the cart down one of the aisles, his eyes first watching to see if she was giving any sort of subtle signal, then searching the rest of the room. Nothing. She picked up the book and followed him down the aisle. He shoved the cart into an alcove, tucked the gun under his jacket, making sure she could see it, and strode beside her. Once they were around the corner of stacks with volumes on Carolingian Gnosticism, which Baker had rightly surmised would be devoid of readers, they sat down opposite each other at a remote study carrel. She appraised him narrowly. "I don't think I have ever in my life seen a man who looks less like a librarian."

Baker grinned. "Thanks for coming." He reached into his jacket and withdrew his wallet, flipping it open to expose the RCMP ID. He remembered Theo Marti's reaction. "My bona fides. All I've got."

She barely even looked at it. "I've checked you out. And your story about Joan." Seeing the alarm on his face, she added, "Using a common work station that dozens of people have access too, and using a scrambler."

Baker visibly relaxed, remembering the deaths of Bergerant and Williams. "So what do you have?"

"Your surmise was correct. Someone is most interested to keep the incident quiet, but I do not know whom. I could not use the computer records in case the search could be traced, and given that the incident happened so long ago I knew there would a record on our old microfiche system in the archives. Only there isn't. The particular MVA you are interested in, the one in which Christian Von Bessel and his son died, has been . . . what was Joan's favourite term? Sanitised."

Baker saw Von Bessel flit between two rows of stacks, behind Haus, listening intently. He nodded at Haus as she continued. "Given the fact that the records are missing or inaccessible, I need to know precisely why this particular accident is of interest to you and what you are looking for."

He filled her in on the anomalies Joan Chan had identified. She tugged thoughtfully at the sleeve of her suit. "Well, I did search the staff duty logs for the night of the incident. I found the traffic officer who responded to the MVA call and was first on the scene. He was off duty today, but he was at home and I talked to him there."

"Did he remember the case?"

"Everyone in this city remembers what they were doing the night of Schweizerhalle. It is something we here in Basel will not soon forget."

"I'm listening." He was wondering how Von Bessel would react to all of this.

"Terrible case. The bodies were badly burned but it was clear they were of an adult male and a young boy. Frau Von Bessel was of no use during the autopsy. Identification was made based on the serial numbers on vehicle parts and the dental records. The dental records were judged to be the conclusive evidence. You can't fake those, as you know."

The big Mountie was deep in thought. "Did the officer mention anything unusual at all about the accident and its aftermath?"

"Just one thing. When he went to close out the file some weeks later, he noted that the report from the insurance company hadn't arrived. When he checked further, he found out why. The wreck had been sent to the wrong impound lot, then transferred a few days later to the correct one. They quickly got that straightened out and the claim settled. Nothing else out of the ordinary. These things happen sometimes, even in Switzerland."

Something was fishy, but Baker couldn't put his finger on it. "So forensics on the vehicle were done later than they otherwise would have been?"

"Yes. But nothing was found. Why, is it important?"

Just as Baker was thinking, they wouldn't have found anything if the car had been already cleaned to remove traces, he heard the faint sound of sobbing. Haus looked around, startled. "Marie Françoise," he called softly. She came around the corner, wiping her eyes.

"Frau Von Bessel?" asked Erika Haus uncertainly. The disguise must be better than he'd thought. She looks like a lost little waif. He wanted to confide some of his suspicions to the inspector, but not with the environmentalist in this state. What with fear, exhaustion and the still-lingering trauma of her family's violent death, it wouldn't take much to push her over the edge.

The two police officers looked at each other. Haus walked over and put her arm around the tiny woman, whispering something in her ear.

After a few minutes Haus asked where they were staying. Told it was yet another seedy hotel, she had offered to put them up at her home. The offer was gratefully accepted. They agreed to get their belongings and meet her there. The inspector made a pointed remark about catching up on their sleep, which Baker knew, was the woman's way of telling him to make Von Bessel go to bed and stave off exhaustion. Once in the woman's small home, Marie Françoise went straight to bed, Haus went out and Baker sat on the sofa and thought.

At 8:40 that evening he came to a decision. He dialed a number on his cell phone. "Fewer Kommandant? It's Staff Sergeant Douglas Baker."

"Herr Baker, I am very glad you called. I have thought a great deal about what you said concerning Schweizerhalle and I must say that I now believe you to be right. I must also say that I think helping you is something my employer would want me to do. I've done some checking."

"Thank you, Kommandant. Go on."

"I had staff do some research through our finance department. They are usually able to trace former employees, but not Klaus Staffel. As you say, he has disappeared. No place even to send his severance and pension checks. Most unusual." There was a pause. Marti had something, but he didn't want to say it.

"Go on," encouraged Baker. "Anything at all."

"Before I tell you, I wish you to understand something," said the fireman stiffly. "I am an honourable man."

What on earth was he talking about? "I know that already," replied the mystified Mountie. Then he remembered the stocky man's eyes flickering at the Bier Stube in Muttenz with Marie Françoise. What had been the question that had prompted the shifty response?

"I repeat, I am an honourable man who likes to deal with plain facts and not conjecture. Guessing is for fools."

"Kommandant, I understand." Baker was leaning forward now, tense with anticipation. "What is it?"

"You asked if I could think of anyone at Schweizerhalle who would have had enough expertise to handle volatile nerve gas components on almost a daily basis and not be found out. Someone in a responsible position who had probably been there for many years with a spotless reputation. I don't know if you have thought of this, but it would also have had to be someone with unquestioned access to every part of the facility, including the finance department where Staffel worked."

"Go on."

"I repeat, I am an honourable man who does not traffic in innuendo." Baker resisted the urge to sigh. The Swiss Germans could be stubborn, unbending and unimaginative, but in the best of the breed there was a granite integrity that had always inspired his utmost respect.

"An honourable man who does not speak ill of the dead."

"I beg your pardon, Kommandant?"

"I have wracked my brains and I can think of only one such person who was at Schweizerhalle in 1986 and before."

"Who?"

"I thought of mentioning it to you in the Bier Stube, but I couldn't under the circumstances."

C'mon, c'mon, thought Baker. For Christ's sake spit it out. Who?

"Christian Von Bessel."

Baker said, idiotically, "Mrs. Von Bessel's dead husband?"

"Yes. He was senior vice president in charge of research and development for a number of years. I . . . liked the man. He was brilliant, a very nice fellow who didn't deserve the comments to the effect that the only reason he got his job was due to Frau Von Bessel's father. No, he was a very hard worker. I only tell you all this because he would have had access, but I can not for an instant believe he was involved. I hope this information is helpful to you. If I find out anything more I will let you know."

"Thank you, Kommandant Marti. You have been most helpful." He rang off, his mind racing. He looked at his watch. Time to call Colin.

****

"Everything okay?"

"Yes," replied Stewart. "Finally got what triggered the big trace hunt on Joan. Given the age of the file, it must've contained a hidden trace command activated automatically when an intruder was detected."

"OK."

"The dental records on Christian Von Bessel. When she got shut out there, she started searching for anything on the name Tousignant. Because there was nothing locally, she tried all of Switzerland and Germany. Blank. Finally she tried a nation-wide search in France. Bingo. A missing person in Paris. In fact, four of them, all named Tousignant, all missing at almost exactly the same time."

"Four Tousignants?" asked Baker incredulously. "Missing when?"

"Within a few days of the fire," said Stewart. "Now it gets really interesting. Joan's hit activated another sleeping trace command. The two sets of files - the dental records and Tousignant - are obviously connected and obviously protected by someone with the same style of computer programming."

Baker remembered the click he'd heard on the line during their last conversation. "Have they traced you?"

"They're trying. I've re-routed my connections but I'd better go. You have anything?"

Quickly Baker filled him in on the information he'd got from Erika Haus and Theo Marti. There was a long pause on the other end of the line. "You've got me there," the Englishman said finally. "Delayed forensics on a mis-delivered vehicle. Very suggestive. I'll think on it. Where to next?"

"I think it's time to audit somebody's books."

"Good idea. Be careful. If he's in hiding, I doubt he has the experience to do it himself. He's being guarded or watched. Doug, I have to go." He rang off.

THIRTY EIGHT

Erika Haus's home, although attractive and beautifully furnished, was like the country in which it was situated: very small, and made mountainous, like the Alps, by steep narrow stairways; you were always climbing. Baker felt like a mutant Ninja warrior in a dollhouse - he was always banging his head on the low doorframes. Marie Françoise had the only guest room, located on the main floor, while Baker had the short, narrow couch in the living room to sleep on. As he looked at it he could still feel the crick in his neck and the tight hamstrings from his previous two nights uncomfortable accommodation. "Wonder if this qualifies me for a disability pension," he muttered under his breath.

They had completed the next day's strategic planning about half an hour after the inspector had finally arrived home. Erika turned in, retiring to her second floor bedroom. Baker wanted to get to sleep himself. He'd been waiting fifteen minutes to use the main floor bathroom, presently occupied by Von Bessel. He strained his ears. Not a sound. Had he missed her leaving the room and going to bed? Shoeless, he walked to the door and listened. Not a sound. The door was ajar. He pushed it open, to see the back of Marie Françoise's half clad body, dressed only in a short T-shirt and cranberry coloured panties. Tooth brush in hand, she stared blankly, as if catatonic, into the mirror. She didn't even seem to notice that he'd entered the room.

He'd seen that look before. Bad sign. Gazing at the slender body, he remembered what had happened in Vancouver. "Marie?" He touched her shoulder and a convulsive tremor ran through her. She reached back for his hand, holding it, bringing it forward to rest against the skin of her bare midriff. Slowly, haltingly, she turned toward him, her upcast eyes, those dark pools of sadness seeking him out, pleading for understanding. "Pourquoi?

"Why what?" he asked gruffly.

"Why is all of this happening? What does it mean? Why weren't Christian and Daniel in that car? Where are they now?"

"I don't know. They probably were in the car. We'll find out."

"Sometimes I feel I shall go mad. That I am mad." Her eyes searched his. "Promise me."

"Promise you what?"

"Promise me that I will never have to go back to an institution. Being there is like . . . being in the cellar. Trapped. Promise you'll protect me. Swear on your soul and on the eyes of your daughter Valerie."

As he looked into her imploring, desperate gaze, Baker didn't know what to say. He could refuse. He could lie. His first instinct as an honest man was to say that he couldn't make such a promise, that it would be dishonest to promise something he couldn't guarantee. Then he decided that Marie Françoise's sanity, at this moment, was more precious than telling the truth. A lesser man would have felt guilty. But Baker knew what he was going to say before he even formulated the thought. He was doing his duty, taking charge to protect the weak and the innocent, making an intelligent decision under difficult circumstances. Showing some character. "I swear on my soul and on the eyes of my daughter Valerie."

Tears rolled down her cheeks and she clutched him like a woman just saved from drowning. He kissed the top of her head. The chestnut hair was warm and spicy, smelling of cinnamon and sandalwood. As she raised her head and kissed him, as he felt the wonderfully soft lips and the hot strawberry tongue searching his mouth, he remembered Colin Stewart's crack about a lapse in his professionalism. As he swept her off her feet to carry her into the bedroom he thought, to hell with that.

An hour later, they lay in each other's arms, Marie Françoise snuggled against his chest. As the scorching heat of passion cooled to the cosy warmth of well-banked embers, Baker found the investigator in him once again starting to take charge. He knew it wasn't the right moment, was probably a crude thing to do under the circumstances, but he had to know.

He had liked Fewer Kommandant Theo Marti from the moment he'd met him; they were a couple of peas in a pod. Marti was a cool-headed professional with an appraising way, a man you couldn't fool for long, if at all. And Marti, a man whose opinion Baker respected, had said he liked Christian Von Bessel. Did he not know about the womanising, the executive's other side? Or did he not care? Unlikely, thought Baker, Marti was a principled man.

Baker rolled over on one elbow. "Marie Françoise," he whispered, "I must ask your about your husband. Tell me more about him."

"Why do you want to know about him?" She was obviously startled and reluctant to talk, but he had to press the point.

"What kind of man was he? What were his interests, apart from his work? What sort of family did he come from?" He thought about the dental work. "Why did he travel so much, and where did he go?"

"He was a very intelligent man who lived for his science. He had no other interests. He never talked about his family, except to say that he was an only child who had been unhappy and that he had loved his father very much. He never talked about his work or his trips. He said they were all business related." Baker could see she thought she was making her late husband sound cold and neglectful, as she added defensively, "He was also very good to myself and Daniel. He adored his son."

Something was wrong. She was hiding something. "He was good to you?"

"As I told you before, he was very generous, always buying me presents and showering me with attention."

Yeah, thought Baker, when he was home. Guilty conscience? Or some sort of act? "If he loved his family so much, why was he unfaithful to you?" He knew how insensitive this sounded, saw the wound appear in the eyes, tried to make up for it. "If you were mine, I'd never be unfaithful to you." As he saw the wild hopeful light dawn in her face he thought, damn, too much - I've overcompensated.

But the next moment, he knew it had worked. "I don't know why he was unfaithful to me." She hesitated. "May I ask you a question?"

"Sure."

"Am I a bad lover?"

He was about to make a joke of it when he realised she was absolutely serious. Suddenly he remembered the first time they had made love, her clawing violence, the fact that he'd had to restrain her, make her slow down. What had been her remark then? 'I had no idea it could be gentle like that.'

He stroked her face. "You are a wonderful lover. Maybe the best I've ever had." Women always liked hearing that. "Now how do I rate amongst the lovers you've had?"

She lay back as her eyes searched the ceiling. "The best by far. But I haven't had a lot of experience. I've only ever been with two men. The gardener who raped me and Christian."

Douglas Baker felt an icy hand squeeze his heart. He wasn't a man prone to pity, but he felt a sudden stab of terrible sympathy for this lovely, lonely, damaged woman. The clawing violence - as if she thought making love like that was normal. Her only experience of sex had been with the rapist and with her husband. 'I had no idea it could be gentle like that.' The stab of pity was replaced by a spike of rage. All of a sudden, he knew he disagreed with Theo Marti. He didn't like Christian Von Bessel.

Then the realisation hit him like a thunderbolt. The man had been unfaithful to this woman. He had to be unfaithful. She was his wife, he was employed in his wife's father's company. If he was sexually violent, he could only go so far with her. He realised he hated the man even though he'd never met him and never would. Burned alive, he thought. Good fucking riddance.

He gazed at her face. Her lips were trembling as she tried not to cry. He kissed her eyes. "You know what we say in North America when something hurts?" She shook her head.

He pulled her towards him. "You have to kiss it to make it better."

THIRTY NINE

Basel, Switzerland, March 23

The alarm clock jarred them awake. Baker looked groggily at his watch. "You want some coffee?" Von Bessel yawned and nodded sleepily. "I'll make coffee, you use the bathroom first."

He padded into the kitchen. Erika Haus had left a note telling them to meet her at her office at lunchtime. Based on the previous evening's discussion, he knew where they were going to go. He put the aromatic black grounds into the automatic espresso coffee maker and poured cold milk into the steamer unit, then turned the machine on. He went to the phone and called Colin. All he heard was a hollow hiss. He tried again. Same thing.

He felt a sagging sense of unease as he showered, shaved and dressed, then drank his coffee. The dye had come out of his hair and he didn't care. It had come out of Von Bessel's too. Fuck it. Come and get me, you bastards. As Von Bessel completed her preparations he opened his briefcase and contemplated its contents. He selected a couple of fake credit cards, just in case. Next he chose a rectangular silver object about the size of a Swiss army knife and another object of roughly the same size, only made of blue plastic. He lifted a compartment and took out a red plastic case. From it he removed four tiny flat metal disks, each about the diameter of a pencil eraser but as thin as a dime. He took out a small envelope, dropped them in and sealed it. Next he removed an earpiece, a tangle of wiring and what looked like a small Sony Walkman. He dropped these various objects into his pockets and closed the lid just as Von Bessel came into the room.

They caught a cab to the downtown area, browsed a bit, then ate an early lunch at the Frisco Bar next to the police station. After coffee Baker smoked a Camel, then looked at his watch and stood, throwing a wad of francs on the table as they walked out the door.

The headquarters of the Basel City Police was located on Spiegelasse. Monopolising half a block, it was a four story grey and cream concrete structure of recent construction, as ugly and utilitarian as any other police station in the world. As they walked through the single white wooden door under the sign marked 'Polizeiposten' and into the entrance, Baker realised that it even had the same smell as other police stations, a compound of coffee, cigarettes, half-eaten lunches abandoned on desks, and the faint scent of gun oil. Erika Haus was there to meet them, so they were able to avoid the bullpen and the multi-desk squad room. They went directly to her office.

"Sleep well, the two of you?" she asked sardonically. Baker realised she would've seen this morning as she left that he was not on the sofa.

"Just fine thanks." He noticed Von Bessel was colouring slightly. "What's the agenda?"

The inspector's eyes flicked upward and Baker followed her gaze. There was a video camera recessed into the vent in the wall. "Let's go for lunch, shall we?" She directed them down the corridor to a bank of elevators, keeping up a friendly banter all the way to the basement. Exiting the elevator compartment, they entered the parking garage and her Peugeot. With a finger to her lips, she gave the message and in silence they drove the three kilometres north to the City Hospital.

Down in the basement, in a long dully-lit corridor painted the same institutional bird shit green of older hospitals the world over, she stopped them and finally spoke. In a hushed voice she said, "Sorry for all the secrecy, but this case has got me a bit paranoid. Who knows who might be watching on the video cameras in the office, and it's possible even my car is bugged. Sorry I missed you this morning, but I was anxious to get back to the office to act on the very interesting information you provided last evening from your friend in Canada and the Fewer Kommandant." She looked at her watch. "We can talk as we walk. He's waiting."

As they headed down the corridor, listening intently, she continued. "First, the accident. I cannot access the computer files and, as I have stated, the microfiche archives have been sanitised and I have no way of knowing what is missing. We are going now to speak to the medical examiner, Dr. Hans Knick, who handled the bodies the night of the accident. Then, as you requested, Staff Sergeant, we are going to talk to the forensics people who examined the remains of the vehicle."

"What about the missing persons business with Tousignant? Or rather, the four Tousignants?" asked Baker.

Haus nodded. "How long has your friend been trying to find that name in the computer?"

"Almost a week now," replied Baker. "Why?"

The inspector smiled and shook her head. "Sometimes the old ways are the best ways. I simply checked the archived EuroNews files going back six years. I was looking for any reference to the name. I came up with four where deaths or missing persons reports were filed around the time of the Schweizerhalle fire."

At last, Baker thought. Joan had said this man was the key. "What have you got?"

"Jacques Tousignant, reported missing October 23, 1986. His son Mark, reported missing October 29, 1986. Both never found."

"Never found?" queried Baker.

The inspector shrugged. "The man was in the process of getting a divorce from his wife. It is possible he abducted the child and they are living somewhere in Europe right now under different names."

"Go on," urged the Mountie.

"His estranged wife Louisa and their thirteen year old daughter Alma were found in Lac Lutzern on November 3, dead by drowning. They had apparently taken a tour boat. No one saw anything. They simply found the boat drifting, then the bodies a few days later. They were too far gone to determine whether there had been any foul play."

The Mountie frowned. "I'm pretty familiar with cases involving ugly divorces and custody disputes. It's possible Jacques

Tousignant murdered his wife and daughter, then fled with the boy."

"It's possible," said the inspector.

"But what does any of this have to do with Schweizerhalle and the fire?" asked Von Bessel.

"Good question," said Inspector Haus. "Now we must consider Monsieur Tousignant's past employment. He was a sergeant with the French Foreign Legion. Most recently he was working in Paris as a plumber, but there are rumours he was not above a little freelance work on the side, mainly bank robberies and such. His military record is sealed but it appears he was an expert in explosives and incendiary devices."

Baker remembered what Theo Marti had said about the possibility of arson at the Sandoz facility: 'You'd have to be an expert. . .' Before he could ask any questions, Haus said, "Here we are. Frau Von Bessel, this will not be pretty and you may hear some disturbing facts. The doctor is rather peculiar and has no bedside manner at all, which is no doubt why he deals with dead patients instead of live ones. We call Knick . . . Dr. Death. He loves it when we call him that."

The morgue was a model of Swiss precision, with bright, shiny stainless steel cupboards and pale green ceramic tile. There were several stainless steel tables with runnels down the sides to carry away body fluids. But even Swiss cleanliness couldn't hide the ugly realities of death and dissection. The body of a man lay on a table at the far end, half covered with a towel. The top half of the corpse was chalk white, the bottom half liverish-purple - Baker knew that when the heart stopped pumping gravity took over and blood settled. Baker glanced at Marie Françoise - most people found their first morgue visit a deeply unsettling experience. She was very pale and he stuck close, just in case she fainted. She turned her head away as they passed a huge jar filled with some sort of bright yellow preservative, in which floated huge wormy sections of intestine. It was a particularly busy day and three pathologists and their technicians were hunched over the nearest dissection tables. Apart from the body on the far table, Baker saw an old man of about eighty, his chest already cracked open; a man of about twenty with a purple-rimmed hole in his temple, the top of his cranium already sawed off; and a blond girl of about twelve who even in the flaccid paleness of death was remarkably pretty. Baker turned his head away. The death of the young was something he found unbearably sad, and his parental instincts kicked into overdrive as he thought of the possibility of the same thing ever happening to his own daughter. As they walked Erika plucked pale green gowns off a shelf and donned one, motioning for them to do the same. She pointed to the far slab and Von Bessel's footsteps faltered as they approached the table and the pump. A door opened and a gaunt beanpole of a man in a white lab coat stepped into the room and stooped to examine the purple and white corpse.

"Herr Doctor Knick, I have some visitors for you," she said in English. "Have we come at a good time?"

"Ah, Erika my dear, always a good time to see a pretty face. Healthy, pink and alive, a bonus. Yes, now is a very good time. I'm about to have liver, my favourite. Ha! Want to assist? Wouldn't be the first time. No? So who do we have here? This tall fellow who looks rather grim and the lady who is as green as one of my clients?"

"Hans, this is Staff Sergeant Douglas Baker of the Royal Canadian Mounted Police and his assistant, Constable Lisse. They are here to ask you some questions regarding the MVA you worked on the night of the Schweizerhalle fire."

"Ja?" He removed a scalpel from a tray and waved it in the air, watching the light glint on the razor sharp blade. "Why would our Canadian friends be interested in such an old case?"

"It might involve a recent attempted murder that is related to the case."

"Aha! The case is still alive, so to speak!" He grinned, and his tobacco stained teeth looked a crooked row of aged tombstones. Baker decided he didn't care for Dr. Death's sense of humour. "If you insist. You gave me the details over the telephone and I have the file here." He picked up a manila folder and leafed through it, frowning. "I do not think I can provide you with any information that is not already in the file."

"Doctor," said Baker, "is the information in the file you are holding the same information that is in the file at the police department?"

"Ja. I never cut anything out. Ha!" Another frown. "Perhaps you are here because someone has done a little cosmetic surgery on the police file? Radical surgery? Ha!"

"I cannot comment," said Inspector Haus in a no-nonsense tone.

Dr. Knick cleared his throat. "I see." He flipped through the folder. "Night of November 1, 1986. I performed the autopsies at 7:30 the next morning. Herr Von Bessel and his son. Both burned beyond recognition. Cause of death, impact with a concrete wall. That St. Jacob's exit is a nasty one." He flipped some more. "Tsk, tsk. High blood alcohol content. Foolish, foolish."

"Doctor," said Baker, "this raises an interesting point. Is there any way at all, whether as a result of the by-products of combustion or some other cause, that could account for a high blood alcohol level other than consumption of alcohol?"

The pathologist blinked twice. "No. Injection, of course, but no one injects alcohol. Why do you ask?"

"According to the dead man's wife, he never drank."

Another blink. "Well, she must have been mistaken." Flip, flip. "I am not mistaken," he said decisively.

Baker tried another tack. "Was it you who confirmed the identification of the two victims?"

"Ja. Given the condition of the bodies, confirmation could only be made through dental records on the father. I understand the wife was indisposed at the time."

"Do you know where the records originated?"

Dr. Knick blinked, then consulted the file. "Yes. Paris. Does it matter?"

"Paris, and not the medical insurance office at Sandoz?" asked Inspector Haus. "Isn't that odd? He would have had a company dental plan."

"There were no records at Sandoz. Lost or misplaced, as far as

I can recall. But the dental office in Paris had the complete records."

"Constable Lisse," Baker said to a very pale Marie Françoise Von Bessel, "didn't you find similar information in your investigation?"

She was as white as the corpse on the table. "What?"

Baker stared deep into her eyes, as if holding her gaze would hold her upright. "That Christian Von Bessel's dentist was in Paris."

She focused with a visible effort. "Yes," she whispered. "His dentist was in Paris. On the Boulevard St. Germain. Dr. Bocuse."

"That is correct," said the pathologist.

Baker folded his arms, thinking hard. "Tell me, doctor, was there anything unusual about the dental work?"

"Unusual in what way?"

"Not up to French or Swiss standards?"

"Ah. As a matter of fact, yes. While most of the dental work was of excellent quality, it appeared that Herr Von Bessel had dentistry performed outside of Western Europe. Some of the fillings were gold. Rare to find such work today, except in old people."

"Any guesses where the work might have been done?"

"Third world. Communist bloc. Africa perhaps"

Haus interrupted. "Thank you, doctor. You've been a great help."

The gangly pathologist's eyes were shrewd. "I can't imagine how, but you're welcome anyway. Would you like me to send you an uncut version of my file, to replace the, ah, dissected version of yours?"

"Please," said Haus. "Now, we will let you go back to work."

"Thank you. Good day to you all." He waved the scalpel again. "I'm having liver. My favourite! Ha!"

They walked out to a series of sniggering cackles.

Out in the hall, Marie Françoise's knees sagged and Baker put her in a chair. "Lean forward," he instructed, "put your head between your knees and breathe slowly."

He turned to Inspector Haus. "Did we learn anything?"

She nodded. "The information about the dental records originating in Paris, and the name of the dentist, had been excised from our file."

"What the hell for?" growled Baker. Haus stared at the top of Von Bessel's head and didn't answer.

When Marie Françoise recovered, they got back into the car and drove to the impound yard where a forensics team had gone over Christian Von Bessel's wrecked car. Von Bessel was still pale, and Baker knew the sorts of questions he was going to ask might shatter her sanity. She nodded gratefully when he suggested she stay in Erika's car. As the two of them walked into the shop, dead car hulks were mounted on hoists, or lying half-dismembered in bays. The charred wreck nearest to them was stained with soot and, on the hood, a fan-like spray of what looked like blood. Most of the other vehicles looked like they'd been crushed; this one looked like it had exploded. Baker sniffed. Cordite and something else he had smelled before but couldn't recall the name of. As they stood in the doorway on the stained concrete floor, a man built like a fireplug walked over, wiping his hands on a greasy cloth.

"Hello, inspector."

"Hello Jacob." Haus introduced Baker to Jacob Strauss, manager of the forensics team. He smiled apologetically and spread his huge greasy paws. "Forgive me for not shaking hands, but I like to work with my men."

"So what do you have?"

"I have gone over the file. Two hundred kilometres an hour into a concrete wall. Fire. What else could there be?" He shrugged.

"Did you do a complete forensic examination of the vehicle?" asked Baker.

Strauss shook his head. "Just routine. We were informed that alcohol was the probable cause of the accident, and there was no indication that we should look for anything else."

"So you found nothing out of the ordinary?" probed the Mountie.

"As I said before, two hundred kilometres an hour, then a fire -

there wasn't a lot to look at, not even with a big well-made BMW. It was obvious from the extent of the fire that the gas tank was completely full at the time of the crash."

"Any sign of explosives or tampering?"

"We didn't test for explosives, but usually there is obvious visual evidence. There was none." He frowned. "There was one thing a little unusual though."

"Yes?"

"The steering column had been severed in a peculiar way. Not a twisting, tearing, torsion sort of movement but more of a shearing. Then again, at two hundred kilometres an hour, you can find some pretty strange distortions in the metal remains."

"Was there any evidence that the wreck had been cleaned?" asked Baker.

Strauss wiped his hands meditatively. "Cleaned?"

"It had been delivered to the wrong impound yard, where it sat for four days until someone realised the mistake and sent it here. The wreck could have been interfered with during that time. Cleaned of residues of explosive charges."

The forensics manager shook his head. "It may have been, it may not have been. Impossible to tell."

And that was that.

They went back to the car. "One hit, one miss," said Baker. He pulled from his pocket the piece of paper containing the address of the grocery store in Dietekon where someone named Hanna Werner had made the mistake of using Klaus Staffel's credit card to pay for groceries. Underneath it he had scribbled the information Erika Haus had been able to discover. "Apartment 603. Time to audit somebody's books. Let's go."

FORTY

They sat in the Peugeot, facing the cluster of five high rises in the residential section of Dietekon, eleven kilometres outside of Zurich. Baker scanned the post office and shops that made up the ground level commercial complex. He pointed. "There's the grocery store. How do you want to play this?"

Inspector Haus pulled a piece of paper out of her jacket. "We have the phone number of the apartment and some information on Hanna Werner's friends, one of whom is very ill in Geneva. I suggest getting the woman out of the apartment, if she is there. I will phone pretending to be a nurse from the hospital and tell her she must come to Geneva immediately, that her friend is asking for her. Then we will go in and have a chat with Herr Staffel. If we can get into the building."

Baker nodded. "Sounds like an okay plan to me. You let me worry about getting in."

Haus went and used a pay phone in the post office, then returned to the car. Five minutes later a worried looking blond drove out of the underground parking garage in a badly rusted yellow Fiat. Haus squinted at the license plate. "That's her."

The three of them walked to the front entrance and opened the main door. In the foyer, the two women stood guard as Baker took a square metal object out of his pocket, about the size of a Swiss Army knife. He examined the lock and grunted. With an expert flick of the wrist two needle-like pronged objects appeared. He slipped the third out of the sliding case. He knelt and jiggled the three in the lock. After seven seconds it opened. He held the door as the women entered. They took the elevator up to the sixth floor. Both Baker and Haus drew their guns at the door. Haus had her badge in her left hand. Baker and Von Bessel pressed against the wall and the inspector kept to one side as well. She rapped sharply on the door. "Herr Staffel? Klaus Staffel?"

After a few moments a muffled voice came from the other side of the door. "Who are you? What do you want?"

"Police," said Haus. "There have been two burglaries in the building in the last twelve hours and I am interviewing all of the residents. I will not take more than five minutes of your time. Please open the door, Herr Staffel."

They heard the sound of bolts being slid and locks being turned. Slowly the door creaked open about two inches, still held by a stout chain. Erika smiled a dazzling, friendly smile and flashed her badge. "Herr Staffel. May I come in?"

Apparently reassured by the smiling female face, Staffel opened the door and they all marched in. The accountant was in his early fifties and in the course of his life had obviously eaten too much sacher torte with whipped cream and schnapps. His pale eyes goggled behind thick glasses and his double chins shook as he saw there were three of them. He ran a flabby hand over his thinning mouse brown hair.

"Burglaries?" he squeaked. "Was anyone hurt?"

"No," said Inspector Haus, looking around as she walked down the hall into the living room. "Nice place. Been here long?"

Scurrying after her, Staffel licked his lips. "About two, three months."

"The apartment is registered in the name of Hanna Werner. You realise that according to the law the names of both tenants must be registered?"

The fat man gulped and stammered, "No, I didn't know that." Then it struck him. "Then how did you know my name? Let me explain. I mean, it's nothing really, there is no need for an explanation. I. . ."

"Sure there is, Klaus," said Baker in German. "You have to explain Schweizerhalle."

Staffel's mouth opened and closed like a fish. Beads of sweat the size of small pearls were forming on his balding forehead.

Finally he shrilled, "I want to speak to my lawyer!"

"Lawyers," said Baker. He put a big hand on the man's podgy chest and shoved hard. The accountant bounced into a chair. "I really hate lawyers." He drew his Glok and theatrically checked the clip, then pointed the gun at the fat man's heaving chest. "You look a little warm, Klaus. Want me to install a ventilation duct?" The fat man squeaked like a mouse confronting a lion.

"Staff Sergeant," said Inspector Haus dryly, "please do not threaten the witness." She leaned over and stared into the wet goggley eyes. "And you are a witness, Herr Staffel. It's not often a man has the Western world's intelligence services hunting for him, and is able to evade them as well as you have. Not to mention what you did at the Sandoz facility for so many years. You must be very clever, Herr Staffel. Very clever indeed."

The accountant pulled himself upright in his chair. The Mountie couldn't believe his eyes - the man was actually preening. You are one smart woman, thought Baker. He holstered his gun and decided to play along. "You'll have to forgive me, Herr Staffel. I only pull the tough guy stuff on hard cases. And you are one hard case. We know that although you were one of the key men in the operation, you weren't in overall charge. All we can tell you is that if you cooperate, we can cut some sort of deal. Isn't that right, inspector?"

"Yes," said Haus. "A deal. I mean, all you did was fiddle some papers. It's not like you killed anyone."

"That's right," said Staffel eagerly. "Not like I killed anyone." He looked at Von Bessel, who was wearing her dark glasses and nondescript clothes, as if trying to remember something.

"The thing of it is," said Baker, "we can't figure out how the hell you did it. Why don't we start with that, with the operational stuff? We can get to the rest later." As he was speaking the Mountie was scanning the room.

Staffel didn't tell them anything more about the bogus manifests and the shipments than they already knew. As he talked, Baker walked around the living room and into the kitchen. He went into the bathroom and closed the door. The toilet flushed, then he opened it again. He checked out the two bedrooms and then strolled back into the living room, gazing out of the picture window.

"Then there was the discovery in Hamburg, that that particular manifest was false. I never even heard about the freighter exploding, and then there was the fire." Staffel licked his lips. "That was a complete surprise to me. Complete. I had nothing to do with it."

Inspector Haus leaned forward intently. "So all you knew was that you were falsifying manifests and certifying them. You had no idea what was in the shipments?"

The fat man's cheeks wobbled as he shook his head. "The first I heard was a few weeks ago when it was on the news about it being arson, a terrorist attack to destroy evidence of nerve gas."

Baker interrupted smoothly. "So now we have how and what. We don't have the why, and I don't think Klaus can supply us with that." He leaned forward, pretending to think hard. "What's next? Ah yes. Who."

He pointed a finger in the accountant's face. "Does the name Jacques Tousignant mean anything to you?"

"No." No hesitation, no flickering eyes, nothing. Truth.

"So who were you working with at Schweizerhalle, Klaus? Who actually handled the stuff and gave you your orders?"

Baker half-expected to see the fat man slowly deflate like a punctured tire, but he didn't. "I can tell you that. It was Christian Von Bessel. But that won't lead you anywhere. He's dead. He died-"

"We know how he died." He looked over at Marie Françoise. She was perfectly erect, her hands on her knees, like a statue of a seated Egyptian queen. But despite the static pose he knew she was anything but relaxed - she was stiff with shock. He had to be fast. "Who was Von Bessel working for?"

"I don't know. My only contact was Herr Von Bessel."

"What was the ultimate destination of the false shipments?"

"I don't know that either."

Haus said softly, "Herr Staffel, we can't cut a deal with someone who isn't fully cooperative."

The man started to look frantic. "I swear, I don't know any more!"

"Why did you do it, Klaus?" asked the Mountie.

The accountant looked both hunted and guilty. "Money. Lots of money. But at first—"

"At first what?" probed the Canadian.

The fat man looked at the three of them, pleading for understanding but obviously not expecting to get any. "For years I have gone to clubs. Special clubs. For people with . . . special interests." Suddenly Baker remembered who this repulsive man reminded him of: Peter Lorre in Fritz Lang's creepy movie M, about a compulsive paedophile. "He threatened to tell. He said I would lose my job and I would be blacklisted everywhere." His shoulders heaved in self-pity.

"So, after the fire, and the death of Von Bessel, you stayed on." stated Inspector Haus.

"Yes."

"Why?"

"I didn't want to. I was afraid that the investigators would find out. They went through everything. I was so scared."

"Why did you stay?" repeated Baker.

"I was ordered to. The money kept coming in, and I was told to."

"Who told you?" snapped Haus.

The jowls wobbled at her sharp tone. "I never met him. It was always by phone, by pay phone. He told me to stay put, to stay at my job, and to report to him immediately if there was any indication that anyone had stumbled on evidence. But no one ever did."

Baker bored in. "Do you have any idea at all who this man is, or who he works for? Does the name Colonel Aziz Hamani mean anything to you?"

The fat man shook his head. "All I know is that he has a foreign accent. Very slight. I don't know."

The Mountie scoffed. "Come on, Klaus. You're a smart man. You must have some idea."

He frowned. "His vowels. And the way he pronounces the letter 'l'. Sort of clipped. Like an Arab. Hamani is an Arab name, right?"

Baker nodded. "Close enough. Iraqi."

Staffel stared for a moment, then continued. "The years went by, everything went back to normal. No more fake documentation, nothing. Not even any more phone calls. I forgot about the whole thing. The only reminder was the money every month, and pretty soon even that just seemed normal too."

Erika crossed her long slim legs. "Klaus, there's a reason why you quit so suddenly, why you're in this apartment."

"He phoned. The man phoned. First time in years."

Baker asked, "Your usual contact? If it was, then it was probably Colonel Hamani."

"Yes. He said the reason for the fire was about to be discovered, and that I would be discovered too. I wanted to run but he said I was valuable to them, that they would take care of me until it blew over. They told me to come here and live with Hanna. They look after me very well."

Baker nodded. "Of course. Because you are so important."

Staffel nodded with the disingenuousness of an overgrown, particularly stupid baby.

"Klaus," said the Mountie, "I want the phone number."

"What?"

"The phone number your mysterious contact gave you to call."

The fat man stared. Baker stretched to his full height and clenched his jaw muscles. "Now, Herr Staffel, or we will have to take you downtown."

He scrambled to his feet and rummaged in the desk. He scribbled something on a piece of paper and thrust it at Baker. "Thank you. Herr Staffel, we have some very important information we must share with you, but we cannot do it at this time. Information that not even your mysterious contact knows about. We will be in touch very soon. Ladies, shall we leave?"

Inspector Erika Haus was staring at him, baffled. "Now," said Baker, slowly winking his right eye.

She nodded briskly. "Herr Staffel, you have been most cooperative. I shall inform my superiors. I suggest you do not leave this apartment, and that you do not inform Hanna Werner that we were here. It will go hard with you if you do."

The fat man nodded pathetically. Haus handed him a card. "Here is my cell number. You may call me at any time."

Von Bessel was motionless in the corner chair. As far as Baker could tell she hadn't moved a muscle in the past five minutes. "Coming?" No response. He walked over and grabbed her arm, lifting her to her feet. She did not resist. At the door, Klaus Staffel was wringing his fat hands like he was trying to twist water out of them. Baker looked at him and forced himself to smile. "Once again, Herr Staffel. Thank you for your cooperation." In his mind he added, you fat, repulsive little pervert.

Just as Haus opened the door, Marie Françoise came to life. She tore off her glasses and stared at Staffel with wild eyes. He backed away, recognition dawning in his flabby face. "Mein Gott! Frau Von Bessel-"

"Liar!" she shrieked. Her head lunged forward like a cobra's and she spat in his face. Her hands came up and she went for his eyes as Baker grabbed. The fat man slammed against the wall, his hands up in a gesture of terrified surrender. She slashed at him and a raking claw opened four parallel red lines on his cheek. Baker caught her by the waist in mid-slash and swung her around in a circle. Momentum kept the arc of her talons in flight and Staffel got a couple of vents cut in the front of his shirt. Baker carried her out into the hallway. She was hard hanging onto because her arms and legs were pinwheeling like a windmill caught in a force five gale. He heard the door slam and the bolts shoot home. They were halfway down the corridor before she started to sob and went limp. Half dragging her, half carrying her, they made it to the car.

Panting, Baker threw open the back door and gently placed her in. She lay on the seat, sobbing convulsively, rocking back and forth. He turned to Haus. "What do you suggest?" The inspector nodded. From her briefcase-sized purse she extracted a small syringe and an ampoule of clear liquid.

"Jesus," said Baker. "What the hell is that?"

"Mild barbiturate," replied Haus. "I find it comes in handy for situations like this." Baker said, "Would you do the honours?" She tore the plastic wrapper off the needle, removed the plastic sheath and punctured the turquoise rubber seal on the ampoule, drawing up one cc of liquid. She flicked the syringe to remove any air bubbles and handed it to Baker. "Subcutaneous or muscle, doesn't matter. You don't have to jab hard." Baker looked down dubiously. "Doesn't have a lot of fat on her." He leaned over and slipped the needle into Von Bessel' rear. She didn't even notice. In a moment he had depressed the plunger. Within seconds she was quieter, and a few seconds later had stopped rocking.

Baker handed the used needle to Haus, who capped it and put it back into her purse. "I'll have to remember this. Works like a charm. She going to be okay?"

The inspector nodded. "It'll wear off in about half an hour or so. Better than having her hysterical, possibly violent, in the back seat while we're driving."

Baker nodded. They got into the car and the policewoman turned to him. "Why did we leave so quickly?"

"Hold it." Baker got out of the car again and spent several minutes searching it inside and out. He threw himself back in. "No bugs on this car that I can find." He started pulling things out of his pockets. He was fiddling with an earpiece, some plastic wiring and what looked like a Sony Walkman. He plugged everything in and adjusted the volume, then dropped the Walkman into his jacket pocket. "You asked me why we left so quickly. Three reasons. First, it was far too easy to get to this guy and get him to talk. It's some sort of trap, and I'm damn sure it wasn't set for us because they would've sprung it." He swung his head toward the back seat. "Second, I was afraid of her reaction once Staffel mentioned Christian Von Bessel. Third, that apartment has more video cameras in it than an electronics warehouse and I don't like the sensation of being watched."

Inspector Haus raised her eyebrows. "I didn't see anything."

"Quite clever. You had to know what you were looking for. I

hope the watchers got a thrill out of watching me take a leak as I scoped the bathroom. You know, it's hard to pee when someone's staring at you."

"Why did you suspect the cameras were there in the first place?"

"You saw what the guy was like. Stupid, arrogant, a slave to flattery and a coward. He might have been a good accountant, but the slightest pressure and he comes apart. If I was trying to hide this guy, I'd have cameras all over the place too."

"What's with all the equipment?"

Baker grinned. "Bugs. Four of them, hidden strategically around the apartment. That's why I did the walkabout. They're nifty little things. Hide 'em in the palm of your hand, lean against a wall or press your hand on something, bingo. Adhesive. They'd never survive a sweep, but I'm pretty sure when I placed them that I was out of the cameras' angles of vision."

Haus said, "You want to go to the next stop, or stay here?"

"Let's go to the next stop." He looked at his watch. "But first, I have to make a phone call. Wait here." He ran across the road to the post office and phoned Colin Stewart. He did the special ring sequence once and there was no answer. He did it again. Christ man, where are you?

He heaved a sigh of relief as he heard the familiar voice. "Colin, when you didn't answer this morning I damn near had a heart attack."

"Sorry mate. Been a busy boy. I've finally got the low-down on Tousignant from Joan's files."

"So do I," interrupted Baker. Quickly he filled Stewart in on everything he had learned from Theo Marti and Dr. Hans Knick. He told him about Tousignant and his family, the Accountant and his surveillance, Christian Von Bessel and Colonel Hamani. He also gave him the telephone number he'd got from Staffel.

There was a long silence. "Very interesting," Stewart said finally. "One piece of information you don't have."

"What's that?"

"Christian Von Bessel and Jacques Tousignant both had the

same dentist in Paris."

"What?"

"That's right. Dr. Ferdinand Bocuse, Boulevard St. Germain."

Baker's mind was racing. "You mean they switched dental records?"

"Yes."

"So just like Joan said, this Jacques Tousignant was the key man. Expert in explosives and incendiary devices. The Iraqis tap him to torch Schweizerhalle, then they have to get rid of him. Von Bessel too, since he also knew too much. The car is tampered with so he dies in the . . . wait a minute."

"Precisely," said Colin dryly.

"It was Tousignant who died in the car?"

"So it would appear."

"And the little boy?"

"Was his five year old son Mark."

Baker ran his hand through his hair. "What about the wife and daughter?"

"I haven't the faintest idea."

"So how on earth would they get him and his son into that car? Ex-Foreign Legionnaires aren't exactly plates of jelly. Where are Christian Von Bessel and Daniel?"

"I don't know," said the Englishman meditatively. "But there is one other thing you just brought up that is very interesting."

"Okay, I give."

"In the course of pursuing my investigations, I've discovered a little more information about Colonel Aziz Hamani. In fact, I even have a photo. You said you were calling from a Swiss post office?"

"Yes."

"Leave me on the line and get a fax number I can transmit to."

When Baker had made his request at the counter he came back to the phone and gave Stewart the number. "Transmitting," said the SAS man. "Now, the information is that Hamani's wife died a few years back. Word is she was sexually tortured by someone pretending to be our friend Major Hakim Guramda, who was then tortured in turn by Mukhabarat. Only reason he survived is because Hamani intervened. Ever since then, the two have been working together, apparently at the direct command of Saddam Hussein himself. All of this - the leak to Von Bessel, the attack in Brussels, the attack in Vancouver, the death of Marta Rudd, all of it - has to do with whoever it is they are trying to flush out. I think the person they are trying to flush is the person who brutalised the Colonel's wife to death.

"Why?"

"I don't know. What I do know is this. We know the Iraqis used chemical weapons against the Kurds, and that they likely used them against Allied forces in the Gulf War, although it's never been proven. What is also known is that an area a couple of kilometres outside a particular Iraqi village was bombed on January 20, 1991, based on the vaguest of intelligence rumours. The village of Al Asad. What's interesting is that virtually all of the inhabitants died."

Baker was puzzled. "I thought you said they bombed an area two kilometres away from the village."

"That's what I said. Enhanced satellite photos taken that day and the day after are not of very good quality, thanks to bad weather, but they appear to show damage to an underground facility of some sort, and a greyish fog creeping over the landscape toward the village. Then tanks and bulldozers move in, dig a pit, bury everyone and cover it up."

"Nerve gas," breathed Baker.

"Precisely. I think that the two chemical precursors being stored at Schweizerhalle were ultimately bound for Iraq."

"And the clincher," said Baker, "is involvement by Guramda and Hamani."

"Your perspicacity never fails to amaze me. And of course Saddam Hussein cannot possibly let the world learn that he was not only making and using an incredibly lethal new form of nerve gas, but that he was actually trans-shipping the stuff across European soil. The absolute bloody nerve of the man gives me gas, if you'll pardon the pun."

Baker grinned in spite of himself, then frowned. "But why

now? The Schweizerhalle is old history. Why now?"

"Don't know. But it's obvious our Iraqi friends regard it as being of terrible urgency."

Baker's mind was racing. "Why would they leak all this stuff through Marie Françoise and the Phoenix Foundation?"

"Because they are a source of irreproachable integrity. Doug, would you believe a single syllable of anything you got directly from the Iraqi government?"

"Good point. So what do we do now?"

"You say the Accountant is being watched? And that he's bait for a trap?"

"Yes."

"Stick close to him, and for God's sake watch out for Von Bessel. I have a funny feeling we are nearing endgame on this one."

"How's that?" asked Baker.

"I've done a little flushing myself in the past couple of days. The Accountant is bait for a trap but he doesn't know it. I've been setting a couple of traps of my own. One of them has me as bait, the other has you. I'm sorry about this, but I simply couldn't think of any other way of saving everyone's life and career."

"Colin, what the hell are you talking about?"

"Sorry, my dear fellow, I can't tell you any more because I don't know what predator is going to come sniffing along your trail. All I can say is, one will, very soon, and the situation is critical. As far as the RCMP and CSIS are concerned, you've fled the Force in a criminal conspiracy, carrying stolen computer information vital to national security, not to mention abducting one of Europe's most famous politicians and compromising a National Defence employee. It's shoot on sight, I'm afraid. Keep your eyes open at all times. And Doug?"

"Shoot."

"Sometimes the faces you know are the ones you should fear most."

Click.

Douglas Baker stared into the middle distance as he hung up the receiver. He walked slowly to the counter and picked up the fax, paid for it. He looked at the handsome face of Colonel Aziz Hamani, the head of salt and pepper hair. He memorised it, crumpled it into a ball between his big hands and threw it in the wastebasket. Thinking hard, he trudged across the road to Inspector Haus's Peugeot.

****

Hanging up the receiver, Colin Stewart surveyed the loft and the proliferation of equipment he'd acquired, thanks to Ned Flanagan. The three screens choked with information windows glared at him. He typed in the phone number Staffel had given to Baker and did a quick search. He smiled. "Idiots."

He leaned over and pressed the intercom.

"Yes, Colin?"

"Ned, could you come up here, please?"

He heard the quick footsteps outside, then Flanagan's laughing green Irish eyes were around the doorframe. "What's up?"

"I know it's your home, old man, but I must ask you to leave, just for a day or two. There may be a bit of unpleasantness around here and I don't want you involved. You've done far beyond the call of duty and friendship as it is."

"Colin, I'm not leaving you in the lurch. I'll-"

"No, you won't," said Stewart gently. "In fact, you'll be doing me a favour." He reached over to the computer console and picked up a sealed envelope. "Be a good fellow and deliver this to Claire, will you? But not for forty-eight hours."

"Colin, I-"

"Go," said the Englishman. The pained eyes in his haggard face told Ned Flanagan all he needed to know.

"God speed, old friend."

Stewart listened to him head down the stairs, throw some clothes into a suitcase and close the front door. He waited until he heard the car roar to life and cruise down the driveway. He raised his fists in the air and hammered his useless legs four times, as hard as he could. Breathing heavily, filled with frustration at his immobility, he finally leaned forward again to the computer console.

On one screen was an e-mail message he had composed two hours earlier. He read it again, then added a couple of paragraphs. He copied the text, then inserted it into a new message with a new address. Satisfied, he keyed the sequence to deliver both messages. He waited a few moments, then flipped two toggle switches on a black box the size of a large dictionary.

No going back now. As he reached for the bottle of Glen Morangie Highland single malt he had a sudden vision of the telephone wires his skill had looped and backtracked onto themselves for the past week suddenly straightening out, all blocks cleared, firing messages like bullets across the now crackling wires.

Here I am, he thought. Here's the bait. Come and get me. He poured six ounces into a crystal tumbler. Wafting the glass past his nose, he inhaled deeply. He took a deep swallow, then raised the glass to the banks of computers and spoke aloud. "Here's to you, Douglas Baker. In Christ's name, I hope you're as smart and tough as I think you are." He opened a drawer and took out five spare clips of ammunition, placing them in his lap. Then he picked up the loaded Sig Sauer automatic and rolled the wheelchair over to the loft window to contemplate the pounding grey-green waves of the Pacific Ocean.

Waiting.

FORTY ONE

Douglas Baker threw himself into the car and slammed the door.

"Are you all right?" asked Erika Haus as she pulled the car away from the curb. "You still want to go to the next stop?"

"Yeah," Baker said curtly. "If the watchers were going to attack us, they would've done it while we were in the apartment. That's another reason I cut it short, just in case they were dithering and finally decided that even though we weren't what they were expecting they'd take us out anyway. The big question is, who are they expecting? And, if everything works okay, we'll find out, courtesy of my extra ears. Where's the restaurant?"

"Near the train station in the town centre. Not too far. You're sure you still want to check it out?"

Baker looked over into the back seat at Von Bessel's glassy eyes. "Apart from the Accountant, the restaurant where Heinrich Weigel disappeared from was one of the first pieces of information we got. Worth a visit. Apart from that, I'm starved and I could use some good Italian food."

It was Italian, all right, but it wasn't good. They'd talked to the staff, and Baker could tell in a couple of minutes that the Turks who ran the place were being completely honest. The restaurant had obviously been selected as a meeting site at random, and the proprietors had nothing to do with Weigel's disappearance. Then they sat down and ordered some food.

Baker got halfway through his veal picatta and threw his napkin down in disgust. "Christ, I hate it when they use stale garlic powder instead of fresh garlic." He lit a Camel to get the taste out of his mouth. He picked up a bun. "This thing is so old it should be in a museum. How's your fettucine gamberi?"

Haus took a long swallow of water. "Absolutely disgusting. It's not fettucine, it's egg noodles, and the shrimp are on the verge of being bad so they've used the old trick of washing them in chlorine bleach to get rid of the rotten smell. I'm going to notify the health department."

"Good idea. I hope you don't die of food poisoning before you get around to it." Baker signalled impatiently for the bill.

"I'll get it," said Haus. "Expense account."

"Thanks. No tip."

"No tip," said Haus. As she signed for the bill, she saw the Mountie reach for his earplug. "What is it?"

He wrenched the piece from his ear and stared at it. "Let's go!"

They dashed for the Peugeot and screamed off into traffic. Von Bessel was sitting up in the back seat, her eyes clearing rapidly. During the drive Haus was on her cell phone asking for backup. They were at the apartment complex in five minutes. Haus rang the outside buzzer to Staffel's apartment. No answer. Swearing under his breath, Baker knelt and fumbled once again with his picklocks. Throwing open the door, they bolted for the elevator, guns drawn. "Stairs!" shouted Baker, and they plunged through the emergency exit and bounded up the stairs, a still feeble Von Bessel bringing up the rear.

On the sixth floor, Baker slithered along the wall from the stair well. Erika dodged across the hall and took up a mirror pose to his, her weapon drawn. Baker's hand was behind him, waving Marie Françoise to stay exactly where she was. Staffel's door was ajar. Off in the distance he could hear the faint 'hee haw hee haw hee haw' of European police sirens. He signalled to Haus that he was going in, then crouched down, kicked the door further open with his right foot and lunged, hitting the floor in a controlled roll. Erika followed, swinging her gun around to provide Baker cover.

"Polizei! Put down your weapons!" No response. Quickly they moved from room to room. Nothing. As Haus fetched Marie Françoise, Baker went into the bathroom. Marie Françoise moved down the hall towards him and was just approaching the bathroom door when there was the tearing sound of the shower curtain being pulled back. Baker put up his palm to stop her. Too late.

Marie Françoise uttered a strangled scream. Baker covered her eyes. Erika Haus sagged against the doorframe.

Klaus Staffel's completely nude and badly beaten body was held vertical by bound wrists strung over the shower outlet. His head was canted unnaturally to one side. A broken neck. Numerous purple-red welts over his face and upper torso were just beginning to show, as if he had been pummelled repeatedly and mercilessly with a blunt object. There was some blood from the welts but a steady flow escaped from his mouth, running down his chest, to drip into the tub in a monotonous cadence. His tongue had been cut out, turned, and stuffed back in so the muscular trunk of it held the mouth open.

Von Bessel darted to the sink and heaved convulsively, dry retches. Thank God she hadn't had any lunch, thought Baker. His eyes narrowed as he noticed a crystal swan sitting on the edge of the sink. He'd heard something once before about crystal swans. What had it been? The swan was sitting on top of what appeared to be a piece of paper. He reached for it and picked up the piece of paper. Only it wasn't paper, it was a photograph with some writing on the back. Marie Françoise lifted her head and wiped her eyes, saw the crystal swan. She snatched the photo from his hand. Baker saw her eyes widen, with an expression he was sure he had never before seen on a human face in all his years as a police officer.

The sirens outside reached a crescendo and fell silent as Von Bessel sagged to the floor. Baker caught her just as he heard padding footsteps sounding in the hall. Erika swung around toward the door, her gun out in both hands.

"Don't shoot! It's me!" came a familiar voice in English. A male hand came into view, waving quickly in the doorway and then vanishing. "It's me!"

Baker struggled to recall the voice, from another time and place. He signalled to Haus to keep her gun up. He wanted to drop the limp Von Bessel but couldn't.

"It's me!"

"And who the fuck is that?" he roared. His jaw dropped as the man came round the door, his hands in the air.

FORTY TWO

"Doug, we have to get out of here! There's nobody in this place you can trust, and sure as hell no one on the police force. They'll be here any second. Come on!"

Baker knelt to pick up the photo Von Bessel had dropped, grabbed the crystal swan, then slung her over his left shoulder and headed for the door, his finger still around the Glok's trigger. At Erika's Haus's questioning glance he said softly in German, "Don't take your eyes off of him, don't put your gun away and for God's sake don't let him get behind you."

At the door, Baker paused. "After you." After a moment's hesitation the man turned and led the way. They fled down the hall to the stairway at the far end. From the other stairwell they could hear the sound of thundering feet. They dashed up one flight to the seventh floor and followed the man's back to an open door. Apartment 703. Last through the door, Baker closed it, panting heavily. The suite appeared to have the same layout as the one directly below it, but otherwise they couldn't have been more different. He laid Marie Françoise on the sofa and placed the crystal swan and the photo on her chest, all without taking his eyes from their surprise visitor, his gun at the ready. The man was watching him carefully, as if waiting for an opportunity. Baker looked around. There was a terrible smell, like burned wool or charred meat. He motioned to Erika Haus to stay against the wall, then aimed his gun. He walked up to the man and felt roughly under his coat with his left hand, finding the holster and removing the Smith & Wesson nine millimetre.

"Hey, what are you doing? We're on the same side, remember?"

"I'll be the judge of that," said Baker, pocketing the gun.

In German he said to the inspector, keeping his tone as conversational as possible, "I'm going to take a look around. Stay close to Von Bessel. Don't take your eyes off him. If he so much as blinks, kneecap him." She nodded.

The dining room contained banks of audio, infrared video and electronic recording devices, as well as computer terminals and a communications satellite set up. Baker knew a first rate surveillance unit when he saw it. He had known that Klaus Staffel was being watched, but he'd had no idea the watchers were just above his head. He felt cold sweat break out on his forehead as he saw two motionless, bloody forms. One was draped over a computer console, the head twisted to one side. The other was in a chair, the arms flung out and the head thrown back, mouth open, a black and unblinking third eye in the middle of the forehead.

A bloody trail snaked from the dining room into the kitchen. Two more corpses lay on the floor, their throats slit. There was another man sitting on top of the oven. Here the burned smell was overpowering. The man had a tennis ball rammed into his mouth, held in place with several twists of masking tape that wound around his head. He had been tied down onto one of the burners on top of the oven. His trousers and legs were badly charred and Baker could see the raw flesh where the skin had burned away. The man's face was a rictus of agony, but even with the distortion of unendurable suffering he could still recognise Major Hakim Guramda. He looked closer. Someone had stuck a gun in his left eye and pulled the trigger - the back of his skull was spattered against the white tile behind the oven. He stared at the mess of brain tissue and bone fragments. He holstered his gun. Using a handkerchief, he opened a couple of drawers until he found one that contained utensils. He took a dinner spoon and poked at the slaughterhouse mess behind Guramda's exploded head. The stuff had slithered halfway down the wall. He scraped some of it and frowned, thinking hard then tossed the spoon into the sink.

Baker walked into the bedroom, saw another man lying on the bed, also with his throat slit, as if he had been peacefully taking a nap when he'd been murdered. The place was a charnel house. His mind clicked away like a camera, registering everything. They all looked like Iraqis. They were dead, all six of them. Seven if you included the Accountant, the bait in the trap, a trap that had obviously gone terribly wrong. He thought of his previous encounters with Guramda, the man's skill. How the hell did you get a superbly fit military man and professional assassin to eat a tennis ball, then sit on a stove while you turned the burner on? Ask pretty please?

He walked back into the living room. Not much time. The police in the apartment downstairs might figure things out and be up here very soon. He contemplated the man standing in the middle of the floor, the man Haus was watching without blinking, her gun half raised. "Und so?" she asked.

Baker replied in German. "Six. All dead. One tortured to death. Major Guramda." He saw the man's eyes flicker. So, he thought, you recognise that name in the midst of this guttural thicket of German. "They've been dead for some time, certainly for at least an hour, maybe more."

"You mean, they were already dead when we were interviewing Staffel?" asked Haus.

"Yes." He thought for a moment. "Maybe not Guramda. He would've taken a while." He walked over to the phone. It had a call display LED. He hit 'automatic redial display' and recognised the number Klaus Staffel had given him. Hamani's number. His eyes searched the equipment in the dining room. The video cameras were still recording and he could see the grainy black and white images of police officers milling around in Staffel's apartment downstairs. No one was yet peering suspiciously into a video camera lens, but it couldn't be long now. He punched a button and stopped an audiotape. He rewound it, then hit play, heard the faintly distorted voices: 'Mein Gott! Frau Von Bessel. . . "Liar!' Scuffling sounds, screaming, the sound of a door being slammed and bolts being shot home.

He turned it off and walked back into the living room. He faced the man, drew his Glok and switched to English. "Hello, Steve. Betrayed anyone lately?"

"I don't know what you're talking about."

Baker gestured at the phone, still showing Hamani's number. "Have a nice chat with your boss?"

"I don't know what you're talking about."

"You already said that. Anyone ever told you you're a God-awful liar?" Baker turned to Haus. "Inspector Erika Haus, Staff Sergeant Steve Owen, RCMP. Long way from Vancouver, Steve."

"I could say the same about you, Doug."

"I suppose so. But I wasn't following anyone, I was being followed." To Haus he said, "Snoop and traitor, as well. Tell me, Steve, E Division still leaking like a sieve? Or were you the only hole?"

Owen was silent.

Baker waved an arm to encompass the room. "Your handiwork?"

"Of course not."

The big Mountie contemplated Steve Owen. For the first time he noticed that the California surfer good looks hid a glimmer of weakness around the eyes. Steve was weak. He thought of what Colin Stewart had said: 'I've been setting a couple of traps of my own. One of them has me as bait, the other has you. I don't know what predator is going to come sniffing along your trail. All I can say is, one will, very soon. . .'

It all started to come back to him. Inspector Jim Wattington saying that Owen had volunteered for the job of guarding Marie Françoise Von Bessel on her visit to GLOBE. Owen asking Joan Chan to do a deep backgrounder on the environmentalist, then discovering to his horror that she had dug too deep, was even better at this kind of thing than he thought she was. What was it Joan had said about Owen's response to her discovery of anomalies? 'He said, so what? We have no jurisdiction . . . let it go.' Then the decision to shut her up by running her down. Owen had been in charge of the GLOBE three team when they'd asked for backup at the Waterfront Café. What was it Barry Nakamura had said, in response to his asking when Owen was going to arrive? 'Another ten to fifteen minutes. GLOBE three says Her Highness isn't the only VIP who needs protection around here.' He realised now that

Owen was giving Guramda and his team time to attack, time to kill Marta Rudd. Calling Owen from the Dunsmuir Street Vancouver College campus after their escape, and having Guramda show up out of the blue. The attack on his apartment, by both CSIS and Guramda, when he had escaped with Von Bessel in the Valerie. The attack on Colin Stewart's home.

With hindsight it seemed so obvious. Steve Owen was the leak at E Division. He had been the one to sling the trace on Joan Chan, from inside the building. He'd been the one who'd made the connection between himself, Chan and Stewart. He was the one working for Colonel Aziz Hamani.

And now he was here, in a room full of dead people, far from home, pale, scared and disarmed, watching a grim Douglas Baker meditatively heft his gun.

"How'd you find me, Steve? At Colin Stewart's home?"

Owen smirked. "I knew you and he were friends. I'd one of our people cruise around Stewart's place, and there was your boat, anchored off the beach. Didn't have to be Sherlock Holmes."

"How'd you find me here? How did you know I was going to be in this apartment building, in the suite downstairs? You somehow manage to plant a locator beacon in my skull?"

Owen eyes flickered. "We intercepted a message. Or rather CSIS did. A message saying that you would be paying a visit to Staffel downstairs, and practically naming the time."

Having just told himself that nothing he ever heard again would surprise him, Baker's eyebrows headed for the ceiling. "CSIS? They told you? Why the hell would they do that?"

"Because I work for them too. I was recruited as a black op because they wanted to keep an eye on any disaffected cowboys on the Force, guys who might get funny ideas once they had their intelligence work taken away from them. I couldn't believe my luck when they approached me. Of course I said yes. I was now in on both the Force and CSIS. The Iraqis were pleased too."

The Mountie digested this. "You work for the RCMP, CSIS and Colonel Hamani? A triple agent? Now that takes real talent. Although you must get awfully confused at times." Baker was thinking hard. The intercepted message must have come from Colin Stewart, the cunning bastard. The SAS man had known that whoever the traitor was at E Division would be sent to find him, not knowing that he had already been warned to expect a predator on his trail.

"Hey Steve. You ever hear the saying that sometimes the faces you know are the ones you should fear most?"

"No. Where'd you hear it from?"

"From the guy who sent the message concerning my whereabouts, a message he intended to be intercepted. I was the bait that would finally draw you out into the open. Guess it worked."

Owen blinked. "You're lying."

Baker shrugged slowly. "Why do you think I didn't greet you with hugs and kisses, you stupid bastard? Because I'd been warned."

The blond traitor looked confused. "Then the trace we did on the message-"

The big man could almost hear the wheels clanking, so he finished the sentence. "Was also something deliberately intended. If you've decided to sic Hamani's people or CSIS on Colin Stewart, based on that trace, I think I can guarantee they're going to be walking straight into a very nasty surprise."

Steve Owen's eyes flicked to the telephone.

"Too late," said Baker, swivelling his weapon. "Might as well tell me about it, Steve. Your part in this little plot is over. Why'd you do it?" He knew that right now someone in the young Mountie's position, so long as he thought it was hopeless, wanted to do one of two things - brag, or spill his guilty guts to achieve some sort of absolution.

"Thrills."

"Thrills? That's it?"

"And money. Lots of money. Hamani approached me when I was assigned to the team that was trying to get Dr. Gerald Bull back to Canada. I'd joined the Force to do intelligence work, and then the government decided to take that work away from the Force and give it to CSIS. I didn't want to give up my seniority and

I thought the guys I'd have to work for at CSIS were a bunch of assholes. I was pretty bitter, and I bit at Hamani's offer. Then CSIS came along and asked me to watch out for any renegade cowboys on the Force. It was hilarious, them not knowing that I was the biggest renegade cowboy of them all."

Baker thought of his own bitterness at what had happened to the Force but for the first time, felt a wisp of respect for CSIS - they knew about Owen and his three sidedness and were using him. "Keep talking."

"Vancouver is a hotbed of international espionage, and not just Pacific Rim stuff. It also has a significant population of transplanted Iranians and Iraqis, plus three major science-based universities and a multi-ethnic population, many of whom are economic or political refugees. It's no wonder Hamani saw it as a good place to develop a network."

He laughed, a little hysterically. "It wasn't until later I realised I'd sold my soul to the Devil."

"You're breaking my heart," growled Baker, disgusted at this display of self-pity. "You want sympathy, you little prick, go tell it to Anne Landers."

Owen suddenly looked cunning. "I listened to the tapes when I got here and found everybody dead. Just before you left you said to Staffel that you had some very important information to share with him, information that even Hamani didn't know about. What is it?"

"It was a ruse," said Baker briefly. "I figured if the watchers decided to crash through the door, they wouldn't kill us until they found out what that information was. I was trying to buy us a little time, just in case."

Owen looked disappointed.

"So," persisted Baker, "these dead watchers were Hamani's men? And the Accountant was the bait in a trap?"

"Yes."

"A trap for who?"

"Mohammed's Sword."

"Whose sword?"

"A mysterious figure called the Sword."

"What is this, a fucking Marvel comic book?"

"That's his code name," insisted Steve Owen. "A renegade scientist, some sort of genius. I don't know the details. All I know is that, like me, only years ago, he was recruited by Hamani. To make nerve gas and other chemical weapons for Iraq. Now he's gone bad. That's why they have to bring him out into the open. That's why they used the Accountant as bait, leaked his whereabouts to draw the Sword in." He waved his hand at the inert forms scattered throughout the apartment, each in its own pool of congealing blood. "As you can tell, it worked."

Baker thought, calculating rapidly. Now it was coming together. The Sword must be the person who got rid of Christian Von Bessel once his usefulness was over. Maybe Tousignant as well. Thinking of the two deaths, a thought struck him. "One guy couldn't possibly kill six trained professionals, and certainly not Guramda." He walked back into the kitchen and looked at the bodies on the floor, the way they were lying with their throats slit, then into the bedroom. Gazing at the peaceful corpse on the bed he remembered something. Swiftly he walked to the front door and searched. He found an unmarked aerosol container on the floor near the front closet, as well as a slim eight-foot length of coiled hose. One end had a pressure screw valve that was obviously designed to fit onto a similar fixture on the aerosol bottle. He walked back into he living room.

"Specialist in chemical weapons, eh? Obviously portable ones too. Snaked the hose under the door and turned on the gas to knock everyone out, then jimmied the door and murdered them at his leisure." The smell reminded him. "Except of course for Major Guramda, whom he trussed up like a turkey and tied to the stove when he was unconscious, to have a little barbecue when the guy woke up. Must've been something personal."

He dropped the container and the hose on the floor. "These guys have been dead for more than an hour. That means they were killed just before we arrived to interview Staffel." He looked around. "But if they were all dead, then who killed Staffel? It had to be this Sword character."

Marie Françoise Von Bessel moaned. She was finally coming to. Again Baker saw the crystal swan and the photograph. Suddenly it hit him, as if a pail of ice water had been dumped over his head. "He was watching us the whole time, on these monitors." He walked over to the screens. The police officers downstairs had called forensics, and on the bathroom camera he could see a still photographer taking shots of Staffel's body from every angle. His eyes searched the other screens. "He would've seen me plant the bugs. He would've known that I'd be listening after I left. So after we left he went downstairs, got Staffel to open the door, and tortured him to death, knowing I'd hear and we'd come back."

He turned back to Owen. "Why didn't he attack us when we were downstairs?"

"He must've had his reasons. Maybe he wants to take his time, play with you a little bit."

Baker looked again at the swan and the snapshot. "And he left those two items."

He walked over to the sofa and picked them both up. "For Marie Françoise. Why?" He turned to Owen. "So it was the Sword who was trying to kill Von Bessel?"

"Yes. According to Hamani, he has some sort of thing about her, I guess because of Schweizerhalle and her broadcasting the information that the colonel leaked to her. I gather the guy is a real sick twist. Wants to kill her personally for some reason. That's why he missed at Brussels. Insisted on being the one to take her out, but the guy's not a pro shootist."

"So why did Hamani have Guramda kill Marta Rudd?"

"She knew too much and was getting too fond of the woman. They were afraid she'd talk. They didn't want to kill Von Bessel - they wanted to abduct her, to hold her hostage so that the Sword would come hunting for her and they'd be waiting. Rudd had to die because it was essential that Iraqi involvement be kept strictly out of it until the whole thing was over. Once the Sword was dead it didn't matter, because it's him they wanted all along."

Baker contemplated the crystal swan and the photograph.

"Why now? They got away with the while Schweizerhalle thing. Why get frantic now?"

"It has to do with the Sword. He's gone bad and he's threatening to take out an entire major city somewhere in the world with nerve gas and blame it on Saddam Hussein. If the Western powers get the idea that Saddam was behind something like that, they'll turn him into a grease spot in about five seconds. And the Sword isn't fooling. He almost took out half of Baghdad before they found the device he'd planted."

Baker stared. "A city?"

"Yeah. Like I said, the guy is one crazy fuck. Either Von Bessel dies or a city does."

"Jesus Christ," said Baker.

"If you'd just kept out of it, it'd all be over." He pointed at the environmentalist, who was sitting up on the sofa, a maniacal certainty burning in her eyes as she stared at what Baker held in his hand. "She'd be dead, the Sword would be dead, and the world would be safe."

"Yeah," snarled Baker. "Safe for traitors like you and murderous psychopaths like Saddam Hussein."

"It doesn't matter," said Owen. "I entered Klaus Staffel's apartment before you arrived a few minutes ago. I knew it had to be the Sword who killed him. I saw the swan and the photo and called Hamani. He now knows where to go to find him. He's on his way right now." He sneered. "It might be over for me, but it's over for you too. Your prints are all over the place downstairs, you still face a charge of fleeing the Force and kidnapping Von Bessel, you still have the CSIS hard drive and they'll crucify you for that. And if CSIS doesn't get you Hamani probably will, sooner or later. Welcome to the big leagues, asshole."

Baker shifted the gun to his left hand and hit Steve Owen with a hard straight right. The punch landed on his cheekbone and the big Mountie heard it crack. The other officer was not a small man, but he sagged to the floor like a sack of cement. "That was for Joan Chan. When I get through with you, I swear to God you'll wish you'd died as easily as Guramda."

Inspector Erika Haus looked stunned. "Staff Sergeant Baker. What do we do?"

Baker glowered down at Owen, who was clutching his face. "How does a crystal swan and a photograph tell Hamani where to go to find the Sword?" He stared at the photo. It was a colour shot of an adolescent of about eleven or twelve. He was standing in front of a collection of what looked like stone farm buildings, and it appeared as if there were people in country working attire dress behind him, but it was too blurry to tell for sure. The kid was handsome and had startling emerald green eyes. He turned it over and frowned as he read aloud the writing on the back - his spoken German was better than his written. "Taken Christmas Eve, 1990. Neuchatel, Switzerland." He looked at Haus, then at Von Bessel. "Neuchatel. Her maiden name was Bertrand. The family home is there." He glanced again at the photo."

Suddenly Marie Françoise lunged and snatched the snapshot from his hand. She stared at it with crazed eyes, a low keening moan coming from deep inside her.

"Marie Françoise," said Baker, "what is it?"

"My son Daniel," she whispered, clutching both the photo and the swan. "He's alive. Look, he's a young man."

Baker knelt and rammed the barrel of his gun into Owen's mouth. "What is this?"

He was so intent on Owen that he didn't expect what happened next. Marie Françoise lunged from the sofa and snatched the gun from Erika Haus's hand, then in the same motion snatched Owen's .38 Smith & Wesson from Baker's pocket. She swung the guns back and forth between Haus and Baker. "I have to go to Daniel," she said flatly. Too late, he remembered how fast she could move.

Owen made a twisting motion and Baker rammed the Glok even further into his mouth, grabbing the man's neck to hold him still as the traitor flinched, the metal barrel breaking one of his teeth.

"Marie," he said softly, "it's another trap, just like the one downstairs. Why do you think the Sword left the crystal swan and the photograph? Because he knew the effect they would have on you. He's trying to lure you, using Daniel. Your son probably isn't even there. Maybe the photo is a complete fake - they can do stuff like that nowadays. If you fall for it, he'll get what he wants - you, in his clutches." Briefly he wondered how the Sword would know about the swan and the boy, but let it pass. Maybe Hamani had told him.

"I have to go to Daniel." She edged toward the door. The gun barrels were wavering all over the room and she was twitchy as hell. Her eyes were hot and vacant at the same time, the pupils like pinpoints but somehow unfocused. Baker realised that in this frame of mind, she would do anything. He removed the gun from Steve Owen's mouth and stood, walking slowly toward her, his hands spread, the Glok loose in his hand.

"Stay where you are!" she screamed, pointing both guns so inexpertly that the Mountie winced. She could drill them all without even meaning to. He stopped. Von Bessel turned to Erika. "Your car keys. Give them to me. No. Instead, give me your purse. Throw it on the sofa. Slowly."

Haus did as she was told. The woman rammed the photo and the swan into the bag, rummaged until she found the keys, pocketed them. She edged toward the door. Just as Baker was about to speak her eyes suddenly flicked to something behind him just as he heard the sound of Steve Owen lunging to his feet. He felt the younger man's arm around his neck. With a savage twist he rammed, first with his left, then with his right elbow. Liver and right kidney, respectively. As Owen convulsed in agony, Baker crouched a little to reduce his height, threw his head forward, then back as hard as he could. He was free. He spun, to see Owen's flattened nose streaming blood. He threw a hard right to the solar plexus just as he heard Marie Françoise scream. He moved to one side as the traitor sagged to his knees, intending to throw a right uppercut.

Two deafening explosions, as Marie Françoise Von Bessel shot Steve Owen. He took one slug in the left shoulder, the other in his left pectoral. Heart shot. Baker spun in time to see the look of horror on the environmentalist's face as she realised what she had done. She dropped both pistols as if they were suddenly red hot and lunged for the door, throwing it open and sprinted for the stairwell. Motioning Inspector Haus to look after Steve Owen, Baker handed her his gun, lunged for the door and ran into the hallway. He stopped.

He heard the sound of thundering feet on the stairwell and three armed police officers burst through the doors, shouting orders and aiming a variety of weapons directly at him. Instantly Baker fell to his knees and raised his hands in the air as the officers advanced. Good thing he'd given his gun to Haus. He heard more footsteps coming up the stairwell behind him. It sounded like there were a dozen of them. Where the hell was Von Bessel? Suddenly he saw a slim figure move from the shadowed alcove right by the stairwell and slip through the door, darting down the stairs. He was about to yell something when he saw several sets of staring eyes and the muzzles of large weapons pointing straight at him from about two meters away. The men looked tense and unnerved, and after what they'd seen in apartment 603 he couldn't blame them. Not a good time to start shouting and gesturing.

They spread-eagled him against the wall and patted him down. Then he was cuffed and roughly shoved into 703, where Inspector Haus was cradling a mortally wounded Steve Owen. Same routine. The officers went ballistic when they saw the five corpses, particularly Guramda. One young officer vomited into the kitchen sink. An ambulance was called for Owen, but he died five minutes before it arrived without saying another word. With her purse and police-issue weapon gone, Haus had no ID and in Dietekon she was outside her jurisdiction. It took almost half an hour of arguing, yelling and phone calls before her identity was established, and another twenty minutes while she explained to her superior officer why she was freelancing on a case that had not been cleared by anyone at Basel police headquarters. She impressed on him the urgency of the situation without giving away any essential details. Finally the explaining was over and Baker was uncuffed. Remembering the leak at Basel police headquarters, he quietly briefed Haus to stay silent about any details for at least another six hours.

When he was finally able to get down to the parking area, Haus's Peugeot was gone. So was his gun - confiscated as unlicensed. He went to the post office and asked the location of the nearest car rental place. It turned out to be just two blocks away. At the rental agency, he used one of his fake credit cards to rent a big fast Mercedes. Taking a map from the rack, he asked the clerk to identify Neuchatel. It was good two hundred kilometres away from Zurich as the crow flies. He used one of the phones in the office to make a couple of calls, finally determining the precise location of the Bertrand family chateau. He sprinted out the door, threw himself into the car, and roared off.

FORTY THREE

Neuchatel, Switzerland, March 23

Eight kilometres south of the city of Neuchatel, in the French sector of Switzerland, Marie Françoise slowed the Peugeot. It had taken her an hour and a half to drive south through Neuchatel, on to the outlying suburb of Pesseaux and her final destination, a remote vineyard over looking Lac Neuchatel. It was dusk and the setting sun illuminated with tones of gilt and bronze the square clock towers, hexagonal spires and brown tiled roofs of the ancient medieval city situated on the western shore of the lake, tucked into rolling hills surrounded by vineyards and forest. Ordinarily the sight would have moved her deeply, but now her thoughts were as dark as the approaching night.

The car's wheels crunched on the gravel of the long, tree-lined avenue that led from the main road to the chateau, isolated behind its high stone wall. In the dusk the tall linden trees looked grim and foreboding, arching over the vehicle like the nave of some organic cathedral. The huge wrought iron gate was ajar. At the sight of it an involuntary shudder ran through her frame at the memory of what she had endured in this place in the past, and what she might now find. The place was supposed to be closed up. She stared at the huge rusty padlock, hanging open on one of the gate's metal spikes. Her legs as heavy and numb as logs, she got out of the car and with an effort pushed the gate open. It screamed as if in pain. She got back into the car and drove through. It was a good half kilometre to the chateau. She passed tilting, decaying work sheds and low, sway-backed barns. Ahead she could see the three story, masonry and wood country chalet, with its rough-hewn wood balconies running the full length of the front of the house on the second and third floors. There was a single light on in the house, shining from one of the upper windows.

She parked the car under a huge spreading oak and got out. The heavy iron-studded door leading into the kitchen was ajar. She drew a ragged, determined breath, crossing the threshold into the blackness of the pantry. Her right hand searched in the darkness for the familiar light switch on the entrance wall. She flicked it. Nothing. She tried to remember the layout, moving forward with her hands outstretched. She started violently as she brushed against what she knew must be the rack of copper pots and colanders next to the kitchen sink. In the dead silence the clashing sound was deafening. Finally she found it. First the cool sleek surface of the stainless steel refrigerator, then the electrical panel to the left. She located the pull-tab and opened the thin metal cover. She fumbled with the banks of breakers until she found the one toggled to the OFF position. She flipped it and was rewarded with an explosion of light. Momentarily dazzled by the brilliance, she shook her head to clear the spots that danced before her eyes. Standing at the end of the aisle way was a squat figure dressed completely in black camouflage fatigues, a black balaclava covering his head. He was aiming a machine pistol straight at her.

"Who are you?" she sputtered in French. "Where is my son?"

The intruder waved his hand. "Frau Von Bessel. This way please." Reluctantly, she followed him to the far end of the kitchen. He stopped at the doorway and pointed downward.

The cellar. Peering into the darkened maw that led down the familiar stairs, the old insidious fear clutched her heart like an icy hand. "Non," she whispered. With an oddly polite gesture, the man gestured again. "You must," he said. Seeking support in the darkness, her right hand slid across the rounded granite stones of the stairwell wall, instantly eliciting a tactile hallucination of childhood terror. Suddenly she was a little girl again, and hell existed seventeen steps down from the kitchen, in the cellar of her own home. Only the thought that her son Daniel might be alive and waiting for her down below made her move on numb legs down the stairs. When she was halfway down she detected a bright light shining in the basement, off to the right.

As she reached the cellar floor, suddenly she heard a voice, so familiar and yet so jarring. "I am so glad you received my message and decided to join us."

She peered at the man standing next to the bright light. He was tall, also dressed in black combat fatigues, also wearing a black balaclava. Why was the voice so familiar? Slowly he reached up and removed the headgear. He was blond, with chiselled features, his mouth hard and unsmiling. She did not recognise him. But there was no mistaking the emerald green eyes. She felt a terrible confusion descend on her. "Daniel?" she whispered. "Where is Daniel?"

The sound of the name caused the man to stiffen, as if an electric charge had suddenly passed through his frame, but still he said nothing, his eyes as green and unblinking as a viper's. She tore her gaze away and looked around the stone room. Set into the far wall was the steel door of the bomb shelter. It was open. On the other side of the bright light a man was sitting in a chair. He was bound with rope and his head sagged on his chest. As he raised it with an effort she saw that his handsome face was a welter of bruises under the full head of salt and pepper hair. His bloody lips moved but no sound came out.

She stared again at the man standing by the light. "Daniel?"

He spoke again, and as he said the words she felt her fingernail grip on sanity loosen another millimetre. "How soon they forget. All women are faithless, selfish bitches. My dear Marie Françoise, don't you recognise me?"

The scream that tore from her throat was so loud she felt a piece of cartilage pop in her throat. "Christian?"

FORTY FOUR

Douglas Baker slid into the turn as the wheels of the big Mercedes screamed. He'd never driven so fast before in his life, and he knew how dangerous it was to travel at such speed on these narrow, winding country lanes.

His eyes flicked to the clock on the dash. He'd made good time, even in the early evening traffic of Neuchatel and Pesseaux, as he had prayed that the traffic cops were drinking beer and eating schnitzel instead of cruising the roads and hiding at intersections. Now, on the lonely country road that skirted the lake, the huge trees flashed past like pickets in some shaggy fence. It must be very close.

He was travelling so fast that he shot by it. He slammed on the brakes and left two smoking black trails of melted rubber on the road. With a rising whine the car reversed and he swung into the lane. Gravel fired like grapeshot from under the wheels as he sped down the long, tree-lined avenue toward the chateau. As he reached the high stone wall and the open gate, he slid to a stop. He was unarmed and had no idea what to expect. He peered into the gathering gloom but could see nothing but the dim bulk of the chateau several hundred meters away. He turned off the ignition and felt in his jacket pocket, found what he was looking for. He squeezed it in the palm of his right hand as he opened the driver's door with his left. In the last remaining light of the faltering day, he searched the road ahead for any sign of movement. Nothing. He slipped through the gate and started to run.

Five minutes later he was holding on to the rough surface of the barn's rock wall to steady his rubbery legs, gasping for air. Jesus, he thought, why the hell do I smoke so much? He wiped sweat from his eyes and tried to steady his ragged breathing. The chateau was less than a hundred meters down the gravel driveway. Between him and the building were a couple of dilapidated sheds containing farm machinery. He could see Erika Haus's Peugeot under an oak tree and a slash of bright light coming from a half opened door in the dwelling, right across from where the car was parked. Lots of cover between him and the house. He smiled grimly. For himself and whoever might be lurking and on guard. He slipped over to a vine-laden stone wall just a little taller than himself, and started to move through the shadows toward the house.

He paused as he realised there was an arched entrance in the rock wall. Although he could see nothing in the arch's inky blackness, some sixth sense kicked in. If a watcher were going to hide anywhere to protect access to the chateau, he'd hide here. Baker tried to remember how much noise he'd made on his approach. None at all, as far as he could tell. He was glad he'd avoided the noisy crunching gravel of the driveway, instead running soundlessly on the deep damp grass of the verge, under the row of trees.

Not taking his eyes from the arch, he crouched soundlessly and felt at his feet for the large stone he knew he had seen there. Hefting it in his left hand, he raised his right hand, his forefinger finding the trigger on the blue plastic container. He stretched out his arm so that his hand was at about the level of the average person's head. With a sudden flick of his wrist he tossed the stone toward the planking of a nearby shed, about ten meters to his left. The rock struck the wood with a terrific bang. A black figure suddenly materialised from the blackness of the archway, machine gun at the ready, pointing toward the sound. Baker fired at the man's hooded face, then ducked.

As the cayenne pepper-based spray caught the guard full in the face, he swung the gun around, then dropped it, clutching his throat. There was not a sound as he fought for the breath that wouldn't come, not even enough air to moan, much less shout or scream at the searing pain that blinded him and paralysed his lungs' capillaries. Baker seized the machine gun and stood again, knowing he had enough time to mix himself a martini if he wanted.

Holding it by the barrel, he swung the gun sideways as if swinging a baseball bat. The butt caught the guard flush on the temple and he dropped soundlessly to the grass. He quickly frisked the unconscious form, removing a pistol and a sheathed dagger in a harness. Tugging up his pant leg, he bound the knife to his right calf. He dragged the guard through the archway so he couldn't be seen, then picked up the machine gun, the pistol and the man's communications unit.

Crouching, guns at the ready in case there were more watchers, he covered the remaining distance to the Peugeot. He paused behind the car, weighing his options as he squinted at the light streaming from the half open door. Suicidal to go in there. He'd slip around the side of the house, try to find an accessible window. Just as he was wishing he had a flashlight, he heard it.

Too late. He spun in his crouch just in time to see the sole of a parachute boot aiming for his head with the heavy inevitability of a piston. A burst of stinging stars, and suddenly he couldn't control his limbs. The last thing he felt was the gravel biting his cheek as he fell to the ground face first.

****

The shock of cold water being dashed in his face brought him around. Sputtering, he squinted through a crimson film flooding his left eye. He realised he was in what looked like a kitchen, sitting on the floor, propped against something. Blearily he saw two pairs of black-clad legs and the muzzle of a gun pointing straight at his chest. In front of his face was a gloved hand grasping a dripping serving ladle. The gun twitched as he raised his hand to his face touched it with his palm. Felt like raw hamburger. He stared at the blood that dotted his palm. Probably looked like raw hamburger, too. The gun twitched again. Time to get up. He rose unsteadily, having to brace himself first against the lower cupboards, then the kitchen counter. His head felt as if wasn't properly attached, like it might fall off if he moved too suddenly. He winced as one of his captors ground the muzzle of his pistol against the base of his skull and said something he couldn't understand because of the ringing in his ears. He was being propelled toward a dark open doorway and a flight of stairs leading down a chute of stone. Staggering, he had to grab the rickety handrail. He tottered, doing his best to appear even more unsteady than he actually felt. He thought desperately. No way out. He could tell from the unfamiliar pressure against his calf that they hadn't found the knife.

As he groped his way down, he could see a blinding light at the bottom, could hear voices. He heard a woman's voice scream, "Christian?" Just as his right foot touched the stone paving, a sudden shove sent him flying forward. He crashed into a chair and fell heavily. Slowly he became aware that he was on his hands and knees, staring blearily at the floor. As the bright red coins appeared on the dusty paving he thought for a moment he was hallucinating, then understood he was only bleeding. He felt his arms give way and rolled onto his side, a heaving wave of nausea convulsing his stomach. He blinked at the concerned face that gazed down at him. Marie Françoise Von Bessel. It must have been her who had just screamed. What had she screamed? He couldn't remember. He lay back, the stone cool against his aching head, and closed his eyes. Someone was mopping his face. Must be her. Desperately he tried to concentrate. It was very important to remember. What had she screamed?

From very far away he heard a man's voice, warm and insinuating. "So this is the policeman who has caused so much trouble. The loyal guard dog, brought to heel at last." The tone changed abruptly. "Chair!" he barked.

Baker was heaved to his feet and thrown into a chair. For a few moments he concentrated on not falling out of it, swaying from side to side. Finally his head began to clear, although he tried to appear as groggy as possible as he looked around the room. There was a bright light, and some sort of large machine with a canvas cloth thrown over it. There were three armed guards. He squinted to his left. Marie Françoise, also in a chair. He peered ahead. A tall blond man. Another man in a chair bound and bloody. As he watched, the tall man strode over to the man in the chair and threw a hard right fist into his face. As the head whiplashed Baker recognised him, from the head of salt and pepper hair. Colonel Aziz Hamani. He remembered Steve Owen, the photo and the crystal swan. Those two inconsequential seeming items had lured them all here. Suddenly he remembered what the woman had screamed.

He fastened his gaze on the tall man, now staring at him with a smirk on his handsome face. Baker spoke slowly, not much caring about the words, concentrating on assessing his options and regathering his strength. "Well, if it isn't Mohammed's Broom, or whatever you call yourself these days, Herr Dr. Von Bessel."

FORTY FIVE

Hidden by the curtain of the second floor window that faced out onto the tree-lined driveway and the dense forest beyond, Colin Stewart waited and watched in the wan dawn light. The loaded Sig Sauer rested in his lap, just in case his plan went wrong. A thin smile creased his haggard face as he saw it.

First had come the dark ones, in their combat gear, just as they had come to his home. He saw them slip from tree to tree, no doubt thinking he was asleep in his cripple's bed, an easy target. Then he saw the others. He smiled again knowing they had been present for hours, even before the dark ones had arrived. Waiting, just like him. When they finally made their move, it was all over very quickly. The element of surprise was crucial, of course, but as he watched the CSIS operatives pounce on Hamani's assault team he had to admit he was impressed. CSIS might have its flaws, but the military precision with which they dispatched the Iraqis was a model of lightening fast efficiency. He heard only three bursts of automatic weapons fire and a couple of pistol shots. Then it was over. He watched until he saw the five captured Iraqis and a couple of dead ones tossed into the van with the armed guards, waited until he knew CSIS was about to launch the assault on the house. Spinning his wheelchair, he rocketed first down the ramp, then up the other side. Quickly he scanned the connections, then the information on the computer screens. He picked up the mouse and laid it carefully and precisely on the pad, then flexed his fingers. He hefted the Sig Sauer and adjusted his chair behind one of the heavy desks, now turned on its side to provide a reasonable screen against most bullets. Waiting.

Five minutes later he barely missed detecting the stealthy footfalls on the landing outside the room. They had no doubt checked the rest of the house and deduced that he must be in this room, the tracking devices homing in on the distinctive electromagnetic signature emitted by the computers. He saw the doorknob turn. Locked. He waited.

The door flew open. The lead man came in low and to the right. Another man came through, low and to the left. Colin fired a burst left and one to the right to force them to huddle in the centre of the doorway, then fired over their heads, to make them crouch down so low that they couldn't get a clear shoot at him, safe behind the over turned desk. He spoke as loudly and as rapidly as he could without sounding strained.

"Good morning, gentlemen. I do not intend to fire again unless I am fired upon. I congratulate you on cleaning up our friends outside. I am pleased to see that the message I sent you was read with care. I have a good idea what your orders are, but you will disregard them. I will tell you what to do. Understood? You may say yes."

A muffled 'yes' came from somewhere near the floor. "Good," said Stewart. "Leave your weapons on the floor, raise your hands above your head and rise to your feet." He raised his voice so it would carry. "If anyone outside this room tries to come in, I will shoot you down."

The Englishman gazed into the two sets of hostile eyes that glared at him. "You notice the mouse I am holding? Good. If I click the right mouse button, everything that is on Joan Chan's hard drive is automatically delivered, electronically and instantly, to the headquarters of every intelligence agency in the Western Hemisphere. Incidentally, it is now all decoded."

He heard a faint shuffling noise outside and the sound of urgent whispering. "On the off chance that you have had the wit to think of jamming my transmissions, the same information is stored in a computer in a remote location. That information will be automatically transmitted to the aforementioned intelligence agencies in precisely twenty-eight minutes, unless I instruct the program to abort."

A voice came from outside the room. "What do you want?"

"Some information, a little understanding, and a guarantee."

"Talk."

"There's a spy at E Division. He or she is the person who set up Joan Chan and aided and abetted the attack on Von Bessel at the restaurant. He or she is in the pay of a Colonel Aziz Hamani, the same Iraqi officer who dispatched the assassination team you have just rounded up so smartly. As I predicted in my e-mail message to you, that team was dispatched to this address this morning in response to a second e-mail message I deliberately let Hamani's people intercept, so they would know where to find me. That message also provided information on the whereabouts and itinerary of Staff Sergeant Douglas Baker. I provided that information so that the E Division spy would be flushed out."

The voice came again. "We already know who it is. Steve Owen. He's dead. Based on what we hear from the Swiss police, he was shot to death."

"Good," said Stewart. "And where is Douglas Baker now?"

"According to a Basel police officer named Haus, he was headed for a place on Lac Neuchatel, pursuing the Von Bessel woman and some guy named Mohammed's Sword."

The SAS man frowned. "Mohammed's Sword?"

"Yes."

"Not Christian Von Bessel?"

There was silence. "Never mind. The important thing is that you understand why Staff Sergeant Baker behaved as he did, why he fled with your hard drive and with Marie Françoise Von Bessel. None of it would have happened if Steve Owen hadn't been an Iraqi spy. Now for the guarantee. I want Baker to be cleared."

More muttering. "Sure. Why not."

Collin smiled. "Not that I don't trust you fellows, but I want a personal guarantee from the head of CSIS." He glanced at his watch. "We now have twenty-seven minutes before the remote program kicks into transmission mode. Give me the man's phone number and I'll call from here. Once I get the guarantee this Mexican stand-off is at an end."

He scribbled the number down as it was given to him. "One more question before I call. How is Joan Chan?"

"She's awake and talking. She's going to be all right. We're getting the complete story from her now."

"Good," said the Englishman. He picked up the phone and dialled. As he waited for the call to go through, he tried not to think of what Baker might be facing at the moment.

FORTY SIX

"Christian?" whispered Marie Françoise.

"In the heavily altered flesh," said the tall man with the emerald green eyes. "Plastic surgery is truly amazing these days."

"Where is my son? Where is Daniel?"

The change in mood was instantaneous, the scream deafening. "Your son? Your son? My son!" Again he strode over to Hamani and punched him viciously around the head. "He's dead. He died during the Gulf War. The Americans killed him when they bombed the village."

Baker's head swivelled as he heard Hamani croak, "No they didn't. You did. Your precious XP29 killed him."

"Shut up!" shrieked Christian Von Bessel. The big Mountie shook his head to clear it. He squinted at Hamani. In the battered, bloody face, the eyes shone with both desperation and penetrating intelligence.

What's this guy's up to thought Baker. As he saw the enraged green eyes and the veins bulging in the neck, he tried to remember what Colin Stewart had told him. "That's right," he said. "The bombs didn't land anywhere near Al Asad." Von Bessel's head jerked around, astonishment on his face. Even Hamani looked surprised. "And what kind of irresponsible jerk are you anyway, keeping your son with you in such a dangerous place in the middle of a war? It's your fault he's dead."

Baker braced himself as Von Bessel flew across the room. He tried to roll with the blows to minimise their impact, his arms up to protect his head. Fortunately the man was so enraged that the punches were largely ineffectual. He realised Marie Françoise was clutching the man's arm, hanging on for dear life. With a convulsive gesture he threw her to the floor. Baker saw the clenched fists as he turned on her. Rapidly he spoke again, a shot in the dark to distract the murderous rage about to be vented on the helpless woman. "Death by nerve gas is an awful way to die. Maybe it would've been better if he'd died in the car, the way Jacques Tousignant and his son Mark did."

It worked. Christian Von Bessel spun around, his eyes mere slits. "Pretty clever," the Mountie continued desperately. "You tapped him to torch Schweizerhalle, but how the hell did you get him to commit suicide in that car? And how did you switch the dental records?"

Unexpectedly the man burst into laughter. It appeared to be genuine amusement, even though tinged with hysteria. "I am amazed. I have underestimated you."

"So," continued Baker, "how did you do it?"

The Sword gestured at Hamani. "My old friend Aziz came up with the plan. With everything discovered, the warehouse had to be destroyed and I had to disappear so I could continue my work. Tousignant was convenient, one of thousands Aziz has all over the world." Baker thought of Steve Owen. "He had several strengths and one terrible weakness. As an ex-Legionnaire, he had mercenary instincts, a fundamental toughness and expertise with incendiary devices. His weakness was his love for his family. The colonel arranged for the wife and daughter to be kidnapped and held hostage to ensure that Tousignant would do as he was ordered. He was told how to enter the facility and how to plant the devices to most effectively burn the place to the ground. While waiting for the fire to ignite, the colonel's men plied him with kirsch, then told him to get in the car with his son and drive to a predetermined location to receive instructions as to how to find his wife and daughter. He was given very little time to get to his first objective, to ensure that he would be driving at a high speed. The car they provided was of course my own, with a full gas tank to ensure complete combustion and a special modification. While on route back to the facility Tousignant received a call on the vehicle's cell phone.

The signal triggered an explosive bolt that had been fixed to the forward suspension system. Afterwards, Aziz arranged for the car to be mis-delivered, so it could be cleaned of any traces of the explosives, and for the dental records to be switched. The only reason Tousignant was chosen was we shared the same dentist and because he had a young son, and because I had made it clear that I would not leave Daniel behind. Once the man and his son were dead, we had no further use for the wife and daughter."

Baker felt a chill trace a cold finger down his spine at the cold-bloodedness of it all.

"Non! Non!" cried Marie Françoise. "You couldn't possibly be my husband! He never would be this cruel, tell these terrible lies!"

She was on her knees, arms outstretched, beseeching. At the sight of her frantic, pleading face, Baker remembered. He had to find out the truth, and he had to do it in such a way as to preserve the environmentalist's sanity. "So you never loved your wife at all. I don't believe you have ever loved any woman. Senseless brutality is all you know." He pointed at Hamani, who was staring fixedly at him. "That's why you tortured his wife to death. Face it, your marriage to Marie Françoise was a fix from the word go. Why?"

Von Bessel snarled. "Because of my father. He worked for her father, for old Bertrand, before he was fired. My father was a genius, and that greedy, ruthless bastard ruined his career. After he died, and I did away with my stinking bitch of a mother, I swore I would get revenge. The only way to do that was to work for the old man's firm. That's why I pursued you, my dear. I had intended to sabotage your father's company, to arrange his financial ruin, but then Aziz came along with a better idea. Your father never made the connection between my father and myself, because though I may not have liked it I have my mother's maiden name."

Again he started walking over to the colonel, who seemed to have almost recovered his wits after the beatings he had endured. Baker knew that if they were to escape he would need every ally he could find, even if that meant it was the Iraqi. He pressed his left leg against his right calf, felt the reassuring presence of the knife strapped there. Strapped it to the wrong leg. To get it quickly with his right hand, he should have attached it to his left leg. Cursing himself for his stupidity, he saw Von Bessel preparing to rain blows on the helpless Hamani. When the time came he'd have to go for the knife with his left hand and hope for the best. And he would need Hamani, which meant the man couldn't be beaten senseless.

To distract the Sword, he said, "So why did you fall for Hamani's trap, if you're so clever?"

Von Bessel stopped and slowly turned, his jaw muscles bunching. "Hamani's trap?" Once again a burst of hysterical laughter. "You mean the Accountant, leaking information to her. . ." he waved a contemptuous hand at his wife, "and the rest? Hamani's trap? I see several people caught in a trap, but it is not his I assure you!"

Urgently Baker continued. "So now that you have us, or rather your wife, you won't have to destroy the city."

A look of indescribable cunning and cruelty settled on the Sword's face like a mask. "On the contrary. I have special plans for my wife. I have certain . . . urges I have up to now been largely unable to gratify with regard to her. Now, it will be different and it will be done very, very slowly. Much more slowly than the gardener ever did, here in this place you believe to be so terrible-"

"Non! Non, how could you know about this place, about him?" wailed Marie Françoise, stumbling across the slender ledge that was her sanity. "You could not know of this. I told no one."

"My dearest, you surprise me. Yes, you did tell someone, your doctor in the sanatorium. You see, I've made a point over the years to keep an eye on you, care for you, looked out for your welfare especially at the sanatorium.

Numb with confusion, she felt herself falling, capitulating. She was beaten. Only her deepest human instinct caused her to blurt through sobs, "Non, please. You can not be Christian. He loved me."

"Oh, in my way, I loved you. Have you forgotten what it was like when you lay in your hospital bed, so helpless, so moist, taking all that I had to give, unable to resist me."

His words, so relentlessly cruel, triggered a mental image of the man in her dream, the one attacking her in her hospital bed, over and over. The pain, the inability to move to react. And in that instant, part of the dream became clear. It was this man who now stood before her who had taken over her dream, her life.

Von Bessel, the picture of sick arrogant power, exclaiming with relish. "I intend to destroy you. It really is amazing how much you resemble my hated mother. "But first. . ."

From the corner of his eye Baker saw Marie Françoise shrink back in horror, cowering.

Von Bessel strode to the canvas-covered machine, seized a corner of the huge sheet and yanked. Baker stared at a large mechanical assembly. There was a bronze-coloured Mylar coated sphere, surrounded by three cylindrical stainless steel canisters equipped with pneumatic pistons. There was an array of electronics and blinking LEDs. There was a low groan from Hamani. The Sword waved at the device like a magician performing a conjuring trick.

Marie Françoise sobbed. "You cannot be Christian. He loved me. I know he loved me. He could never be so hurtful. He would never do this!"

Von Bessel sneered. "The amazing female belief that they alone know and understand love. You were a means for me to revenge myself on your father and when he was gone, you served in his place. You were the incubation unit for my son, nothing more. And without my son, there is nothing but revenge."

He patted the top of the bronze sphere. "Do you recognise it, Aziz? There are eleven more just like it."

"Where are they?" asked Baker.

"Paris, Washington, London and Baghdad," said the Sword matter-of-factly. "And here. As far as the kill ratio is concerned, each of the twelve is the equivalent of a four megaton nuclear blast, although of course only people are destroyed, not infrastructure."

He reached inside his black fatigues and pulled out a cellular telephone. "Each unit is activated by electronic impulse once a specific number is dialled and received."

"I always knew you were insane," said Hamani, in a controlled, neutral tone. "I should have killed you myself, years ago."

"But you didn't," said the Sword softly. "By the way, did the maid Fatima follow her instructions? Did she tell you how much I enjoyed your wife?"

A feral snarl appeared on Hamani's battered face. The Sword smiled. "Good."

Again he waved the cell phone. "When I dial the number, the receiver on the unit will send an electronic command. The pistons will compress their contents into the central mixing chamber. Then, when the brew is good and toxic, boom!"

He turned to Marie Françoise. "You and I will escape before the explosion. And we will be together again. I assure you I will make it last as long as possible, and very soon this cellar you dread so much will begin to seem like very heaven in comparison."

Baker remembered his promise to Marie Françoise. On my soul, and the eyes of my daughter Valerie. He braced his feet on the ground, ready for what he knew would come. "I've had your wife as well, you pathetic sack of shit. In a way you'd never imagine. I had her passion. And I can tell you she loved Daniel more than you ever could. You're a pitiful excuse for a man, for a father."

The Sword was shaking with rage. He pulled a pistol from his belt and strode up to Baker. He aimed but at the last moment, with a superhuman effort, he pulled himself together. Instead of shooting, he swung with a hard left hook. The Mountie tried to roll with it but still saw stars. He plucked at his trouser leg. Mustn't lose consciousness.

Von Bessel was staring at him, panting, eyes narrowed. "It won't work," he said shortly. "I won't kill you quickly. I won't deprive you of the experience of my best work." He raised the cell phone and pressed the recall button. He held his finger over the send button.

In one fluid motion Baker seized the knife from the sheath with his left hand and lunged. He caught Christian Von Bessel clumsily under the ribs and twisted, then pulled the knife out. Missed the heart. He heard one of the guards shout and pulled the Sword to him as a shield, scrabbling to get the cell phone out of the man's hand as the gun hit the paving with a metallic rattle. He dragged him toward Hamani, who was frantically straining at his bonds and rocking back and forth in the chair. The Mountie saw the guards moving, trying to get a shot at him without hitting the struggling Von Bessel. He flinched as he heard the shots, then realised it was Marie Françoise, firing the Sword's gun at the guards. She dropped one and the two others spun around, looking for cover. Once again he'd forgotten how fast she could move. He reached Hamani and slashed twice at the rope with the razor sharp bloody knife. The colonel struggled briefly, then he was free. As he staggered to his feet, Baker yelled, "The phone!"

He grabbed for the unit. Too late. The Sword pushed the send button. Baker was dimly aware of the remaining two guards lunging for the tunnel, to escape before the device exploded. Hamani ripped the cell phone from Sword's hand and knelt, frantically dialling a number. The Mountie struggled with the writhing wounded man, who was making a series of eerie keening noises. He heard four shots being fired - the fleeing guards were being cut down - then the banging sound of booted steps sprinting down the tunnel. Four ghostly forms materialised from the brick-lined chute. It took Baker a moment to understand they were clad in gas masks and camouflage chemical warfare gear. He shoved Von Bessel away from him, unsure whether the new arrivals were friend or foe. He heard Colonel Hamani bark orders in a language he didn't understand, then stand before the bronze sphere, his hands clenching and unclenching in frustration as the suited men spread around the room. They carried boxes that looked like medical kits. One of the figures paused in front of him and thrust a mask into his hand. He saw another do the same to Marie Françoise. One of the men nearest the door had opened the case he was carrying, removing handfuls of cylindrical clear plastic containers about the size of Baker's thumb.

As it dawned on him that they were Hamani's men, the Mountie moved over to where the Iraqi was standing. "What's going on?" he shouted.

The colonel seized a mask from one of his men. "Put it on!" he ordered. He gestured to the man holding the ampoules. The figure quickly knelt and ripped the plastic off a needle. Fixing an ampoule to the end, he rammed it into Hamani's thigh as the Iraqi gasped.

Now the suited figure had grasped Baker's thigh and was about to do the same. As he prepared to belt the man Hamani said, "Pyridostigmine, diazepam, and atropine-oxime. Nerve agent anti-toxins. You will feel very ill, but it's better than dying." Baker gazed into his eyes and saw nothing but truth there. He nodded, then gasped and winced as the needle rammed home.

"Fuck, that hurts," he hissed. He saw them do the same to Marie Françoise. The Sword was crawling slowly across the floor, leaving a slimy dark red trail, his green viper eyes fixed and staring as he descended all the way into madness. He had no mask and had received no injection. "Won't the masks save us?" he asked Hamani.

"No. The toxin can be absorbed through the skin."

Baker stared at the device. The pistons were on their deadly march towards the centre. Hamani was pawing frantically at the mass of electronics at the base of the device. Just as Baker saw the man's skin turn a sickly greenish yellow, he experienced a wave of nausea so intense he almost collapsed. Focusing with difficulty on what Hamani was trying to do with his suddenly shaking hands, he tried to concentrate on not vomiting. He felt the peculiar helplessness that comes from being in a life and death situation and having absolutely no influence over the outcome.

"Then what are you doing?" he yelled at the colonel, his voice muffled through the mask. He swallowed bitter bile and tried not to faint. "We're going to die anyway."

Hamani shouted back, over the rising, steam-kettle hiss of the device's mixing chamber. "The wiring looks the same as on the device we found in Baghdad. It has a 'blow-by' system. About two percent of the payload does not form XP29 by the time the explosive charge is scheduled to go off. It must be vented. That is why we have the masks and the anti-toxin - they will enable us to survive the venting of the imperfectly mixed raw gas. But if the whole thing blows, we're all dead."

His trembling hands fumbled at the wiring. "Hold this out of the way!" he shouted. Trying desperately to control his sweaty hands, Baker seized a double fistful of red, green and yellow wiring and held it to one side as Hamani worked frantically. "He has delayed the time between plunger activation and explosion to ensure he had time to get away. It is impossible for the cell phone sequence activating the other devices to work underground, in this cellar. He obviously intended to do it once he had activated this device and got above ground."

Frantically he pulled at the wiring. Baker felt delirious, almost gagging with nausea.

"Twenty seconds to venting! Thirty seconds after that, it blows!" Hamani gestured wildly. "Get out! Everyone out!"

Baker lunged at Marie Françoise, picked her up and carried her to the cellar staircase. One of the suited figures grabbed her limp body and hauled it up the stairs as the three others followed. Baker looked back at Hamani, who had sagged to his knees. He looked longingly up the stairs, then made his decision. He would stay. Although it was hard to see in the gas mask, he saw Christian Von Bessel lunge to his feet and stagger toward the staircase, trying to flee. Baker hit him as hard as he could, right on top of the wound below his ribcage. The chemist flailed his arms and fell to the floor. Hamani was slumped over the device and seemed to have passed out. Baker shook him hard by the shoulders. The Iraqi roused himself and continued working like a man possessed. His voice was so faint with nausea Baker barely heard him as he shouted, "Shut the door!" Baker slammed the cellar door and staggered back to the Iraqi.

There was a vicious hissing sound and a jet of what looked like grey steam shot from one of the pistons. The device was venting. Thirty seconds to detonation. He heard a terrible scream and turned. It was Christian Von Bessel. His lips were blue, his emerald green eyes bulging from his head. As Baker watched in horror, he saw the whites of his eyes turn egg yolk yellow. The Sword's hands, rigid as claws, raked his chest as the gas corrupted and dissolved his pulmonary system. He could no longer scream. His bared teeth were bright red with arterial blood and his face was swelling like an inflating balloon. His legs suddenly convulsed as if he had grasped a live electric cable and he slammed against the stone wall, limbs twitching. Slowly he slid to the floor, his face as grey-green as that of a long-drowned man, the emerald eyes rolling back in his head as a torrent of blood flooded from his open mouth.

Baker looked back at Hamani. The Iraqi was staring at him though the goggles of his mask, holding up a single black wire. The Mountie tried to make his way to him but his legs suddenly gave way. Half crawling, half-rolling toward the device he touched it as the colonel sagged sideways. Leaning over the man he saw him slipping into unconsciousness and knew the same fate was his. No explosion.

They'd done it. And then he was falling down a long black tunnel.

When he awoke, he was in a cold dark room, drenched in cold blood. It took him several moments to comprehend that the darkness surrounding him was the Swiss night, and the coldness was the night dew on the grass. The kitchen door was still ajar but everything was silent. Painfully he rolled onto his side. Someone had taken off his mask. Beside him lay Marie Françoise, also maskless, her chest rising and falling as she breathed. Beside her were several empty ampoules. The same beside him. Hamani and his men had obviously administered more anti-toxin to ensure their survival.

Groggily he looked around. The Iraqis were gone.

He heard sirens coming down the lonely dark lane to the chateau. He lay back and closed his eyes, breathing the sweet, sweet air.

EPILOGUE

San Pedro, Belize, April 12

He inhaled deeply, breathing the moist tropical air, heavy with the scent of bougainvillaea and frangipani. Bright sunlight flooded through the loose fitting louvers of the open air, ground level veranda of the restaurant. She smiled at him and he smiled back. The place was empty except for them.

There was a rustle as the beaded curtain was brushed aside. An elderly, skinny man approached the table and hovered. "Señor. Señorita. There is another visitor. He is waiting outside. Shall I send him in?"

Baker tore his eyes from Marie Françoise. "Of course, Señor Paz."

Moments later, a dragging, slapping cadence sounded on the flagstones. A young man with a crutch expertly turned the corner and hobbled up to their table. Baker grinned. "You're getting so good with that I bet you'll miss it when you're fully recovered."

"Fat chance," said Barry Nakamura.

"How was your flight?"

"Excellent," replied the young constable. "I've never been fussed over by so many gorgeous stewardesses in my whole life. Maybe I'll keep this damn thing after all, just for airplane flights. Where's the party?"

Baker tilted his chin. "Outside on the patio. Everyone's catching some rays and drinking too much beer."

"Sounds good to me. I've been hearing about this damn Belekian beer for years now. Time I tried some." He headed for the exit onto the patio just as two other figures came through the door. One was in a wheelchair, the other also on crutches.

"Well, if it ain't hop and long," called Baker. "A person might almost think this was a convention for the disabled."

"You should talk. Your skin still makes you look as green as Mr. Spock," said Colin Stewart severely.

"Yeah, smart mouth," interjected Joan Chan. "You be nice to me or I'll have to kick your butt once I'm fully mobile."

"I still think you crazy people should be in a hospital and not partying in a tropical paradise," said Marie Françoise. "Oh, what's the use." She stood and walked over to the cooler at a nearby table. Expertly she twisted off the cap and slugged back a mouthful of brew.

"You're getting awfully good at that," said Baker. "We'll turn you into a regular person yet."

"Voyou," she sniffed, smiling. At Nakamura's questioning glance the big Mountie said, "Hoodlum." The constable nodded. "And here I thought you were just a clumsy oaf. Woman's sure got your number."

Baker grinned lazily at the petite Swiss environmentalist. "You got my number?"

She tossed her head of chestnut hair. "Yes. And don't forget," she said with mock severity, "that it is a dedicated line!"

He raised his glass in salute. "I can live with that."

The End